A Novel of Barsoom®

GAUNTLETS OF MARS

THE WORKS OF
EDGAR RICE BURROUGHS

TARZAN® SERIES
Tarzan of the Apes
The Return of Tarzan
The Beasts of Tarzan
The Son of Tarzan
Tarzan and the Jewels of Opar
Jungle Tales of Tarzan
Tarzan the Untamed
Tarzan the Terrible
Tarzan and the Golden Lion
Tarzan and the Ant Men
Tarzan, Lord of the Jungle
Tarzan and the Lost Empire
Tarzan at the Earth's Core
Tarzan the Invincible
Tarzan Triumphant
Tarzan and the City of Gold
Tarzan and the Lion Man
Tarzan and the Leopard Men
Tarzan's Quest
Tarzan and the Forbidden City
Tarzan the Magnificent
Tarzan and "The Foreign Legion"
Tarzan and the Madman
Tarzan and the Castaways
Tarzan and the Tarzan Twins
Tarzan: The Lost Adventure (with
Joe R. Lansdale)

BARSOOM® SERIES
A Princess of Mars
The Gods of Mars
The Warlord of Mars
Thuvia, Maid of Mars
The Chessmen of Mars
The Master Mind of Mars
A Fighting Man of Mars
Swords of Mars
Synthetic Men of Mars
Llana of Gathol
John Carter of Mars

PELLUCIDAR® SERIES
At the Earth's Core
Pellucidar
Tanar of Pellucidar
Tarzan at the Earth's Core
Back to the Stone Age
Land of Terror
Savage Pellucidar

AMTOR™ SERIES
Pirates of Venus
Lost on Venus
Carson of Venus
Escape on Venus
The Wizard of Venus

ERBURROUGHS.COM

The Wild Adventures of Edgar Rice Burroughs™

*The hapless green man looked up in astonishment as
a strange, red man plunged toward him.*

A Novel of Barsoom®

GAUNTLETS OF MARS

CHRIS L ADAMS

*Cover art and
interior illustrations by*
DOUGLAS KLAUBA

EDGAR RICE BURROUGHS, Inc.
Publishers
TARZANA   CALIFORNIA

Wild Adventures of Edgar Rice Burroughs Series Editor: James Sullos

Special thanks to Kathleen Bonnaud, John Burroughs, Douglas Klauba, Janet Mann, Jeffrey J. Mariotte, James Sullos, Cathy Wilbanks, Charlotte Wilbanks, Mike Wolfer, and Bill Wormstedt for their valuable assistance in producing this book.

First paperback edition

Published by Edgar Rice Burroughs, Inc.,
Tarzana, California
EdgarRiceBurroughs.com

ISBN-13: 978-1-945462-88-7

- 9 8 7 6 5 4 3 2 1 -

Dedication

With warm gratitude, I dedicate this novel to the hardworking folks of Edgar Rice Burroughs, Inc., and to the small army of fine editors, proofreaders, artists, and cover and interior designers who worked tirelessly behind the scenes to make the publication of this story a possibility.

Thank you, Jim Sullos. If not for your early support my Barsoom tales would be but bits and bytes on a hard drive.

Thank you, John Ralston Burroughs, the first person on the West Coast to read Dat Voga's exploits.

Thank you, Cathy Wilbanks, for your tireless efforts to keep Edgar Rice Burroughs relevant today, and for all the fresh and exciting new works coming from Edgar Rice Burroughs, Inc.

Thank you, Charlotte Wilbanks, and Janet Mann. Your efforts are crucial in keeping Edgar Rice Burroughs, Inc., on an even keel, and books flowing into the hands of readers, which is most important and much appreciated. My gratitude extends to those who have come and gone in your warehouse and shipping department; I appreciate their work since books don't yet ship themselves.

Thank you, Joan Bledig, Robert T. "Bob" Garcia, Jeffrey J. Mariotte, and Bill Wormstedt for your excellent editorial work. I appreciate both your criticisms and your plaudits, especially the critiques that help me hone my craft.

Thank you, Christopher Paul Carey. You wear more than one hat at Edgar Rice Burroughs, Inc., so thank you for your excellent editorial work, and for your interior design work on my first two novels published with Edgar Rice Burroughs, Inc. It has been a real pleasure working with you on *Dark Tides of Mars* and *Gauntlets of Mars*.

Thank you, Mike Wolfer, for your fabulous cover design on both books. Excellent work!

And thank you, Douglas Klauba, for the beautiful artwork you have supplied for *Dark Tides of Mars* and *Gauntlets of Mars*. It was a real pleasure working with you on this latest novel.

In closing this dedication, I wish to express an opinion I have formed since working with Edgar Rice Burroughs, Inc., that the work of an author is at best fifty percent of the effort, give or take, of what readers ultimately hold in their hands. I hope that this dedication makes it obvious that a lot of work goes on under the hood, work that some may have no knowledge of, but which is crucial in order that the best quality product comes to market. It takes a team effort, and I really appreciate all these folks.

Chris L Adams

TABLE OF CONTENTS

A Note on Measurements

Measurements in this novel are given in Barsoomian units. While these terms should be understandable via context, their specific Earth equivalents may be found below for the curious Jasoomian reader.

haad A Barsoomian "mile" (equivalent to about 1,949 feet).

ord A Barsoomian "year" (equivalent to about 687 days).

sofad A Barsoomian "foot" (equivalent to about 11.694 inches).

tal A Barsoomian "second" (equivalent to about .885 seconds)

xat A Barsoomian "minute" (equivalent to about 2 minutes, 57 seconds).

zode A Barsoomian "hour" (equivalent to about 2 hours, 27 minutes, 42 seconds).

DAT VOGA STEPPED BACK to surveil his handiwork, having perforce to gaze upward into a bright, cloud-dappled sky to do so, for he had just descended eighty sofads after furling a topgallant due to a recent change in the sea breeze affecting the ship's tacking. A zode later, someone might very well follow new orders, climbing the same mast and unfurling the same sail. Such, he had come to learn, was life at sea.

Having completed this final task of the day he looked forward to a pleasant evening, short though it may be due to the increased workload of late. He hoped, barring the unforeseen, of course, to spend the short half zode before retiring to his bunk in the company of Azaria of Horz.

He had stumbled upon the beautiful girl months ago lurking in the hold of the *Prachus*, a stowaway on the ship sailing under the flag of Horz, in the name of Hal-Roh-Kim, merchant, shipbuilder, and—most importantly—Azaria's father. The *Prachus* was the same ship, in fact, that months before had rescued him and his friend, Thuria of Zoquan, from an island in the middle of nowhere, upon which they were marooned.

"That was good work today, Dat Voga!" avowed Roh-Du-Von, clapping the red man on one of his sun-kissed, reddish-bronze shoulders as he passed the Heliumite on his way aft.

"Thank you, Roh-Du-Von! And I appreciate the help with that Horzian thumb knot earlier!" he replied. "Gar-Noh-Dar was to show me that trick weeks ago. We've been so busy . . ."

"After we lost our comrades to those pasty-faced fish-men," put in First Osar Bim-Gon-Dar, pausing beside Dat Voga, "we've been busier than a boat full of prachus in a Plaezorian swimming hole, for sure. Get some rest, both of you."

"You don't have to tell me twice, Osar. Fair sailing, Dat Voga!" cried Roh-Duh-Von, waving and continuing abaft.

"Fair sailing, Roh-Du-Von," the red man called out. He nodded at Bim-Gon-Dar. "'Til morning, Osar." Now Dat Voga made haste for his bunkroom to freshen up before seeking Azaria and perhaps grabbing a bite in the galley. But while he was in his quarters, the gauntlets of Daxxus Nahl came to mind.

"I did promise Thuria that I would spend every moment possible working with them," he mused aloud.

Cocking his head on one side to listen for traffic in the narrow passage outside his door, he crouched before his sea trunk to retrieve the precious gauntlets. "Could I but decipher their key, these could send Thuria and me back to our own time." Then he reminded himself, "And if I do not, we shall remain here . . . one million years in the past." That last was a sobering thought. The harm they might cause were they to remain in this time was not lost upon him.

"What cipher did you use, Daxxus Nahl?" he muttered, sliding open the plate to expose the panel where he was supposed to enter a cipher of some unknown value—unknown to him, anyway. He stared at that panel a moment, but in his imaginings abruptly rose the vision of Azaria's perfect features. He shook his head. "I think tonight it must remain a secret . . . but soon I will definitely put more effort into solving this riddle."

Before he placed the precious items back into his sea

chest he took a moment to glance at the registered time counter, ticking away the tals that had accumulated since he and Thuria arrived here in the past. This value would be all-important when he returned to the future, for he must use it to return to a specific moment in time, no sooner and no later. He did some rapid figuring in his head based on the value he read there.

"Nearly eight months! Issus!" Swapping out his sweaty harness for a dry one and transferring any necessary equipage such as his ever-present pouch and dagger to the new harness, he scanned his chamber, saw that all was right where it should be, and headed aloft. Now deckside, he went first to sternward. Azaria often lingered there, watching the wake from the back of the ship where she would not interfere with the sailors' duties. Instead, he found Thuria, his fellow companion from the future, alone.

"And just what is the most beautiful girl from Zoquan on the entire ship doing sitting here alone?" he teased.

Thuria grinned impishly. "Dat Voga, you know full well that I am the *only* girl from Zoquan on this ship, beautiful or otherwise! Now tell me of your adventurous day before I go mad, for mine was filled with mending tackle and cleaning fish for the galley."

He spoke briefly of his day but caught a look in the young woman's eye that caused his brows to knit in wonder. "What is it, Thuria? Your mind was a million haads away just now. Or was it a million *ords* away?"

"That's just it, Dat Voga. I have wondered all day how long we have been here—in the past, I mean. Since coming here, it has all begun to feel so natural that at some point I ceased to track the passage of time. I admit, it caused me a moment of panic. Am I being ridiculous, Dat Voga? Oh, tell me I am not!"

"No, you are not at all ridiculous," the man hastened to reassure her. "It happens to me, too, Thuria. Today, in fact. Do you know you are speaking to a lesser noble of modern-day Helium? A padwar of the Heliumetic Navy, the most powerful navy on Barsoom, mind you? And formerly, I suppose I should append, Ambassador of Helium to Ptarsas and Zoquan? Why, the last time I was in Xanator, where we are now headed, the city was abandoned and home only to great white apes, one of which was nearly my undoing."

"Yes, it is all so strange, I can hardly wrap my mind around it," Thuria admitted. "One moment in my thoughts I might find myself sitting in the garden with my mistress, Tahn Dih, or dancing at the gala in the Grand Ball Room of Ptarsas, or squatting in one of those terrible cells in that dungeon of Daxxus Nahl's. The next, I am skinning fish on a sea that is, in our time, covered in yellow ochre moss and drier than a bleached bone."

"What's drier than a bleached bone?"

The two looked up in surprise to find Azaria standing above them, looking, to Dat Voga at least, mesmerizing in the evening light, which cast all manner of beautiful colors into her lively eyes and caught entrancingly in her auburn locks.

"Why, my hands from cleaning all those fish today," Thuria replied naturally, holding them up to view.

Azaria looked, "Thuria, you poor thing! Come with me this instant. I myself was busy with the mundane labors of the day, but ugh—I'd rather clean the bilge than clean fish!"

Once more Dat Voga found himself watching the two chatting women walk away, leaving him alone at the rail.

"Speaking of fish," he muttered, "I'm starved! I hope Thuria cleaned a boatload."

Chapter One

Trapped in the Past

Dat Voga actually kept a closer count of their time in the past than he admitted to Thuria. He figured the two from the future were marooned for six months on what he liked to call his "island in the middle of nowhere" and had now spent nearly two months lost at sea aboard a sailing ship of a far-gone time. It had been but three weeks by his reckoning since the attack of the fish men where they had lost so many friends when a watchman in a phlega nest a hundred-forty sofads aloft shouted the words that one and all anxiously awaited—land had been sighted.

Dat Voga sensed the eagerness as every eye strained to see the blessed sight. Although much of his experiences at sea had been incredible, yet could he scarcely wait to set foot on solid land again, if only for a few days. After their brush with death on the grim sea, he needed a respite from it. He did not know it, but he had arrived at the understanding all sailors eventually realize, that the sea is a harsh mistress, and one whose embraces are best not wooed lightly.

Excited beyond measure, he rushed forward to grip a gunwale, his own eyes straining as he awaited the moment the ship should crest so that he could see across that watery plain. Finally, the ship climbed to the top of a swell and there it was: a shoreline! With his heart slamming in his chest in pure delight, Dat Voga recalled the words of the odar: "You should see them when we raise the sight of land after many long weeks a-sea!" He smiled, for now he understood.

The sight of the distant coast galvanized the crew, causing them to act as though they had taken draughts of a wondrous potion. They laughed and slapped each other's backs. They sang chanty after chanty, sometimes scarcely finishing a song ere they started it again from the beginning.

For Dat Voga, this was a treasured glimpse into a time that would become iconic in his peoples' histories and legends, for these songs were unknown in his day. That afternoon, as they sailed toward what someone eventually recognized as the Plaezor Archipelago, he learned them all, singing and working as lustily as all the others and grinning just as widely.

Although saddened by the loss of their comrades, they knew their grief would be with them for the remainder of their lives. Meanwhile, they would celebrate as was their wont when, after weeks at sea, they sighted land. Also, they celebrated for those who had perished, believing the songs somehow cheered their shades. The red man agreed and sang with as much gusto as the others.

"This archipelago," Odar Gan-Toh-Gan informed Dat Voga, "lays southwest of the port city of Xanator."

The distance to the island chain could not be covered quickly enough for these land-hungry sailors. But, as with all journeys, eventually the end hove into view and, with feelings of elation and curiosity, Dat Voga looked upon a primordial city for the first time.

Val Statt crossed his mind as he gazed at it. He knew the old historian would die for such an opportunity. Soon he forgot about old Val Statt, though, as he took in the miraculous vision of a city whose name had possibly not even survived to his time.

Knowing nothing of the intricacies of navigating a harbor, he joined Azaria and Thuria on the command deck, which afforded a better view than would standing at the bow. He heard Azaria chatting away about something, but she stopped when she realized no one was listening. Her friends were enrapt, taking in the scenery.

These docks were much shorter than those with which Dat Voga was familiar. He mentally compared them with the immense examples of the future, which ran for haads out into the desert. Then he considered that these docks did not have the extensions added, this only having occurred after the seas receded. The thought caused his heart to leap, and he stared even more intently. The harbor was so full of color and movement he scarcely knew where to look first.

Ships moved in and out of moorings while small boats wended their way between their larger cousins. The ships at the docks were being loaded or unloaded, the whole creating a mosaic of color, sound, and movement.

The city's sea wall became the backdrop for a boardwalk up and down which was enacted a veritable hive of activity. Places of business bustled next to shanties. Wares of every conceivable kind hung for sale or were displayed upon vendor tables and stands. And everywhere people walked, talked, ate, begged, haggled, fought, bought, shouted, sold, stole, and hawked.

The smells wafting across the marina were a mixture of foods cooking over fires and the sweet odor of smoked meats commingling with the reek of the harbor's seawater and unwashed bodies. The sights and smells were both wonderful and foreign to the two of modern days.

Dat Voga saw cargo being lowered to the docks using simple tackle and pulley systems. In a cacophony of voices, merchants haggled with sea odars for their goods while other traders, expecting goods from Xanator, Horz, or other distant cities, loaded their packages and bales onto carts. These they then hauled away amid the chaos using titanic, eight-legged beasts that Dat Voga suspicioned were progenitors to the future zitidar. He later learned that these beasts of burden were called zytogonths.

These gargantuan creatures did not appear to be as volatile as the zitidar, appearing much more docile. And it was a good thing they were so quiescent since in between the giant beasts wove a crowd of people that included street urchins, dock workers, merchants, sailors, vendors, and soldiery—people from every vocation and walk of life.

Some of these sought transport to the mainland that lay but a few days sailing to the east, while others, newly arrived, made their way up the narrow street and through the city gate in search of lodgings.

A small boat soon made its way to the side of the *Prachus* and hailed her. One of its occupants was an oily harbormaster with whom the odar engaged in the most heated negotiation Dat Voga had ever witnessed, over a spot to berth the ship.

During this discourse the odar's face turned nearly as red as Dat Voga's. The exchange revealed a side of Gan-Toh-Gan's character the padwar had not known existed. After much haggling during which first one would scream and yell while the other countered, both parties finally reached an agreement and, the price agreed upon, they were told where to berth.

The harbormaster gave a small flag to the odar, which indicated the amount of time the *Prachus* could berth, together with her assigned slip. Every ship in the harbor flew a similar pennon, as any ship *not* doing so would be subject to being boarded by the Harbor Guard, and either fined or impounded. The odar's beard fairly bristled after the animated exchange. Muttering something the padwar could not repeat, he stormed off, shouting orders to his men.

The decks of the *Prachus* bustled as final preparations were made to make port. Naturally, all were anxious to leap to the docks and immerse themselves in the life of the city, but much work remained to be done. Although these islands were not their ultimate destination, Dat Voga learned they might find better trading, since in this out-of-the-way island chain many of the goods they carried would be worth more here than upon the mainland.

To determine who was granted shore leave and who would remain aboard, the osars used a tried-and-true method. Naturally, Dat Voga wished to accompany Thuria and Azaria. Yet, to be fair, all must abide by the system, and the odar assured him he would provide an adequate escort should fate decree otherwise than the outcome for which Dat Voga hoped.

Although crime was rare in this time, kidnappings were not unheard of. This archipelago was, after all, a melting pot of humanity, containing people from all over this hemisphere, most of whom had migrated here to make their fortune in the mines for which it was famous.

To settle the issue of who was granted shore leave first, Osar Gar-Noh-Dar came on deck bearing a leather box with a soft, slitted hide for a cover. Inside the box were an equal number of both light-and-dark colored viands, of a type that were very hard until prepared by boiling. Each man now approached the box and inserted his hand into the slot, retrieving a single viand. The ones who withdrew the pallid viands were the ones who were permitted first shore leave.

As he watched, Azaria and Thuria each drew a white. Now it was Voga's turn to draw. By this time all aboard knew of Dat Voga's affection for Azaria. In their hearts, each hoped the likable red man would pull a white viand from the box. With the sailors' eyes upon him, he inserted his hand and pulled forth—a black!

A collective groan went up among the crew. Immediately, a dozen men offered to trade their white for his black.

But Dat Voga was an inveterate sportsman, and not one to take advantage of their good fortune. He insisted he abide by the rules, and that they take their leave.

If it had not been for the fact that all knew of his affection for Azaria, and his close friendship with Thuria, he might have traded. But he felt that he would be the recipient of pity and did not wish to prevent someone who had won his shore leave fairly to lose it at the last instant. Nay, the noble from Helium accepted his loss with aplomb, assured by Gan-Toh-Gan that the women would be escorted by his son and could not be safer if they were aboard the *Prachus*.

Chapter Two

Fate of the Plaezors

CATCHING THURIA ALONE, Dat Voga gestured at the equilibrimotor belt about her waist, and suggested she leave it in her quarters. When they first came aboard the ship and did not know if they were among honorable folk, they had worn the items to keep them safe. But it was one thing to wear the strange items among friends who saw them daily and now paid them little heed, and something else altogether to parade them around strangers from all over this corner of primordial Barsoom.

"Street vendors will be on a constant lookout for interesting peculiarities," he explained. "The belt and gauntlets might draw unwanted attention, possibly making us the future target of thieves. While it is true theft is rare in our time, we cannot be sure it is that way now. The rabble of any city is certain to contain any number of shady individuals."

Thuria agreed to place the belt in a drawer containing her few personal items. Dat Voga had his sea chest beneath his bunk where he kept spare leathers and various items, and it was in this chest that he secreted the gauntlets when he was not wearing them. He was not concerned about anyone aboard the *Prachus* rifling through his effects, but one never knew who might board the ship while docked, making him feel it for the best that they were out of sight.

The padwar went topside to pitch in unloading their

cargo using a new hoist he had fabricated in the ship's workshop weeks ago; it was one of many small things he had done to ease the burden of a people he had come to love. Unaided, he could haul great loads skyward that would typically require the combined efforts of many men.

Since this was the hoist's first, practical use, there were many interested spectators, chief of whom was Odar Gan-Toh-Gan. But also watching were those aboard nearby ships and docks, their eyes widening in wonder when they saw Dat Voga, with very little effort, haul great loads out of the hold.

Gan-Toh-Gan instantly noticed these curious onlookers. Never one to miss an opportunity, he called out to the padwar, "Dat Voga, come up here." The odar leaned against a rail on the command deck, from which vantage he had been observing the red man at work.

After turning the handling of the device over to a nearby sailor whom he had instructed in its use, Dat Voga sprinted up the stairs to the command deck. As he came to a stop beside Gan-Toh-Gan, the odar surreptitiously indicated the curious audience keenly watching the sailor using the hoist.

It did not take Helium's ambassador long to perceive the object of the onlookers' curiosity. He grinned, but with his face averted so the odar did not see him smile. He regretted he could not build all the contraptions that sprang to mind, many of which would cause this simple tool to pale in comparison. But to reveal too much was to risk revising history. He had agonized over the mechanism, which was advanced for its time, but, in the end, watching his fellow sailors toil with simple rope and pulley decided the matter.

"They seem interested in my hoist. Do you have any idea what you're going to do about it?" he asked innocently. By now, Dat Voga had figured out a quirk of the odar's personality that proclaimed itself when it came to haggling.

The odar, a salty old sea calban, scowled. This part of his

job he took quite seriously. "Of course, I know what I'm going to do about it, you young gantahn! You and I are going to make more of these devices of yours, these . . . what do you call them?" The odar gestured with his hand as he grasped for the word.

"Hoists?" Dat Voga provided.

"Yes, these hoists! They're going to make old Hal-Roh-Kim a fortune."

Dat Voga smiled at the bristling odar. He did not tell him that, in the future, this device had been outmoded for millennia because they accomplished all heavy lifting in that time by utilizing the miraculous eighth Barsoomian ray to negate gravity. "Of course, Odar, we can begin this instant."

Gan-Toh-Gan, still scowling at thought of the looming fierceness of haggling in which he must engage to guarantee the profit he wished for his master, followed by Dat Voga, hiding as best he could how amusing he found this comical peculiarity of the odar's, went belowdecks.

Making their way to the stern they came to a small, but well-equipped workshop where Dat Voga had constructed the prototype. Here they were to take stock of the materials on hand, making a list of anything Dat Voga required to build more units.

By now, those who had won the shore-leave lottery were disembarking, including the two women who were accompanied by Gar-Noh-Dar. Dat Voga and the odar, deep in the hull of the ship, were not idle while these prepared for their outing. The odar helped compile the list of needed items while telling the young man of the archipelago, this port being located upon the largest island of the chain.

After its initial discovery by a Xanatorian trade vessel, the existence of the islands had remained undisclosed for some time. The Xanatorians hid its discovery and location from the rest of the world for as long as possible, for they had discovered the chain to be flush with valuable minerals.

Chief of these were veins of white gold, and a particularly rare type of blood-red diamond with distinct, black, subterraneous patterns.

"For many years the archipelago was simply called Plaezor's islands, or sometimes simply the Plaezors, named after the odar of the vessel who discovered it," explained Gan-Toh-Gan. "A lively mining colony was established, and steady shipping of rare stones and precious metals began.

"Out of a chain consisting of over a hundred islands only the three greater ones are inhabited. Many of the minor ones are not much larger that the deck of this vessel. Nearly every island, though, regardless of size, has at least one mine established, and piers, the miners being ferried to and from the mine they are working."

The islands were rough in every respect, causing them to be difficult to build upon, this being especially true of the lesser ones, which tended to be more rugged and steep. Many of the mines were accessible only by foot, the miners hiking over terrain that was far too difficult for the ponderous, eight-legged zytogonths to navigate, forcing the workers to pack the ore out of the mountains on their backs.

The main island had digs that showed no sign of depletion even after thousands of years of harvesting ore. The young scientist was dutifully impressed. Of course, over the years, knowledge of these rich mines leaked out. Gradually, there began an influx of merchants, opportunists, and adventurists. The area grew from a colony to a village, and thence to the busy city it was when Dat Voga visited.

"The islands are a hodgepodge of nationalities, but also include a native population that has never set foot on the mainland. They know no other life than that of being an islander," said Gan-Toh-Gan. "And why leave? With the constant bustle of activity and people coming and going, a merchant can become wealthy on his imports and exports. The island populace covets wares from the mainland, and trade is brisk. It would be interesting to live here."

Dat Voga grinned, guessing why the odar might feel this way, imagining him at the docks negotiating with merchants. Dat Voga also learned that the region was still volcanically active. One of the islands was barely twenty years old, having risen from the bottom during a violent eruption. The seabed activity at the time, the odar told him, caused the surface to boil and slew millions of fish.

"Killed a bunch of fish-men, too," he grunted. "And good riddance!"

A thought occurred to Dat Voga when he learned of the substantial volcanic activity in this area. When he and Thuria arrived in the past, they had become confused during the storm that eventually marooned them on the island where they lived for months. Since arriving in the past, they had never known precisely where they were geographically. Now, he thought he did. The odar had told him roughly where lay the ruins of ancient Xanator, and he had recently learned that these islands lay northeast of that city.

While pondering this he recalled that he had flown over an area in roughly this location while on maneuvers. He did not remember any land formations rising from the dead sea floor, however, but instead he recalled a deep depression, covered naturally in ochre moss.

Of course, the distances were difficult to judge precisely. At the time, he had been aboard a flier, while now he was reckoning by inconsistent sailing speeds. If this were indeed the area over which he had flown, then at some point in the future a catastrophic event must occur to cause the archipelago to sink.

He guessed the calamity to be related to the volcanic activity still forming the islands. He did not care to envision Plaezor vaporized, yet after nearly perishing in that manner himself once, he appreciated the very real possibility that thousands of years from now all of this could suddenly and violently cease to exist.

Chapter Three

DAT VOGA'S EPIPHANIES

THE ODAR HAD LONG SINCE LEFT HIM to attend to his duties, and Dat Voga realized he had been in the little workshop for some time. Wishing to see Azaria and Thuria before they left, he rushed up the stairs onto the deck. As he walked toward the women's quarters, however, a sailor stopped him short. "Kaor, Dat Voga! If you seek Azaria, you just missed her. Gar-Noh-Dar and the women just left!"

He thanked the man, disheartened to have missed seeing Azaria. He wondered why the women had not come to say good-bye. For some reason, the thought depressed him, for if Azaria cared for him at all, would she not come to see him before leaving? He would have sought her, were the situations reversed. He felt suddenly silly and ashamed of the direction of his thoughts.

"She has never avowed any feelings for me, so I have no reason to expect such considerations from her. After all, it is I who am moonstruck, not she." Suddenly, the young padwar felt as though there were fofals fluttering around in his belly, and an icy fear gripped him. "Truly, she must not care for me at all!"

The young man had never experienced the doubts and trepidations that can assail one in love. After remaining steadfastly unaffected by the importunities and flirtations of the many beautiful and desirable women of Barsoom's gleaming cities, and causing as many hearts to flutter in ballrooms as he had stilled in times of war, he had finally himself succumbed to that most vulnerable of emotions. The smallest thing now took on mountainous proportions.

Misgivings assailed Dat Voga. In his mind he invented scene after scene of Azaria with other men; Azaria—cool, aloof, and indifferent to him. "What if she is in love with Gar-Noh-Dar?" he mused. "They are lifelong friends and it would be completely natural for her to fall in love with him. He is a handsome man, and one of her nationality for whom she may already harbor feelings after a lifetime of association."

Instant, intense jealousy of Gar-Noh-Dar filled his heart. Reacting instinctively, he clenched the handle of his dagger. Mortified, he jerked his hand from the hilt as if it were red hot, disgusted by his action. "What am I doing? Gar-Noh-Dar is my friend whom I have grown to love and respect!"

Downcast and confused, he spun toward the hatch to return to his workshop when he heard a tinkling of laughter . . . Azaria's laughter! Sprinting to the rail, he saw the three of them then, just stepping off the pier onto the boardwalk.

As he gripped the rail with whitened knuckles Azaria turned her head, possibly for a look at the *Prachus* from the quay. But although he was certain he had heard her musical laughter, her expression was somber as her eyes quested down the length of the ship.

Then she saw him standing at the rail and he could not recall ever seeing anyone's face illumine with such joy at sight of him, unless perhaps his mother's had done so. The young woman's face beamed with a wide smile that showed all her beautiful teeth, and the sun glinted magically from her eyes. She waved her hand to get his attention, not knowing his eyes were already devouring her.

When he waved in reply she blew him a kiss—a friendly gesture which, however innocent, caused the young man's heart to pound furiously in his breast. His breath came in ragged gasps, his skin was burning hot and glowing with excitement. He managed another quick wave before, pulled along by Thuria, she disappeared in the crowd.

He waited by the rail, hoping for one last glimpse of her, but she never reappeared, for the crowds that parted to receive them swept closed and swallowed them.

"Gods," he exclaimed. "How is it I am only now becoming aware of the prodigious depths of my affection for this girl—and her an Orovar from a million years in my past?"

As insecure as he felt around her, even he could not deny the obvious joy she displayed just now when she saw him. He had noted the desultory expression her face wore just prior, and then the great change the sight of him wrought upon her demeanor. It gave him hope.

But on the heels of those epiphanies more unwelcome doubts assailed him. He felt an icy stab of fear with the realization that the future could not possibly hold for him the outcome for which he so deeply longed. There existed no possible path for him to remain in this time and have a normal life with Azaria.

"How can I ask her to become my mate," he asked himself, "when to do so would forever revise the timeline of the future? The branching of family lines for a million years would be irrevocably altered. Who knows what manner of indiscriminate destruction will result should I willfully pursue a life with Azaria in this time? One thing is certain—untold millions would simply cease to exist."

Such is youth, thinking they will live forever, and that the world will end if they are not there to save it. It was his next thought, however, that stopped him in his tracks.

"Issus, how is it that this has not occurred to me ere now?" he quizzed himself. "It must be that a kind providence hid it from me, knowing my mind incapable of coping with the calamity I know I have inadvertently wrought! What in the name of my first ancestor have I done? What was I thinking?

"I saved Azaria's life during the attack of the fish-men when she nearly drowned! That single act has already affected the future timeline. Yet even Thuria did not reprove me for it. She is so sensible that she would simply say I could not have acted otherwise. The fish-men's attack occurred so suddenly. I acted purely on instinct and the impulses of the moment in the defense of my friends and the woman I love."

He quickly analyzed the events as they most likely would have occurred without his interference. "If Thuria and I had not gone down to meet the crew of the *Prachus* when they landed on the island after the storm, then the encounter with the fish-men would have occurred as it must have in an unmodified past, in which Azaria would have perished in that attack."

The thought made him ill. "And then I come along and change everything. Thuria and I join the crew of the *Prachus*, we work side by side with them, we make friends with them, and I fall in love with one of them. Eventually, I save Azaria's life when she would have surely drowned. But that is not all I unwittingly changed."

Dat Voga felt increasingly uneasy as he considered the other events of the encounter. Suddenly his heart began hammering, yet this time not from a great love, but from fear. For the gross level of his meddling had not ended with the saving of Azaria's life. No, he was guilty of much more than saving the life of a single individual.

"In the original past not only Azaria, *but the entire crew of the* Prachus *must have perished*!" he cried, slamming a fist onto the workbench.

The drama in which he took part had played out in a different version in which he did not exist. He was now certain that originally there were no survivors of the fish-men's attack. Therefore, he had been instrumental in saving the lives of *all those who survived*. Everyone had acknowledged it. Sailor after sailor had come to Dat Voga to thank him for saving their lives.

Those hearty thanks and exclamations replayed in his mind: "Thank the shades for you, Dat Voga!" and "By the shades, Dat Voga, I don't know how you turned that brobdoganth on the fish-men like you did, it was remarkable!"

Were it not for him telepathically controlling the brobdoganth, the great fish would have rammed the ship from below and sent her to the bottom, together with every able-bodied sailor, including Azaria.

He could not begin to fathom the wreckage he had wrought on the future. If Thuria or he blinked out of existence the next instant, it would not have surprised him.

Cold with dread, he stumbled to his quarters, the odar and the new hoist forgotten. At all costs, he must solve Daxxus Nahl's cryptic, and he must solve it now. They simply must return to their own time, and quickly. The thought of having to leave these people, especially Azaria, left him with an unswallowable knot in his throat.

He only hoped that, when that time came, he could go through with it.

In his quarters he worked feverishly on the cryptic input screen of the gauntlets. The door suddenly burst inward, and Odar Gan-Toh-Gan rushed in behind it. "Dat Voga! There you are, by the shades! Kun-bor just returned. The City Guard arrested Gar-Noh-Dar and detained the women!"

"What?" shouted the astounded padwar, exploding to his feet.

"Apparently," continued the odar, "Thuria caused a good deal of excitement in town. You two look so remarkable with your red skin! Anyway, word of her appearance spread, and they were eventually confronted by an officer with a contingent of warriors that we believe was sent to apprehend them.

"They demanded that Thuria come with them. When Gar-Noh-Dar refused, they attacked him! They rounded up all three because Azaria came to Gar-Noh-Dar's defense after they wrongfully accused him of maliciously attacking an officer. Come on, you can play with your silly armbands later!"

But Dat Voga had already dropped the gauntlets into his sea chest and was strapping on his sword. Slamming the chest shut, he faced the odar. "Let's go!"

He would spill the blood of every able-bodied fighting man on this island if that's what it took to free his friends and the woman he loved. Gone were the fumes of jealousy of moments before; gone, the panicky fear of the repercussions of his actions in the past. Those emotions were now displaced by the cool, measured thoughts that typically guided him in all his actions.

The two men rushed up the companionway to the upper deck, where Gan-Toh-Gan ordered Kun-bor, a steersman, to lead the way.

Pausing at the gangway, Gan-Toh-Gan instructed his first osar, "Bim-Gon-Dar, no one is to leave this ship but for runners to return all hands from shore. In the meantime, ready the *Prachus*. It may be that we will need to leave in a hurry."

The odar, the padwar, and Kun-bor then dashed down the gangplank, onto the pier, and into the crowded street. Racing through the gate, they headed toward the inner city.

Chapter Four

Teufels

OLLOWING THE LEAD OF KUN-BOR, the padwar and
the odar raced through the winding streets. There
was no time for the sightseeing Dat Voga had anticipated, and the densely packed masses obstructing him
were only hindrances around which he must weave. He
heard several cries after the fashion of "Look! He's got red
skin!" and "It's another of those creatures!" He ignored them,
and the pedestrians seemed fearful of impeding him.

They finally arrived at a palatial building in which resided
the government of this island. Kun-Bor indicated the structure with a nod. "They were taken in there."

When Dat Voga asked about speaking with the jeddak,
Kun-Bor explained that, unlike in most cities upon Barsoom,
no jed governed this island city, but rather a tribunal of
elected native islanders.

The practice hearkened to the days when this was a
colony of Xanator. Because of the distance, the jeddak
decreed they choose three of their own to rule locally. A
further requirement was that a member of the tribunal
report to the mainland several times per year. The intent
of the compulsory trip was clearly to assert control, as any
one of the many vessels departing daily could have borne
this report to the jeddak.

There was a time when the islands wished for their

autonomy. Blows were traded. In a surprise move, rather than wage war with the colonials, of whom many were of Xanatorian descent, Xanator conceded, ordering the return of its warriors. This then required the Plaezors to form their own defensive force. In the past they had drawn the attention of seafaring green men seeking slaves and victims for torture, so the withdrawal of Xanator's warriors had left them temporarily defenseless.

The sallow fish-men also plagued their shores, surfacing just long enough to clamber aboard a vessel or onto the docks to drag a victim into the sea. The locals would say, "If a fish-man gets you in the water, you're a goner," as the bodies of those taken in that manner were never recovered. The common belief was that they were dragged into the depths and devoured.

Dat Voga saw that a great confluence had congregated in the square outside the guard keep, which was where he guessed their friends were located. Initially, they had no trouble weaving their way through the crowd, until Kun-Bor stepped on a fellow's heel, causing him to turn with an oath unfamiliar to the Heliumite. But rather than releasing his oaths upon poor Kun-Bor, the diamond miner stared wide-eyed at the red-hued Dat Voga.

Without pause, the man shouted, "A *teufel*, by the shades!" In an instant all became utter bedlam. Fists were raised, weapons flashed, while others of the crowd in their closest vicinity executed a general withdrawal from them, as if out of fear. Those in the rear, however, began forcing the others forward so that the three men found they must pull their swords to defend themselves.

They continued to force their way toward the steps of the barrack where they put their backs against a wall of the structure. Those present then witnessed the most splendid display of swordsmanship they had ever seen.

Thinking only of Azaria and the others, Dat Voga fought as though inspired, for the stakes were incalculable. He had the evolution of a million years of sword-fighting techniques at his disposal. The voice of his illustrious instructor, John Carter, the greatest swordsman on two worlds, sounded in his ears as though the Warlord fought by his side.

"Mind your balance, Dat Voga! You grip your blade too tightly."

To the padwar, it seemed like the enormous clangor filling his ears became muted as he focused on that inner voice expertly guiding his blade. With each conjured whisper from the Warlord, the red man adjusted his feet or his grip until his blade appeared a living thing.

Two Plaezorian guardsmen charged at him with swords raised in double-fisted grips. The Heliumite's sword flashed. One guard's hand sailed into the mob still gripping the handle of his weapon, his appendage neatly amputated. The second's sword was knocked nearly free from his grasp on a vicious backstroke. The man managed not to drop his weapon but recovered too late as Dat Voga's point found his heart.

The odar and Kun-Bor wielded their gaffs, with Dat Voga now witnessing just how effective these were against an antagonist. The odar surged forward, his curved bill catching a guard behind the neck. Hooking his catch, he drew him in. Dat Voga had seen sailors do similarly when fishing. Kun-Bor slammed the sharpened point of his gaff into the guard's chest, the point blasting through the warrior's leather breast plate to pierce his heart.

With a savage wrench, the steersman pulled the point free as Gan-Toh-Gan jerked his bill from the man's neck and planted a foot into his gut, propelling him backward into his fellows who fell atop his dying form. All of this took but a moment.

The padwar had been engaged by an adversary who had managed to achieve a higher level of skill than his fellows. The sword Dat Voga was using, although they called it a longsword, was shorter than the swords of his day. Also, it had a much heavier, clumsier blade unlike the slender, razor-sharp blades of his time to which he had been accustomed since breaking his shell.

He would have given much to have the sword he had when Daxxus Nahl captured them, but he had not seen it since succumbing to the fumes in the upper cavern during the fight with the Banaalians. The swords of his time were so sharp a mere flick of the tip in the hands of an expert could open a man's throat from ear to ear.

But he was finding he could acquit himself admirably even with this unfamiliar blade. Since it was considerably heavier than that to which he was accustomed, he snatched a heavy dagger from his belt with his free hand. The extra weight on his opposite side offset the bulkiness of the sword, and afforded him a weapon for his unguarded side, upon which crept a dirty-faced miner with an iron bar.

This was his first sword fight since arriving in the past, and he quickly realized the benefit of his augmented stamina. His physique had never been better tuned. Combining his body's enhanced ability to absorb oxygen and having spent weeks at sea performing demanding labor had done much for his muscular development. He felt like he could fight all day, and the realization that he had an edge on his foes brought a smile to his lips.

With a renewed feeling of self-confidence, he fought on with what his enemies seemed to consider an intimidating and irksome smirk on his face. He fought tirelessly after his friends began to wax weary and his foes to stagger. The enemy, however, did not suffer from exhaustion as much as did the two sailors, for the latter were forced to fight continuously, while the guards and the inflamed mob could step back as they wearied and allow others to take their place.

Deflecting a simple stroke that the youngest martial student of the padwar's time could have parried, the padwar turned to face the attack from the man with the iron bar. He was about to brain Dat Voga, already having swung the bar back behind his head to the pinnacle of the arc the bar would describe in its descent upon the red man's skull. But he had not reckoned on the quick reflexes of the padwar.

As quick as a striking banth, Dat Voga drew his dagger and flung it toward the miner. Dagger tossing had long been a favorite pastime in the navy, and most warriors excelled at it to some degree. After releasing the weapon, the padwar did not bother to survey the damage, renewing instead his onslaught against another foe. There followed a quick flurry of steel where the padwar's swordpoint seemed to be everywhere at once, confounding the man.

Faster than any eye could register, Dat Voga's point swept across the man's throat, unintentionally severing the leather chin strap securing his helmet. The man staggered back, his helmet sailing from his head into the face of an incoming miner lunging with a fishing spear. Dat Voga ducked beneath the stabbing spear and withdrew his dagger from the heart of the dirty-faced miner, whose iron bar lay on the flags near his stiffening fingers.

Rising, he ran his sword through the miner holding the fishing spear, who collapsed onto a pile of bodies so thick Dat Voga could hardly maneuver for their presence. He stole a quick glance at his friends, noticing they were starting to really show signs of fatigue. They had not spoken for several xats, each having been too busy gasping for air, and trying to stay alive.

The scientist turned in time to block a vicious cut. This he followed by hammering the pommel of his sword into the grimacing, flushed face before him, observing at close quarters as the man's teeth caved-in from the crushing blow. But the guard would not have to worry for long how this would affect his smile. When Dat Voga pulled his sword back, he came across with a slash from the dagger that once more drank deeply of a member of the Plaezorian Guard.

The padwar knew they could not maintain this pace. The numbers against them were overwhelming, and they could not face every direction at once. Then the melee took a new turn. The swordsmen on the front line withdrew, allowing the advance of spearmen.

Shortly, the three were surrounded by two rows of spears, the men in the rows being staggered so that a man in the front row did not impede the cast of the man behind. It looked as though they were to be wholesale slaughtered. His breathing slow and measured, the red man paused, crossing his arms across his breast—a dripping sword in one hand and a bloody dagger in the other.

Breathing heavily, wiping sweat and blood from their brows, the two sailors came and stood beside the padwar. So far, none of them had suffered an injury, only superficial nicks, cuts, and bruises. The look on Dat Voga's face was angry and his brow was furrowed in a scowl. It was frustrating that his efforts to free Azaria and the others had come to naught. But he was a patient fighter and a cool tactician. He would wait for another opportunity.

His gaze was level and focused as he scanned his enemies, seeking an avenue of escape. The guards and mob against whom they had fought now stood behind the spearmen. No one spoke. They appeared to be awaiting someone of note—perhaps he who would issue the command to slay them.

They did not have long to wait. Three or four figures were visible making their way through the crowd. They stopped behind the front row of spears, out of reach of the weapons of the men of the *Prachus*.

The Heliumite saw that these were the ones in authority. Rather than waiting for them to speak, he addressed them first. "What is the meaning of this attack?" he demanded. "Where are our friends and why have they been detained?"

"Silence, creature!" A man with long robes and a strange headdress stared at Dat Voga, his mouth curled in scorn. He directed his next comments at those who accompanied him. "This is the male counterpart to the other. Place them with the others. In the morning, we shall flush the evil from these teufels in the depths of the quays!"

Gar-Noh-Dar exclaimed, "Teufels? This man is no teufel, you imbecile! You're making a mistake."

Dat Voga did not recognize the word, but to him it connoted something of death, or of a creature returned from death. Their captors ignored every attempt to communicate with them and, having no choice in the matter, they relinquished their weapons but continued to voice their dissent. Eventually, the guards beat them with their spear hafts and shouted at them to shut up.

Forced at spearpoint, disarmed, and bound, they were marched into the barracks. There they were brought before a large man sitting behind a desk. The man was writing meticulously in an enormous tome that lay open upon a table of volcanic glass, chiseled from a mound of the material that was still attached to the floor. The hieroglyphs he scribbled were indecipherable to the red man.

The man did not immediately acknowledge their arrival but continued to scribe in his ledger in his small, neat handwriting. When he finally looked up from his work, he studied the three captives' faces briefly, his eyes lingering on Dat Voga. Turning to their leader, he spoke in a monotone that dripped with tedium. "Report, Osar."

Returning his gaze to the prisoners, he studied each of them in turn as the osar reported. As the osar described Dat Voga's exploits with the sword, and the numbers of slain, the man behind the desk focused his gaze intently on the Heliumite. Dat Voga could sense a growing animosity within the man, if the muscles jumping in his jaw and his narrowed eyes were any indication.

At last he exploded, turning on the padwar. "Enough! You invade our island! You attack our citizens! You slay our soldiery! The quays are too good for you. I shall speak to Kyper Tron. Perhaps he shall grant us the exquisite joy of torturing these unclean shades before they're purged!"

Odar Gan-Toh-Gan interjected, "No one here is an unclean shade, you simpleton! We've been trying to explain this, but no one will shut their mouths and open their ears long enough. I never heard of anyone taking those childish teufel stories seriously. They're tales to frighten children to their sleeping dais, not to goad men into acts of barbarity!"

A collective intake of breath followed from their guards, as though they could not believe Gan-Toh-Gan could be so brash as to utter such blasphemy and heresy. The large man came to his feet, one finger stabbed truculently in the odar's face.

Glowering, the man said, "Utter not one more word, on your life. Osar! Take these daksors to their den and put them with the others. I go to speak to the High O-Von. Once he hears of this heretic's remarks, I believe he, too, will find his sentence too lenient." With that, the large man stormed from the room.

Upon his exit, the soldiers, beating the prisoners about the head and neck with the flats of swords and spear hafts, drove them into a different passage from that which they had entered. They were then forced to follow a dark path, deep underground into the base rock of the island. The red man knew after trekking for a considerable amount of time down this steep path that they must be far below sea level.

From the abandoned and broken implements scattered along their path, it became clear to the prisoners that they were descending into a former mine. Their captors, accusing them of being supernatural creatures, had decided to imprison Dat Voga and his companions in the darkest of pits, with the prison cells above being reserved for ordinary offenders. They apparently took no chances with those found in the company of teufels, either.

Here and there, reflected in the light of the torches carried by their captors, were the glints and glitterings of unmined veins of ores. The padwar saw Barsoomian white gold, platinum, and other rare minerals and metals. That these veins remained unmined testified to the riches contained in these islands.

Dat Voga never knew for how long they walked, but eventually they arrived at a heavy doorway set in a tunnel wall, which was apparently their destination. Opening this, their guards prodded them into an unlit room and slammed the door shut behind them, leaving them alone in the darkness.

Chapter Five

Prison beneath the Sea

WITH THE ECHOES OF THE SLAMMED DOOR yet resounding in their ears, Dat Voga and Odar Gan-Toh-Gan made their way carefully across the room, feeling their way forward slowly in the pitch blackness with their hands extended and sliding their feet forward, seeking obstacles, or openings in the floor. The voice coming to them from out of the dark void surprised them.

"Who are you? Have you come to release us?" The padwar recognized the voice as that of Gar-Noh-Dar. So, too, did Gan-Toh-Gan.

"My son!" cried the odar.

Dat Voga recognized the joy and relief in the voice of the odar. He was understandably grateful to have found his son, after being buried beneath the sea in this fathomless hole. After his first exclamation of shock and surprise, however, the odar's voice resumed its familiar tone of formality.

"Report, Osar! Where are the women, Azaria and Thuria?" he barked.

Before the osar could answer, Thuria cried out, "We are here!"

"Odar, what of Dat Voga? Is he here?" the voice of Azaria asked.

"I am here," the man from the future answered. He exhaled in relief to have found Azaria and Thuria both safe.

He stumbled toward Azaria's voice, his fingers finally finding hers. Pulling her close, he felt her face and limbs for any sign of injury. "You have not been hurt, Azaria?"

"No, Dat Voga," she replied.

Only then thinking of Thuria, he asked sheepishly, "Thuria, you are also unharmed?"

"I am unharmed. But I had hoped you were negotiating our release!"

"It seems my sword could not speak quickly enough," he replied.

Unable to contain himself any longer at contact with the woman he loved, the padwar wrapped his arms about Azaria's slight frame and kissed her forehead, at the same time inhaling the fragrance of her thick mass of hair.

"Gar-Noh-Dar fought like a banth against those ulsios, Dat Voga!" Thuria said excitedly. "He kept himself between them and us until the cowards cast blunt spears and hit him in the head, knocking him unconscious."

"What's a banth?" Azaria asked.

"Ulsios?" Gar-Noh-Dar queried.

The red man smiled. It reminded him of the times he and Thuria stumbled as they learned the names of creatures of which they had never heard. He did not inform their Orovar friends that banths and ulsios did not yet exist. As with the primitive zytogonth, those modern creatures were most likely known by different names in this time as their primordial cousins would be housed in different forms, necessitating many more millennia before becoming the creatures of his and Thuria's time.

Instead, he said, "Well done, Gar-Noh-Dar! I'm so glad that if it could not be me, that you were there to defend these two whom I treasure above all others. My sword is at your feet, my friend!"

Gar-Noh-Dar had not heard the modern term of placing one's sword at another's feet, yet he caught the insinuation instantly.

Although telepathy existed in these prehistoric people, it was not as highly developed as it would become in Dat Voga's time. Else, he would have perhaps used that medium to express his gratitude to his friend. Based on his observations thus far in the past, the pasty fish-men had a keener development of the art.

The padwar recalled mention of Gar-Noh-Dar having been knocked unconscious. "Gar-Noh-Dar, were you injured when they struck you?"

The sailor replied that, besides a gash over his temple and a slight headache, he was whole and hale. He then recounted their adventures. They had traversed much of the city, each enrapt as they took in the various sights of this bustling, seaside cosmopolis. It was Azaria who pointed out they had developed a small following.

Initially, they had thought little of it. Shortly, however, members of the city guard approached them with two others who, from the description, wore the same headdress and robes as the man who had accosted Dat Voga and his friends in the square outside the barracks.

The robed man, whom they heard called Kyper Tron, questioned Thuria. Apparently disliking her responses, he grew annoyed. Accusing her of being a teufel, he abruptly ordered them all seized. At this point, Gar-Noh-Dar stepped between Thuria and her accuser, shouting for Kun-Bor to hasten to the ship to warn his father.

When he had left the ship, Gar-Noh-dar had taken with him only a dagger. This he used to good effect, but his resistance proved to be valiant but futile; mere moments into the fight someone threw something at him. This had struck him a glancing blow, he said, but it was enough to knock him out cold. When he awoke, he lay in this dark cell with the two women.

At this point, Kun-Bor took up the tale. "A guard grabbed me, but I twisted out of his arms and ran. I escaped down an alley that let onto a main thoroughfare filled with zytogonths pulling wains and people moving in every direction. It was an easy matter to disappear in the crowd. I then made my way back to the ship."

Now that they were reunited and everyone appeared uninjured but for minor abrasions and bruises, they huddled together in the darkness to plan. They chose an area of the floor away from the entrance so they could converse in hushed whispers without fear of being overheard, having no idea if the enemy had an ear to the door.

Dat Voga considered retrieving his modern pocket torch from his pouch, which he still had about his waist. Although he and the others had been relieved of their weapons, the sailors of the *Prachus* yet retained their waist pouches, due no doubt to their innocuous location beneath the thigh-length utility straps depending from their harness belts.

This distinctive feature of Horzian sailors had not caught on elsewhere. In addition to being extremely useful on the ship, the straps now proved to have an unintended value in that their pouches had escaped the notice of their captors.

He knew he should take out the light and examine their prison, which would possibly facilitate their escape. However, he hesitated. If he did, he would have much to explain to his prehistoric friends. His light, after all, was a million years ahead of current innovation. As intelligent as these people were, this fact would not go unnoticed, just as it had not escaped Azaria's quick eye in the hold.

As he considered this, he felt Azaria's light touch on his arm. She leaned in close as the others whispered together. Speaking low, she said, "Dat Voga—your light! I saw it the day you discovered me in the hold. I know you do not wish others to see it, but we need light if we are to escape. Please!"

"Azaria—" he began.

The odar apparently overheard a portion of her hastily whispered plea. "See what, Azaria? Out with it, you young gantahns!"

Dat Voga gave Azaria's hand a quick squeeze, then admitted to the odar, "I have a light; just a moment."

The next instant, the entire floor in their midst became brightly illumined, light sparkling and glinting from raw gems and refracting from the veins of precious metals threading throughout the floors and walls. It also showed the amazed looks on all the faces but Thuria's, whose expression reflected only her kind understanding.

He looked at her sheepishly, for it was always he who stressed the need to keep a low profile, to be careful of what they said so as not to affect the future or bring suspicion upon themselves. He smiled at her when he saw her look of approval, and the brave smile she flashed him.

The odar drew a deep breath. But, before he began an interrogation, Dat Voga stopped him. "Odar Gan-Toh-Gan, I beg you, do not ask me to explain at this time. It may be that I can never do so. Suffice it to say, I have this light, and it shall serve us now in our moment of need. Please, let us examine our cell before our prison door is thrown open to admit our jailers—and perhaps our executioners."

The odar sighed. "Very well, Dat Voga. But someday." With that, the padwar, with the others trailing along, began a detailed inspection of the room. They discovered they were imprisoned in what, hundreds or even thousands of years ago, had been a chamber where workers slept and stored their gear between shifts in the mines.

Carved into the walls were shelves and storage areas, while about the periphery were tunnel openings, each blocked by a wooden door. This, then, was a crosstunnel of mine shafts. Emblazoned over each door were fading hieroglyphs that none in their party could read. It was evident that men had lived here, deep below the sea, and that from this point they were dispersed through these shafts to their labors.

In the middle of the chamber an enormous column stood, left in place when the miners excavated the room from the mother stone. Ledges protruded from this column bearing human dimensions of width and length, stacked vertically to the ceiling, forming sleeping platforms. The room's design seemed maximized for use of the space and was approximately a hundred sofads in diameter.

Dat Voga guessed that when these shafts were active this room had been a hub, with man-powered carts brought through here on their way to the surface. Nor was he incorrect in his guess. In some areas, ruts, carved by years of use by wheeled contrivances, were in evidence, the marks of their passage engraved in the stone floor.

They found the door through which they had passed because it was the only one locked from the outside. If that had not been enough, the dust of ages was ample evidence of where they had trampled. Spaced out approximately every fifteen sofads about the periphery were the entrances to mine shafts. The ceiling was of a vaulted type, with the gigantic, left-in-place column stabbing upward into the apex of the vault.

Dat Voga thought it strange their captors would imprison them in a room with so many exits until he considered that to try to traverse these shafts without a light would have been suicidal. To enter the wrong shaft might send the escaped convict deeper into the bowels of the island, and further beneath the sea.

For all he knew, these shafts dropped sheer to the ocean floor. Whichever path they chose to take, he realized that pursuit would be quick, since the deep dust on the floor would point the way to their avenue of escape.

Before deciding which tunnel to enter, they traversed each optional corridor for a short distance to see if it took a downward trend, which they certainly did not wish. In this manner they eliminated many shafts. The group came to a consensus on the route they would take, and without further delay, they set out. The corridor they chose ran level for a time and then began trending upward.

The hike provided Dat Voga an opportunity to ask the odar why he never accused them of being the teufels these fanatics believed them to be, and, since he was familiar with these islands, why he had not foreseen the danger in coming here. They had discovered in the worst possible way that a powerful and fanatical religious force was at work, controlling both the tribunal and the military.

"We haven't made port here in a few years. I had never heard of this strange order that *purges* men in their quays and believe this to be a recent development, perhaps related to an influx of folk from somewhere these beliefs hold sway.

"Our people believe the shades of our ancestors protect us as they are able; that they bless us, give us advice, and guide us from pitfalls. These people follow a distortion of that, believing shades return to this world, and that they can destroy them as though they were living men. The people of Plaezor would be better off purging these so-called O-Vons and turning from this ridiculous folly."

They continued to follow the path upward, with Dat Voga and the odar bringing up the rear. Dat Voga held his modern light so that it illuminated the floor, that they might avoid hazards. The walls and floors of the tunnels they followed were so rich with precious bounty that the light, reflected and scattered in every direction, gave them excellent visibility in what otherwise had been the true darkness of a pit.

The well-worn floor of the passage meandered, generally climbing, although a couple of times it tended downward, alarming them all. They needed to reach the surface, and their ship. Quite often they found themselves again in large, cavernous areas where miners had formed quarters or storerooms.

In these rooms were the stone ledges for sleeping, and the mouths of new tunnels. Each time they came upon one of these, they must of necessity decide which tunnel to follow, hoping they guessed correctly. They also often discovered additional branches from their tunnel, running off to the left or right, and sometimes in both directions simultaneously.

At these intersections, they would decide whether to remain in the current shaft or to branch off. This they decided by the same manner as before, by traveling down each briefly, or simply by flashing their light down the dark passages and taking the one that appeared to incline upward the most.

Their worst fear was that the only path to the surface might be that which the guards had brought them, and that eventually all tunnels terminated below sea level. If that were true, it would be catastrophic. But they did not believe that to be the case because the air remained not only breath-able, but fresh—as though new currents were somehow being directed into these subterranean shafts.

Chapter Six

A Desperate Plan

I F DAT VOGA KNEW WHAT A HAT WAS, he would have mentally taken his off to the ancient Plaezorian mining engineers who designed these delves. But also, after tramping the tunnelings, he began to wonder that the entire mass of the island above their heads had not caved in with such an extent of the substratum so perforated with voids, tunnels, and cavernous chambers.

To his trained eye, it was obvious this mining operation had been active for thousands of years and that the only reason so much ore remained in the walls and floors was that if they had mined it all, the tunnels would have collapsed.

Eventually, he heard an inevitable sound—echoes of the voices and footsteps of pursuit. The guards would move more quickly than had they, having only to follow their prints in the dusty trail, while the escapees must seek the wisest course, hoping the shades of their ancestors guided them. It was impossible to gauge the distance to their pursuers. All they could do was push onward.

Soon, the sounds of the voices came to them more clearly. But coincidently from ahead, Gar-Noh-Dar claimed he saw a soft radiance and swore he smelled the sea. The red man extinguished his torch, and they waited anxiously for their eyes to adjust. After a few moments they saw a dim glow ahead.

They rushed forward, coming to an ancient mine entrance carved in the face of a cliff. They guessed the miners utilized a rope system, which no longer existed, to send ore down. The sun was just rising and sat low in a leaden sky. They had spent the entire night, then, traversing the tunnels. And now they were at an impasse, for the slope before them was perpendicular and treacherous.

Dat Voga realized that to attempt a rapid descent of these rocky faces might result in injury or death. And to have their enemy come upon them from above while they descended—he did not need much imagination to figure out the outcome of such a scenario. Far below him he could see the city beginning to stir, while further away, sitting peacefully in her berth, sat the *Prachus*.

Gods, how he wished they had a handful of equilibrimotors, or the flier in which he and Carthoris had sailed to Ptarsas! That seemed like such a long time ago, but a million years must pass before that flight occurred. A hundred things flashed through Dat Voga's sharp mind, but none of them placed the power to save his friends in his hands.

An idea struck him. Wait—he did have a power! These fanatics believed he and Thuria possessed dark powers, and that they could destroy their evil spirits by submerging them in the waters of the quay. Obviously, they were unconcerned that it would destroy Dat Voga and Thuria as well. He did not debate it any further. He turned to the others, who noted the look on his face and realized he had an idea.

"What is it, Dat Voga? Quickly, man, we have mere xats!" cried the odar.

"All of you descend those cliffs now! Thuria, come with me. You and I shall come again to the *Prachus* by another path."

Gar-Noh-Dar protested. "Dat Voga, what do you have in mind? I do not wish to see Thuria in danger. "

The padwar saw that Gar-Noh-Dar appeared to have developed more than a passing interest in Thuria. But their personal feelings did not matter right now. For himself, he dearly wished he could accompany Azaria. But he knew he had another path he must follow. He laid his hand on the man's shoulder.

"I understand, Gar-Noh-Dar. But these people seek Thuria and me, so it shall be the two of us they find. My hope is that they will be content with us long enough to allow the rest of you time to escape. You must trust me— we shall join you aboard the *Prachus* in time to sail with the tide. Now, go! And keep a sharp eye for us near the anchor chain."

"The anchor chain?" asked a confused Gan-Toh-Gan.

As the others started down the cliff, making their way slowly and carefully to avoid a fall, Dat Voga looked at Thuria and smiled. Bravely, she flashed him an impish grin. She guessed what he had in mind. Taking her hand in his and flashing on his light, they sped off into the darkness of the tunnel they had just exited.

Running as quietly as possible, they retraced their steps back to one of the intersecting conduits they had passed earlier. Here, he guided Thuria up one of the other branches for a distance and waited, switching off his light and returning it to his innocuous pouch.

They heard the voices of guards and saw a faint light coming up their tunnel. Dat Voga had already informed Thuria as to his plan, so now they walked slowly toward the oncoming guardsmen. At sight of them, the men shouted and rushed forward, while he and Thuria paused, appearing to be placing themselves into their power of their own accord.

An officer came forward, his short sword drawn on the pair. His face wore a dark scowl. "Where are the others?" he demanded.

Dat Voga looked at him inquisitively, and hoped the guards were no more familiar with these long, abandoned mine shafts than were they. "We were forced to devour them," he said, "as we were beginning to feel weakened from privation. We just now followed this tunnel to a dead end and were returning. This is the second tunnel we have followed that ended in a chamber with no exit."

The officer recoiled in horror and fear. He and the others would have fled but for fear of their odar, above at his desk, and the High O-Von. The padwar noted their reactions and inwardly smiled. Aloud, he said, "Do not fear. With our hunger assuaged you are in no danger—for the moment."

The two from the future could hear mumblings among the guards. The officer swallowed hard, then steeled himself and turned to an underling. He then fired off, "Run up the other tunnel and recall Bek-Bin-Badha and the others and tell them we have the prisoners. Meet us at the intersection. Go!"

The man ran off to intercept the other soldiers who had just started up the tunnel that let onto the cliff. Dat Voga sincerely hoped he would reach the guards before they arrived at the end of the tunnel and discovered his friends descending the cliff.

The officer turned to Dat Voga. "Teufel, you will accompany us back to the upper levels. The odar awaits. The time approaches for your purging."

Dat Voga and Thuria were escorted by their guards back to the intersection where they awaited the arrival of the others. None of the warriors seemed anxious to crowd about the two, giving them a wide berth before and after. The red man noticed with amusement that the rearmost guard ahead of him constantly cast glances to his rear to make sure he stayed well ahead of Dat Voga and Thuria.

Upon the arrival of Bek-Bin-Badha with his usar of ten warriors, the prisoners were marched back to the original room in which they had been confined. From that point they continued back up the long path they had traversed earlier, to the first room where sat the huge man behind the desk, he whom their officer referred to as odar.

Once more the giant man glowered at them in anger, with no sign of the fear his men showed. His eyes squinted to two slits of rage as he exploded, "Where are the others?"

The officer of the guard stammered, "They devoured them! Only the shades of our ancestors prevented them from eating us, too! We checked all the tunnels; none remained alive!"

The padwar sensed that the giant man did not believe the story. The odar approached him, leaning his face close to the Heliumite's, glowering all the while. The man did not show the respect due a creature of the underworld, Dat Voga perceived.

"You do not have much fear of teufels," Dat Voga noted wryly.

The odar leaned in closer so that none might hear, and sneered, "You have renewed their waning faith—*red man*."

More loudly the man boomed, "The others can wait! There is no escape from those tunnels, except the doorway through which you just walked. The O-Von is anxious for the purgings this morning."

"At least we had a last meal," Dat Voga commented sarcastically, referring to his prevarication about having devoured his companions.

Glowering, the enraged odar turned to the officer of the guard, and snapped, "Bring them along!"

Forced at swordpoint, the group exited the barracks into the square and began the trip back through the city toward the quays. Presently they paused outside an imposing building that Dat Voga took to be the seat of their perverse religion. From it came forth the High O-Von and his retinue along with the tribunal and a multitude of guards and retainers. It appeared this purging would be quite an event.

As they proceeded down the streets and avenues toward the harbor, the padwar hoped he had not overestimated his and Thuria's abilities. The further they proceeded, the larger the following became, some of whom were wanton in their callous remarks, while others were simply curious.

Before long it became clear that knowledge of the forthcoming event had spread; a crowd was gathering upon the sea wall and along the quays and docks. The red man and Thuria were led out to the end of a pier where a pivoting framework stood with rope attached. Upon arriving, the High O-Von addressed both the prisoners and the crowd of onlookers.

Dat Voga paid little attention to the words of the O-Von as he was more interested in observing the preparations. He did catch one part in which the sentiment was expressed that when they returned to the surface, the evil shade causing them to be teufels would be gone. The O-Von opined that he hoped they would survive the purging, but if they did not, then at least the waters of the harbor would have rid their bodies of the dark shade, that their own might find eternal rest with their ancestors.

"Praise the Shades," responded Dat Voga.

"Attach them to the purging rack!" commanded the Hi-O-Von, one eye twitching with annoyance at the lack of fear and respect in Dat Voga's tone.

Two warriors roughly tied their hands and feet, and then added weights to their ankles. Finally, the ropes binding their hands were attached to the rope hanging from the pivoting framework. Dat Voga was nervous on one account: that they might send them beneath the water one at a time. The High O-Von did not leave him wondering long as to that, however, announcing that Thuria would descend first—and alone!

"Oh, praise the First Teufel!" Dat Voga exclaimed with obvious relief.

"What? What did you say?" blurted the high priest.

"Oh, nothing much. Only that I am very happy to be spared the horrors of being first into the water. It would have been especially awful were we purged simultaneously, where I would have to witness her thrashings," he finished.

The High O-Von did not meditate long on the matter. "They shall go down together!" he concluded, with a leer at Dat Voga. The padwar put on his best crestfallen expression.

The red man felt a flood of relief now that it appeared they would be sent down together, as the new development dovetailed nicely with his plan. Soon, they were hauled up and swung out over the harbor, dangling at the end of the wooden frame. As their guards lowered the two into the cool, briny water of the harbor, the crowd became hushed in breathless expectancy.

He did not have to tell Thuria to prepare herself for their immersion—she had already begun taking in lots of air, her beautiful skin now glowing as her modern physiognomy reacted to the massive amounts of oxygen she inhaled.

Upon seeing their skins deepen in color to almost a glow, the O-Von, fanaticism plastered across his face, shrieked, "See their vile perverseness! In moments, wicked shade, thou wilt be no more! Into the sea with them!"

As they were lowered toward the dark surface, he fairly preached the blue out of the sky with his shrieks, calling on the shades of their ancestors to purge these bodies of the evil shades that inhabited them. Then the cool waters of the harbor closed over their heads, thankfully cutting off the odious sound of the O-Von's rantings. They went down for about seventy sofads before they settled upon the sand and rank mud of the bottom.

Dat Voga went to work as soon as they ceased their descent. He dragged enough slack to enable him to begin working at his pouch, a difficult feat with his hands tied because of its location beneath the utility straps upon his belt. Eventually, he clutched the object upon which he had based his entire plan, the bit of blade that saved him from the green men a million years ago—in the future.

First the padwar went to work upon the rope that bound Thuria, to free her hands. Once this was finished the rest went smoothly. Soon, carrying the weights from their ankles in their hands to steady them, they began walking along the muddy bottom of the harbor, seeking the keel of the *Prachus*, whose location the padwar had noted as they were led to the wharf of death.

He had to wonder how many falsely accused unfortunates had gasped out their last breath at the end of a rope, squirming in that slimy mud while having their so-called *evil shades* expunged in the chilly depths of this rancid harbor.

At last, they found the ship they sought and now discarded the ankle weights they had carried from their point of immersion. Swimming up along the anchor chain they surfaced, and using the chain links as a ladder, they clambered aboard. The crew was ready for them, raising anchor and casting off even as Dat Voga, coming last, slipped over the gunwale.

Glancing down the length of the harbor he could see the crowds near a vacant pier. A large commotion could be heard. He shook his head sadly. He felt sympathy for these people. He had no doubt that Kyper Tron would use their vanishing as proof of their supernatural origins, proliferating belief to keep the people in a state of terror and obedience and the High O-Von in an exalted position of power.

With his customary aplomb, he put the incident behind him. They had escaped. For now, that was enough. As he scaled the side of the ship, he heard Odar Gan-Toh-Gan barking orders, the sweetest sound he had heard all day: "Kun-Bor, point us toward Xanator—and don't spare the sail!"

Gar-Noh-Dar's smiling face was the first thing he saw as the big, tenderhearted sailor put a warm wrap about Thuria's slender, shivering body. Casting a smile of gratitude to Thuria's benefactor, the sailor led the beautiful, red damsel toward her quarters.

And then Azaria appeared by his side, smiling up at him. She, too, held a warm wrap in hand and a steaming brew they made from leaves of which Dat Voga had become particularly fond. He had become so keen on many of the—to him—strange, new consumables in this time that he did not know how he would live without them when he returned to his own age.

He sighed when he considered the future, and then pushed the thoughts from his mind. He did not want to think of leaving this place and these people. They had just escaped a precarious situation with no loss of life. He could not ask his ancestors for much more than that.

Chapter Seven

John Carter Comes to Ptarsas

S IR! THE DWAR ASKED ME TO REPORT TO YOU that Tars Tarkas is on the wireless set and is asking to speak with you." John Carter nodded his thanks and headed for the command bridge of the *Tycheus*. Entering, he found Dwar Brik Lakko at the wireless controls. The dwar handed the set over to the Warlord and resumed his own seat.

"Tars Tarkas," he said. "John Carter here. I wondered when you would arrive. We have been in position for three days. What have you to report?"

The voice on the other end of the connection responded at once, crisp and clear over the wireless device. "John Carter! We ran into difficulties along the way, which I shall elaborate on another time—around the campfires of Thark, perchance! We have captured two Ptarsans who manned observation posts in the mountains. They seemed quite surprised to see us." Tars Tarkas chuckled.

"These Ptarsans are brave men," he continued. "Even after their capture they maintained eye contact without flinching. Knowing our reputation precedes us, we found that impressive. Dostet Beeda was all for giving them a sample to loosen their tongues last night, but I forbade it, wishing you to be able to interrogate them while they were intact, and presentable."

John Carter had known the great Thark for many years

and heard the grin in his voice as the green man baited his close friend and ally. Smiling, John Carter replied, "I applaud the restraint of both yourself and Dostet Beeda; I know the temptation must have been enormous to tickle a rib!

"Shortly, a six-man flier will approach your position," John Carter continued. "Do not shoot it down! Signal the pilot to pick up the senior of the two Ptarsans. I do, indeed, have questions for him. The other, however, I wish to leave in your delightful company for leverage, should we need it later."

In short order, the flier returned with a dwar of the Ptarsan Forward Observation Guard. The man's face showed his astonishment when he climbed from the flier onto the deck of the immense vessel of war. Without preamble, John Carter said, "Follow me, Dwar, if you would, please."

The Ptarsan opened his mouth to argue but thought better of it. The charismatic tone of this man's voice commanded obedience. His superbly muscled physique towered over the slighter dwar by at least a head, his balance and poise serving to accentuate his powerful carriage.

After ordering the dwar to follow, the Warlord turned and strode off without bothering to note the effect of his words, as though he *knew* the dwar would follow him. The action was a stark indicator that here was a man accustomed to having his orders followed without undo pause, and with no need to repeat himself. The dwar followed.

The stranger led the Ptarsan on a detailed tour of the vessel, the likes of which the dwar had never in his life beheld. The mechanisms, once explained to him, were inconceivable in their destructive capabilities. If the intent of the tour was to make an impression, it worked.

One thing mystified him, however: the fact that his captors had not asked him any questions. The dwar was quiet as he walked the companionways of a vessel filled with five thousand strong. He saw strange devices and airborne weapons by which an assault might be launched. He also saw fourteen other ships identical to this one, spaced evenly and low against the horizon where they were virtually unnoticeable.

Lastly, his captors led him through a series of bulkheads, concluding with them stepping into a room commanding an extraordinary view. Here was such a control array as to baffle the eyes. The vessel's actions in battle would be controlled from this room. The man who had conducted the tour proffered him a seat. A woman of staggering beauty was here ahead of him, her level gaze boring straight into the eyes of the rattled dwar.

"Who *are* you people?" he exclaimed nervously, unable to hold his tongue a moment longer.

The tall, white-skinned man ignored the dwar's question, and instead asked one of his own. "What is your name, Dwar?"

"Vimont Vidarro," the Ptarsan replied at once. He swallowed hard, guessing this was the preamble to an interrogation. He wondered if it was to be torture and glanced nervously at the mysterious controls.

"Dwar Vimont Vidarro, sometime back, my son and another young man were sent to your country on a mission of great import to Barsoom. Note that I said of great import to Barsoom—not to our own city of Helium. We have had no communication with your city for a thousand or more years, and rather than arrive upon your doorstep in the manner that you see—"

Here, John Carter's hand swept in an inclusive gesture, encompassing the other ships of the flotilla visible through the special light-gathering viewscreens.

"—we chose instead to send two envoys to represent the empire to your government. We have adhered to an agreed-upon timetable and even extended this somewhat to give our young men ample time to accomplish their ambassadorial mission and return home. Yet they have not. Our ground force, whom you had the pleasure of meeting, found not a trace of them en route. This brings us to the conclusion that they made it safely to your country."

John Carter began to see signs of animation flit across the man's face. "You have seen and had explained to you the awful capabilities that lie within the hull of this ship. Do you have any doubt, Dwar, that we could lay waste to your city?"

Vimont Vidarro, a look of sudden understanding on his face, said, "I am sure that you can do all you suggest, and more! But there is no need to, I assure you! Accompany me to Ptarsas—in a smaller vessel, please, as I do not wish to cause a panic within the city that the sight of this vessel would surely cause. You may rest assured that we are as mystified by your friends' disappearance as are you."

John Carter caught the eye of Dejah Thoris, and Dwar Brik Lakko. The man's voice had the ring of sincerity.

"Sir," the dwar continued, "a good friend of mine named Ran Tasis, a padwar of the Royal Guard, became quite close with Carthoris and Dat Voga, the two men of whom I can but assume you speak as you mentioned no names. We of Ptarsas wished them no ill will, you have my word."

Within a zode, John Carter, together with Dejah Thoris—who refused to remain aboard the *Tycheus*, stating that she wished to hear any news of her son immediately—stepped into the council room in the city of Ptarsas. It was the same room in which the Heliumites had addressed the Ptarsan Council.

The room was filled beyond capacity, for a state of emergency had been declared. Rumors had spread through the city of a vast armada of warships, of a size and type never seen, hovering a zode to the west.

John Carter had begun to doubt these people had anything to do with the disappearance of Helium's ambassadors. He did not wish to terrorize the populace needlessly, but he was determined to get to the bottom of the mystery. But if information was not soon forthcoming, he suspected Dejah Thoris might begin handing Ptarsan officials over to Dostet Beeda, the Thark.

The green men had openly approached the city with the remaining captured range guard, having arranged to meet John Carter's flier just inside the city gate. Upon entry, they relinquished their prisoner, who seemed astounded to escape with life and limb from the clutches of the horrible green men. Their reputation did indeed precede them.

Tars Tarkas, with Dostet Beeda, stood beside John Carter and Dejah Thoris. Ptar Ras entered. The room became quiet—all eyes were now upon the Jeddak of Ptarsas. The Warlord observed the man curiously. He wished he were meeting this jeddak of a forgotten people under different circumstances, but he made sure the expression on his face told Ptar Ras nothing.

Then Ptar Ras did something surprising. He approached the representatives from Helium and, where all expected him to stop before John Carter, he paused instead before Dejah Thoris. Smiling down into her face, with a hint of regret in his voice, he took both her hands in his.

"Princess Dejah Thoris. Although we have never met, I recognized you the instant I entered the room as your son bears a remarkable resemblance to his mother. Yet I must say, that although he made a heroic attempt to describe to us the profoundness of your beauty, I see that he but grasped for words of adequacy; for absolute beauty cannot be described but must rather be witnessed."

The jeddak gestured to his guests. "Please, sit where you shall find a measure of comfort and I will detail, insofar as I know it, what we have gleaned of your son's and Dat Voga's disappearance. It is a disappearance, mind you, that includes members of our city, and also that of Zoquan. These vanishings have caused as much alarm in our hearts and minds as I am sure the loss of Helium's ambassadors has in yours."

So saying, he led the planet's most beautiful woman to the table, at the same time motioning John Carter and the green men to be seated as well. John Carter appreciated the astute compassion of the jeddak that caused him to display such deference to the Princess of Helium. It showed that the jeddak understood the great love of a mother for her child. Extra seating having been fetched, Ptar Ras began an interesting narrative.

The jeddak appeared to omit nothing, even admitting to his own grave doubts about entering an alliance that would bring foreigners within the walls of Ptarsas for the first time in a thousand years. "It was a situation for which we were not sure we were ready. And I admit, I cast relentlessly my many misgivings at poor Dat Voga. Ah, but the passion of your delegate from Helium! We were all very much impressed and were eventually, one and all, won over by the ardent young man's arguments.

"We spent many long days cloistered in meetings, ironing out details of the mining operations. Your two from Helium became fast friends with my daughter and Thuria, her best friend; and with my sons, who took them on regular excursions, eager to show them our city and its surrounding countryside."

His eyes narrowed in anger. "And then came the night of the gala, when Zat Simpus drank too deeply of his cups and showed his true colors. Your son, Carthoris, came to my daughter's defense, Princess, slapping Zat Simpus to the floor like the craven calot he is!"

John Carter's chest swelled with pride upon hearing the exploits of his son, and how both men had comported themselves. Dejah Thoris blinked away tears, but smiled, for she was at all times the proud mother of her son. Their actions had brought honor both to themselves and to Helium.

Ptar Ras resumed his story, telling them how he watched the visitors from Helium board their ship with his own eyes.

"With them went Thuria, close friend of my daughter, a native of Zoquan who accompanied them to visit her family. Also, there had been Voss Borgas, our newly appointed ambassador to Zoquan, in whom I had laid much hope in healing the tattered relations between our two countries.

"When weeks turned into months and they had not returned, I sent an inquiry to Zoquan. Within a day my man returned, bearing with him Darfa Quan, Thuria's father, who is the ambassador to Ptarsas. He wished to know everything. Only then did we learn their vessel never reached its destination.

"Together, our two nations scoured the flight path Carthoris was to follow, working in concert to find our missing. For the last several weeks we have combed the rugged barrens, the nearby gorge, the dead sea bottoms, the cliffs, and peaks of the Ptarsan Range—a massive area, but to no avail. It is like seeking a thoat tooth in a moss-covered seabed. Then without warning, a Banaalian vessel approached the walls of Ptarsas.

"We received them cordially enough," said Ptar Ras, "not knowing their intent. I assumed it to be related to my expulsion of Zat Simpus, that I had offended the jed, who is as difficult to deal with as is his surly son. We were mistaken. When the envoy was ushered into my presence, he presented me with a declaration of war, to be rescinded upon the return of Zat Simpus! So, now we had another missing vessel—that of Zat Simpus, who had been expelled weeks earlier!"

Ptar Ras paused before the Warlord. "John Carter, if you heard how Zat Simpus threatened us with death, saw the hate in his eyes, you would leap to the same conclusion as did we. I believe it to be no coincidence that both vessels went missing simultaneously. Also to be considered is the fact that the ship of Zat Simpus was of the armored, so-called *courser* type, which, if you are not familiar with it, is specifically designed to attack *from behind its prey.*

"Only then did we begin scouring the flight path for blast marks and radium impacts. And we found them—on the south wall of the Ptarsan gorge. We had been looking for visible wreckage and had not found it. But we certainly found evidence of a running battle, and finally of an impact and crash site on the floor of the gorge, but with no sign of wreckage or debris. At least, not at first.

"The site was easy to miss, for the searchers were looking for signs of twisted metal that would be visible from several hundred sofads above the ground. But upon closer examination, the signs of a skidding impact were discovered. But we never found the actual wreckage of any vessel.

"As mysterious as this may sound, it is as though someone purposely obfuscated the search by removing any evidence of the ships. John Carter, we can show you the crash site and the pockmarks from radium detonations in the gorge. We can introduce you to a hundred witnesses to corroborate our testimony of the threats made by the person of Zat Simpus, which were directed against your ambassadors, and indiscriminately against everyone in that room.

"We attempted to display this evidence to the Banaalians, but they would not hear of it. They blame us for their prince's disappearance, while we believe it is he who is to blame." Ptar Ras exhaled an exasperated sigh, "We just do not know what became of those ships!"

Chapter Eight

A New Alliance

A T THIS POINT PTAR RAS, his frustration plain upon his face, paced to a nearby window where he glared out over the gardens of the Ptarsan palace. Having collected his thoughts for his final words, he turned to his guests.

"John Carter, we hope that you will join us in the search for your missing ambassadors, and further, that you will use this mighty armada you have at your disposal to come to our aid in this, our moment of need. Our defenses are outmoded, as you have seen. Oh, they have been adequate for our survival until now, but with the arrival of the Banaalians, and now your force . . .

"I believe it is time Ptarsas formed new alliances, although the change will be difficult for many. I have something I wish to show you that, instead of any flowery words I might say, will be my final plea. After that, all that remains is for you to decide if you believe us—or the Banaalians."

John Carter rose to his feet. "Ptar Ras, I consider myself an excellent judge of character. From what I have seen, the comportment of your people, from your lowliest to yourself, has been that of only honor, and bravery in its purest form. Tars Tarkas remarked how your men faced their green captors unflinching. That is quite an avowal, take my word for it."

Ptar Ras smiled. "Nevertheless, my friend, I believe that you, and certainly your princess, shall be extremely interested in what I intend to show you, as it means much to all of Barsoom, if I understood correctly the one who explained it to me—that being none other than Ambassador Dat Voga."

Garr Karosa, speaker of the Council of Jeds of Ptarsas, handed Ptar Ras a leather satchel. Ptar Ras approached the table where John Carter stood beside Dejah Thoris, and together they pulled forth the contents of the satchel.

Inside was document after document, signed in the unmistakable handwriting of Carthoris and Dat Voga, alongside the signatures and seals of the Jeddak of Ptarsas and each member of the Ptarsan Council of Jeds. These were the treaties and accords upon which they had all worked zealously for weeks. These documents officially made Ptarsas an ally of Helium and under her protection, by Heliumetic law.

Stunned at this turn of events, John Carter looked at Dejah Thoris. She, too, grasped instantly the significance of the documents. Helium could no more make war on this city than they could Hastor or Gathol. Indeed, there now existed no reason to do so. After the detailed narrative of all that had occurred during the visit here of the two delegates, they found themselves convinced of the culpability of this Zat Simpus of Banaal.

The Banaalians would have quite a surprise awaiting them should they arrive upon the Ptarsans' doorstep. Indeed, soon they would behold the unwelcome sight of the battleships of the Heliumetic Navy confronting their insignificant city.

With mixed feelings, Dat Voga watched the Plaezor Archipelago fall astern and disappear below the horizon. It was a relief that the *Prachus* had escaped with all her crew intact, yet he was saddened at the turn of events that ended with their fleeing for their lives, pitying the people for the decadence to which they had fallen because of the foothold of fanatics.

He was also glum because he knew he would never see these islands again. For he now understood what had before merely perplexed him. Since learning the geographical location of the islands in respect to Xanator, he had been unable to place the archipelago in his memories except for the great depression in the seabed lying, in the future, in the same vicinity from the former mainland.

From what he had observed of their mining operations, extreme overmining had compromised the bedrock of the island chain. If it were not for fear of collapse, he had no doubt there would not be a drop of any of the rare ores remaining in the shafts through which he had trekked.

He guessed that in the future a massive seismic subsidence occurred, or perhaps a hypercenter of super volcanism would form beneath the island chain, either of which might destroy the archipelago. The latter made sense. The tunnel-riddled bedrock, possessing too little mass to direct the force of an eruption through natural vent tubes, would burst through walls thinned from thousands of years of tunneling, resulting in the vaporization of the landmasses to some distance below the seabed.

He sighed and returned to the bow to find Azaria. In his heart, he knew the destruction of these islands, along with the monumental loss of life, had its roots in the greed of man. It disheartened him to admit that the future he was from was little different.

Thinking of his own time, he wondered what had happened in the control room of Daxxus Nahl's laboratory. Did Carthoris yet live? Had John Carter come in search of them? Surely by now the Navy of Helium had sailed for Ptarsas. Then he recalled that, unless he perished here in the past, none of that had yet come to pass. Nor would it, for he had every intention to return and—

He sighed and returned to the bow to find Azaria.

"Dat Voga! There you are." Gar-Noh-Dar ran lightly down the stairs from the command deck and approached him, the ever-present affable smile upon his face. However, as he stopped at the railing beside the young scientist, his face became somber. From the sideways glances he cast at the padwar, Dat Voga guessed this was not a simple, friendly visit.

The Horzian sailor joined the Heliumite in looking out over the ocean horizon. "Dat Voga," he said, breaking a long silence, "I have something of import I need to discuss with you. I know you and Thuria have secrets that you and she only speak of when no one else is around. I also know that I'm a good judge of character and that I trust you both implicitly, with my life and with the lives my crew.

"I don't understand the import of the odd contrivances you both have in your possession, the gauntlets you wear occasionally, and the strange belt Thuria wore when she came aboard this ship. I also do not understand how you possess knowledge of things no one ever heard of and yet are unable to identify the most common fish of the sea."

"Gar-Noh-Dar—" started Dat Voga.

"Please, let me finish. I know the two of you are different. I've never seen a woman who looks like her, nor a man like you. I know there is something about where you come from that you cannot discuss, and it involves this secret you keep. The way you two can hold your breath is baffling. I want you to know that I would never betray you. Nor would anyone aboard this ship."

"Gar-Noh-Dar, I appreciate—"

"I wish to ask Thuria to become my mate," Gar-Noh-Dar blurted out. Not giving the padwar time to object, he rushed on, "When I first met you, I thought the two of you were in love. But I know now that you were, and still are, acting as her protector. I cannot help but feel that the shades of my ancestors chose you above all others to protect her, treating her with the care of a brother. I have come to realize,

Dat Voga, that Thuria is precious beyond all measure. Forgive me! My heart understands the depths of my feelings, but my tongue possesses not the eloquence to express it."

Dat Voga unobtrusively probed the mind of Gar-Noh-Dar, for he considered this serious business. Dat Voga did care for Thuria as if she were family, and he needed to know that no guile lurked in the sailor's intentions. He saw that the man's feelings for her were sincere. And to think, only the day before he had been jealous that Gar-Noh-Dar might be a rival for Azaria's affections!

"Gar-Noh-Dar, I wish I could explain the complexity of the truths about Thuria and me. And one day I hope to. For now, what you need to know is that there is but one path that will allow you to be with Thuria if such is her wish. That path I cannot outline today, so I need your word that when I am able to disclose everything to you, you will do as I command, instantly, as all our lives may hinge upon it.

"Further, not only our lives, but millions of lives that you know nothing of may hang in the balance. Can you make me this promise, Gar-Noh-dar? If you cannot, then a future for you and Thuria simply cannot be, my friend. And that is as near to the truth as I can come for now. You must trust that I have your and Thuria's, and countless others', best interests at heart."

He stopped and waited for his friend's reaction. He realized this was much to ask and guessed the man might hesitate. The sailor surprised him, however. As soon as Dat Voga ceased speaking, the hearty giant grasped his forearm, in the Barsoomian sailor fashion of a million years before Dat Voga's time.

Smiling, Gar-Noh-Dar exclaimed, "Yes! When you say the word, Dat Voga, whatever you ask, I will do it. I trust you. And now, I must go see Thuria!"

Flying across the deck to the entrance to the next level, he disappeared, heading for Thuria's quarters with his heart in his hand and a smile on his handsome face. The red man shook his head. His mouth wore a whimsical smile. He felt honored to have just now stood in and performed this duty for Thuria's father, and content that Gar-Noh-Dar understood his position without his having to explain it.

He had been considering many things since panicking for fear of how he might have revised the future by saving the *Prachus* and her crew from the brobdoganth and the ravages of the fish-men. He could not know what changes he had wrought, but now he knew a way that these two could be together. If Thuria wished a life with Gar-Noh-Dar, he would see to it that it happened.

Dat Voga strolled slowly upon the swaying deck toward the bow. The day had turned out indescribably beautiful, with the bluest sky he had ever seen. The stacks of clouds in the sky were so deep and appeared so soft and fluffy that it made him wish heartily for a good flier. He imagined how he would love to explore this new world from the air, to see these strange new vistas to their farthest horizon.

His youthful fancy conjured images of flying low above the sea, of coming upon the mainland and rising in elevation until he burst through the low-lying clouds, observing the swiftly changing landscape beneath his keel.

He arrived at the spot where he and the two women met every evening. Leaning upon the gunwale, he continued to daydream until he felt a feather-light touch upon his arm. Turning, he met the smiling visage of the one he loved, his primitive and beautiful princess—or at least, the one he wished to call his princess.

He became instantly contented in his soul to be right where he was in time and space, on the softly rolling deck of this ship, with this beautiful young woman. Without a word, she leaned against him, and together they looked out over the horizon, seeking Xanator with their eyes—their next stop, shades of their ancestors willing.

Chapter Nine

Xanator

THE DAYS THAT FOLLOWED were ones of blessed normalcy, the crew finding the open sea refreshing after the harrowing events of Plaezor. During this time, the son of Odar Gan-Toh-Gan approached Dat Voga with a new request, and one Dat Voga was willing to immediately grant.

Gar-Noh-Dar's father had spoken many times of the red man's uncanny command of the sword that he witnessed firsthand in Plaezor, detailing glowing accounts of Dat Voga's skills until Gar-Noh-Dar at last expressed an interest in having the padwar instruct him. Swordplay was an important skill to master, enabling one to survive a violent world and protect loved ones in times of peril.

Gar-Noh-Dar proved to be an apt pupil, quickly absorbing Dat Voga's futuristic style of dueling. Some might think the padwar had gone back on his oath to do nothing to endanger the future by instructing this prehistoric sailor. However, if what he had in mind came to pass, this instruction would have no ill effects. More importantly, the man's sword might one day stand between Thuria and danger, and for that the padwar was willing to risk much.

The crew gathered when they sparred, hanging from yardarms and beams to watch them go at it as if their lives depended on the outcome. Dat Voga had spent so much time in the presence of his own master, John Carter, that his teaching style began to mirror that of the consummate Virginian's. Whether he drew his blade in war or drill, it became an extension of his body, his instructions to Gar-Noh-Dar sounding much like the Warlord's as he honed his pupil's proficiencies.

One thing he realized acutely during these bouts was that the heavier blade of these primitive swords was a hindrance. He advised Gar-Noh-Dar to hold a heavy dagger in his off hand for balance, and could but curse when he tried to teach a fine point and found it difficult to execute with the—to him—clumsy weapon. In those times, they simply did their best with what they had.

At the same time, Gar-Noh-Dar took it upon himself to instruct Dat Voga in the use of the primitive gaff the sailors preferred, used more often as a tool than as a weapon. The padwar found it fascinating to learn its use, all knowledge of it having evaporated with Barsoom's oceans. The weapon remained unknown in his time, as he had seen no surviving examples. If one had been depicted in an ancient mural, he had not seen it.

Although the days sped by quickly with work and training and whiling away zodes with Azaria, Dat Voga's heart leaped excitedly when he heard the cry they had all yearned to hear—that of the lookout announcing the sighting of land. Once they identified the coastline, they realized they were only a few haads north of Xanator. With high anticipation, they turned their bow south.

After long months, the newest ship of Hal-Roh-Kim at last heaved within sight of her original destination. The last few xats before the city came into view were long ones for Dat Voga. He could not tell the sailors gathered with him at the rail that the last time he was here was a million years in the future, when he and Carthoris had tangled with a horde of great white apes.

Awe filled the padwar when they sailed within sight of

the city. He could scarcely reconcile this shining metropolis with the timeworn structures he remembered. This city was perhaps more beautiful even than Helium. Hugging the shoreline, it was constructed of gleaming stones and enduring marbles—stonework which survived to his time.

He now realized that time and wars had taken a toll on the beautiful facades of the remains of his day. The scene he saw looked so pure, white, polished, and reflective that it almost hurt the eyes to look at it. He could not begin to recognize any landmarks, as the city differed so much from the ancient ruins.

He could see that the empty areas of the future between enduring structures were, in this time, filled with wooden homes and shops built in quaint, architectural styles that were possibly dismantled over time for the valuable materials of which they were built. He guessed this information could change the population calculations of these ancient cities by savants such as Val Statt.

Although she had never visited ancient Xanator and so had no images of it in her mind to compare to this much younger version, still, Thuria appeared enthralled. Dat Voga smiled at the sight of her and her friends standing on the command deck, watching the seaside city drift by a quarter haad off their port side.

The docks lay farther to the south, as they had heaved in sight of the city just north of them. A great deal of the metropolis they passed was residential, with the buildings becoming larger the farther south they sailed. Mostly hidden from their vantage point were the inland portions of the city, which disappeared enticingly behind low hills and tropical coastal verdure.

Considerable foliage was visible, nestled in parklike vistas, while the sea fronting the city teemed with shipping while lacking the chaos of Plaezor. Many pleasure craft were at sea, with people fishing and swimming, while couples, consumed only with themselves, occupied other vessels, the lovers oblivious to those navigating about them.

They found the harbor, when they came to it, masterfully coordinated, and the *Prachus* berthed without difficulty. The odar set off down the dock chatting gaily with a member of the Port Guard, with whom he appeared to be acquainted, to take care of the required paperwork. There would be no haggling over fees or tariffs, making it clear that corruption was not rife here as it had been in Plaezor.

The crew had, as usual, work to do after making harbor. However, this time there would be no need to draw viands to see who would go ashore; because the shore leave at Plaezor for the second group had never occurred, they were automatically granted leave in this instance.

Claiming Dat Voga had no business walking about a city with which he was unfamiliar, Azaria resolved to accompany him. The padwar was so anxious to view this magnificent and historic metropolis that he forgot to bid Thuria farewell. When she called out to him from the railing he spun with a guilty grin and returned her wave. He understood now how the two women had left without telling him farewell in Plaezor. Then, dragged forward by Azaria, the two merged with the multitude along the quays.

"Come on, Dat Voga!" Azaria headed straight for the barter district, a place she obviously adored. The man from the future found the merchants' stalls fascinating. He scrutinized each table they passed, committing what he was able to memory, wishing to regale Val Statt, of the Society of History, with as much detail as possible should he regain his own time. Not for the first time he found himself wishing for his photo-chronicler, abandoned on their flier in the Ptarsan Gorge and now lost to him.

They eventually sauntered out of the bazar, each grasping a sweet confection from a vendor who guilted the red man into buying the treat for Azaria, whom he assumed was Dat Voga's sweetheart. The padwar had yet to bring up their budding relationship to the girl, conflicted due to his strange circumstances. He desperately wished her for his mate, but realized the futility of pursuing her since he must eventually return to his own time.

Still, the plan he had in mind, and the argument he would make to those it would impact, encouraged him, and offered a gleam of hope for him and Azaria.

They passed through several districts before coming to a series of huge, regal edifices he knew must belong to the seat of government of Xanator. In one of these structures would be the jeddak.

Dat Voga had met jeddaks in his time and knew many on a personal level, finding them to be among the most colorful men he counted as acquaintances. How he should love to meet a jeddak of the ancient world! Here was an undreamed-of opportunity, but he had no idea how to make it happen. As he finished the thought, Azaria eyed him, her face expressive.

"Dat Voga, how would you like to meet the Jeddak of Xanator?"

The man could scarce believe she had come out and said the very thing that had just passed through his mind. Out of curiosity, he asked what caused her to mention it.

Reflecting, she replied, "Honestly, I don't know. It was the strangest thing, but in that moment, I just knew it would be of interest to you."

The coincidence notwithstanding, Dat Voga became skeptical. "Why would he take time to see us? I am an unknown, a nobody, while you are the daughter of one merchant among many who trade here—albeit the fairest, for sure."

She grinned mischievously. "The fairest? Why, Dat Voga, I do believe that is the first compliment you've ever paid me! But you don't know what I know. I have been coming to Xanator since I broke my shell. When I was young, Hal-Roh-Kim, my father, arrived here from Horz just as the jeddak's barge began to sink. We rescued the jeddak and his retinue and struck up a friendship that endures to this day. My father never fails to visit him when in Xanator."

Grinning, he said, "In that case, Azaria, I would love it!"

As she continued to chat away, happy and carefree, Dat Voga wondered if he had unconsciously shared his thoughts with her. He felt he would have been aware of it if he had. It was rare for such to occur, and typically only between those whose minds were unclosed to one another. He thought of the great secret he hid, and felt that could not possibly explain it, yet he was positive he had influenced her invitation.

The street they walked down was quaint and beautiful. The city planning had conserved areas of shade trees when laying out the city, creating a delightful, almost magical, ambiance for the man to whom trees were exceeding rare, and those limited to but a handful of varieties. The dappled sunlight upon the ersite-cobbled streets was mesmerizing.

Stepping from beneath these trees, Azaria grasped his hand as they crossed a street toward an impressive structure whose top was not yet within sight due to its height and the overhanging verdure that presently obscured much of it. Its loftiness impressed him, considering the era of its construction, the stonework soaring hundreds of sofads into the sky.

As they passed from beneath the overhanging limbs of a tree long extinct in his time, the red man drew a quick breath. Issus! It was the very monolith over which he and Carthoris had flown! They had found it memorable with its four corner towers, only one of which remained standing in their time, the others having fallen into the roof and nearly gutted the building, but for the outer walls.

Shades of the ancestors! The padwar recognized the grand foyer entry where great white apes had loitered the last time he saw it. He let his eyes leap to the top of the tower closest to him, to the left of this entry. There it stood, that lone, surviving tower—new, intact, and beautiful!

Chapter Ten

Py-Noh-Dok

DAT VOGA PAUSED IN THE MIDDLE of the street to stare at the tower, other pedestrians simply parting around them. Ignoring their curious and occasionally irritated glances, he allowed Azaria to draw him on across the wide boulevard. As they arrived on the other side of the thoroughfare, he indicated the tower. "Azaria, would it be possible to visit that tower? I would love to look over the city from that vantage point."

She pursed her lips, before replying with a shrug, "All we can do is ask. I cannot recall the purpose of these towers. The jeddak began these years ago, but then ceased all work on them of late. If not that one, would one of the others suffice?"

He glanced longingly at the mysterious southeastern tower. "Yes, I suppose. But I would really love to visit that one."

Members of the Palace Guard intercepted them as they approached the palace vestibule, inquiring as to their business. Azaria introduced herself and presented Dat Voga as a visiting emissary from a mysterious nation called Helium. Dat Voga did not disavow them of the belief that he came from a far, unknown land, as it lent greater credibility to his story. And it was mostly true since, although it did not yet actually exist, it would in the future, and it helped explain his appearance.

A majordomo informed them of a short delay before their request to meet the jeddak could be approved. Azaria was optimistic an audience would be granted as even the warriors and palace functionaries were impressed with Dat Voga, both by the mystique of his unknown homeland and the uniqueness of his physiology.

Azaria assured her friend that he and Thuria need not worry on account of their distinctive appearances here. Although the people of Xanator believed the shades of their ancestors to be spectral beings to whom they would speak and supplicate, those beliefs had not become debased here, as in Plaezor.

The Xanatorians were typical in that they would often beseech their ancestors for assistance or blessings but would then strive their uttermost to attain that which they desired or needed. Afterward, they gave thanks to their ancestors as though the shades had accomplished all, for they knew not if it were their own efforts, or the beneficent blessings of an ancestral shade, which brought them their heart's desire.

While waiting, they wandered about the front portion of the palace that was open to the public, a vestibule the red man found captivating. It was stately, with winding stairs, reminiscent of his visit to Ptarsas, which contained a beautifully blended mixture of new and picturesque architectural styles. He guessed that eventually these stairs would be replaced by ramps.

Leaving the vestibule, they entered a room of massive, evenly spaced columns. In the center of the room, two hundred sofads over their heads, was a skylight set in the roof of the attached rotunda. Through the glazed pane, a sky filled with colossal, billowy clouds was visible. The Heliumite gazed upward in wonder. The scene was one rarely encountered in his time, in which clouds were an anomaly.

In this anteroom was housed an incredible collection of artworks. Displayed upon the walls were paintings and statuary wrought by local artists alongside exotic pieces of foreign origin. Painted murals on the walls were also present, with these having a greater degree of freshness, contrast, and saturation than the time-softened examples seen in abandoned cities from this epoch, which wore layers of accumulation from untold millennia of neglect.

As the two walked about in admiration, animated voices suddenly rose in a heated debate. One voice claimed, "On that particular day—and I recall it as if it were yesterday, mind you—the jeddak wore his yellow cape—not the red! And he carried not his staff!"

This voice was at once rebutted by another: "I, too, recall the day distinctly—is it not fixed as vividly in my memory as the ignorant expression upon your face is this very instant? You think of the color of the jeddarra's robes. I tell you, the jeddak wore his yellow robe, and he carried his staff!"

Curious, the two visitors stepped around an enormous, life-size statue. The sculpted scene, captured in an ebony gneor, was of a jeddak upon a zytogonth trampling the bodies of a number of vanquished slain. It was mounted upon a massive, gergite base that itself stood head high. On the other side of this monument, they discovered two of the most aged, grizzled Barsoomians Dat Voga had ever seen outside of Val Statt.

The ancients stood before a half-finished mural, clutching paintbrushes that they pointed and jabbed at one another's faces to add emphasis to their "recollections." Splattered and bespeckled with whatever color was on the other's brush, they wore only the scantiest of leathers from which were suspended several receptacles bearing paint of various hues, while from pouches hanging on cross straps protruded brushes of sundry sizes and other tools of their trade.

Upon the wall behind them sprawled an unfinished mural of a most intense and realistic appearance. Dat Voga imagined how a million years would soften the vivid colors, and realized that, although the denizens of his time always respected the artists of this glorious period, they could not have dreamed of the brilliance these works had when new.

Dat Voga became absorbed peering between the two combatants at their mural and failed to realize they had ceased to argue. When he did, the two oldsters were whistling and painting side by side, and talking about what they were doing for dinner, and where they were planning on fishing that evening.

He glanced at Azaria, who made a poor attempt not to giggle. The two wizened elders never glanced at the two as their masterful brushstrokes added detail and depth to the depiction of an event that may have happened fifty years before, for all he knew. Somehow, this was not how Dat Voga imagined these timeless pieces of art taking form during their act of creation.

Not for the first time, he smiled in wonder at how different he was discovering this ancient world to be from his former imaginings and saw that he must be willing to relinquish any preconceptions of the past. They were still watching the artists when a youth appeared. "You are the daughter of Hal-Roh-Kim? The jeddak will see you now, if you will follow me."

Up a set of stairs the fellow conducted the two, and then along a curving, wood-paneled hallway overlooking the grandiose display of statuary below. The youth paused at a door, rapped lightly, then opened it to reveal a softly lit room with stained-glass windows. The room had a faux ceiling over it, for it lay well below the true roofline. This had been set with glazed panels to allow natural lighting to enter from the skylights far above, and the glazing set in the outer walls.

Set in the ceiling, Dat Voga saw, for the first time since arriving in the past, examples of radium lighting. It appeared to him that these were reacting to the amount of visible sunlight entering the room. Those set toward the farther walls, where it was darker, glowed more brightly, while those near a glazed panel allowing in natural light glowed more softly. Their design resulted in a gentle illumination of the room.

The youth, softly announcing the two to the room's sole occupant, brought Dat Voga's attention back from his ponderings. "Lady Azaria, daughter of Hal-Roh-Kim of Horz, and Dat Voga of Helium, my jeddak." Then, turning to the two visitors, he said, "Py-Noh-Dok, Jeddak of Xanator."

His simple introduction complete, the youth left the room and closed the door. The jeddak rose from his seat and approached, taking Azaria's hands in his. In a voice that sounded every inch a jeddak's, he boomed, "Azaria, little princess! Where is old Hal-Roh-Kim? Busy fishing monarchs from the sea, no doubt! What a man. And what a ship builder! But wait! He was here, seeking you. What has happened?"

Without waiting for an answer, the gusty jeddak continued, "He swore he would find you if he had to cross uncharted seas to do so. And he said something about having sent one Zit-Tar-Phak home with a well-planted foot to his hinder parts, saying he would annoy you no further. Come, girl; let us hear this story from the phlega herself."

Azaria had tried to get a word in, without success. Finally, she had consigned herself to wait until the jeddak had finished. The man fairly brimmed with enthusiasm. Although he could turn on the courtly charm and manners when needed, his personality was very much akin to those of the boisterous sailors filling his harbors. He was comfortable being himself around Azaria, and for this Dat Voga was grateful, as it gave him a glimpse into what kind of man this jeddak was—a man he found to his instant liking.

Azaria narrated to the jeddak all that had happened. She spoke of running away from Zit-Tar-Phak with whom her father had, at one time, wished her to mate. She told of hiding away on the *Prachus* on her maiden voyage to escape the unwelcome nuptials, of the great storm that nearly destroyed the ship, sending the vessel thousands of haads off course. Lastly, she explained how they discovered Thuria and Dat Voga, who themselves were lost and marooned on an unknown island in the middle of nowhere.

She then detailed all that had occurred since the padwar had joined them: of how he saved them from the brobdoganth and the fish-men, and of their misadventures in the Plaezors. When she finished, the jeddak folded her in his arms, just as though she were his own daughter.

"Azaria, I am grateful the ancestors delivered you through these calamities, and that you have met a man who meets your stringent expectations." He winked at Dat Voga and unfolded his arms from about the girl.

"But my jeddak, Dat Voga and I are not—" she faltered. Dat Voga grinned; Azaria was not easily flustered, so this was new to see.

Interrupting her, Py-Noh-Dok continued, "Dat Voga, my city is yours! You have saved the lives of good friends of mine. I know every soul aboard the *Prachus*, for I have been good friends with Azaria's father for years. They are good men, and excellent sailors, too, or that ship would be at the bottom, mind you, and make no mistake about it!

"Your exploits with the brobdoganth and the fish-men are epic! My son, these are noble deeds, and I intend to chronicle in our histories that sad day, and your eventual triumph. You should know that this girl is like my own daughter. I not only thank you—I salute you."

The boisterous jeddak of Xanator clasped Dat Voga's shoulders with his hands, an expression of respect that needed no interpretation, for had it not been handed down, unchanged for a million years, to his own time? Angry at their treatment at Plaezor, the jeddak waxed wroth. "I shall send my navy to pay the archipelago a visit and depose Kyper Tron and those sycophants!"

Azaria found an opening in the conversation and mentioned the towers, explaining Dat Voga's wish to view the city from the southeastern tower particularly. The jeddak switched from wrathful to enthusiastic, but went on to explain that this specific tower, the last of the four he had built, was unfinished. "You are still welcome to climb it if you wish. Oh, why not? I shall go with you myself, but we must visit all four! Each holds its own unique charms and distinct views."

The padwar felt chills of anticipation run up his spine as they climbed the nearest tower, which happened to be that to the northeast. He found it eerie, knowing that this tower would one day collapse into the structure, from war or some other misfortune, along with two others, caving in the roof and destroying this beautiful palace.

He tried not to focus on the fragility of humanity's creations nor the whimsy of fate which would preserve here, only to destroy there. He saw that man often invested so much wealth and labor only to see it destroyed in the end. It caused Dat Voga to consider the lofty towers of Helium. Were they, too, destined for destruction in some unknown, future calamity? Xanator's example forced him to mull the possibility.

The jeddak explained that his original intention in building these towers was for observatories to view the heavens and to overlook the great beauty of this wonderful city. But as his builders completed one, the jeddak filled it with beautiful pieces of his accumulated artwork.

Their excitement had peaked by the time they passed beneath the lintel of the doorway at the top of the first tower. Glazed windows hung in the embrasures that were easily swung open. This they did to introduce a breeze from the coast. The views were remarkable. One could overlook the city in its entirety. Set about the loft were comfortable seating and tables for refreshments so that visitors might sit and enjoy the sweeping vistas.

One by one, they circumambulated the palace counter-clockwise, climbing the towers, each having something unique and remarkable that caused it to differ from the last, either in its views of the city and surrounding countryside, or its collected artwork that was set in niches and upon ersite mantles protruding from the walls as one climbed the helical stairs.

Dat Voga grew anxious as they approached the entry to the southeast tower, the one he most wished to visit. This was the last one, and the only one that would remain in his own time. He realized it would contain nothing that he could go back later and recognize, for Py-Noh-Dok had already said it remained unfinished.

Just as the jeddak said, this tower was nothing more than a barren, empty space. No artwork adorned the niches, and no murals festooned the walls. The view, however, was magnificent. From this perch, the padwar could see the harbor. The verdant forests of tropic vegetation near the coast were in stark contrast to the whiteness of the city and its beaches. There were no glazes, so the loft was open, allowing for the entry of the fresh-smelling sea breeze.

The padwar must have had a smile upon his face that the jeddak noticed. Py-Noh-Dok nodded in obvious agreement. "I see you approve, Dat Voga. This is my favorite, too. I would like to see it completed, to see it filled with wonderful artifacts from all over the world, and the walls artfully adorned by Gai-dos and Vai-dos, those crusty old zytogonths!"

Then he exclaimed, "I know what I shall do! I told you I wished to chronicle your triumph over the fish-men, for it is a story that must be told to future generations. In gratification of your appreciation of this tower, upon this very wall I shall have that worthy pair illustrate your victory. Azaria, you must stop and describe the scene in detail to my historians. Those two thrive on minutiae! Oh, it shall be magnificent! When next you visit, it shall be complete."

Continuing to describe his enduring creation, the jeddak

descended the spiral stair with his two visitors. It saddened the padwar to think that he may never return this way to see the outcome of the work by the two wizened masters.

Returning to the first chamber, the jeddak asked Dat Voga about Helium. The padwar told what he might without revealing that the city did not yet exist. He told of her beauty, her museums, and the character of her people. He told of her attempt to be a beacon in a wicked world, coming as she did to the aid of those in need. He next regaled the jeddak of the nobility of Helium's warriors and recited many stories of derring-do by individuals such as John Carter and Carthoris, among others.

But he never mentioned radium rifles or fliers, or eighth rays, or anything that would give away the fact that these tales took place a million years from now. Instead, Dat Voga spoke of his studies of science and physics, at which mention the jeddak became fascinated.

"Dat Voga, you simply must visit the most illustrious scientist Xanator has to offer while you are here! His name is Arkaff. I've no doubt you will find his laboratory of interest. If you wish it, I shall have you escorted there. He dwells a few haads outside the city, where he has a compound in which he conducts his bizarre experiments.

"I implore you—visit and speak with him. You will have a great deal in common. I cannot, however, allow my guests to take their leave without sustenance. You shall have food, and drink, the best in Xanator! Dat Voga, you would not believe how your visit has revitalized my waning interest in finishing the towers. They have lain dormant while I have focused on other interests. I intend to speak without delay to my architects about finishing these enduring monuments to my time on Barsoom."

Chapter Eleven

ZIKKA

D AT VOGA THRILLED AT THE OPPORTUNITY offered by the jeddak to meet a prominent scientist of ancient Xanator. This man would be one of the red man's peers. It would be extremely enlightening to see his laboratory and speak with him about his work. Not to mention, if he did not visit the scientist, he would one day have to face Val Statt and explain himself.

Many secrets of ancient technology were lost to Dat Voga's time, such as radium lighting, whose mystery eluded the scientists of his era. One theory was that certain materials simply no longer existed and that viable candidates for substitution to reproduce the lost art had not yet been discovered. Be that as it may, the young Heliumite viewed this as the opportunity of a lifetime.

The idea interested Azaria as well, as she had never stepped foot in a laboratory. She was filled with excitement. The same youth who had conducted Dat Voga and her from the art room to meet with the Jeddak now guided them through the streets of Xanator to arrange with the Wall Guard for safe passage to the facility of Arkaff, the city's famed scientist.

They passed interesting shops and places of business along their way, from apothecaries to butchers. Nearing the outer limits of the city, the buildings began to thin and decrease in size. The streets were still paved in ersite cobbles, but now they found greater expanses of trees and vegetation left in-place.

As they walked past it, Dat Voga recognized a sound that would remain unchanged even in his day—the clang of hammer and anvil in the shop of a blacksmith. The sound reminded him of the problems the heavy swords of the day caused him and Gar-Noh-Dar, and the ensuing difficulties met in performing many of the maneuvers of modern swordplay.

On an impulse, he persuaded his guide to take a detour to this shop. Entering the smoke-darkened doorway, the smells of molten metal and burning wood smote their olfactory senses. Azaria and the effete youth wrinkled their noses, but to Dat Voga the sights and smells were ambrosia. The interior of the stone building was literally black from soot.

As soon as they entered, a courteous, but firm, voice hollered out, "Hoy! Stay over there 'til I call ye." The hammering continued unabated while they stood in the small entry, watching as the man would pull a metal object from the cinders of a blast furnace, beat upon it, shaping the metal, and then reheat it only to strike it yet again, further contouring the shape to his liking.

At last, he was satisfied. He quenched it in a staved wooden drum, the liquid hissing in protest and sending up clouds of steam. He skated a file across the piece, grunted in satisfaction, and then hung the object on a rack suspended from the ceiling. He had forged the hook for a new gaff.

Implements devoted to fishing and weaponry hung upon any wall space not occupied by raw materials. Racks filled with metal instruments for the control of vegetation, scythes, brush axes, and the like—tools that were unnecessary in Dat Voga's time—caught his eye. In every other conceivable space hung an assortment of small arms and pieces of armor of every description.

When he spoke, the man's speech bore an interesting

accent, differing from that of the other Xanatorians Dat Voga had met, which admittedly, he could number on one hand. The smithy was a huge, imposing monster of a man, looking to be at least a palm and a half taller than the padwar.

The man's face, black with soot, split in a welcoming grin, his teeth standing out in stark whiteness against his grimy face upon which white streaks were visible where the sweat from his brow made runnels in the ash caking his cheeks and forehead. His forge sat next to the furnace where he constantly stoked his fire, pumped his billows, and bent his huge frame over superheated metals.

His hair, a thick, deep brown, would have cascaded to his breast were it not tied back with a leather thong to keep it from his face as he labored.

"Hoy, I am Zikka. Now, what can be done for ye?" he asked, after closing the doors on his furnace and adjusting a damper.

Inside, the shop seemed smaller than the building looked from the outside, the crowded rooms being given over to supplies of various metals and the wood necessary to feed the furnace. One small area had been set aside with a table; toward this spot he guided them, it being slightly cooler there than the rest of his shop as it was farthest from the forge, with windows thrown open to allow in fresh air.

The man ushered them into chairs, hanging his filthy work apron on a wooden peg. He washed his hands and face in a basin and then joined them, heaving a hefty sigh as he eased his giant girth into a chair. He offered them a vessel of water that they declined, having but just left the board of Py-Noh-Dok.

Realizing this man lived by his craft, the padwar got right to the point. "I am called Dat Voga. We were on our way elsewhere when I heard you forging. I have in mind a certain sword design I want you to fashion. On second thought, I would like two of them. I have little money, being far from home, but my—Azaria, here—has said that her father has credit in Xanator that she will sign for, one Hal-Roh-Kim, of Horz? Are you familiar with him?"

The man's face lit up at once as he nodded his head. "Hoy, but of course I know old Hal-Roh-Kim! I wish they were all cut from the same cloth as he. Now, if I heard ye right, ye have a design in mind, so I'll not waste your time showing ye my completed pieces. But mind ye, I'd like ye to consider whether your piece could be fashioned by modifying one of them, as it will affect your price if such is not the case."

Dat Voga answered instantly, "Alas, no, my friend, for the material alone will be different from those—that is, if you're able to create this alloy I have in mind. Also, the blade length will be longer, not shorter, so cutting one down will be out of the question. But first, I need to know if you have these materials, or suitable substitutes?"

Pulling a piece of parchment from his pouch and picking up a writing instrument the smith had lying on the table, he handed the items to Azaria, asking her to write as he dictated. He proceeded to detail a list of materials and their properties in case Zikka must make a substitution. The smith read the list, written by Azaria in the smithy's language, for the red man knew not the written form of Xanatorian, although his companion did.

The smith muttered to himself as he read. At last, he said, "I have all but this one. But I do have something I believe will make an adequate substitute. Come, let me show ye."

The two threaded their way through the small shop from one materials rack to another, speaking of melting temperatures, quench durations, and various metallurgical details. Dat Voga mentioned the intense temperature his alloy must reach for forging, a point the smith seemed concerned about.

"The temperature is roughly double what this forge puts out using wood," Zikka said, "but I have an idea." Chortling as if at an inside joke, he went to a radium light fixture set in the ceiling. He flipped a release and took off the glazed covering, and then dropped a small, flat circular substance into his palm.

"I'll try a trick my father told me," he said.

"What is that?" the padwar asked, curious.

"This is a gagandium-radium compound, what my father called a radium cake. The story goes that he found an odd metal once, scratching about in an old mine. When he tried to melt it down, it would not budge, resisting every effort and remaining solid and unformable. So, he grabbed this piece of material from what, at the time, was the newest form of lighting—the radium light."

"He took the material out and tossed a chunk of it into the forge, his thought being that, since it glowed bright enough to create light, it might create extra heat. It singed the hair off his head when it blew his furnace door through the wall of the shop! After it settled down, it burned right fierce. He tried to measure the units, but it was off his scale. He figured it probably reached double the normal output. I think it'll work for your alloy, but, truthfully, it's a guess."

Seeing the radium compound sitting in the smith's open palm, Dat Voga's brow furrowed with concern. "Zikka, is there any danger it could explode in the daylight?" Naturally, he thought of the future radium-infused projectiles with which he was familiar. "I do not wish to risk blowing up your shop and anybody getting hurt. These swords aren't worth the price of your life."

However, on that score the smith reassured him. "There be no risk of that," he said, waving a hand dismissively. "That propensity is controlled by the additives they blend with the radium when they produce the compound for the light, gagandium being the primary stabilizer base. It causes the radium compound to release its energy slowly, in the form of light, rather than instantaneously as an explosion."

"What I do have to be careful with," he continued, "is adding too much of the compound at once, as my father mistakenly did. Although I've never attempted it, my theory is that you must add it in small amounts, spaced out, as it is very powerful. It's something I've never attempted because I never had the need before. But my father did it, and now I will attempt it."

Upon hearing this bit of information about the radium lighting, Dat Voga became keenly interested. Radium lighting remained one of future Barsoom's greatest unknowns. No scientist had ever solved the mystery of how these ancient alchemists accomplished this miraculous lighting. All they knew was it worked. A million years later, and the lights were still burning brightly in all the ancient, deserted cities.

He found it extremely intriguing to hear this man propound upon the topic as if it were nothing and to learn of this formerly unknown compound, gagandium. He guessed something in that compound must be the missing secret ingredients that had eluded millennia of scientists, preventing them from replicating this wonderful invention.

"Zikka, what can you tell me of gagandium? Where does it come from? Do you know anything about the use of it in manufacturing radium lights?" He was eager to hear what the man would say. Could Zikka but answer his questions, he could lay to rest for future Barsoom a riddle that modern engineers still yet sought to decipher.

"Well, I cannot say exactly as to what the proportion of gagandium is to radium. I can tell you that our processing plants synthesize gagandium from common seawater. Why do you ask?" the swordsmith inquired.

Dat Voga smiled. "Just idle curiosity."

Seawater! No wonder the secret eluded them. With none of this necessary ingredient available, Heliumites would have gone extinct before they guessed it. Old Val Statt had been correct, then, when he surmised that the ancients had used a material that no longer existed to produce the radium lighting, that being the long extinct seas!

The young scientist found the smith to be highly intelligent, there being little that the man did not instantly grasp or was at least familiar with. His depth of experience and ingenuity were impressive, and Dat Voga had thoroughly enjoyed the story of the man's father's apparent reckless abandonment when it came to advancing his craft. It was the sign of a true savant.

Men like these forged their own paths, increasing their knowledge by experimentation at the risk of life and limb, where others were content to follow their lead. At some junctures, however, Zikka literally wrote down exactly what Dat Voga told him, if the process differed greatly from his own experience and customary way of doing things.

The red man detailed all the minutia of the weapon's dimensions, but noted where the design could be open to interpretation. He was not looking for an exact replica of his weapon from home, but rather a worthy substitute that possessed the essence of it.

The weapons hanging about the room indicated this man was more than a mere metallurgist, a science that anyone might learn, but also an artisan—an ability not so easily grasped. Dat Voga had no doubt the blades would be things of beauty, wrought by this master's hand, and he counted himself fortunate to have discovered him.

A thought came to the young padwar as they rose to leave that caused him to smile. He imagined returning to his day and age and bringing this new sword with him. He would walk into the Hall of Antiquities, lay it upon the desk of old Val Statt, and regale him with a tale of how it had been forged by the hands of a Xanatorian metalsmith one million years in the past. The look on the aged historian's face would be quite amusing!

Zikka gave Dat Voga an estimated time for completion of two to three weeks and inquired as to whether he should deliver the items to the *Prachus*, or if the padwar would fetch them. There was no hurry, so Dat Voga replied he would return to pick up the swords. Then, bidding the man farewell, they set off for their original destination—the laboratory of Arkaff.

Chapter Twelve

Arkaff

RKAFF'S FACILITY LAY IN THE COUNTRYSIDE several haads beyond the city. Dat Voga had declined the jeddak's offer to travel by zytogonth directly to the wall garrison, preferring to take the opportunity to tread these ancient streets afoot. After meeting Zikka, he was glad he had done so. Since leaving the metalsmith, the cobbled ersite slabs had ceased, and they continued their walk on pebbled paths meandering between rural homes of quaint design.

At the limits of the metropolis, where the city wall stood as a barrier between Xanator and the wilds of the jungle, they picked up the armed escort that the jeddak assured them was necessary to safely travel through the forests. The wall guard informed them that after leaving the protection of the city, they could be in danger from wild beasts. Here, they mounted zytogonths and, exiting through a gate, entered a primordial forest where lush ferns quickly obscured the city from view.

In addition to predators such as the giggurtta and the asygurrok, he heard mention of one creature their escort specifically wished to avoid—a beast they called "Arkaff's bordubor" to which they attributed a malign intelligence. But they offered no explanation as to why they associated this beast with the mysterious scientist.

The area they traversed was one of dense forest made up of many tropical varieties. When they came to a fork where a branch diverged from the track they were following, they took it, and wended their way through a jungle of simply immense trees and softly swaying, giant ferns whose tops reared three hundred sofads over their heads, disappearing in a misty, green canopy filled with sundry flitting things.

They were several haads inland, so the breeze here held no scent of the sea, carrying instead the moist, earthy smells of forest and decaying jungle vegetation. They continued along this road until Dat Voga wondered if they should ever arrive at Arkaff's.

The ferns gradually gave way to a dense growth of enormous hardwood trees whose limbs were home to a variety of wildlife in the lower, middle, and upper terraces. He guessed it would take twenty men holding hands to girt the circumference of these giants that stood several hundred sofads tall, blocking much of the light from above. The light that penetrated did so in dancing, dappled patterns on the jungle floor.

Before long, they climbed a small hillock, the crest of which was barren of growth due to a rocky soil there which formed a natural clearing. From here, they obtained a view of their surroundings. Below them lay a compound bounded entirely by forty-sofad-high walls.

In size he guessed it to be roughly a half haad in length, and perhaps a quarter that in width. This was no mean compound. Armed guards were atop the walls, and a primitive but effective portcullis was set in a barbican. If this were the requirement to abide here, this forest must hold formidable predators indeed. They descended the hill to the gate where a guard admitted them entry after their escort vouched for them.

They were not kept long in waiting, having just entered the foyer of the foremost building, a simple affair constructed more for endurance than architectural beauty, when

Arkaff entered. The guards had informed him of the visitors' approach, they having been visible the instant they crested the hill.

He was a middle-aged man, dressed in the pocketed vesture of a scientist, with two equipment belts hanging upon him, one about the waist and the other slung diagonally across his breast. He sported a short, immaculate beard and sharp, bright blue eyes, and his hair and beard still held a considerable amount of the ash blond of his youth.

Arkaff looked first to their escort to introduce his guests, who informed him these were friends of the jeddak. Upon hearing this, he became a warm and congenial host, appearing excited to have such a man as Dat Voga visit him in this out-of-the-way location.

"You say you are a scientist in your city?" he asked after the guards' introductions. "But this is wonderful news! There are none here with whom I might discuss my ideas—none who understand me, anyway. What is your field of study, Dat Voga?"

Dat Voga might have recited a list of futuristic disciplines but could only reveal that he studied radium and planetary phenomena. His list of studies, and many of his fields of research, did not yet exist. To divert attention from himself, he asked, "The jeddak did not go into the specifics of your discipline but said that I should find a visit here interesting. What exactly do you do here?"

For answer, Arkaff gestured for the visitors to follow him. They did so, traversing dim halls illuminated by skylights that appeared too small to be adequate, only occasionally encountering small radium bulbs set in the walls. Their path through the building complex had a dismal, unwelcoming atmosphere that neither Dat Voga nor the Horzian girl found agreeable.

When asked about the dim lighting, Arkaff explained, "You must consider the wild beasts with which we contend here, Dat Voga. Many of them are . . . rather cunning.

Large skylights might allow ingress to certain, determined predators. And they would broadcast our presence more broadly. We keep the lights dim where brightness is not necessary, such as in these passages."

Curious upon a point, Dat Voga asked, "Why then did you locate your laboratory so far from the city?"

"To answer your question, I must go back to a time when there still stood an ancient wing of the palace that was part of the original structure built during the reign of Kong-Py-Zett. Py-Noh-Dok held a gala in that part of the palace one evening. During the merrymaking, a section of wall came forth, falling among the guests and killing many. One of the dead was the jeddak's young son."

"I'm sorry to hear that. He didn't mention it."

The scientist nodded, "No doubt. Months later, an agent of the jeddak visited me. The engineers had learned that a climbing ivy, which had covered the exterior of the building, had breached its facade. Veins of the invasive plant had made their way inward, weakening the stonework and causing the collapse. The battle is constant to keep the jungle, which always looks to permeate our city, at bay. We must be vigilant, or shortly Xanator would be inundated. The gardens, were they not carefully checked, would flow into the streets!

"You've surely seen the hardiness of the growths. When the jeddak summoned me, I was but a specialist in horti-culture where I utilized my art to enhance the natural beauty of landscaping for the beneficence of wealthy patrons. Already, I experimented with controlling unwanted variet-ies and enhancing those that were desired. In short, the jeddak tasked me with inventing new ways to combat the attack of nature upon our fair city.

"It made the most sense to build this compound here, in the midst of the enemy. On your approach you journeyed through fern and hardwood forests; southeast of here lie marshy swamplands—the most difficult to tame. We are at the forefront of the battleground. At the same time, there are varieties of beauteous plants that we dearly love, but which only thrive for mere short weeks each year. These we seek to enhance, to increase their life span.

"To this end, I experiment with the interbreeding of various florae to develop newer, hardier, or radically different species, while concurrently seeking methods to reduce the number of harmful plants. That reminds me, I must show you the crown jewel of all my creations! Py-Noh-Dok was amazed when I explained its properties to him. I have made vast inroads since then, and it is nearly ready for use. When we come to Building Four, I shall elucidate further.

"In recent years," he continued, "we have begun experimenting with crossing various species of wildlife to manufacture breeds that will feed on unwanted vegetation. Alas, this has largely proven fruitless. They always prefer lush grass, tender shoots, and soft, leafy foliage instead of the tough briars or viny growths we attempt to eradicate."

Dat Voga was incredulous. This man was the opposite of the people of his own day, who sought to recover lost vegetation, cultivating what they might along their canals. The Ptarsans would be particularly saddened to learn of this epic state of warfare that existed against the very thing they held most dear: to wit, a green growing thing.

To clear his head of these morbid thoughts, the padwar changed the subject, saying, "The guards mentioned a creature they called *Arkaff's bordubor*. We assume you are the namesake?"

"Not my finest moment," admitted the scientist. "For a time, we experimented with crossing the base strands of men with carefully selected animals, but with such horrific results that we ceased further research along those lines. The experiment they referred to produced creatures dangerous in the extreme. Make no mistake, they are not to be trifled with."

Dat Voga assured him that their escort had warned them

of the danger. But, to learn that Arkaff had engineered them! Arkaff explained that the goal was to blend certain physical traits of a white-furred simian found to the north, renowned for its strength and agility, with the cells of men.

"The hope was to create a superior warrior, one with man's ingenuity and the strength of a beast. Toward this end, twenty criminals under sentence of death were selected, male and female, and trials began. For a year we administered specially developed treatments with no results.

"Then, almost overnight, the subjects began to show the physical traits we had hoped for—that of increased strength and agility. I discontinued the treatments and observed the subjects for a period. Given that they were convicted criminals, we kept them in powerful cells from which escape was impossible; after seeing the subjects' enhanced strength, I was thankful I took those precautions.

"But it soon became clear that the cellular mutations were not finished when the subjects continued mutating even after the treatments were stopped. The subjects exhibited bizarre, outward manifestations, with some of the mutations varying from both parent species."

The test subjects, Arkaff said, developed growths beneath their arms that burst forth in hideous fashion as new appendages, an intermediary set of arms although the simian used in the experiment was of a two-armed variety. The shape of the skull began to change, with the subjects crying out in hideous agony during these transformations.

"It became so alarming that I at last deemed it best to destroy the poor creatures to put them out of their misery. They must have overheard the guards speak of it for they cried out against their destruction. By now their very voices had become guttural, beast-like, and practically unintelligible. With the decision to conduct their destruction approved by the jeddak and the experiment deemed a failure, I sent a detail of warriors to carry out the sentence.

"When they arrived, they found the creatures covered in their own filth and blood and lying dead upon the floor of their holding chamber. The guards threw open the door and entered to inspect the remains. Only then did they realize they were the victims of a ruse!

"Those hideous travesties rose from the floor as the warriors triggered the trap. Designated individuals attacked the guards while others rushed the door to prevent it from being shut and locked. The raucous din of those growling beasts, mingled with the screams of agony from the guards as the creatures pulled them apart limb from limb, was appalling. The mutants destroyed the guards to a man. None of the mutations were slain during the melee. They all escaped over the compound walls."

Since then, Arkaff believed the monstrosities had mated and borne young, as their numbers seemed to have been augmented. Safe travel in the area about the compound became impossible, with visitors venturing to the site only under armed escort. Arkaff was quick, however, to assure his guests that the creatures had never managed to penetrate the laboratory defenses.

The jeddak later ordered forays into the wood to destroy them, but the bordubors were extremely elusive, and these sorties resulted only in the complete annihilation of Xanator's warriors. Not even the bordubors' haunts were ever discovered, leaving Arkaff guessing they had bedded down deep in the forest.

Occasionally, a perimeter guard spotted a member of these aberrations staring fixedly at the complex, as if in contemplation of an overthrow of the men who created it, as though it recalled its lost humanity with resentment.

The Heliumite found Arkaff's tale captivating. The thought that these people were this intelligent one million years before his time, engineering a method to cross the structural strands of two unrelated species to create a new species, was mind-boggling.

He admitted, "Arkaff, this is astounding! Is there any possibility of seeing one of these creatures?"

Arkaff scowled. "Dat Voga, were you to see one, it would

likely be the last thing you ever saw. For your sake, I hope you do not see one. Let me show you something that is not depressing and dangerous. I believe you will find this fascinating!" The scientist seemed reluctant to speak further of what he considered a catastrophic failure, so the padwar dropped the subject.

Arkaff led the way toward the greenhouses located upon the side of the compound opposite that upon which they had entered. That he and Azaria were curious would be to put it mildly, as both wondered what strange things they might witness. They exited the main building into an area given over to the study of hydroponics and flora.

Here were examples of strange, hybrid plants, their host pausing before each to explain their purpose. This one was for insect control, while another was a "warning plant" that screeched when disturbed, and so forth. Dat Voga was careful *not* to disturb that latter. The scientist guided them through various buildings until they came to one located against the outer wall.

They entered the greenhouse that Arkaff referred to earlier as Building Four. Not for the first time, the red man saw families of mosses, ferns, and fungi, having observed many varieties of these on the island upon which he and Thuria had been marooned, the forest floors and the boles of trees often having coverings of these long-extinct plants.

Upon the entire surface of Barsoom in Dat Voga's day, only the hardy, ever-present ochre moss remained of these growths. Of ferns, there were none, unless it were that the Ptarsans had examples of these delicate plants tucked away in a corner of their kingdom.

Arkaff led them to an anteroom and thence to a rather large terrarium sitting on a table. The bottom of the terrarium was covered with what the padwar guessed to be the test subject—yet another moss variety. The Heliumite had by now seen so many of these that he found his interest in them had begun to wane, but he was determined to humor his host.

"Here, Dat Voga, is the crowning achievement of my career!" said Arkaff. "What you see here is an entirely new variety of moss, created entirely in this laboratory. This special strain was requested years ago by Xanator's city planners to drain the northwestern morasses and wetlands for possible expansion, and to create new, irrigable farmlands.

"They tasked me with designing a hybrid plant that would absorb water from swampy regions, but it was my own idea to release the captured moisture as oxygen into the atmosphere. Were the moisture released as a vapor, it would merely turn back into precipitation and the cursed cycle would never end.

"This moss has been years in development, but it has only been in these last months that the experiment has shown success. It is my belief that this will one day prove to be a lucrative export commodity for Xanator." The scientist watched his visitor's expression closely, obviously expecting to see shocked surprise at this miraculous, man-made, newly formulated flora.

Dat Voga realized that Arkaff expected him to see in this moss a unique variety that he had never encountered, being unaware that Dat Voga was unfamiliar with the plant life of this time and would be unable to recognize the subtleties between different varieties of prehistoric mosses.

However, regarding this specific moss, Arkaff was mistaken if he assumed the moss would be unrecognized by the Heliumite.

Slowly, for the idea was preposterous, the realization dawned on Dat Voga that he had indeed encountered this specimen—for it was the ochre yellow moss that covered every dead sea bottom of his own time!

Chapter Thirteen

Triumph of the Moss

As HE BROUGHT HIS FACE CLOSE to the plant to examine it more minutely, Dat Voga envisioned the dead sea floors that had surrounded him his entire life. Upon closer scrutiny, the plant was unmistakable. It was brighter in color—but the possibility existed that it would change over the course of a million years. With no water to feed the moss of the future, its colors had most likely dulled until reaching the ochre color with which he was familiar.

As the padwar stared in shock at the unassuming plant, Arkaff added a beaker of water to the terrarium, which was covered in the man-made vegetation. The Xanatorian leaned over the chamber to watch the vegetation consume it. "Quickly, observe this, Dat Voga!" he said eagerly. In less time than seemed possible, the moss absorbed the water, the plant brightening and swelling during its vampiric feeding.

Whence came his next, portentous thought he did not know. As he watched the insidious vegetation gulping that beaker of water, an abrupt epiphany brought him upright with peals of doom sounding in his mind. The hair on the back of the padwar's neck stood on end from the truth of his realization.

It came to him that this moss would obtain a foothold

in the oceans where, invisible to those above, it would spread and silently drain the seas. Unable to plumb the depths, humanity would never guess what caused the loss of their waters. Even had they, they would be powerless to prevent it. After the unstoppable desiccant was introduced to the seas, it would destroy a world ignorant of its impending doom from beneath the shrinking waves while they, oblivious, went about their daily lives.

The young padwar felt staggered by this unforeseen, crushing blow. He remained at a loss to explain how the engineered desiccant would obtain its foothold on the sea floor. It was heartbreaking to realize the Orovars, a people looked upon with veneration in his time, were responsible for the coming calamity.

What the scientists of his day assumed to have been natural causes he was now convinced was an experiment gone awry. It was horrible! And to think that one school of thought from his own era credited the ochre moss as the salvation of Barsoom, claiming it insulated the arid upper crust of the planet and prevented precious topsoil from being stripped away by solar winds!

Arkaff was speaking again, bringing his focus back to the ingenious Xanatorian scientist; a man whose name was unknown in the future, but who Dat Voga feared to be single-handedly responsible for the destruction of the planet, and the loss of untold billions of lives.

"Well, Dat Voga, what have you to say? Is it not marvelous?" The scientist bent again to his creation with his eyes filled with pride. The red man did not know how to respond; his eyes remained fixed on the ochre moss, except when he stared at the back of Arkaff's head.

He knew that, of all men down through the course of time, only he understood the latent destructive capability within that plant. If any other had guessed the awful truth, their knowledge had surely died with them, for the theory had never been propounded among the scientists of his day.

How could he explain this to Arkaff without rewriting the future and wiping out entire civilizations himself?

How could you say to a man that he had made the greatest blunder of any single individual—ever? That he should not be experimenting with nature in this manner? Is that not precisely what scientists did—Dat Voga included?

Had he not bent his own keen wit to the completion of a device that would allow one to travel through the amplitudes of time? Was he not as guilty of the same reckless abandon in the field of experimentation that he now laid at the feet of Arkaff? He sighed. Yes. One could easily become absorbed trying to improve with the human mind what nature conducted with consummate ease and perfection.

When he answered, his voice was listless and bitter. "Yes, Arkaff, it's ingenious. You are perhaps the only scientist on all Barsoom who can claim to have created a new species. But whether your creation shall be judged evil or divine will remain for the future to determine, and that by judges not yet conceived."

Arkaff looked quizzically at the Heliumite but did not question him on the meaning of his cryptic reply, for he had grown used to the criticism of many who felt he dabbled where humanity ought not. Instead, he said, "Come, now you will see the result. Lower your face close to the moss."

The sides of the observation chamber were not high, so he leaned over it as he saw Arkaff do. Azaria, too, who had remained out of the conversation, voicing neither acclamation nor dissent at this man-made creation, leaned over the sides of the incubator to experience the result of the experiment.

With their noses held just above the moss they easily detected the release of oxygen. Taking too deep of a breath, Dat Voga became giddy, his skin gaining a palpable glow from the fresh, pure oxygen.

Noting his giddiness, Arkaff laughed. "Do you see?

This wonderful moss would do wonders underground, where we could channel water to it to oxygenate mine shafts. Its uses are limitless!"

Dat Voga imagined effervescent bubbles floating to the surface of the seas for thousands upon thousands of years, the enriched oxygen content of the sea causing a veritable explosion of life. He closed his eyes to force the horrible thoughts away. Finally, Arkaff indicated they would continue the tour, and they left that place.

At the doorway, Dat Voga turned for one last look at the moss container where he could see the tops of the moss plants in the incubator of the deadly time capsule. Shaking his head, and with his thoughts disconsolate and jumbled, he turned away. Hand in hand with Azaria, they followed Arkaff back the way they had come.

Although the remainder of the tour of the facility would have normally proved intriguing to a man of science, the red man could not shake his depression. Afterward, he could recall almost nothing of the complex. Listlessly, he followed the scientist about as one in a trance, his mind a million years away. Arkaff did not notice, for he did not know the padwar well. He continued to speak with wild enthusiasm of first one experiment then another. But Azaria noticed.

Dat Voga wished he had never seen the moss, and then that he had never heard of Arkaff. He should be ecstatic touring a facility run by such an exemplary peer! He understood this was an opportunity old Val Statt would slit his throat for, yet he could not enjoy a moment of it.

While Arkaff spoke to an assistant about some detail, Azaria laid a hand on her friend's shoulder. Her brow furrowed in concern, she said, "Dat Voga, are you ill? You've been out of sorts ever since we left the building with the moss."

The young woman seemed to sense something was not right. She could not, of course, know what the man's state signified, but her voice betrayed her apprehension. He suspected that her heart had begun to beat rapidly with fear of the unknown.

He forced a smile to reassure her, but he could not shake off the ponderous weight of what he knew: that men from her time, men revered in his day, will have destroyed their world. That they had unmade civilizations and completely revised the planet's future. That today marked the beginnings of the red man of the future—his race, which had been spawned during the calamities.

When the jeddak's detail informed him that they should leave to avoid traveling at night, Dat Voga bid Arkaff farewell. He genuinely liked this fascinating scientist and tried not to condemn him, although he knew the blame for what would come was his to bear. The red man knew the moss had not sprung from an evil heart, but from a perceived need. And for that he could not condemn Arkaff without also condemning himself and every other scientist down through the ages.

Chapter Fourteen

Bordubors

D AT VOGA COULD NOT PUT INTO WORDS how he felt about their host. When Arkaff bid them safe journey, his own response was wooden, muttering something he later could not recall.

Mounted on zytogonths, they traversed the shadowy primordial woods one must navigate on the return journey to Xanator, the most dangerous portion being the bordubor-haunted tracts on the outskirts of Arkaff's compound. Dat Voga noticed the guards casting wary glances into the surrounding trees and to their rear, as though fearing pursuit.

His curiosity aroused, he asked, "Warrior, what do you seek?"

The man's answer reminded the Heliumite of his conversation with Arkaff: "Bordubors!"

Another warrior added, "These forests are cursed with them. I am no coward, but I hate traveling to Arkaff's creepy laboratory! And now it gets on toward evening—it's a bad time of the day to travel this stretch of woods. On second thought, it's never a good time to be in these woods. We won't be safe until we've put some haads between us and the complex."

Despite Arkaff's warnings, the inquisitive Dat Voga wished he might catch a glimpse of one of the hybrid humans. Yet, with Azaria present, he also hoped they would not encounter any. He did not wish to endanger her just to satisfy a point of curiosity.

Thinking of his primordial princess, he glanced to where she rode alongside him at the precise moment a hideous creature dropped from the branches of a tree and landed on the back of her mount. A startling cacophony of roars and growls erupted. From all sides, a dozen creatures leaped from the trees and foliage along the trail.

Lighting upon the mounts, the hideous-looking things began mauling the riders, tearing them from their seats to slaughter them in the dank vegetation of the trail. Warriors, dragged into the forest by the brutish abnormalities, gave vent to pitiful cries of terror and agony that were awful to hear. Although its voice was gruff, so guttural in fact that he barely understood it, he heard a creature bark, "No kill woman! Kill warriors!"

The creature that alighted on the rump of Azaria's mount, which had been about to rend her before being warned not to by his compatriot, tossed her roughly over one shoulder and leaped agilely into the branches of the trees from which it had emerged. The woman's weight was nothing to the brute strength that precipitated the arboreal monster from the back of the beast.

The red man needed no invitation to follow. That same instant he, too, bounded to his feet and leaped for a branch in the same tree into which the creature had disappeared. He was soon glad that he was unencumbered, unlike the bordubor, for he would have been no match for its speed and agility upon this arboreal highway.

However, Dat Voga had two arms free while his foe must keep one wrapped about Azaria to prevent her from falling, thereby slowing his pace from what it would be had he traveled unhindered. As it was, the padwar's greatest efforts were barely enough to keep them in sight as the hybrid ape-man leaped agilely from tree to tree, forty sofads above the ground.

The creature had no idea it was being followed, for

Azaria's screams had drowned out any sound of pursuit until, tiring of her yells, the monster cuffed her in the head. Azaria immediately went limp. Enraged, the red man involuntarily called out at the cowardly blow: "Calot! Stand and fight!"

The manlike creature spun and saw its pursuer for the first time. Dropping Azaria's limp body across an immense limb, the bordubor threw back its head and roared. The hideous, bestial sound was chilling. Dat Voga was not the type, though, to recoil from a sound which could not by itself harm him.

He dropped from a higher limb onto the branch upon which his enemy stood over the prostrate Azaria, hoping the violent cuff had not slain her. The padwar's face was dark with rage, but his chest rose and fell slowly, the exertions of the past several xats having caused him little labor thanks to his evolved physiognomy. He drew the heavy short sword that was slung across his back, initiating a charge from the beast-man, who now ran nimbly along the branch toward the Heliumite.

The apish caricature of a man was roughly human in size and conformation, but there any similarities to mankind ended. The body of the creature was nearly covered in a sparse, dingy white fur and from beneath its armpits hung inchoate limbs. Having not even the strength to hold them out of its own way, these pendulous appendages flopped about uselessly.

Its skull featured a sharply sloping forehead with an exaggerated supraorbital ridge that lent its eyes a sullen, sunken appearance. The hair on its head stood stiffly erect, strongly reminding Dat Voga of the great white ape of his day, the scourge of the dead cities. Its body was powerfully muscled, giving it the appearance of immense strength. He had seen evidence of its power as he watched it hurl its own weight, combined with Azaria's, from branch to branch as it traversed the forest.

With no weapons beyond its yellowed talons and a mouth filled with heavy tusks, the monster charged the puny human who dared contest its rights of spoil. The curving, barked surface of the limb made for unstable footing for the man who was unaccustomed to this arboreal battlefield, while the bordubor seemed completely at home as it closed the short distance between them.

Displaying no fear, the beast charged with no consideration to the padwar's sword, almost like a beast that never had contact with man. When it snapped its arms closed around what should have been its prey, it clutched only empty air. Looking downward, the beast discovered a length of cold steel thrust to the hilt into its abdomen. The Heliumite had ducked and dropped from the limb to another directly below.

Roaring in pain, the creature tore at the weapon protruding from its vitals, doing much more damage to itself than the initial stab wound had produced. In anguish and frustration, it loosed a roar of rage, but it was far from being whelmed.

The beast tossed the weapon aside in anger, and it disappeared in the leafy verdure, the man hearing it clanging from branch to branch on its way to the forest floor. Now the creature followed him to the limb upon which he had precariously leaped. The red man had little experience in clambering about in trees but for a few instances while marooned on the island. His efforts to do so now were not as adept as those of his apish foe, who stalked him in its native habitat.

Having lost his sword, he now drew his dagger, his last weapon of defense. Should he lose it, he might be doomed, knowing he was no match for this beast barehanded. Making his way to a point below Azaria, who lay on the limb above him, he called her name, hoping to awaken her. His gut was wrenched with fear, wondering if she had survived her mauling, and fearing that she might fall from the limb.

Pressed by the ape-man, he faced his antagonist. He was certain the creature was mortally wounded if its internals were located where he guessed them to be. Naturally, he could not know if its mutation had relocated its vitals. The thing came at him, though, with full vigor, as if it were uninjured.

They grappled!

Chapter Fifteen

Battle in a Primordial Forest

THE BORDUBOR LUNGED FOR HIS DAGGER, and Dat Voga quickly discovered just how appalling its strength was. Having learned a lesson with the short sword, the creature nearly snapped the Heliumite's wrist in its attempt to wrest the sharp, pointy thing from its foe. With its free hand it grasped Dat Voga behind his neck and drew him toward massive, mutated jaws that snapped ferociously at his face as its rank breath nearly overwhelmed him. The red man's own strength was barely equal to holding the yellowed tusks from his flesh.

Dat Voga silently thanked whichever ancestor bequeathed him his short nose, for he swore if it had been any longer, he would have lost it in the toothy maw of the ape-man, so close did its jaws snap to his face.

If he were to have any chance of victory, he must conclude this fight on the jungle floor, knowing this unstable field of battle would be his undoing if he remained in the branches of the tree. The beast had hold of his hand with the knife, so he decided to apply what John Carter called pugilism to the end of the deformed ape-man's nose to hopefully free himself.

He jerked the arm the ape-man clutched. Likely thinking the man sought to escape, it instinctively tightened its grasp and was drawn toward the puny man. Dat Voga pummeled the beast rapidly in the face, its head snapping back with each hammering blow. The padwar then slammed a knee into its groin and, risking all, lunged forward with all his might, pushing the bordubor off balance. Wrenching his dagger free of the surprised creature's grasp, he pushed the bordubor and himself off the branch.

Falling from a great height is a fate all arboreal creatures inherently fear, and this creature was no different in this respect than its less-imaginative cousins. These might flit from branch to branch as confidently as one might cross a busy street, but the idea lurks in the back of their mind that they might fall, just as a pedestrian might fear being struck by a ground flier as he crosses a busy intersection in his modern-day metropolis.

The instant the bordubor felt itself shoved backward off the limb, it sought to save itself, an instinct of self-preservation that kept it from mauling Dat Voga's face, which again came uncomfortably close to the beast's savage fangs. The red man clung to the filthy ape-man, keeping its body between him and the ground.

As they fell, Dat Voga scrambled for whatever purchase he might find. He sunk his dagger into the creature's shoulder, eliciting a savage roar of pain that nearly deafened him, reminding him of the white ape he had faced in the flier fleeing Xanator. His empty hand, missing a grab for the ape's elbow, closed instead upon the anemic, withered lower arm that swung pendulously, flopping about its waist.

They fell for twenty sofads before they hit a limb. This limb bent to the combined weight of the two falling bodies, eliciting a howl of pain from the apish travesty that struck the limb. The blow to Dat Voga's own frame was softened by the rancid-smelling flesh of the bordubor that was between himself and the limb.

They rolled from the limb and continued their fall, with the man now on the bottom. Realizing this calamity, he let go of the dagger that remained stuck fast in the bordubor's shoulder. Grabbing a fist full of hair on the furry shoulder of the bordubor, he managed a midair twist, putting the creature once more on the bottom. No sooner had he done so than they crashed into yet another branch, and then another, the last finally ripping them apart.

In the ensuing violence of their separation, the monster's tiny, useless limb was torn free in the grip of a desperate Dat Voga, unseated from its socket where the padwar gripped it relentlessly. They then continued their journey toward the floor of the jungle individually, the dismembered beast howling in agony.

Letting loose of the grisly, underdeveloped arm, Dat Voga clutched at leaf and limb, but still only barely slowed his fall before he dropped the final distance to smash into the deep, lush jungle rot of the forest floor. He looked as though he had wrestled a banth and he would have testified that he felt worse than he looked.

He arrived upon the forest floor alone because the more agile bordubor had grasped a limb and stopped its own fall. Growling in pain and rage it descended rapidly, wishing to inflict its terrible vengeance upon the man-thing responsible for its maiming. It ceased growling and fell quiet. In silence now it came, the only sound that of the faint rustling of foliage above the prostrate man.

Barely conscious from the impact of the fall, the padwar frantically looked for a stone or anything he might turn into a weapon. He knew if the bordubor slew him, no one would succor his princess. His did not fear for himself, but for her. Then, as if placed by a beneficent ancestor, his blindly questing hand fell upon a sword hilt—his sword, which the creature had earlier cast aside.

He grasped it, turning over upon his back as the hideous face appeared above him. Snarling in triumph, the frightful travesty launched itself out of the foliage above him, straight for the prostrate man's throat.

Too late, the bordubor realized the man held the blade. The tip of the sword entered its gaping mouth between its parted jaws and shot down its throat into its heart and lungs. The weight of the creature, and the impetus given its body by its downward leap, knocked the wind from the red man. The sword handle, crammed to the hilt against the yellowed fangs of the plunging beast, was driven into the man's temple.

Dat Voga had no idea how long he lay thus when, from a great distance, he heard someone calling his name. It cost too much effort to answer. Finally, he opened his eyes and looked about him. His thoughts were incoherent. He was lying on the ground but could not recall how he had come to be there.

Near his face, upon a jungle blossom, perched one of the delicate, prehistoric fofals. Miraculously, it and the flower had somehow escaped being crushed during the violent scuffle. The colorful insect watched him, its four sets of wings slowly opening and closing while its delicate antennae moved this way and that as it assessed the smells carried by the breeze.

As he watched, its wings whipped up and began to rapidly spin. With a soft hum that reminded him of the flier motors of the future, it flitted away, gracefully wending its way between the limbs of the forest.

The red man heard the voice again. "Dat Voga! Where are you?" Above him, peering from amid the foliage, appeared the face of Azaria. Spotting him below her, she began to descend. He started once to sit up but groaned and lay back down. The bordubor lay nearby, dead.

The Heliumite's head throbbed from the concussion it had received from the sword hilt. He managed, "My pri—that is, Azaria! Thank the ancestors you are safe!"

Azaria smiled. This strange man came closer and closer to calling her his princess, words she now longed to hear.

But she knew he did not know she was aware of the fact, nor did it anger her. She was confident he would declare for her in his own time. Still, she could not resist adding a noticeable accent of her own to his name, as he did with hers.

As she finished descending the tree, she replied, "Yes, my—*Dat Voga*! Thanks to you!"

She shot him a knowing little smile as she dropped to her knees beside him. Then she gently picked up his bleeding head and pillowed it in her lap. The man groaned, but then sighed in apparent relief at her soft touch.

They sat thus while he recounted what had happened after the bordubor knocked her unconscious. While they spoke, Dat Voga watched the sunlight filter through the young woman's hair, creating beautiful highlights as she bent over him.

He announced that he would like to try to stand, so Azaria helped him to his feet. They were both in considerable discomfort from their injuries, but they retrieved his sword and started in the direction they had last seen their escort.

When they heard voices calling for them, they followed the sound and discovered the dirt track they had taken to Arkaff's, and their escort soon after. The warriors had lost half their number in the attack but had rallied and beaten the bordubors into a retreat, and then instituted a search for them. They eventually called off the search and were about to return to the city to report the visitors missing, when the senior officer admitted he was loath to do so and delayed their departure. He felt it would be a death sentence to leave them in this forest if they yet lived, and also for him, were he to return without them.

The warriors' mouths gaped in astonishment when they learned that Dat Voga had single-handedly wrested Azaria from the ape-man. Many had witnessed the bordubor make off with the young woman and had given her up for dead, while others saw the padwar scramble into the tree and take off after her.

They grinned and slapped Dat Voga on the back as rough men will, causing him to groan, for he had literally been beaten black and blue both from the fight with the bordubor and from the fall. He truthfully could not attest to which had given him the more bruises and was but thankful he had suffered no broken bones. The act earned him their fierce respect.

The warriors kept after him until he told them the story of his chase and hand-to-hand battle. Although the clash had been short, and he assured them he had triumphed primarily by luck, they respected the courage that prompted the chase, and the fact that he had taken the battle to the bordubor in its own haunts. Also were they impressed with his modest nature, and he heard his name mentioned among their numbers as they journeyed to the city—on foot now, for the zytogonths had fled in panic during the attack.

During the return journey, Dat Voga was thoughtful. The final part of the battle kept reminding him of when he and Carthoris were attacked in modern-day Xanator by the great white apes. The thought had come to him that perhaps these were the ancient progenitors of those beasts. Arkaff told him that he had created them by blending the structural strands of a white-haired simian found to the north with that of the convict specimens.

Dat Voga had stolen a close look at one of them and found the similarities striking. Although this creature's extra set of intermediary limbs were underdeveloped and currently useless, he guessed that would not remain the case. Already had their bodies adopted the white fur of the simian, while the hair on their heads, short and stiff, was unlike human hair at all.

He suspected that eventually the white hair upon their bodies would disappear, but the stiff shock of hair upon their heads would remain. He wondered idly what would occur during the succeeding millennia to cause them to arrive at the immense height and mass they would eventually attain.

The Heliumite shook his head at the thought that Arkaff had perhaps not only single-handedly brought about the destruction of the planet's seas with his genetically engineered moss, which was responsible for the deaths of untold billions of people, but might also be responsible for one of the greatest menaces of future Barsoom—the dead-city-haunting, great white Barsoomian ape.

Chapter Sixteen

The Dejection of Dat Voga

WHEN THEY RETURNED TO THE SHIP, Dat Voga was quiet and thoughtful. After receiving treatment for their superficial wounds and telling rapt listeners the extraordinary tale of their visit to the palace, and of Zikka and Arkaff, and of their encounter with the bordubors, Dat Voga and Azaria finally retired to their berths, where they slept like the dead.

However, such is the resilience of youth that within a day or two they were mostly back to their normal selves. The red man now bore a scar upon his temple that he would carry the rest of his life, where his sword hilt had struck his head during the battle with the bordubor. He shrugged it off, as it did not bother him. If it bothered his mother, he told Thuria, he would see the great medical genius Ras Thavas about repairing it.

For several days he remained aboard ship, recuperating. He laughingly told the sailors that he had won the fight with the bordubor but lost the encounter with the tree. His youthful body was battered and bruised from his fall, for one does not lightly rebound from the injuries incurred in falling limb-to-limb from a jungle giant.

But his joking demeanor was a front. The things he learned at Arkaff's greatly disturbed him. When he could speak to her alone, he told Thuria what he saw, and explained his theories about the moss and the bordubors. But he warned her not to mention either of these things to Azaria or the others.

He and Thuria had a responsibility to do nothing that might affect the future, although he realized mistakes had been made—and mostly by him, he would admit. He hated keeping secrets from the one he loved above all others and hoped eventually to reveal the truth to Azaria in its entirety, trusting that she would forgive him for what he had concealed.

The coincidence was not lost on him that he had discovered the very answer to the question Daxxus Nahl planned to seek here in the past. That Daxxus Nahl selected a time frame so near the actual event he found astonishing. Considering the scientist's propensity for diabolical accuracy, however, he should not have been surprised the man had divined so precisely the time of the beginning of the seas' vanishing.

The Heliumite wished with all his being to stop this wanton destruction, fully as much as Daxxus Nahl, although each possessed different motives for so wishing. He kept returning in his mind to the opportunity he had to stamp out this vile moss before it wrecked the world, understanding that it would be a different world to which they returned—if they managed to recalibrate the gauntlets.

However, were he to revise the timestream, he and Thuria would most likely cease to exist, the change resulting in the potential loss of billions of individuals and the formation of new family trees. Even if they did not cease to be, few of the cities with which they were familiar, and none of the people they knew, might exist.

Arkaff's actions were destined to change the surface of Barsoom into that with which he and Thuria were familiar. He wished there were a way to save the seas and spare the people the suffering to come while preserving those of the future. But, to do so would take the efforts of a god, which he was not.

He recalled what he had learned as a schoolboy of the calamities, of the mass migrations and uncounted deaths. His heart was crushed by grief for the untold horror to be suffered by those yet unhatched—and to think he was able, yet at the same time powerless, to stop it! Wars, pestilence, draught—all were related to the loss of the seas.

He knew the history, but now those historical facts and figures were much more real to him than they had been a million years from this moment, when he was sitting, detached, in a classroom in Helium, with all of this in the past and the anguish having been suffered by others long dead.

He was now living and walking among those others. No longer were they faceless and nameless. Oh, to be sure, the worst would occur in thousands of years from his present time, but the coming apocalypse seemed much more real to him now. What if it were Azaria, or one of the others, who fell prey to the awful tragedies his world would soon suffer? The thought was too horrid, so he shook his head to clear it.

He became absorbed with the idea of killing Arkaff, having to force the notion from his mind. To travel that road was to descend into madness and went against everything noble he represented. He was no murderer. And yet, would he not be guilty of the deaths of billions by not acting? He could not answer such colossal questions, so he threw himself into his work, hoping to dampen the pain, the confliction and the anger raging within him.

After spending days aboard the ship convalescing, he began making excursions into the city with his friends. It was strangely haunting to walk the beautiful streets of Xanator, animated by its populace, and to realize the ruination he knew to be its destiny. The city was so beautiful and alive!

At times, he would see the two women in lively discussion, often catching them glancing at him, and knew they were discussing him and Azaria. Thuria told him she had encouraged her friend to be patient with him. In the face of his obvious love and affection for the beautiful girl from

Horz, the Heliumite had not yet declared for her, and Azaria was understandably confused. She sensed he held her in deep affection, yet he refused to speak of it.

"It is my intention to declare my love for her and ask her to be my princess only when I know for certain that we can be together," he explained to Thuria. "Only, I am reluctant to do so while the future is so unsure. I wish to do so when I can devote myself entirely to her, as she deserves. Right now, I cannot do so."

Yet he had thus far made no progress toward unlocking the gauntlets. While they remained locked, he and Thuria would remain trapped in a time where they should not be. Even the crew of the *Prachus* should not now exist. If he had not intervened, they would be in the bellies of the fish-men, their remains littering the bottom of the Throxeus after the brobdoganth sank their ship.

Something finally occurred, however, to brighten the padwar's outlook and draw him out from under the pall of gloom he had been under since the excursion to Arkaff's complex. He had forgotten all about Zikka, but Zikka had not forgotten all about him.

Dat Voga sat coiling new ropes before taking them below for stowage. He had not purposely avoided Azaria, but he had been so busy preparing to leave port that they only spoke briefly of an evening after completing the day's work. Today she sought him out, smiling as she paused to watch him leaning over his work, his sun-bronzed red fingers standing out in stark contrast against the brand-new white rope he sorted and coiled.

The sounds of voices and footsteps abound upon a vessel, so the padwar did not notice the approach of two figures behind him, paying them no attention at all, for, was he not among friends? A voice boomed directly behind him, startling him from his concentration. "Hoy, Dat Voga! Tis I, Zikka. Did ye think then to escape my fee so easily?"

Chapter Seventeen

A Precious Gift

DAT VOGA SPUN AT THE SOUND of the quaint and recognizable accent of the giant metalsmith. Zikka was cleaner than the last time he had seen him. The smith had made the long journey from his shop to the barter district and thence to the ports to visit the red man aboard the ship of Hal-Roh-Kim. He wore a huge grin on his face, obviously enjoying teasing the Heliumite.

Still grinning, he reached into a long, cloth satchel he carried and retrieved a sword, handing it hilt-first to the red man, the blade running parallel along his massive forearm. Dat Voga's eyes lit like flames when he saw it. The workmanship was stunning.

Zikka said, "Ye said ye wanted the mark of my skill on the blades. Well, the white gold took some doing to get my hands on, but hoy! When ye do custom work for the jeddak, it opens doors for ye."

Dat Voga gazed enthralled at the beautiful gold inlays. "But Zikka! This is a much costlier blade than I expected," he stammered, wondering how he was to pay for this. He stopped in midsentence, losing his train of thought as his eyes devoured the beautiful workmanship.

Zikka winked at Azaria, who smiled back at the jovial artisan. The blacksmith said, "He's in love, Azaria. Now, Dat Voga, don't ye fret none about the gold and the baubles. They were Azaria's idea. She said to spare no expense for ye."

"Azaria's?" questioned the Heliumite. The blade drew him powerfully, and he forgot the odd comment about Azaria's requesting no expense be spared. The blade was a sofad or so longer than the swords of these primitive Barsoomians and less than half their width and thickness. The specially blended alloy he had specified yielded greater strength than the thicker blades and was more flexible and lighter.

The Heliumite brought the hilt close to his face, angling the blade toward the sky where he could watch the play of light as he gauged its trueness with a discerning eye. He recognized the telltale shimmer of the nearly indestructible, nontarnishing steel of the future.

Assessing its edge with his thumb, it easily shaved the top layer of dead skin away as if the edge were only the thickness of an atom. When he held the blade out to evaluate its balance, he realized fully Zikka's mastery of his art form. The blade balanced perfectly! He stepped away from the crowd to a broad, clear area of deck.

Running through simple warm-up maneuvers, he gathered speed, the sword becoming a blur as he wove a net of steel about him. The weapon appeared to the onlookers to become an extension of the red man's mind and body. From hand to hand, his motions sped, faster than the eye, the blade always in motion. He felt it cut the air as he slashed and speared imaginary foes.

His fellow sailors and Azaria stood by in silent awe at a display the likes of which they had never witnessed. Even when he and Gar-Noh-Dar had dueled they had not seen swordsmanship of this nature. Then, he had been handicapped with the clumsy blades of the day, while now he gripped a weapon of comfortable familiarity, and it was like stepping into the home of an old and dear friend.

Zikka's eyes grew moist as he watched his weapon in the skilled hands of the padwar.

Dat Voga brought the sword to a stop and stared in fascination at the masterpiece he held, unaware of his awed admirers. They had all been impressed at the skill he displayed when he and Gar-Noh-Dar dueled, but they now knew they had only gauged the tip of the red man's prowess. With a familiar weapon in hand, his abilities became godlike and confusing to the eye.

The grip and hilt were an artful blend of a metal heavier than the alloy utilized for the blade, giving it the right amount of balance in the grip to counter the weight of the blade's length. White Barsoomian gold, with accents of rare, black diamond, were set in the handle, which was equipped with a nonslip hold even if one's hands were damp.

The pommel and guard were of bronze, the contrast of the whiter metal and the black diamond striking. The flats of the guard and pommel were artfully inlaid with ships and sea creatures, together with a series of Xanatorian hieroglyphs. These last he could not read but he was astounded to recognize one of them, having seen its like on unusual, ancient swords in museums that had been discovered in archaeological digs and were renowned for their advanced metallurgy. He now realized that Zikka was the man who had fashioned those blades!

Blinking hard to force from his mind the fact that Zikka had obviously continued to manufacture his exotic blades, whose design and specifications had been set down for him by Dat Voga, he asked Azaria to decipher the inscription.

She bent her face close, examining the weapon a moment and quietly marveling at its beauty. Then she read aloud: "It reads, *Sword of Dat Voga of Helium*, and here it further says, *Fashioned by Zikka, Son of Zikka, of Xanator*. The sword is beautiful, Zikka! Your father would be so proud."

The metalsmith beamed at her. "My thanks, Azaria.

Hoy, Dat Voga, here is the companion blade you requested. I left it uninscribed, for I knew not for whom it was intended. And, although you did not request it, I fashioned each its own scabbard. A sword needs one—at least, to my way of thinking." He handed Dat Voga a scabbard for his blade.

The padwar sheathed the sword and passed it to Azaria. Taking its companion in hand, he recognized hieroglyphs he had seen on his own blade, knowing now they were Zikka's maker's mark. Zikka's blades were literally the only ones from this era to survive, making him not only the most famous sword maker of the time, but the *only* known sword maker of the time.

The opposite side, where his blade bore his name, was instead covered in beautiful, elaborate carvings. The engravings were different, consisting of creatures of the sea and bearing an anchor on each side of the pommel, a fitting adornment for the son of a sailor, for whom Dat Voga intended it.

As did its cousin, this sword boasted white gold with black diamond accents in the grip. The sword's beauty dazzled, and Dat Voga looked forward to gifting it to Gar-Noh-Dar, who was not on board at that moment. He turned to the metalsmith.

"Zikka, trust me when I say a million years will not see your equal. These are unbelievable. I had no idea what to expect, but you have exceeded every expectation. And while these are things of beauty, it is their balance which impresses me most. The poise is so perfect the blade feels weightless."

Zikka smiled, apparently satisfied with the red man's praise. Zikka's own estimation of a weapon clearly paralleled the padwar's—beauty must follow functionality. "By the shades, Dat Voga, I know not where you learned your own art, but it is plain you have studied under a master. Indeed, I would title you master after that display. I cannot say how happy I am this blade rests in the hands of one so capable and worthy of its stewardship."

The red man replied, "If you name me master, then he who instructed me is a master of masters."

After a time Zikka declared he must return to his forge while Dat Voga, accompanied by Azaria, took the swords to his quarters. As they walked, he glanced at her. "Thank you for the swords, Azaria. I shall repay your father, rest assured. At last, I finally feel as though I am satisfactorily armed! I've never felt quite as confident with these heavier, ancient short swords."

She replied with a chuckle. "Ancient? I hardly think they are that old, Dat Voga."

He glanced sidelong at her. To divert her attention from his slipup, he said, "Why did you ask Zikka to add the gold and diamond? Won't your father object?"

She turned to face him, her tone losing its playful notes and turning serious. "I asked Zikka to do so because you are worth it, Dat Voga. And my father will not object to the cost because I paid for them myself. I did not come aboard empty-handed, my friend."

There was a space of three to four weeks before the odar would be ready to sail for Horz, so Dat Voga took advantage of the remaining time to further his friend's lessons. To say that Gar-Noh-Dar was thrilled with his new sword would be an understatement. He thought so highly of the blade that he said he considered it a fitting gift for a jeddak of jeddaks. He could not thank Dat Voga and Azaria enough.

Now indeed, Gar-Noh-Dar told the Heliumite, did he understand what his friend had meant about the clumsiness of the heavier swords. Dat Voga was pleased to see Gar-Noh-Dar finally began to master the new techniques prior to their landing at Xanator, maneuvers that the former found he could accomplish now that he gripped the type of weapon around which those movements had been designed.

Gar-Noh-Dar also found that Dat Voga was correct in his assessment of the importance of balance for these maneuvers, many of which they had both cursed while attempting to execute with the shorter blades. Their mock combats became more intense as the osar's skills increased.

Dat Voga's friend told him that at first he was confounded by the sword's greater length. But once he mastered this unfamiliar aspect, he soon discovered he had more control than with the shorter swords to which he had been accustomed since he broke the shell.

Orders came down from the odar to prepare to set sail and the trimming of the vessel began in earnest. For days, they off-loaded cargo and loaded new goods and coin, preparing for the return to Horz. The odar was anxious to set Hal-Roh-Kim's mind at ease about both his daughter and his latest vessel.

All pitched in during this time as Gan-Toh-Gan cancelled all shore leave. Everyone had taken multiple turns in the city and Dat Voga paused the sword lessons until they should be at sea where they would have more time.

The sailors went about their work with happy smiles, singing their songs lustily as they heaved together to apply sail, and to wind the capstan to take in the anchor. Having been absent for months, the *Prachus* finally pointed her bow for Horz.

The crew were thrilled to be back on the ocean, not realizing how much they had missed it while they sat at berth for weeks at Xanator. It became obvious to Dat Voga now that, as happy as sailors might be to sight land, they were just as much so, after weeks in harbor, to return to the open sea.

Chapter Eighteen

DOLDRUMS

IN FIGHTING AGAINST A FLASH HEADWIND that severely crippled her speed, the *Prachus* attempted to sail far out to skirt the edge of this stalling wind, taking them into uncharted sea-lanes. Misfortune struck. From contending with a strong headwind, they went to having no wind at all. The sailors cursed—they had stumbled into what they called the doldrums. They sat unmoving, the lack of breeze utter and complete.

Days rolled by with no change. Having no other recourse, they began to row, although the ship was not outfitted for such. This they accomplished by attaching hawsers to the smaller boats and towing the ship, the sailors dutifully bending their backs to the oars.

Dawn of the twelfth day of rowing found their state unchanged and the crew weary beyond belief. It was early morning, and Dat Voga was utterly fatigued from his time at the oars the night before. Asleep in his bunk, he dreamed he heard a rumbling sound beneath the hull of the ship.

The sound was not loud enough to bring him to full consciousness, being one of those sounds that only half awakens one before it becomes incorporated into a dream, lulling the sleeper into deeper slumber because the sound becomes part of the mind's imaginings. The sound Dat

Voga heard caused him to dream of fish-men, and of the eerie cries of brobdoganths in the ocean deeps.

The tension of his nightmare heightened. He relived the anguish of seeing the women and the crew in harm's way. In his dream, he did not have the strength to combat the telepathy of the fish-man who leered mockingly as it directed the whale to attack. The pasty humanoid, watching his efforts, grinned as it urged on the great fish. Dat Voga struggled for air. He must return to the surface or drown!

Desperate now, he fought his way upward, struggling against cold, slimy hands pulling him into the depths from which there would be no return. He gasped as his head broke through the surface; he heard a clamor—the cries of the sailors!

The watch, perched in the phlega's nest a hundred and forty sofads above the main deck, shouted an alarm. Dat Voga also heard these cries coming from the deck above him. This amazed him because, in his dream, he had surfaced some distance from the ship, yet he could plainly hear feet upon the stairs climbing to the command and observation decks.

He bolted upright, awake, realizing that he really did hear feet pounding the decks. Now he heard the cry that filled the hearts of ancient sailors with dread—"Green men!" He burst from his cabin with his new longsword in his hand as Gar-Noh-Dar started down the companionway in his direction.

"Quick, Dat Voga, there are green men upon us! How in the name of the shades did they get so close without being spotted?"

The barrel-chested sailor continued down the companionway, pounding on doors to rouse the work-weary men from their slumbers. His heart pounding with dread, Dat Voga followed. At the top of the stair, Gar-Noh-Dar sheared off, but called back over one shoulder, "I must find the odar, Dat Voga! Take a position and prepare to repel boarders!"

The decks were alive with sailors scrambling for their stations. Dat Voga had heard nothing good concerning these primitive green men. Far less was known in the past about them than what would later be learned about the modern-day green men. He gleaned that these seafaring green men attacked without provocation, leaving no survivors were they the victors. They scuttled captured vessels, sending them to the bottom after plundering their cargo.

It was imperative they prevented the green men from boarding the *Prachus*. As soon as Dat Voga's feet hit the deck, he ran to a rail where he saw a sight he could have never imagined in a million years. Approaching the ship were green men riding upon the backs of gantahns. It was astonishing.

"What in the name of Issus?" he cried.

Observing them briefly, he saw that there was a rhythm to their gait. After several leaps above the surface, the gantahn would dive. The rider held his breath while they were submerged, which was when they made their most rapid progress, with the leaps above the surface being for the benefit of the green man. The pair would burst to the surface while the green man caught his breath and prepared for the next dive, and the cadence was then repeated.

Advancing thus, they attained the celerity of charging thoats. They had this gait down to a nicety and could keep the pace up for zodes with neither man nor fish tiring or suffering from lack of oxygen. If that were not bizarre enough, an even odder sight met his eyes. Bursting above the waves came strange vessels, and just ahead of them, the backs of the brobdoganths who towed the outlandish vessels.

When the vessels surfaced, hatches opened from which green men poured forth, grasping rings set in the top skin for that purpose. The hatches were closed while the green warriors, a boarding party, crouched upon their advancing vessels. Waving their weapons aloft, the air became filled with their fierce cries. Their faces, made hideous by war paint, were made even more so by their scowls of vehement hatred.

Dat Voga swore and wished, not for the first time, for a rifle. How easily might he lay waste to these attackers if he had the automatic from the rear deck of Carthoris' ship! But he did not, and the sight of the brobdoganths, in such numbers, was sobering. He considered himself one who could coolly calculate risks and assess situations; he guessed if these giants were loosed against them, they were doomed.

Briefly, Azaria filled his thoughts. He wondered where she had taken position for the coming assault and hoped she had armed herself. He had intended to find her when he reached the main deck, but the attack was so eminent he dared not leave the rail now. His sword arm would be sorely needed when the enemy was upon them.

Chapter Nineteen

Red Swords at Sea

WHEN THEY REACHED THE SHIP, the gantahns, each wearing a harness to which a green man clung, leaped high into the air a final time with their riders. Timing this perfectly, the green men loosed their grip and sailed through the air. They hit the water and reappeared at the waterline where they instantly began scaling the sides toward rails lined with astonished sailors.

On their heels came the brobdoganths, towing the primitive bathyspheres upon the dripping hulls of which crouched score upon score of green men. As the whales closed, they dove beneath the green men in the water just when the red man thought they would smash through their own forces and ram the *Prachus*.

Skimming over the surface, the green men, crouched on their bathyspheres, launched grappling hooks as they closed on the ship. Their hooks cast, the green warriors, timing it to a nicety, leaped from the backs of their vessels just as the whales dragged their strange carriages below the waves.

Hitting the water, the green men swam for the ship's hull, where they began ascending the sides.

Wave after wave of green men bombarded the vessel with grappling hooks and ropes. These hooks clacked and clanged about the deck, seeking purchase, the rough iron scratching and gouging the vessel's beautiful, oiled decking. The red

125

man did not have to be schooled in this primitive manner of warfare to act. He leaped for the nearest grappling hook and flung it overboard.

Sailors nearby acted similarly. One flung a heavy hook over the rail into the face of a green man below, the hook bloodying the fellow's face and snapping off one of his tusks. This elicited cries of rage and pain. The sailor cursed the green man and flung his gaff straight down the side of the hull into the wounded man's chest, driving him beneath the waves with a chopped-off gurgle.

Despite having never gained any proficiency with the weapon, the Heliumite wished he had one of the powerful bows he had seen the day he met Gar-Noh-Dar. They needed something with which to strike at a distance. Nor was he alone in thinking of bows. A man rushed onto the deck carrying all his arms would hold.

The gaff was obviously not the weapon of choice to meet the strange attack of the green men. It could not reach the green men until they were aboard, unless one relinquished his weapon by casting it like a spear. Their only chance lay in preventing a boarding, and toward that end they must slay the attackers while they were still in the sea.

As the padwar waited for green men in which to bury his steel, he saw that while he and his fellows were distracted with the first wave, a second line of attack approached them from another angle. Lines of gantahns with mounted green men prepared to travel down both sides of the ship, parallel with the vessel.

Behind these lines of attackers were more brobdoganths, the green warriors already pouring from the hatches of their bathyspheres. Dat Voga did not know what they hoped to accomplish by putting so many warriors into the sea, from which position the humans could repulse their attempts to board. He soon saw these new maneuvers were not to be conducted in the same manner, however.

From their perches on their submersibles, spears were now cast at the sailors lining the rails while short, powerful bows were also wielded by the green men, filling the sky with arrows. The sailors, having doffed their gaffs for bows of their own, fired volleys of arrows but found the moving green men difficult to hit.

The green men, however, fired at stationary targets, and in this measure their efforts were successful, with sailors abruptly slumping forward over the gunwales with arrows bristling from their bodies. Roughly half thus stricken fell into the sea, while others collapsed to the decking where they squirmed in agony or lay still in death.

Sailors now pulled additional bows from the weapons racks and distributed them, but Dat Voga felt their requisitioning at this stage might have cost them dearly. As the crew expected waves of boarders, only about every other man had armed himself with a bow while others wasted precious time arming themselves with swords and gaffs. Their lack of understanding of their green attackers' tactics had greatly stymied their defense.

Desperately, the padwar wrested a bow and quiver from the hands of a fallen comrade and laid into the green men in the water. These were easier targets than those racing past on their fishy steeds or charging on their strange submersible craft.

Dat Voga had not spent a great deal of time with the bow, and so had never become very skilled with it. Being a man of war as well as a scientist, he had an interest in anything martial and so of course had examined them and found them interesting. Yet, even with his unfamiliarity he managed to score hits, just not as often as he wished.

Speeding an arrow only to watch it plunge fruitlessly into the sea, and then having the instant disappointment of watching his target continue to advance, caused him to feel that his best effort to defend the ship in this manner was useless. As he struggled to find some way to make a difference in the battle, he spotted a group of three submersibles approaching rapidly.

"There!" he pointed.

On either side of him his friends took aim and fired, dropping green men on the craft both to left and right. One of the padwar's arrows took out a green man while the others went wide, and the two green men standing atop the strange craft in the center continued to approach. One of Dat Voga's friends, Tas-Du-Boh, shouting curses and speeding arrows, leaned far out over the rail to take a shot at the oncoming foe. The next thing Dat Voga knew, the man fell overboard.

Dat Voga had never cared to wait for another to bring the fight to him, and the sight of his friend floundering in the sea, helpless, with green men plowing down upon him, decided it. As the attackers upon the swaying surface of their craft shouted taunts and one of their number leveled a spear to skewer Tas-Du-Boh, Dat Voga leaped to the rail and, before anyone could stop him, drew his sword, and sprang for the two green men who were now nearly beneath the ship.

Dat Voga made for quite a surprising sight both to the sailors of the *Prachus* and the two warriors below him as he sailed through the air toward the green man he had targeted. In another moment, the sword of Zikka would quench its thirst for the first time, with the life's blood of an enemy!

The hapless green man holding the spear looked up in astonishment as a strange, red man, gripping a long slender blade, plunged headfirst toward him. That was the last thing he ever saw, unless his eyes registered the blood-filled waters as his head sank beneath his vessel. Dat Voga continued his dive, splitting the bloody waters himself. He turned swiftly and shot back to the surface in time to meet the second green man leaping at him.

But the Heliumite was not totally unprepared. His sword in hand, he had only to aim. Casting his body quickly to one side, he felt the tip of the sword pierce flesh and then felt himself dragged violently under by the heavy, sinking body of this second victim, who never drew breath after that single thrust found and stilled his heart. Fearing that either the weight of the dead body would drag him to the bottom or he would have to relinquish his grip on the sword fashioned by Xanator's ingenious metallurgist, he wrenched desperately and felt the blade slice through ribs and flesh and come free.

As he gained the surface, the nearby shell-shaped vessel, most likely at the promptings of its pilot, slipped suddenly beneath the water and disappeared. Shaking his head to fling his soaked hair from his eyes, the red man looked up to find sailors crying out to him and Tas-Du-Boh to hurry; a new wave of attackers approached, and already green men were hitting the water. Sheathing his blade, Dat Voga swam for the ship, with Tas-Du-Boh close behind.

"Quick, Dat Voga!" shouted one, while another cried, "Catch, Tas-Du-Boh!" That man and others fired arrow after arrow into the water on either side of the red man and the sailor he would save.

Dat Voga never knew how close the green men came, but any green man who approached the padwar too closely sank from sight, filled with arrows. Reaching the side of the *Prachus*, he and Tas-Du-Boh each grasped a hastily slung rope and clambered back aboard.

"By the shades, Dat Voga! I thought you were a dead man, taking on the green men in their own element! Here!" a man cried. He thrust a gaff into the red man's hands.

"Thank you, Dat Voga!" cried Tas-Du-Boh.

There was no time to answer either man. At that moment cries of dismay rose from the stern, where Dat Voga saw green warriors leaping agilely over the aft gunwale. Here at the starboard rail, fighting with unfamiliar weapons, the padwar felt useless while taking the fight to the enemy with his sword had scored two victories. With the sight of the invaders pouring onto the stern, he knew he would be of more value there with his sword than here with a gaff.

Debating it no longer, he forced the unfamiliar weapon into the hands of Tas-Du-Boh where it could be put to better use.

"Where're ye going?" Tas-Du-Boh cried.

For answer, Dat Voga drew the sword of Zikka. "I go to the stern!" he cried. "Make way!"

By the time he arrived, a dozen green warriors had swarmed over the rail and were wreaking havoc on the aft deck. More followed. Desperate sailors met them with short swords and gaffs. He saw a sailor lunge forward and hook a green warrior behind one of his lower shoulders and jerk him from his feet.

As the green man hit the deck, four short swords found his vitals, and another hacked his head free. The grisly thing began rolling back and forth with the tossing of the ship, which was racked by the wake of the brobdoganths. Within moments a sailor stepped on it, the ghastly noggin sending him sprawling to his back. A green man instantly pinned him to the deck with a spear.

"Zoh-Du!" cried the brother of the slain sailor. The man screamed in mindless rage as he swung his gaff with both hands, the steel bar catching the green man across the temple. Someone grasped the severed head and flung it overboard. A heartbeat later, Zoh-Du's brother was spitted on a sword himself and fell bleeding to the deck where friend and foe alike trampled him in the violence of the fracas.

The padwar could not recall ever having seen more savage fighting. Leaping in close, he speared a warrior on the tip of his blade. He displayed no fanfare as he fought. He sped the tip of his sword into as many green breasts as possible, realizing that only in sheer numbers slain did they have a shred of hope.

A pair of green men charged him, wielding long swords.

The foremost aimed a sidelong swipe at his neck while the second lunged for his heart. He parried the stroke of the first warrior, expertly guiding the blade into the path of the second and throwing off his attack. There was a flurry of swirling steel resulting in the padwar opening a diagonal cut in the throat of one. That one stumbled away and collapsed. The remaining green man redoubled his efforts.

Dat Voga whipped his sword in a blinding, horizontal cut, filleting the man's chest to the ribs. Roaring in pain, the man recoiled. Transferring his sword to an intermediary limb, the green man grasped a nearby sailor and held the hapless man aloft in his upper arms. His wound gaped and bled profusely. Cursing from the pain, the green man tossed the unfortunate sailor at Dat Voga.

There was nothing the red man could do to save the sailor. Throwing himself into a forward roll, he dove beneath the hurtling body, which passed above his head and on over the railing. The sailor's scream was awful, but short-lived, as his wails ceased the instant he fell among the green men at the waterline.

Continuing his roll, Dat Voga came into a crouch at the feet of the green warrior and drove his sword into his enemy's abdomen, burying his blade to its hilt. He wrenched his steel free with a motion that left the green warrior gashed wide open and Dat Voga drenched in a deluge of blood and gore.

The green man's face contorted, but his wide-open mouth was voiceless from hideous agony. His sword dropped to the deck. The padwar shoved the mortally wounded man toward the gunwale where he dislodged another green man just scrambling over the railing. That warrior fell into the sea with Dat Voga's most recent victim right behind him.

Dat Voga leaned over the railing to surveil his handiwork . . . and looked directly into the face of yet another green man climbing the stern. As the attacker clutched the top rail, the padwar reflexively lopped off the man's hand.

Because this was the only handhold the green man had upon the railing, being engaged in grasping various weaponry with his three others, he, too, fell from the rail and into the churning sea.

Chapter Twenty

Green Men

DAT VOGA WAS SO CERTAIN he and his fellow sailors at the stern would be overrun that it was with considerable amazement that he looked about to see only himself and a handful of brave sailors standing amid the horrific carnage. Awash with gore, he stared in fascination at the bodies of both races littering the deck.

Weary from the vicious fighting, the sailors slumped from exhaustion, their hands upon their knees to support their weight while their breath came in ragged gasps. Not so, the red man. His chest rose and fell slowly to his unlabored breathing, giving him the appearance of not being in the least fatigued. He took note of how the defense had gone on the rest of the ship.

Dat Voga looked down along the starboard side but could only see to about amidships due to the curvature of her lines and the intervening superstructure. As he looked, a volley of arrows and spears took out half a dozen sailors along a section of rail. A wave of green men poked their heads up and began clambering over the side. "Issus!" hissed Dat Voga.

He guessed that the main attack would focus upon that side, and that the others were feints to split up the defenses. The padwar made up his mind instantly. There being no officer among the survivors, he took command of the remaining sailors on the stern.

"Ak-Mon-Tu! Roh-Du-Von! You're with me! The rest of you remain here and repulse any green man who dares poke his eyes over that rail." Without a hindward glance, the red man ran toward the green men swarming over the side.

It was only with difficulty that they were able to move toward the breach. The fighting along the path between the railing and the promenade became fierce, and it was not as if Dat Voga could ask them to pause while he and his two men passed.

Near the stern end of the promenade, the Heliumite noticed a tangle of rope dangling within easy reach, its moorings having been severed during the battle. The transparent glazes of the walkway, a once-beautiful characteristic of the ship, were now shattered. Sheathing his sword, he leaped for the rope and scrambled up the side like a bordubor. Ak-Mon-Tu and Roh-Du-Von followed his example.

They climbed above the command cabin to the observation deck, which was free from fighting. Until this point, the bulk of the carnage had taken place along the railings. They ran forward until they reached a point above where the green men poured over the rail.

The first wave to gain the deck stood over the slain bodies of the many sailors who had sought to halt their progress. The green men had set up a perimeter fore and aft of their position to fend off attempts to stem the flow of boarders. The tide of green men pouring onto the main deck seemed unstoppable.

Thoughts of Azaria and Thuria crossed his mind, but he could only dwell on them briefly. The breach made by the invaders must be sealed. If the green men gained control of the deck, they were lost. He forced himself to focus on the task at hand.

Not knowing whether the two sailors would follow him, he clambered over the rail and leaped for the deck below. He plummeted about twenty sofads to land feetfirst on the shoulders of a green man whose charge he had timed with precision.

The green man's shoulders slumped as the padwar's full weight slammed onto him from above. To the red man's ears came the sickening *crunch* of snapping bone, and with a horrid groan the green man collapsed, broken and paralyzed. Dat Voga rose from the man's body to face a horde of surprised green men.

The padwar's blade flew into his practiced hand as he lay into the boarding party with unbridled ferocity. He fought as if he would slay them all single-handedly, and what followed was sheer butchery. He did not enjoy this style of fighting, but he had no other choice. In desperation born of necessity, he slew until he was forced to transfer his blade to his left hand to give his right arm time to recover.

He had slain a dozen or more green men before he noted that Ak-Mon-Tu had followed and taken up a forward position. He took the green men from behind while they fought off their attackers, not expecting the enemy to descend behind them from above. Roh-Du-Von had taken a similar position sternward where he, too, actively introduced the green men to sharp steel.

The green men had not yet penetrated the promenade, perhaps due to their giant stature, the walkway's ceiling being but seven sofads high. Had they done so, the fight would soon have been over, as they would have surrounded the three defenders on four sides.

It did not take long for the green men to realize the three sailors had attacked their rear. Shouts of fury went up, and the invaders turned on them with vigor. Several green men now went on all fours, coming at them through the tunnel-like promenade. The fighting became so intense that it was difficult for the defenders to swing a weapon without endangering their comrades, whereupon daggers were drawn and fists employed.

The red man fell to picking up fallen daggers from lifeless fingers, reverting to his dagger-throwing days in the navy. No sooner would a dagger fall from a dead hand than Dat Voga grabbed it and snapped his arm forward in a savage arc, at the end of which the dagger flew with unerring accuracy.

During this time, Ak-Mon-Tu suffered a gaff wound when a green man cast the weapon spear-fashion. The sailor took the gaff full in the chest, the weight of it slamming him backward where he encountered the rail. Before either of his comrades might come to his aid, he catapulted backward over the rail into the faces of advancing green men scaling the sides, taking those with him into the sea.

The Heliumite saw that conditions were rapidly degenerating for his side. He and Roh-Du-Von would soon be in a hopeless situation from which escape would be impossible. They must find someplace more defensible, for to remain here was to perish. Yelling for the young sailor to follow, Dat Voga gripped a dagger in each hand and looked in the direction in which he hoped to escape—the promenade tunnel where three green men were charging through a shattered opening.

He threw both daggers. The first *thunked* into the top of a green skull as the warrior crouched to pass through the small opening. The second slammed into another's chest. Grabbing a fallen gaff, Dat Voga engaged the last one blocking their passage. That fight was quick and savage. Leaving the gaff impaled in the fallen man's breast, the padwar drew his sword.

They fled through a shattered opening in the promenade, of which not a glazed panel remained. Behind them, enraged green men howled for their blood. Luckily, there were so many attackers that they hampered one another's movement.

The two men dashed down the hall to the stairs leading to steerage, and thence to the observation deck.

They charged up the stairs, occasionally having to stop to fight their pursuers. At last, they gained the observation deck, but with green warriors right behind them. Many of these ran on all fours, using their intermediary limbs like spider's legs. Having lost a number of their men to Dat Voga and thereby gained much respect for the red man's sword, they approached warily.

But when they saw the pair running for the rail, the green men erupted out of the stairway access like insects from a nest. Only now learning of the direction their flight had taken, numbers of them scaled the outer walls of the command bridge, which their great height and reach enabled them to do. The sailors' situation appeared hopeless.

Dat Voga determined that rather than die here he would fight to the side of the woman he loved, that he might fall in her defense. From this vantage point he sought for sign of Azaria, and he spotted her for the first time since the attack began. She was at the bow. Alongside her was Thuria and Gar-Noh-Dar, who had remained by her side to stand in their defense should the green men gain a foothold on the decks.

Only a short leap from the railing was a yardarm, from which point he could scramble up a rope ladder leading toward the phlega's nest. From that mast hung suspended a network of rigging. It was the only path from the observation deck. "Come, Roh-Du-Von," he ordered. Sheathing his sword, he jumped.

Climbing and clambering, the two men rushed in their mad scramble. An occasional gaff flashed close to them, but luckily no arrows, for the boarders had no bows among their numbers.

Before long, they were at the main mast. Far above the enemies' heads, they ran out on a beam and, cutting a piece of rigging free, descended to the deck while their friends, following their advance with their eyes, defended their retreat with bows.

"It's about time you joined the fight, sluggards," roared Gar-Noh-Dar as they swung to the deck. His words were wrenched out with effort. With one arm he swung a gaff, bashing a green head. With his other he darted his sword forward to spear a green man in the throat.

"Hah," roared Dat Voga. "And where were you during the fight on the fantail? It was a battle worthy of the bards!" His sword back in hand, Dat Voga joined the circle of defenders surrounding the two women. He only had a moment to call to Azaria. Glancing over his shoulder, he asked, "You are well, my princess?"

Azaria answered, "Yes, my chieftain!" This she at once followed with, "Watch out!"

Dat Voga turned to see green men rushing them. Everywhere he looked, they swarmed about the ship; the ship's defenses had suffered multiple breaches along the rails through which the green men poured in a continuous flow. Brave defenders of the *Prachus* fell to the bloody decks, to rise no more.

The brobdoganth-drawn chariots had ceased their fusillade of arrows as they now risked hitting their own forces. The faces upon the small contingent at the bow were distraught. Scenes of carnage were visible everywhere. The humans had given an excellent account of themselves, but the death tolls on both sides were atrocious. Many a shade had split the aether to join their ancestors this day.

There came a lull in the fighting upon the part of the green men, and the sailors perceived the enemy falling back slightly. The remnant of the vessel's crew wondered what new stratagem might be employed against them.

"What will they do now, Gar-Noh-Dar?" Dat Voga asked. Thus far, the tactics of the green men had surprised him, each time being in all ways unpredictable.

The older man shook his head. "Who may say? No man has witnessed what we have today, Dat Voga, and lived to speak of it. I only fear that we, too, may be among those doomed to know the answer to your question."

The green men and two-armed warriors alike took advantage of the moment to catch their breath. All, that is, but the man from the far future, who was apparently unaffected by his exertions, although his muscles were taxed from his endeavors.

A tall, dark green man strode among his fellows, passing instructions to them. His darker coloration marked him as a more mature specimen. His highly developed musculature possessed the appearance of massive strength. On his face rested a cruel expression.

Dat Voga and his companions could see the green men making preparations of some sort. They wondered in what form the green men's next attack would take.

The signal was undetectable, yet swiftly the air became filled with hundreds of barra nuts. Closely following the bombardment was a veritable cloud of netting. Dat Voga and the others fought nobly, but when one of the nuts struck him in the head, the red man realized these were modified barras with weight added, converting them into excellent missiles. These were no light, hollow gourds.

Against this strange new form of attack and with their numbers reduced to near nothing, they could not last. One by one they were struck unconscious and tangled in netting. As he fought against oblivion, Dat Voga's last, fading thoughts were first of Azaria. His hopes ebbed for a life of happiness with his primordial princess.

His princess! He relived the moment when he thought they were to be slain outright and he had called her his princess, and she had named him her chieftain. Could it be possible she returned his affection?

With their capture, he guessed they would be tortured

to death, if these green men were like those of his time. He turned his head to look once more into the face of his beloved, only to find her lying as one dead. And then blackness mercifully folded the man from Helium in its dark embrace.

Chapter Twenty-One

FAREWELL, *PRACHUS*

WHEN HE AWOKE, Dat Voga knew instantly they were no longer aboard the *Prachus*, as the motion caused by the ocean current was much more perceptible. Opening his eyes, he saw that he lay on level with the sea, upon the deck of a small vessel.

Sitting up, he found himself securely bound, his arms behind his back and with sharp pain shooting through his eyes from the concussions he had sustained. Sitting or lying next to him were the members of the small band at whose side he had fought. Azaria and Thuria both lay comatose, but Gan-Toh-Gan and Gar-Noh-Dar were sitting up; faithful Roh-Du-Von lay as though dead.

Dat Voga saw they were upon the stern hull of one of the odd, shell-shaped vessels of the green men; the vessel's dimensions were approximately fifteen sofads in diameter, one of the larger variety. Two portals were open through which a simple, bare interior was visible. Inside sat a green man before a control surface focusing intently on something out of the red man's view.

Guarding the prisoners was a green man upon whose hip both his and Gar-Noh-Dar's swords swung. He stood near the hatch holding a large gaff, watching the proceedings aboard the captured ship.

A second green man stood nearby rigorously pumping

a type of bellows device, apparently forcing air into some form of storage tank; much of the air escaped as he attempted to seal it after removing his device.

The red man guessed the odd vessel carried six or eight green men but could not be sure until he obtained a better view of the interior, which contained equipment he could not see. From his position, he could not guess how much of the vehicle lay below the waterline, or whether it consisted of one deck or more.

A massive hawser, tied off to the bow, disappeared into the sea. He assumed this led to the brobdoganth that floated on the surface a hundred sofads away, its horny protuberances clearly visible.

Now he looked toward their ship. From various points upon the *Prachus* disgorged flames and billowing smoke, black from the tars and pitches used in her construction, and mayhap from whatever the green men used to ignite their fires.

There were still several green men aboard, but as he watched, these began to clamber overboard into the sea where some swam to waiting gantahns, and others to the strangely shaped vessels such as that upon which the prisoners rode.

The green man with the captured swords turned to the warrior with the bellows. "How much longer, Tazzor Gobatt, until you finish?" he asked in his gravelly voice.

That worthy set the bronze tip of his bellows upon the surface of the vessel with a grating sound. "I am finished now," he replied.

"Good, they are disembarking. We shall depart presently."

Dat Voga looked down the sides of the ship and saw that they were exiting en masse. Apparently having taken everything they wished in goods and plunder, they would set her afire and abandon the vessel to her fate.

He mourned for the ship, recalling the day he boarded her—the day he fell in love with her. How beautiful she had been! Odar Gan-Toh-Gan caught him once, staring at the ship, his eyes following her lines. Smiling, the odar had approached the young padwar and thrown a comradely arm about his shoulders.

"Ah, young Dat Voga, you have the look of a lovestruck youth! I see you have fallen for the beauty and the wiles of the *Prachus*! And why not? She is astounding!" he had exclaimed.

The damage from the fracas was frightful. Even from his low vantage he could see that her decks were awash with blood and bodies. Everywhere scars of battle were apparent in the form of shattered railings and gouges made from the metal instruments of war upon her hand-carved and polished woods. If that were not enough, smoke and flames leaped from hatches and cabins, finally engulfing her sails and rigging.

He could not imagine what havoc had been wrought inside. He thought of his neat, trim little cabin and felt a sudden, sharp stab in the pit of his stomach as he recalled his small storage chest. Issus! Had the green men retrieved the gauntlets hidden within the trunk, or had they over-looked them?

He sat, lost in thought about the gauntlets, when he refocused his attention on the ship. The green men had retreated from the vicinity of the vessel. He assumed these savages would now take him and the other prisoners to their homeland for torture and slaughter, and that the ship would be abandoned.

But he soon found out that he was off on that score. Shortly, he saw a great disturbance upon the surface of the sea and heard excited yells of jubilation from the green warriors. They roared with laughter and howled battle cries and shook their weapons violently in the air.

With a surge of water as it propelled itself forward with enormous force, the figure of a monstrous brobdoganth sped with the velocity and energy of a battering ram, a green man clinging to the horns behind its head. The swell reminded Dat Voga of the time he had been nearly washed into the sea while on the island, when a similar fish gulped a creature off the rocks right beside him.

At the last moment, the green man leaped from his mount as the giant creature dove headforemost toward the waterline, slamming into the hull of the ship. The green man swam swiftly toward an awaiting vessel.

The sounds of the concussion and the ensuing rending of timbers were terrific. The beast shoved the vessel laterally for over fifty sofads from the sheer force of the impact. In horror, the survivors of the crew looked on as they watched the scuttling of their beloved ship, unable to tear their tear-filled eyes from the spectacle; the mighty odar wept openly.

Dat Voga saw the green men laughing at them and pointing in mockery, and realized their torture had already begun in the act of witnessing the annihilation of their ship, thus destroying any vestiges of hope they might have held.

The brobdoganth retreated and dove from sight while on its heels another charged in, striking the ship at nearly the same location. The flames from the fires the green men set belowdecks were belching thick smoke, the battering the ship was taking sending ash and embers into the sky.

Water gushed into the enormous hole the behemoths had smashed in the hull, and the ship began to list to starboard. She was preparing to lie over. She reached a tipping point, and with a loud groan collapsed like a felled tree, creating a huge concussion of spray when she hit the surface. Her masts snapped off as if made of rotten twigs.

As she filled with water the ship began to drop by the stern. The bow rose high into the air, causing the outstretched arm of the maiden-of-the-prow to appear as though she were grasping toward the smoke-filled sky for succor, as if she could catch hold of a cloud and prevent the pending calamity.

With a sudden rending of timbers, the vessel broke in

two where she had become weakened by the brobdoganths. The forward portion collapsed back into the sea with a tremendous crash, while the stern sank almost instantly. The arm of the figurehead was the last thing to disappear beneath the churning waters. And then she was gone, leaving only scattered debris floating upon the disturbed surface.

The green horde roared in hilarity. In horror, Dat Voga envisioned the once-beautiful ship plummeting, stonelike, toward the bottom of the sea, the lovely face of the ship's figurehead still set in firm resolve, however futile.

A memory of his visit to Arkaff's laboratory came to mind, and along with it the mystery of how the moss became introduced into the seas. The answer to the question just clicked into place.

The sowing of the moss must have been a combination of shipwrecks at sea and the relentless war of the green men against helpless vessels, both scenarios resulting in sending untold amounts of the plants to the bottom. Just as a farmer would walk his rows tossing seed into the soil, these sinking relics of this bygone era would sow the seeds of destruction in the seas, guaranteeing the coming apocalypse.

Had Arkaff not said the moss would become a giant export product of Xanator? Could it be possible that even the *Prachus* carried a shipment of this poisonous product, destined for Horz? Were the first seeds of the calamity that would destroy untold lives and the entire surface of Barsoom even now speeding their way toward the bottom of the beautiful and mysterious Throxeus?

He felt overcome by the horror of his realization. Flooding his mind were thoughts of the moss destroying his world, the destruction of the ship he had grown to love, and the loss of the irreplaceable gauntlets that were right now on their way to the bottom, forever stranding him and Thuria in this epoch. He rose to his feet only to hear a snarl from behind.

"Stay down, you ugly red scum!" It was the hoarse, gruff

voice of the green man who had stolen his sword. Bright lights exploded in his head from the swung gaff of the green man, and for the second time that day Dat Voga collapsed into blackness, this time from a blow dealt not in battle, but in cowardice from behind.

Chapter Twenty-Two

A Journey on a Styth

WHEN DAT VOGA AWOKE it was to a musty, chilly darkness. He lay with his face pressed against an unyielding, metallic surface, a position he must have been in for quite a while, if his cramped muscles were any indication. The sound of rushing water came to his ears.

As he became accustomed to the dimness, he saw that it was not as dark as he thought, there being a faint illumination forward. When his eyes had adjusted, he perceived others lying nearby, but he could not make out their identities. He heard voices speaking in another section of the vessel, but these were low and incomprehensible.

He sat up and found that he could see and hear better, because he was peering over a short wall that had blocked his view when he was lying on the floor. Considering the floor, he noticed that it was unstable, moving as if it were on elliptical wheels, creating an upward and downward motion; occasionally a jerk caused a shudder throughout the craft.

He now saw three green men sitting forward in the vessel. One leaned forward in concentration, staring through viewing windows. Dimly, a hundred sofads ahead of them, Dat Voga saw the gargantuan brobdoganth to which they were tethered. He assumed, then, that they were aboard

147

the craft from which they had watched the scuttling of their ship.

He could see the surface of the sea above them by looking through the thick transparent substance set in the bow of the vessel. The sound of rushing water was that of the ocean passing over the surface of the bathysphere, for they were submerged. The green men said little, as though fearful of breaking the pilot's concentration. It became obvious to the padwar that this man directed the actions of the brobdoganth by telepathic means.

Eventually one said gruffly, "Mab Meebo, direct the beast to take the styth to the surface; we near Nagor, and I find the stench of these humans suffocating." The man called Mab Meebo must have done as he was directed because Dat Voga noticed a sudden upward tendency in the vessel's motion. Soon they burst through to a surface illumined by a sun sinking toward the horizon.

Another green man, crouching in the cramped interior of the vessel, turned a knob until there was the hiss of rushing air. Pushing upward, he opened a small valve that allowed in fresh sea air. The intake of the valve was situated high above the surface in the form of a tube, since the motions of the giant fish occasionally resulted in the vessel dipping below the surface.

Dat Voga could see little from his position in the rear of the bathysphere, his view consisting mostly of a steep, upward angle through which only the sky was visible. He became aware that they neared land only from the comments of the green men.

The one in charge spoke. "Stop here, Mab Meebo. Tazzor Gobatt! Unhook us from the brobdoganth and direct him to go feed, but to then return to the corral."

Dat Voga had already realized telepathy was playing a part in the control of these beasts; he had observed the total absorption with which this Mab Meebo focused on the creature, and he had heard the orders instructing this same green man to command the whale to do this, or to do that.

But the fact that they could issue commands to it, and it would return even after it had left their presence, he found impressive. It called to mind the last command he had given the brobdoganth that attacked the *Prachus* and made him wonder if it yet hunted the fish-men.

He had been tempted to use telepathy on this Mab Meebo's brobdoganth, but did not wish to tip his hand, worried the green men might sense his efforts. He was mildly surprised to have discovered two species with telepathic abilities, but to learn that telepathy had not yet developed beyond its infancy with respects to the humans he had associated with in this time.

He became aware of movement about him and knew that the others must have slept while he had lain unconscious from the blow he had been dealt by the green man in command. He hoped to someday have an opportunity to meet that man on equal footing, that he might repay him for the craven act.

Next, Dat Voga wondered how his fellow prisoners fared and immediately attempted to locate Azaria and Thuria in the murky interior. It was quite dim within the chamber in which they were housed, so much so that he could not see well enough even to verify the identities of the other occupants, though he assumed them to be those he had seen before he was struck down.

The styth came to a halt. The green men threw open the hatches, allowing the light of day to penetrate the interior. Glancing eagerly from face to face, the padwar experienced a stab of sharp disappointment. Azaria and Thuria were not here!

Tazzor Gobatt exited through a hatch and dove into the water, swimming rapidly and efficiently to the brobdoganth where he disconnected the hawser attaching it to the submersible.

The padwar grudgingly admired the versatility and engineering behind these unique vehicles, which were unknown in his time. The smaller versions he saw were towed in the same fashion, but were drawn by gantahns, not brobdoganths. The gantahns were much larger than the riding variety, but clearly members of the same species.

He found it impossible to believe the green men had developed these unique vehicles when all other races used sailing ships, or vessels powered by oars. While he pondered the mystery, the prisoners were directed to exit through a hatch beside which stood the malicious green man, who did not miss an opportunity to heap insult and injury upon his prisoners.

Mab Meebo, the styth pilot, remained at the controls as the prisoners exited the sub. He was in the process of locking the dive planes in preparation for the vessel to be beached or harbored. Glancing at the instrumentation before climbing out the rear hatch, the padwar saw hand and foot levers, used perhaps to regulate elevators to obviate the motions of the brobdoganth. There was not much else in the way of controls.

Once on the smooth, outer surface, Dat Voga and the others were ordered to board a skiff. This vessel seated twelve, and had armed guards fore and aft, with the prisoners seated amidships. Their hands were freed, and they were directed by dint of threats to man the oars.

While they boarded the skiff, Mab Meebo reeled in the hawser and stowed it, attaching the styth to a smaller rope tied to the rear of the rowboat. The red man now saw that the other prisoners consisted of Gar-Noh-Dar, Gan-Toh-Gan, Roh-Du-Von, and two other sailors of the *Prachus*. The only other submersibles carried more green men, but no other humans were to be seen.

He could only hope their destination was the same as that of Azaria and Thuria. Perhaps they had arrived earlier, or they had not yet arrived at all. Reinforcing this hope were other skiffs floating nearby, each manned by four green men and apparently awaiting the arrival of styths that had yet to return. Sighing in resignation that he must wait, he took his seat and picked up an oar.

Chapter Twenty-Three

The Isle of Nagor

D AT VOGA STARED GLUMLY AT THE COAST toward which they rowed. The inhospitable shore reminded him of the western side of the island he and Thuria had called home for six months, it being rocky, craggy, and consisting of near vertical cliffs extending far into the sky.

Following the orders of their green masters, they proceeded into a narrow slot in the cliff face. They paddled through a sea-filled chasm for quite some time, eventually rowing out from between the vertical sides and into a lagoon ringed by more treacherous cliffs, but with visible landings.

At the feet of the cliffs were wooden piers, attached to which were various shapes and sizes of styths. The predominant shapes of these were of patelliform and turbinate shells, natural formations obviously chosen for their hydrodynamics. At the sight of them, Dat Voga's heart beat faster. The sight gave him hope that the women had arrived upon one of the vessels already berthed.

The padwar sought some method whereby their captors scaled these cliffs, as it made no sense to tether their vessels here, where there were no buildings or places of habitation. They paddled to a certain dock where Mab Meebo hopped ashore and tied off the styth. After disembarking, the captives were directed to enter a narrow cave. Their wardens followed.

The path was dark, winding, and steep, climbing upward to at last emerge in the light of day. Looking east, Dat Voga saw a gray sea and a dark violet sky filled with ominous clouds. A storm was coming. At the behest of their captors, he and the others began a downward descent into a rocky basin.

Those initial craggy precipices on the coast were the only similarity to his tropic island. Here was no verdure nor animal life, the landscape consisting of mostly bare rock. Scant vegetation clung sporadically to the stone, but of trees he saw none.

Smoke drifted from chimneys, and firelight flickered in the square windows of rocky, lackluster buildings with no notable architectural charm. What they burned, the red man could hazard no guess, for the place looked barren. He found it difficult to reconcile these rough, stone buildings with the relative complexity and natural beauty inherent in the design of the bathysphere styths.

When they reached the valley floor, their superiors ordered Mab Meebo and Tazzor Gobatt to take the captives to a holding cell, while their commander and the other guards continued toward a larger edifice.

The green men pointed the way the men were to take, which led along a rocky path, eventually leading to an unlit building fashioned, once again, from stone. Their jailers cast open the only door in the edifice, herded the prisoners within, and started to slam the door.

"Wait!" Dat Voga called. "Where are we? And where are our friends?"

The green man who piloted their styth paused. Dat Voga, knowing well the hair-trigger disposition of green men, who were only slightly less mean-tempered in his future than their war thoats, wondered if the man would snap and begin beating him. However, he did not do that.

"I know nothing of your friends. This is Nagor," was all he said.

They heard a ponderous bar dropped in place outside, and they were left to their own devices.

The next morning, Mab Meebo, the styth telepath pilot, awakened the prisoners while unbarring their door. Stepping away from the opening, he called, "Red man, come out. Lodus Voyvott, Jed of Nagor, has demanded your presence. Yours, and the Orovar by whose side you fought on the bow of the ship."

Thus summoned, the man from Helium, together with Gar-Noh-Dar, emerged from the dark interior of their dungeon into a cold, foggy morning. Mab Meebo stood there with his gaff; a grim and businesslike short sword swung from his hip. Another guard stood slightly behind the door, which he kicked closed behind the two sailors of the *Prachus*, dropping the bar into its keepers to prevent any others leaving.

Mab Meebo directed the men, "Walk ahead of me and go where I direct you."

But the padwar hesitated. "What would your jed desire of us, green man?" he asked crisply.

Mab Meebo answered, "That is for him to relay, not I." Indicating the path again with the point of his gaff, he commanded, "Now, walk in that direction."

The two men started up the craggy trail that led sometimes along the edges of steep precipices and at other times through dimly lit caves. In the latter instances, the green men would retrieve radium torches, many designs of which were in evidence where they were stored at either end of the tunnels.

It was some of the roughest topography Dat Voga had ever traversed, being everywhere steep, harsh, rocky, and nearly vertical. Navigating the path along which they were directed was dangerous in the extreme. On every hand were yawning chasms and pitfalls dropping into jagged crevasses, many of which were so deep that their bottoms were invisible, with their sides disappearing into inky darkness.

Often, these fissures crossed their trail. Where they yawned wide, the green men had placed roughly constructed bridges. The narrower ones, where one could see their sides turn and dip downward into darkness, they simply leaped over. The two prisoners wondered if they would successfully clear some of these, since their legs were shorter than those of their wardens.

Eventually they saw further sign of habitation. These new structures possessed more of an appearance of society than the buildings they found on the summit after ascending from the sea. They later learned that those first structures represented an outpost, located at the top of the cliffs to defend the only passage from the harbor.

Here the buildings were still of simplistic design, but not as plain in their rugged composition. They had more architectural styling, and somewhat more care had been taken in their finish. Areas of cultivation were in evidence, including a hardy variety of a fruit bearing tree. But no tropic growths were visible, such as the colossal ferns Dat Voga admired, it being too rocky and cold here for them to prosper.

For the first time, they saw the females and young of their captors. They gathered quite a following as they strode through what eventually became the main thoroughfare of a village. Unlike the modern green tribes with which he was familiar, these did not offer the yells, taunts, jibes, and insults he expected. Many followed out of curiosity, while some only watched. Still others barely ceased their activities to glance at the prisoners. This last caused the red man to believe they did not consider the sight of his kind unusual.

He had little time to study these ancient progenitors of the modern green men during the pitched battle aboard the *Prachus*, although he had noted a couple of distinguishing traits. Now that his path proceeded among so many of them, it afforded him time to study them further, the crowd consisting of members of the race both male and female, young and old.

During the fighting he had noted these ancient green men had slightly webbed fingers and toes, indicative of a quasiaquatic relationship with the sea, causing him to wonder if they bore any relation to the fish-men with which the sailors had tangled.

In stature they were roughly equivalent to the height attained by the modern variant, many of even greater height than their descendants. But these primitive green men tended to be of slimmer build, and their coloration was lighter. Their facial structure was similar, but with subtle variances that would have sent his anthropologist friends in Greater Helium into a frenzy.

This tribe, however, maintained its incubators much as the Orovars did, with family incubators built nearby its dwellings.

When traveling, the Nagors would use their telepathic powers to summon the large, mostly docile, leviathans, including the brobdoganths and gantahns with which the padwar was familiar. To these they would attach towing harnesses and use them to draw their fantastic craft.

Using telepathy on the brobdoganths, they would command them to drag their aquatic chariots across vast, open stretches of ocean in short periods of time. When they wished to travel evasively or with stealth, they would command the creatures to submerge, thereby dragging their carriages underwater, these being equipped with air and provisioned for long journeys at sea.

The green men were renowned for attacking vessels with no provocation, leaving nothing in their wake since they killed all but for the few they carried into slavery, and for torture. They took what they wished from the stores of the vessels, which answered a question Dat Voga had relative to the radium torches and other human-manufactured devices Dat Voga saw among them, and then they sank the ships, leaving no trace.

When they traveled en masse, they used large wains, which were also submersible. If they met with a force too large for them to fight while adequately protecting their women and young, they sent the women and children underwater, and then the warriors covered their retreat before diving themselves.

What astounded him most was the familial relationships. They had family units, unlike their modern descendants. He saw little ones behind stone walls enclosing houses and incubators, and a mother figure was always nearby. Children played in the street, the green women ushering them to their sides as the humans strode past. The relationships between the green men and their women, while reserved, were not callous as in the future. Dat Voga became curious about these odd traits and commented on it to his escort.

"Where I come from, the green men know not their parents, being raised by those best suited to teach them the skills of combat and weaponry, and the like, depending on whether they be male or female. The tribe stores all the eggs, which are kept below incubation temperature until it is time to select from the vast store the few that meet the strictest tests of perfection. The tribe has a common incubator into which these perfect eggs are placed, none knowing their own. But here, each home has its own incubator, similar to my own race."

Mab Meebo looked astonished. "It must be a mad world from which you come, red man, for men and women to know not their own children! When a man takes his mate, he constructs their incubator, for with it lies the hope of the future. He then builds their house, for it is within those walls the young will spring. Finally, he builds his wall, a defensive perimeter from within which he will die defending his mate and offspring. Our children are our future; I cannot imagine a green tribe existing in the manner you describe."

Dat Voga noticed a note of vehemence in the tone of the green man when he answered, so the red man was not entirely convinced Mab Meebo was revealing the whole truth of the matter, causing him a great deal of curiosity. But he decided not to press the issue.

As they proceeded along the street, their path opened into a city square. This became a large concourse along one side of which stood a large, palatial edifice; Dat Voga guessed this structure was their destination. Situated about the periphery of the square were shops that performed services or displayed goods for trade. As Dat Voga saw no monetary units in evidence, he assumed they used a barter system.

The most gripping feature of the square stood in its center. Rising from the stone flags was the imposing statue of a hideous creature that resembled the product of a nightmare. The throng paid it no heed, but the padwar could hardly take his eyes from the horrid thing, it being carved from a single piece of stone and roughly fifty or sixty sofads in height.

They advanced through the crowd to the palace and entered the foreboding pile. The jed was expecting them, so their escort conducted them without delay to the throne room of Lodus Voyvott, Jed of Nagor. Of the throne room, Dat Voga could not see much when he passed through the wide entrance, for a large throng of green men stood just inside the doorway, blocking his view.

As he and Gar-Noh-Dar, with their escort, threaded their way through the crowd, they heard many voices commenting on them.

"They say that red man killed a hundred of Lodus Voyvott's warriors!"

"I could take him! Look how puny."

"Someone said he could pluck a dagger from thin air, cast it halfway around the ship, and kill a man!"

Dat Voga let them continue their diatribe, offering no rebuttals as he preferred to let his sword do his talking. Also, he preferred keeping an enemy confused and guessing, allowing their imaginations to conjure fears that words might otherwise allay. Long ago, he had discovered that a man's worst enemy was his own fears, and that the fear of the unknown was the greatest of these, and the most difficult to conquer.

At last, they forged through the tangled mass of bodies gathered in the throne room and stood before the jed ,where for the first time since arriving in this era, the red man let his mouth gape in astonishment at the sight of the figure before him.

Chapter Twenty-Four

Lodus Voyvott

THE HEIGHT OF THE GREEN MAN, at nearly twenty sofads, would be considered, whether in the past or the far-flung future, to be nothing short of astounding. Aside from his height, the first thing Dat Voga noticed about Lodus Voyvott were the three eyes and two mouths the green man possessed.

One mouth was drawn up in a perpetual snarl, as he apparently lacked the muscular control to shut it properly. Located near his left temple, the mouth angled upward diagonally toward where his left ear should have been, this ear having been shoved further around the back of a skull altogether misshapen and oversized.

A third tusk jutted from the side of his head where his second mouth ended, the tusk curling up and over his head to depend over his forehead between his normal set of eyes. His third eye sat somewhat off center in his forehead above his right eye, but at such an odd angle that, when he looked into it, Dat Voga involuntarily tilted his own head sideways by sheer reflex. The padwar wondered whether these deformities were gestational defects, perhaps from Lodus Voyvott having absorbed a twin after conception.

Abnormalities aside, it was the green man's expression that was most impressive, it being altogether merciless and with eyes of utter cold. Dat Voga had never seen a more debased or crueler countenance on the face of any other being. Seeing this, he became consumed with getting the women away, realizing without having to be told the danger they were in while in this man's power.

Lodus Voyvott stared coldly at the two puny humans standing before him, his deep scowl turning more dour the longer he looked at them. It was quiet as all waited for the jed to speak. The red man heard the green jed grinding his teeth.

The Jed of Nagor finally growled, his voice harsh and angry, "What is this? I see a great hoax has been perpetuated upon me, and by this time tomorrow, I shall adorn myself with the freshly flayed hide of he who has propagated the lies! You there! Mab Meebo! Slay me these insects and remove their corpses from my sight!"

A look of astonishment crossed Mab Meebo's face. To confirm the command, he inquired, "My jed, these are the two you requested. You are sure you wish me to slay them?" The jed was known to issue such hasty commands only to later have slain those who had simply followed his orders to the letter.

The jed snarled, "There is no likelihood that these are the same swordsmen that supposedly slaughtered my warriors! I shall wring the head off the shoulders of Laxx Melda for his scurvy fabrications!"

At mention of his name that worthy came forward, cringing. "But, my jed," he stammered. "I saw them myself! I do not exaggerate! Let them display their skills before you judge!"

This gave the giant pause, during which he seemed inclined to follow his initial course and have them slaughtered outright. He had sat palpably forward during the pronouncement of the death sentence as though eager to see blood spilled.

But now, a bit reluctantly perhaps, he eased his giant girth back somewhat into his stony throne. One of his arms came up to play idly with his oddly placed tusk, appearing to derive some measure of contentment from hearing his raspy fingers rake across its coarse, yellowed tip.

"Very well, Laxx Melda. Give the red man a sword and duel him. If he lives, then I shall know that you did, indeed, not fabricate lies."

Laxx Melda started to object, but then slammed his jaws shut. His eyes narrowing to hate-filled slits, he approached the padwar. He asked a green man standing nearby to give his sword to the red man.

But Dat Voga demurred, "I would use my own sword."

Laxx Melda shouted, "You refuse to fight? Then die!" And he came at the red man, swinging as if he would sunder him in halves at the onset. It was apparent to Dat Voga that the green man did not want him to get a sword in hand, neither his own nor anyone else's.

Desperation will lend speed and ability to most cowards, and Laxx Melda seemed to be no exception. He apparently sensed that if Dat Voga got a sword in his hand, then his life would most likely be forfeit, so he needed to be certain that did not happen.

Laxx Melda could not touch Dat Voga, who rolled and leaped and spun in his efforts to dodge the green man's slashing blade. Naturally, there were many howls of laughter at the padwar's antics to avoid Laxx Melda's blade. But there were also a good many jeers and hisses at the expense of Laxx Melda for what appeared obvious to all as the behavior of a coward.

Unsure how long he could continue to avoid the slashing of Laxx Melda's blade and doubting he had any support from the crowd surrounding the combatants, Dat Voga held out little hope for any aid from that quarter. But perhaps Laxx Melda had reckoned without considering the mentality of the crowd, for without warning a blade skittered from nowhere across the stone flags to stop at the feet of Dat Voga. The Heliumite scooped it up without a moment to spare, though even as he stooped to retrieve the blade, Laxx Melda swooped in for the kill.

But where the sword of Laxx Melda thought to drink deeply of the blood and brains of the red man as it cleft the air toward his scalp, it swung instead swiftly through empty space to slam forcefully against the stone floor, causing sparks and chips of shattered rock to fly in all directions.

Dat Voga stood patiently, awaiting the green man's next move, only this time with a sword in hand. Seeing the red man thus armed, Laxx Melda made an immediate adjustment in tactics, going on the defensive. The padwar saw that he would have to carry the fight to the green man and wasted no time in doing so.

Although the weapon in his hand was not his now-favorite blade crafted by Zikka, he had practiced much with these shorter, heavier blades before coming to Xanator. He adjusted his style to compensate for the difference in weight and balance. After a few passes with the green man, he knew the limitations of his ability with this blade and went at Laxx Melda in earnest.

In a blinding flurry, he cut off one of Melda's ears, placed several specifically located cuts about his face, neck, and breast, and then began working his way down, cutting and nicking the green man when and where he willed.

His skill and command of the blade became obvious to his captive audience. Although many wished to see the green man slice the human into chum, the padwar heard suggestions of admiration for the brilliant dalliance of the red man's fighting style. Dat Voga's blade was never idle. With blurry speed, it wove a continuous barrier between himself and his enemy, leaving the onlookers spellbound and wanting more.

Laxx Melda was wont to broadcast his attacks, his sword remaining almost stationary until he saw what he presumed to be an opening, his eyes then telling his adversary where he would attack with monotonous predictability.

Dat Voga's intentions, however, were impossible to foretell, because his weapon remained in motion, and he had the ability to attack from any position or angle his sword happened to be in when he saw an opening, which he was always quick to exploit.

His uncanny knack of being in the right position at the right time seemingly preyed on the green man's nerves. Soon, Laxx dripped with blood from scores of painful nicks and cuts. His face, made hideous by the permanent grimace of fear plastered across it, as well as the lacerations it had sustained, ran with nervous sweat. His anxious perspiration ran in runnels down his face, creating a bloody mess that he was periodically forced to wipe from his eyes.

Everyone now understood that at any time since the red man had snatched the blade from the floor, he could have run Laxx Melda through the heart and ended the fight. The tension steadily built, and all wondered when Dat Voga would end the nerve-shattered green man's life.

Lodus Voyvott did not appear to care which of the contestants perished, only that someone's life ceased at the end of a blade, and soon. He leaned forward in anticipation, his expression callous and expectant.

Dat Voga had no intention of dying at the hands of this green man. Really, it was inimical to his style to make a spectacle of and to butcher a man like this. But in this instance, he deemed it paramount that Lodus Voyvott be impressed enough with him and Gar-Noh-Dar to preserve their lives. And the cowardly Laxx Melda had earned his punishment by trying to slay him while unarmed.

Gar-Noh-Dar shouted a warning of something amiss. The padwar had perceived that his opponent was attempting to maneuver him in a certain direction, and quickly guessed his intent. One of Lodus Voyvott's warriors was standing out from the crowd where he had positioned himself to trip the red man. With a slight smile on his face, Dat Voga allowed himself to be "driven" in the direction

Laxx Melda wished. A groan sprang from the lips of many of the onlookers who had more sense of fair play. With a whirlwind of gyrations and slashes, he added two more painful cuts to his enemy and maneuvered himself in the exact fashion that Laxx Melda was hoping for..

Laxx Melda seemed to gain the confidence of a charging calban as he rushed the padwar. Dat Voga, giving ground, was apparently at the green man's mercy. Laxx Melda's eyes widened with the lust of imminent victory as the hated red man gave way before his onslaught.

As the crowd waited expectantly for the red man to trip over the green foot awaiting him, and with the sword of Laxx Melda already in a vicious and desperate descent, Dat Voga dove beneath the feet of the tall green man. Laxx Melda's sword, committed to its downward stroke, buried itself to the midriff in the stunned warrior who had treacherously sought to help him.

As Laxx Melda desperately strove to wrench his blade from where it had become lodged in the rib cage of his perfidious conspirator's upper torso, Dat Voga, his breathing unlabored, approached the throne of the Jed of Nagor. Scores of green warriors gripping swords, gaffs and iron bars leaped forward and placed themselves between the human and their jed, for they knew not his intentions.

"Lodus Voyvott," the padwar began. "Is this treachery typical of the manner in which your warriors must fight to win their engagements? Are all your warriors so *brave*? Gar-Noh-Dar and I could slay you all, were it not for the fact that one of your so-called warriors would try to stab us in the back! Now, for what did you summon me?"

An ugly snarl was upon the face of the jed, but Dat Voga could not ascertain if he scowled because of the red man's words, the outcome of the fight, or the less-than-stellar performance of one of his warriors, Laxx Melda's disgrace having been witnessed by all.

At last, the jed said, "Allow the red man to approach—

but take his sword. Toss the body of Mag Satjag over the cliffs into the prachus pit. Add his women to my seraglio and have his hatchlings delivered to Poxx Vorka. Now leave us."

The Heliumite handed over the borrowed sword to the green man who approached with his hand extended. Then he folded his arms over his breast and stared at the green jed. Gar-Noh-Dar approached and joined him, with Mab Meebo in attendance. The remainder of the throng, alternately reviling Laxx Melda and the red man, filed from the throne room. Two of them dragged the body of Mag Satjag with them.

Soon, only the four of them remained, for when Mab Meebo asked if he should stay or go, the jed told him to stay, apparently not wishing to be alone with a man who commanded such bizarre fighting skills.

Lodus Voyvott eyed the two sailors for several tals. "What manner of man are you that wields a blade as you do and has skin the color of the setting sun that no man ever saw before?" he finally asked.

"I come from an island in the middle of nowhere, far from here. There, we all excel at the blade. And I am not, as you allude, the only individual of red skin you have seen. There is another, as you well know."

Ignoring Dat Voga's obvious referral to Thuria, Lodus Voyvott said, "This other man from your ship—he can wield the sword as skillfully as you?"

The red man replied honestly, "Nearly so, yes." Not believing these green warriors to be conversant enough in swordsmanship to make an accurate determination, he added, "I think any of your warriors would find Gar-Noh-Dar a formidable opponent. Why?"

"I wish you to instruct me in your method of fighting. If you do not, your lives are forfeit. My warriors are not always as proficient with the sword as those they face in battle. We rely on our numbers, our styths, and our brobdoganths to even the odds. I did not at first believe what they said, but it is possible that Laxx Melda was right when he said you are the greatest swordsman in the world. That fool might as well have been unarmed."

Dat Voga instantly saw in this an opportunity to serve Azaria, Thuria, and his fellow sailors of the *Prachus*. It might even be possible to barter for all their release. "I will do so . . . but with conditions," he finally said, as if considering the matter.

Lodus Voyvott ground his teeth, his dark, calculating eyes narrowing. "Name them," he finally hissed, his fingers making rapid audible rasps upon his yellowed tusk.

"First, that you free the surviving members of our crew and passengers of the ship you attacked and guarantee their safety. Next, I wish Gar-Noh-Dar and myself returned our own swords, which were taken by one of your warriors aboard the styth that brought us here. Mab Meebo would know his name."

Dat Voga saw instantly that his request was not well received. The jed exploded, "You are prisoners of war!" Regaining his composure, he appeared to reconsider and said, "When I am satisfied with your instruction, we will discuss your release. And I will guarantee their safety . . . for the time being."

Dat Voga gazed into the deeply hooded eyes of the jed. He did not trust the man. His instincts warned him the green jed had just lied through his jaundiced tusks. Yet, Dat Voga had no choice in the matter. At the least, they had gained a reprieve, or so he hoped. He owed it to the two young women and his fellow sailors to do what he could to alleviate their situation.

"And what of the two women who were captured with us?" he inquired, wishing to know more specifically about them. "One of them is to be my mate, and the other is to be the mate of Gar-Noh-Dar here."

The jed replied, "On that score, have no fear, they are safe enough. They are imprisoned in huts near where you your-selves are incarcerated."

Dat Voga saw Mab Meebo snap his head up at that last statement and determined that the jed just unflinchingly lied to him again. But rather than push the issue, which might put the women in danger, he decided to wait. He might be able to wrestle more truthful information from their jailer.

"And our swords?" he asked.

"They were taken by Poxx Vorka, who accompanied us on our styth," Mab Meebo supplied.

"Very well," said Lodus Voyvott. "Mab Meebo, have Poxx Vorka bring those swords before me immediately. I should wring his neck for not showing me those spoils of battle! Fetch him. Leave the red man and the white man here. Quickly, now!"

Mab Meebo left to find the unlucky Poxx Vorka. None saw it, but Mab Meebo smiled. Mab Meebo was not fond of Poxx Vorka. It did not take him long to return with the other green man in tow, Dat Voga recognizing him as the one who had struck him from behind while aboard the styth. The swords of Zikka were in his hand, and he handed them to the jed. "I was going to bring these to you this very day, my jed!" he said.

Lodus Voyvott snatched the swords from the extended hand and said nastily, "I am sure you were! You may leave, Poxx Vorka. And Poxx Vorka, we will discuss this matter later in greater detail!"

Dismissed, the green man spun on his heel and started toward the door, but not before casting a malicious glare at the two prisoners.

By now, the jed was eyeing the Xanatorian blades with palpable avarice, for they were unique and beautiful beyond what pale words might convey by way of description. His eyes widened as they ogled the blades. Catching Dat Voga's glance, they narrowed cunningly once more.

Everything about the Jed of Nagor had the red man's senses on high alert. He had met crafty, cruel men in his time, but none that could lay claim to the level of Lodus Voyvott.

Thus were Dat Voga and Gar-Noh-Dar conscripted into training the Jed of Nagor in the art of swordplay. Admiring the detailed anchors upon the pommel, the jed insisted on keeping Gar-Noh-Dar's sword for his own use, while the padwar once again came to possess his sword from Zikka. As for the inscriptions, Lodus Voyvott could no more read them than could the red man, so they mattered not one bit to him.

Several ironworkers among the green men claimed they could fashion swords approximating the dimensions of the Xanatorian blades. They were, of course, heavier, and Dat Voga knew if they were pushed to their limits that they would snap like brittle, dry bones. They would, however, suffice for the training.

As there were two instructors in this unknown style, the jed tasked Gar-Noh-Dar with training Lodus Voyvott's subordinates while Dat Voga became the jed's personal trainer. Since he was their keeper, Mab Meebo was nominated to be Gar-Noh-Dar's first apprentice.

Chapter Twenty-Five

An Unexpected Ally

MAB MEEBO ARRIVED EACH MORNING to fetch the two trainers, escorting them to the palace where they labored as instructors per their agreement with the jed. In the afternoon, Mab Meebo would return them to their prison. The jed claimed he did not wish prisoners housed in his palace, which suited the two sailors from the *Prachus* for neither did they wish to be separated from their comrades.

But knowing green men as he did, and knowing they feared neither man nor beast, Dat Voga suspicioned the jed was hiding something. Lodus Voyvott possessed a diabolical and scheming nature and therefore suspected everyone else of the same qualities. He trusted no one, for he knew himself to be untrustworthy.

The padwar was unable to obtain any details regarding the two women, or of any survivors of the sinking of the *Prachus*. He had no idea how many survivors there were but felt sure there were more than the six who shared the stone prison.

They viewed the secrecy of the women's location as further evidence of the diabolism of the twisted, devious, and cruel brain of Lodus Voyvott. The jed well understood that while he held Azaria and Thuria, he commanded the cooperation of Dat Voga and his fellow sailors.

The instructors were subject to a grueling schedule, training every day with the horrid jed and his warriors. Weary though he was, the Heliumite found himself missing Azaria so terribly that he constantly racked his brain for some plan of escape, yet he knew not even where they held her.

Because of their forced inactivity, the remaining sailors began to grow disheartened with the chilly gray atmosphere and their dismal prospects. They missed their tropical ports and warm breezes and the freedom of the sea. Lodus Voyvott's handpicked trainers at least escaped their prison every day, even if but briefly; the others were rarely allowed outside, being forced to live in their own filth.

Once a day, the green men allowed the prisoners to walk about in a walled enclosure. Then they were quickly forced back into the dingy, one-room structure. They did what they could to maintain their physical condition but had little room to move about.

Mab Meebo appealed to Lodus Voyvott for better treatment of Dat Voga's shipmates, doing so in the presence of the red man one evening, but to no avail. The jed remained firm that he was holding up his end of the bargain by not torturing and slaying them, which would be justifiable being that they were prisoners of war. Thus reasoned the jed.

Their situation seemed hopeless, yet at these times John Carter's oft-repeated refrain would beat in Dat Voga's mind with the persistence of a war drum: "I still live!" He sought to hearten his fellow prisoners with the words of his mentor, urging them to not give up until their spirits left their bodies. "We still live! And so long as we live, there is hope," he encouraged.

During the training exercises, which now included a great many green men, the padwar was careful about how much he and his own pupil taught their enemies of their futuristic style of fighting. He knew that one day they would cross swords with these green men again. Meanwhile, they must abide until they discovered the whereabouts of the women and any other sailors from the ship—both of which were carefully guarded secrets.

While he eagerly awaited that day, Dat Voga made sure their enemies did not learn all his tricks. At night, he discussed with Gar-Noh-Dar the points they would cover the next day, making the Orovar aware of what they would teach, and what would remain undisclosed.

Although some basic principals were included in the curriculum, for the most part the maneuvers they taught the green men consisted of known, amateurish traps. These were taught, together with their counterpoints, in the Heliumetic Navy, for one must know the proper response to any advance, even if it were one that would end badly for the one who initiated it.

A seasoned swordsman, if attacked in the maneuvers in which they tutored the green men, would have inwardly smiled. He would smile because he would already have his next half-dozen strokes planned and his opponent was already a dead man. These moves, and their proper responses, Dat Voga had previously taught Gar-Noh-Dar. If a green man utilized one of these, the Orovar would have the upper hand.

The path they traveled to their prison was lengthy. Along the way, they spoke with Mab Meebo, often discussing points of the day's instruction. Both sailors found the green man to be not only a stellar pupil and acute of the mind, but also unusually likable. This was to the infinite chagrin of both men, who would have preferred to nurture their dislike of their captors.

Mab Meebo's personality was so at odds with the stereotype of the green man—that of torturer, marauder, thief, and bandit—that Dat Voga decided to broach the subject with him. Before he did so, he decided to ask another question of the taciturn green man, one that lay dearer to his heart.

"Mab Meebo," he said, as they approached their prison. "Could you point out the house where Azaria and Thuria are being held? It would be a great comfort to know just how near I am to the woman I love."

Casting a sideways glance at his prisoner, Mab Meebo sighed. "I have told you, it is not for me to say, red man. You must take the matter up with Lodus Voyvott."Thereafter the green man turned his face resolutely to the trail and became unresponsive. Dat Voga saw that he would learn nothing from their jailer about the women, so he changed the topic.

"This is not my first time in the company of your people. Many times, have I experienced their cruelties. After being convinced for years that it was impossible to form friendship with any of their number, I have since met many for whom I would lay down my life in their defense. You remind me of these. You're nothing like Lodus Voyvott, whom I wouldn't trust to tell me if it were night or day without feeling he lied to advantage himself."

The green warrior snorted cynically, but was otherwise quiet, and Dat Voga thought he would make no reply. As they approached the door to their stone structure, the green man paused. "Not all green men think as do Lodus Voyvott and his sycophants. To survive, these others must obey, while biting their tongues, and girding their intestines against the horrors they must, against their moral fiber, commit."

The green man contemplated the heavens. "Regrettably, those are greatly outnumbered by ones who lust for torture and slaughter. The recalcitrants you will find piloting styths, maintaining the stock, and performing other mundane duties considered unfit by Lodus Voyvott. But it is in those vocations these are insulated to a certain degree from the horrors of war.

"As a telepath pilot, I become one with the creature with which I bond, be it a gantahn or brobdoganth or some other creature over which we green men hold sway. We see the acts of atrocity and often are forced to perpetrate them.

We play the part, because the risk of having one's family tortured or slaughtered is too high a price to risk disobedience. Do you understand me, red man?"

They stopped before the door to their prison. Above them, a twilit sky held shades of purple, pink, and vermilion. Low storm clouds—perpetually upon the horizon when they were not pummeling the stony surface with rain—floated gray and foreboding.

No one was there but the three of them. On impulse, Dat Voga extended his arm, warrior fashion, to Mab Meebo. The green man's breath hissed between clenched teeth. Slowly, he extended his arm to the red man, grasping him above the elbow. His hand, massive in comparison to the padwar's, engulfed the other's arm.

No words were exchanged, nor were any needed. It was a gesture of like-mindedness between two men who, but for their circumstances, might have been friends or comrades. The two sailors turned and entered their prison without a word and the door shut behind them.

Chapter Twenty-Six

BETRAYED!

FOR TWO DAYS MAB MEEBO did not come to fetch the tutors for practice. Neither did he bring provisions. When food finally arrived, a different green man delivered it, one with whom they were unfamiliar. Naturally, Dat Voga asked after Mab Meebo.

The warrior sneered, "Who are you, human filth, to ask about your betters? Shall I have Lodus Voyvott come justify himself to you? You would do better to worry about your own hides, not Mab Meebo's!" After this soliloquy, the green warrior thrust a day's rations through the door, slammed the portal in their faces, and dropped the heavy bar into its keepers.

The days passed slowly and miserably. The prisoners could only wonder what had changed. Dat Voga and Gar-Noh-Dar grew increasingly worried for the two women, whom they had not seen since the attack on the ship. The situation was becoming ever more unbearable, but they were powerless to change it.

Late one evening, the men sensed another storm approaching from out at sea. They heard the grumblings of thunder, and soon a light rain began to fall. On the other side of their prison door, the incarcerated men heard a grunt, followed by a low moan. The grating sound of the bar on their door being withdrawn followed.

Fearing the treachery of Lodus Voyvott, they tensed. A call at this late time of night could be for no good reason. The door crashed open, and a flash of lightning cast their visitor in stark relief. Filling the enormously tall entry stood Mab Meebo!

At his feet lay their slain guard, a poniard protruding from his still breast. Mab Meebo's breath came in ragged gasps, and Dat Voga sensed this was not due entirely to the exertions of the long trek here from the city of the green men.

Feeling the dread of an apocalyptic event on the horizon, the padwar, galvanized by the appearance of the green man, stepped forward. "Quick, Mab Meebo! What is it?" The red man's tone brooked no delay. He knew already that no trivial reason would bring the green man to their den at this late zode and cause him to slay a member of his own tribe.

"I know not, red man, why my illustrious ancestors chose to bring you to my shores. Gods, if only they would spare me this! I have come here against orders, for which my life must now be forfeit. That last evening that I saw you, I was going home when, on a whim, I went to the palace instead, where I appealed to Lodus Voyvott once more to show clemency to you and your friends.

"The jed reassigned me as an outer perimeter guard to our farthest, northern boundary. It is a desultory post reserved for young novitiates—and for those who fall into disfavor. Poxx Vorka was there with a hideous sneer on his moronic face. The shades grant that I live to see the day death freezes that face in its own peculiar grimace!

"I can tell you, Dat Voga, now that my death sentence is upon my head, that the women of your ship were never held in these cold stone huts. They have, this entire time, been locked in cages in the rear of the palace! Lodus Voyvott strictly forbade any mention of their location on pain of death—a sentence that extends to the family of any green man found guilty of relaying this information to you."

If the padwar had feared before for the safety of Azaria and Thuria, those fears were as nothing to what he experienced upon hearing this news. Frantic with fear for them, he was on the verge of some reckless act, a desperate attempt to free them or die in the attempt.

Mab Meebo continued. "Dat Voga, I never knew what they did in the palace at night, for I am wont to spend my evenings cloistered with my family, small though it is, consisting of but me, my mate, and my son. That night, I discovered Lodus Voyvott with his minions, including your friends, Poxx Vorka and Laxx Melda. It appears they are once more in the jed's good graces."

Meebo paused, as if reluctant to relay what he knew he must. "They were torturing one of your comrades from the ship!" he blurted.

"By the shades," cried Gan-Toh-Gan.

"The man was near his end," Mab Meebo continued. "They had removed his eyes, his skin. They were in the process of breaking bones and removing organs. His screams! They were hideous! Not for the first time I am ashamed of my barbarous race."

"But they said there were no others!" Roh-Du-Von cried."That only us and the girls remained. That is what they said!"

"They lied," Mab Meebo said flatly. Then he added, "Yet sadly, that is quite possibly the truth, now."

"Mab Meebo, what do you intend to do?" cried Dat Voga. He was determined to perish here and now on the tip of Mab Meebo's sword before allowing the prison door to shut on them. "It cannot be that you came here tonight to reveal these things to us and then leave! No, my friend, though we have known you but weeks, my mind has tested yours. Honor and integrity are written on your heart."

"Follow me," was all the grim warrior said. And spinning on his heel, Mab Meebo led the way back up the trail toward the hidden city of stone of the green men of Nagor.

And following him, their backs hunkered against the rain, came six puny humans.

Chapter Twenty-Seven

Mab Meebo's Mad Proposal

As RAPIDLY AS THEIR FEET COULD CARRY THEM, the odd troupe advanced along a dark and precipitous trail. Halfway to their destination, the storm broke in all its fury, and so to the list of perils they faced could be added another, for the rocks over which they climbed were now wet and slippery, demanding the exercising of great caution.

Over the racket of the storm, Mab Meebo called out that they would stop by his home to select weapons from his armory. He had an idea, he said, that would take too long to elucidate upon the trail. He would tell them more once they had taken shelter where his mate might be included in the discussion.

The padwar made out one thing Mab Meebo said that gave him hope—they were to leave Nagor, that night, with as many humans as they might save. He thrilled thinking of an imminent reunion with Azaria.

Outside the town, they descended into one of the great crevasses and made their way along its dripping face and down an ancient trail until Mab Meebo deemed that they were within the city. As to sentries, they had little to fear, he said, because these would seek shelter from the storm. The trail they followed over yawning chasms was perilous, but Mab Meebo deemed it a necessary precaution. Any hope of success depended upon stealth.

Dat Voga was relieved when their green ally led the way upward and they stood once more on solid ground. Sneaking through back alleys, they made their way to the rear of Mab Meebo's property. The red man breathed a sigh of relief that these primordial green men had not domesticated the prehistoric equivalent of the calot, as this would have precluded any form of stealthy approach, making sneaking through the camps of the green men impossible.

Scaling the low, stone wall, they approached the sturdy dwelling Mab Meebo called home. The concept of entering the domicile of a green family was strange to him, defying everything he held to be true of green men. He approached the structure with interest.

At Mab Meebo's light knock they were greeted by his mate, Oola Zofta. The woman possessed a tall, slender build with skin a lighter shade than her mate. She would undoubtedly be considered beautiful to a green man. She held a short sword in one hand, her grip on the weapon indicating intimate familiarity.

"Mab Meebo," she cried, as they entered. "Tazzor Gobatt was here but moments ago, seeking you!"

"Tazzor Gobatt? What said he?" asked the green man.

"That thou had no sooner left the palace than Poxx Vorka incensed the jed against you! He claimed you are not worthy to be among the tribe. They do not know that Tazzor Gobatt's feelings align with your own. He said Poxx Vorka maligned your character by claiming you sought an alliance with the humans. He said he knew this for he had witnessed you clasp arms with the red man, as though you had struck some agreement."

Oola Zofta cast her eyes at the humans suspiciously, obviously wondering if there might not be a germ of truth in Poxx Vorka's last accusation.

"Blast Poxx Vorka, that cursed, treacherous spy!" Then, more gently, Mab Meebo said, "Oola Zofta, come, sit here."

He led her to a chair seated before a tiny table. As the dignified green woman took a seat on a chair that would have left Dat Voga's feet swinging in the air like a child's, Mab Meebo took her hands in his and related what had occurred between him and the humans over the last weeks, and what he had witnessed that evening at the palace. He left out nothing, apparently having not spoken of the matter to her before.

She sighed as he finished. She knew her mate well enough to know his decision was final. "I just want to hear that your plan includes saving your own family, as well as these strangers," she said, ignoring the humans, and with eyes only for Mab Meebo. "For now, Lodus Voyvott will forever be thine enemy."

For the first time since Dat Voga had known the man, Mab Meebo smiled, as gentle a smile as any man, of any race, ever cast upon his mate. "Of course it does," he said. "Awaken little Donza and pack for the sea. We leave tonight. I must obtain weapons for these men, as we go to wrest their mates from the hands of Lodus Voyvott. I fear the remaining sailors will have been slain ere now, the poor wretches. Our greatest hope, Oola Zofta, hinges on your success in carrying out your part of the scheme. But first, where went Tazzor Gobatt?"

"He said he went to his abode. Why?"

"Excellent," was the only reply. Mab Meebo began outlining his mad proposal. "I shall go to the house of Tazzor Gobatt and convince him to lead me before Lodus Voyvott as his prisoner, under the pretense that he caught me lurking about suspiciously, having ignored my orders to report to the north."

"No!" cried Oola Zofta. "They will kill you!"

"It is the only way to ensure that all eyes will be in the

throne room, Oola Zofta, as the rare occurrence of one of repute in the tribe being brought before Lodus Voyvott as a prisoner will draw the curious. The jed and his like-minded followers so love torture and death that it no longer matters if the acts be perpetrated upon a man of two arms or four."

While Mab Meebo drew the attention of the guards, little Donza was to lead the sailors to a network of ancient volcanic fumaroles and vent pipes with entry points along the cliff face of the great crevasse circumscribing the city. This chasm was the same as they had used to sneak into the town. Donza was as familiar with the tunnels as he was his backyard, with an entry point lying close to their home.

The cliff wall, Mab Meebo explained, although perched over a seemingly bottomless abyss, was an easy highway, although the recent rain might make it more treacherous than normal. Mab Meebo would instruct little Donza to lead them to an opening at the rear of the palace that would give them entry at the most likely place for the women to be found. If they were not there, Mab Meebo said, then they were quite likely dead, these being the only prison cells in the palace of which he was aware.

Oola Zofta nearly came undone when she heard the part her son was to play in the scheme. It was all Mab Meebo could do to assure the mother of their child that these were desperate times, and that all their lives, not only those of the humans, were at stake.

"After Donza leads the men to the rear entrance of the palace, which should be unguarded if all proceeds in the throne room as planned, he will wait for them," he told his mate. "He will then guide them back. If they do not return shortly, Donza will proceed alone back the way he came, bypassing the house and continuing along the path below the rim to rendezvous with you. He shall be in no more danger than when he sneaks off alone to explore those same tunnels."

Only slightly reassured, Oola Zofta next tried to persuade Mab Meebo into allowing her and Donza to switch roles, considering her own to be the less dangerous of the two. But Mab Meebo pointed out her unfamiliarity with the tunnels. "Little Donza has played in these tunnels his whole life," he said. "He knows them as well as he does his mother's face."

Although tears brimmed in her eyes, she had to agree. The wise green man then came to Oola Zofta's part in the caper. "Yours, my beautiful mate, is the most crucial. You will take the long route to the cliff above the harbor, thus avoiding discovery. There you will call the gantahns, of which we shall require two. You must hitch them to two styths. If you encounter anyone near the berths, they must be slain. On this wretched night, I doubt any will skulk about the quay.

"Your task will be difficult, Oola Zofta. You must hold the gantahns at all costs. When Donza comes, he can take one over, for the boy is unusually skilled. I believe he could command them in his sleep! If I come not, take our son, and flee to the island where we broke our shells. You know the way. If Tazzor Gobatt comes, take him, for he is an honorable man, as you know, and he will fight for you both. You must promise to do this."

"You must come! You *will* come, Mab Meebo!" the woman replied passionately. She leaped to his side and wrapped four arms about him. Looking into his face, she asked, "What if Tazzor Gobatt wishes no part of this crazy plot? What can you and Tazzor Gobatt do after you are in the power of Lodus Voyvott? Oh, Mab Meebo! This is madness! You have not thought this through!"

Mab Meebo interjected, "I have not gone into all the details, but there is no time. The humans, after rescuing their women, can set fire to the rear of the palace. Much of wood and cloth is stowed there. During the ensuing distraction, Tazzor Gobatt and I may escape. It is likely the jed will order Tazzor Gobatt to imprison me. If so, we shall find opportunity to flee. Tazzor detests this way of life as much as we.

"If the humans do not find their women, and if I know Dat Voga like I think I do, they will proceed on through the palace, at which point Tazzor Gobatt will supply me with a weapon and we, with the humans, shall attack the jed and his warriors simultaneously. I shall instruct him to bring along a long sword, and a short.

"Granted, a great deal of this scheme leaves much open to the interpretation of the moment, but we have not the time to come up with a better stratagem. If Tazzor Gobatt will not accompany me, I shall go forth and surrender to Lodus Voyvott alone, pleading that I wish to spare my family by surrendering. Lodus Voyvott will lie and agree, but I am certain he will defer my execution—and I only need him to defer it a few xats while the humans seek their women to the rear of the palace."

It was an unhappy Oola Zofta who went to awaken the young boy. She found him sitting up amid his bedding on his sleeping platform, eagerly devouring the conversation of the adults. She admonished him, but she understood the curiosity of the inquisitive toddler. The two entered the gathering room where she introduced the green boy.

Dat Voga had been an avid spectator of all these things, the idea of a green family still being bizarre to him. He studied the boy, who appeared to be highly intelligent. When Mab Meebo brought Donza over to introduce him, the red man felt a sudden, quick probing of his mind before he could put up his guard.

Shocked, he realized this boy was highly skilled with telepathy. None of the green men had ever attempted to read his mind, their skills not being equal to the task. Dat Voga had not been in the habit of maintaining a mental guard in the past, as he had when in the presence of Daxxus Nahl, and attributed Donza's success to his not understanding the boy's depth of aptitude. His only fear was, what had the boy learned? He did not have long to wait.

"Father," Donza said, excitedly. "Dat Voga is from Helium, a city in the future! They fly around—"

"Now Donza," Mab Meebo remonstrated.

"But, Father!" the boy protested.

"Come," the boy's father said firmly. "We must acquaint you with the details of your role. And I wish to hear no more fanciful fabrications about Dat Voga flying around!"

The two went over to a settee where the green man began instructing his son about the night's events and the part that he was to play. Dat Voga caught the boy looking at him inquisitively. The red man smiled and winked at him. Donza's eyes grew large, and then his face lit up with a grin. The Heliumite knew this boy was all right.

Now armed, the group began their final preparations. Mab Meebo and his family took one final tour through their home, selecting small articles they wished to bring with them. Many times, the red man observed one wistfully pick up an object only to place it back down, for they must pick and choose carefully the items that were truly important.

He felt sorry for them, to be exiled on his and his friends' accounts. At the same time, he would have exiled or slain every member of the green race upon the island of Nagor if that is what it took to secure life and freedom for his beloved. But he did stop Mab Meebo and tell him of his appreciation.

Mab Meebo replied, "This is not entirely your doing, red man. For centuries has the green race adopted martial tactics in the control of the members of their tribes, egg selection, and the like, exactly as you described. How you knew these things, I cannot guess. Our tribe is not unique in this. In the last hundred years, many have become more critical of the eggs they hatch in their family incubators.

"Some have gone so far as to say that the ruling class should select the eggs. Can you imagine a world where a ruling body decides which eggs are fit to hatch? The ancestors forbid that dark day! But those who feel as do we are in the minority. The tribe to which Oola Zofta and I once belonged started down this path, and so we left and joined this sister tribe. Now Lodus Voyvott plots the same dark course."

Chapter Twenty-Eight

The Treachery of Lodus Voyvott

As MAB MEEBO SET OUT for Tazzor Gobatt's, the sailors exited the rear of his home. With their swords attached sailor-fashion to prevent clanging against the surface of the precipice, they followed little Donza over the edge and down approximately thirty sofads where they struck the ancient track.

It was the same ledge they had used to approach the town earlier, a narrow projection formed by a layer of rock that had slid back on the stratum below it. It was enough to give them purchase for their sandaled feet. Along this precarious foothold they clung and cautiously made their way to the tunnel opening of which Mab Meebo had spoken.

Dat Voga saw the green boy disappear into a crevice. When the padwar came to the opening he had to squeeze into it, feeling his way forward with his hands, for it was pitch black inside. He rounded a bend and bumped into little Donza, who only now illuminated the space with a radium torch. In Dat Voga's time, these were rare and price-less museum pieces. Nearby was a pile of them.

When asked, Donza explained, "These are the plunder of trade vessels. Everyone has stockpiles of them. My father gave me these from his stores. I leave them here for when my friends and I come here to explore."

They were of the classic bronze-handle type with the

globe that rotated as the wielder slid a lever in the handle, thereby exposing more of the glowing material. They were beautiful devices. The red man gripped one in his fist, and shoved an additional one into his belt, not knowing when an extra torch might be of value.

Their path was circuitous, following the alternately winding and diving vent tube. Luckily, the floor had been worn smooth, and they encountered no crevasses, for which the sailors were thankful. When Donza stopped, they were once more over the yawning fissure. Outside, thunder and cascades of rain filled the leaden sky. Donza instructed the humans in their next steps and consigned them to the hands of their ancestors.

"Heed, Dat Voga," the boy said. "Continue along the cliff, but not far. Be on the lookout for an unusually perfect split that runs straight upward. I have used this landmark many times to locate the rear of the palace. There are many handholds there, providing easy access to the top.

"Occasionally, when there were prisoners, I could see them when they let them outside briefly. There are several entrances. The door you seek is upon the far right. Inside are the prison-cages of which my father spoke," the boy finished.

"Many thanks, Donza. We shall make haste." Turning to the men, Dat Voga said, "Come. The sooner we return, the sooner we'll leave this place."

They made their way across the vertical face, found the landmark where Donza said it would be, and scaled the cliff. There were no signs of guards or prisoners, so they approached the door on the far right of the palace without incident. The operation had proceeded so smoothly up to this point that Dat Voga felt success was at hand. They entered the unguarded door and discovered the prison cells exactly as Mab Meebo had described.

They were all empty. The man from distant Helium came as near to a panic as he ever had in his life. It was the same with Gar-Noh-Dar. They searched each cell again, to no avail. Finally, Dat Voga stood quietly in thought. His pulse, which rarely became elevated in the dense atmosphere of this time, beat furiously with fear for his beloved.

"I'm going to find the girls," the red man said. "If I must, I will tear every stone from the other, until I have deconstructed this building to its foundations. I don't expect you to go with me. Even now, Mab Meebo is in the throne room, risking his life to divert attention from us. If any man does not wish to continue, let him make his way to Donza. None shall judge you, for this is a personal matter, as you all know."

"Do you think I'll crawl back to those tunnels without my little girl?" asked Odar Gan-Toh-Gan. "She's like my own daughter. Besides, Hal-Roh-Kim would have my hide! So, I'll be coming with you."

"And I!" said Roh-Du-Von.

Dat Voga looked at Gar-Noh-Dar, but he already knew what the man would say.

"Naturally, I'm not leaving without both of them," said the osar. "I love Thuria with all my heart, and Azaria is like a sister to me."

Every sailor maintained that he wished to accompany Dat Voga and rescue the women of the *Prachus*. Gar-Noh-Dar was for setting out immediately, for his sword now lay at the feet of Thuria, right alongside his heart.

As they sought a path from the cell block, the men were glad again for the radium torches. The structure was much larger than any had guessed. They passed through many rooms, halls, and tunnels that appeared not to have been used for eons, judging by the dust of ages upon the floors.

They discovered the route taken by the green men to lead prisoners to the cells and reached a section of the palace that bore the appearance of everyday use. Hearing voices and feet approaching, Dat Voga guided his band down an unused hall, if the undisturbed dust was any indication. They dodged into a passage that looked to have stood unused for ages. Quietly, they drew an ancient portal closed.

They doused their lights, and soon noticed a scattered light emanating from deeper within the chamber. Voices came to them indistinctly, some raised in anger and others in raucous, ribald banter. Moans of agony, too, reached their ears, causing them to believe they had stumbled on the torture chamber of Lodus Voyvott. The men clenched their swords and advanced farther into the chamber.

Proceeding slowly in the dark, for they did not wish to apprise anyone of their presence with the torches, they made their way to the foot of a stone stairway covered in the deep debris of untold ages. The voices emanated from above them. The sailors, led by Dat Voga, treaded lightly up the stairs with not a whisper of sound coming from their sandaled feet, where the accumulated filth of ages dampened their steps.

At the top of the stairs, they discovered a heavy tapestry. Softly diffused light sifted from the opposite side of the hanging through many tiny holes where it had thinned with age. The padwar enlarged one of these with the point of a dagger and placed his eye to the hole. They were overlooking the throne room. Visible below him were the two women, their hands and feet bound, but appearing otherwise unharmed.

Beyond the women stood Mab Meebo, his face bloodied. Beside him stood Tazzor Gobatt, whose eyes were wide as he stared helplessly at his friend. Tazzor Gobatt held one end of a rope attached to Mab Meebo's limbs, which were bound. The room contained two dozen of Lodus Voyvott's staunchest supporters, and Lodus Voyvott stood over Mab Meebo. As he watched, the tyrant delivered a savage blow to the face of the bound man.

There was no more time for plotting or planning. All that

remained was to act. Stepping back from the tapestry that he now recalled seeing upon the wall of the throne room, he sheathed his dagger and pulled his short sword. "For the *Prachus!*" he shouted. And splitting the tapestry from top to bottom, he leaped through the rent.

Chapter Twenty-Nine

Fight in the Throne Room

ONE AFTER THE OTHER, the sailors followed the red man through the slash in the ancient embroidery, dropping to the floor fifteen sofads below. Dat Voga was already slickening his sword in the blood of a green man standing below the wall hanging.

It is doubtful the green men were aware of the existence of the opening behind the tapestry, judging by the dust in the chamber and upon the staircase behind it. It was an ancient deception still in use by modern races. But the green men, never building anything of their own, except perhaps of the most rudimentary form, mayhap knew not of this archaic device.

Since seeing the giant statue in the courtyard, Dat Voga had begun to suspect that another race than the green men constructed these buildings. The structures were obviously ancient, and it was possible that a multitude of races had utilized them since their abandonment.

Jerking his blade free, Dat Voga spun and started for the jed of these murderous cutthroats.

Snarling, Lodus Voyvott roared, "Kill them!" And then he threw himself forward, clawing Gar-Noh-Dar's sword free of the scabbard swinging wildly at his hip.

Poxx Vorka, who now carried Dat Voga's blade, drew the sword, and charged the red man, bloody intent plastered all over his face. That he wished to exact revenge for his perceived wrongs at the hand of the red man was all too obvious.

The Heliumite saw the two giants charging at him. Cries erupted from the green men in the room when they realized these puny humans were bearding the banth in its own den. The red man snatched his dagger from his belt. As he ran to meet Lodus Voyvott, he shot his arm forward and released the slender blade, never at any time taking his eyes from the awful jed who now loomed close upon him.

To battle a foe twice his height, who was endowed by nature with five times his strength, and who possessed twice as many arms that were double the length of his own, with only a puny stick pin of a sword, seemed the height of insanity to Dat Voga. And indeed, being that the padwar had fallen into full battle rage, perhaps he was slightly mad in that instant.

He never felt a moment's fear or hesitation. He performed no mental comparison of the physical attributes of his contestant and himself, seeing instead only the author of his and his friends' hurts, and the one who had caused the death of so many shipmates—he who had incarcerated, threatened, and bound the woman he loved.

"Dat Voga," the jed sneered, crossing blades a half a dozen times with the red man. In his immense paw, Lodus Voyvott gripped Gar-Noh-Dar's impossibly sharp blade. "As you can see, you taught me well! I am glad you could make it to this evening's revelry. I had no idea Mab Meebo invited you, so I am afraid we commenced the festivities without you!" He gestured toward a platform where the remains of a sailor dripped on the cold flagstones.

Dat Voga saw the appalling remains for the first time, having been so busy keeping his opponents in sight, along with the women and Mab Meebo, that he had overlooked this grisly sacrifice sitting at the foot of Lodus Voyvott's throne. His breath hissed between clenched teeth. "Issus," he breathed. "You're a beast."

Lodus Voyvott barked out a harsh laugh at the red man's reaction. "Spineless weakling," he spat. He swung a vicious cut at the padwar's midriff.

Dat Voga parried the slash from the jed that would have cut him in twain had it landed. The odar and the osar had fought their way to the sides of the women, where they were heavily beset. The odds were stacked greatly against them, for they had half a dozen green men slashing and hacking at them with sword and gaff.

However, Gar-Noh-Dar had by now become the equal of at least three of their number. His skill with the blade had been greatly enhanced in the weeks he had spent train-ing with the man from the future, and further still in the weeks of training with various green men where he had received several pointers in private from his friend in their prison cell.

"You see before you an aberration whose like I intend to prevent in the future, red man," Lodus Voyvott said enigmatically.

Slash! Shing! Blade skittered off blade.

"I know you have been spreading your pusillanimous weakness and vaunted humanitarianism to Mab Meebo, who, I am sad to find, has fallen prey to it! I must admit, he had me beguiled. But, in hindsight, I see him for the weak-gutted fool he is."

Cling! Clang!

"But I will change all that! I intend to stamp out any sentiment I deem weak. Kindness has no place in the heart of a modern-day green man. It is a useless, leftover senti-ment from a bygone age. Henceforth we shall strive for perfection, breeding out flaws and instilling strength through the torture of our enemies. Nor shall the might of that army ever know the likes of me, who shall be the last deformed green man to degrade the horde.

"I am hideous, am I not, Dat Voga? Vile red man! I see

the disgust writ plain upon your face! But no more: I shall be the last. I have slowly begun altering this tribe into the shape of the future, where the jed and his council shall select the most perfect eggs, culling the imperfect!"

The red man scowled behind his blade, hearing the echoes of his own day, when the race of green men would expend an excess of time and effort in the selection of their eggs, destroying any that hatched too early, or too late, lest they pass down their defective traits to later generations.

He lunged at Lodus Voyvott. "Why wait for the far future to expunge the aberrations of the horde?"

Lodus Voyvott parried the red man's strike but disdained to take the bait. "I envision a day where the weak tenderness of my warriors' mothers will not be passed on to them, but where they will be raised with a sword in their teeth! They will never know the warm arms of comfort and solace, but rather the steely sinews of warriors who will raise up an army that will not include the likes of spineless Mab Meebo—one who has no taste for war! Now eat steel, red man!"

The green man's sudden and relentless slashes came as close as any to the hide of the red man. He was massive, and, for all his great bulk, hideously fast. Unable to resist, Lodus Voyvott continued to taunt his adversary.

"Once I destroy your pathetic band, I will sample the delights of your women. What a glorious night! To glut myself in torture, and to then spend the night in the sinuous arms of your magnificent mate! But only for tonight! For on the morrow, I shall filet the skin from her wondrous body and feed her hideous remains to the creatures of the deep in remembrance of you. Her cries of torment will provide a fitting dirge for your internment."

Dat Voga fought on, not letting the jibes of the green jed enrage him, for he knew from the teachings of John Carter not to allow an enemy rattle him to the point where he made mistakes. Although Lodus Voyvott had the advantages of enormous reach, strength, and height, there was one enviable quality the jed did not possess—that of endurance, a commodity the red man had in plenty.

Already the jed panted from exertion, his breath coming in ragged gasps. For all his size, he had not the stamina of the padwar. Dat Voga's lungs were one and a half times the size of any human of the day, and his organs had adapted to the rarity of the future atmosphere of Barsoom to such a degree that they absorbed the element in orders of magnitude more than those of this time.

In short, the red man was a dynamo of boundless energy. He felt no fatigue and his eyes were sharp and focused. Something nearby caught his eye—the dead body of Poxx Vorka. It lay with the Heliumite's dagger protruding from the center of its hideous face, right where he had cast it earlier. Lying beside the body, loosely clutched in its dead fist, was the sword of Zikka. His sword!

He backed the jed about with a series of maneuvers and stooped to snatch the blade from the dead hand of the green man. Then he flung his short sword into the face of the oncoming Lodus Voyvott.

The jed took a quick, uncalculated swipe at the whirling sword, very nearly missing it. The blade spun on a disturbed path, grazing down the length of Lodus Voyvott's forearm and leaving a burning path of shaved and furrowed skin.

There was one enviable quality the jed did not possess—that of endurance, a commodity the red man had in plenty.

Chapter Thirty

Reunited

As dat voga battled lodus voyvott, the sailors of the *Prachus* were not idle. The odar and his son defended the women while one of the other sailors slashed the ropes binding their arms. They were soon freed, and then they, too, took up arms. Their fighting number was now augmented by two.

Roh-Du-Von and a sailor called Bhyda fought back-to-back in defense of their piece of ground. They had already accounted for several green men, the hopelessness they each suffered these last weeks causing them to fight with reckless abandon. There were scores to settle on account of their tortured and slain shipmates. The mutilated body near the throne had not gone unnoticed.

Each knew that the longer they remained here, the less were their chances of leaving. They must make their way to the harbor or breathe out their last on this island. Gar-Noh-Dar had witnessed the red man snatch the sword fashioned in Xanator from the body of Poxx Vorka. Gripping his own sword seemed to galvanize the red man, and with renewed vigor he drove the gasping Lodus Voyvott in retreat.

Then Gar-Noh-Dar became hard pressed as a green man leaped at him, swinging one of the newly made long swords, manufactured by one of Lodus Voyvott' armorers to Dat Voga's specifications in mimicry of the swords of Zikka. The sailor recognized the warrior as one of his former students.

He smiled a grim smile when the man entered one of the known setups, taught to the green men by him and Dat Voga. A few quick maneuvers left the man dead at his feet. The green man's blade had snapped off at the hilt as Dat Voga foretold, the steel being too weak to support the narrowness of the blade when hard pressed. Gar-Noh-Dar moved on to another antagonist.

Dat Voga decided it was his turn to taunt the green man, an old trick of John Carter's, who loved to goad his opponents until they became furious, at which point they became reckless.

"What now, Lodus Voyvott? Did a sorak bite your tongue? Did you think I taught you all my tricks, you towering fool? You are unaware, but most of the maneuvers I taught you were classic setups that end with me having you at the end of my blade. And you cannot possibly know which they are, for I feigned defeat with each crossing of our blades. Can you guess which they were, Lodus Voyvott?"

In a trice the green man bled from half a dozen painful cuts following a blur of movements from his smaller opponent. For with the padwar's longer blade in hand, the jed no longer remained just out of reach as with the perilously shorter blade Dat Voga had obtained from the stores of Mab Meebo.

With a half smile on his handsome face, the Heliumite began carving up the jed at will. He cut up his legs and his lower arms, whatever came within range. The jed swung his sword in a monstrous arc, his body pivoting low and bringing his upper torso within reach. His shorter opponent seized the opportunity to sever a tip from one of the jaundiced tusks, which skittered across the floor with a hollow, repugnant sound.

A groan from the green men surrounding the humans caused Dat Voga to risk a quick glance toward the women, fearing the worse. What he saw caused him to smile in earnest. The green men were now being attacked from their rear by Mab Meebo and Tazzor Gobatt! These two had been all but forgotten, for the blow from Lodus Voyvott had sent Mab Meebo crashing to the floor, stunned or dead.

Leaping to the side of the red man, Mab Meebo also engaged the outnumbered jed. Lodus Voyvott was in a sorry state, bleeding from scores of painful nicks and wounds. Dat Voga was not toying with his opponent but rather had found it difficult to locate the giant man's vitals, for the jed's strength and height made him formidable, even for the skilled Heliumite.

But Mab Meebo did not have these difficulties. He was not half the swordsman of the red man, but his great stature leveled the field as far as Lodus Voyvott's advantages. With a shout of "For Oola Zofta!" he joined the fight at the side of his diminutive friend. Dat Voga shouted, "For Azaria!" with the sight of the green man filling him with renewed hope and confidence.

Lodus Voyvott could scarcely defend himself now, for the human's taunts had seemingly struck him stiff with dread. He appeared terrified to attempt the maneuvers the red man had taught him for fear of leaving himself wide open for destruction. He was forced to fall back on his own limited store of knowledge, which Dat Voga knew to be inadequate against his own skill.

With the advent of Mab Meebo, Lodus Voyvott's fear became all the more evident. Slashing viciously at the red man to buy a brief respite, the cowardly behemoth turned to flee. Before he could withdraw his sword arm, however, Mab Meebo brought his sword crashing down on the jed's extended appendage, lopping it off at the elbow. The stricken man's scream filled the throne room.

Clutching the bloody stump of his arm, the jed fled

through the midst of his embattled men, who parted to allow his passage and then immediately filled the gap behind him. Scattered across the chamber were a dozen dead green men. A sailor had also fallen. Through insurmountable odds they had stood their ground but were not out of danger yet. They must escape and make their way to the harbor.

Dat Voga, with the two green men who joined him, ran to the small band of men and women, pausing only long enough to retrieve his scabbard from the side of Poxx Vorka by the simple expedient of cutting the belt from the corpse. The sword Lodus Voyvott had stolen from Gar-Noh-Dar he took from the grasp of the severed arm of the jed, but the scabbard was gone, being still upon the hip of Lodus Voyvott.

Dat Voga went straight to Azaria. "My princess! That I should live to see this moment! Lodus Voyvott has not harmed you?"

The girl sobbed with joy at sight of the padwar. She cried out, "My chieftain, I knew you would come! I told Thuria you would come! We are unharmed, but please, let us flee this horrid place."

Taking her hand in his, they left, retreating through a narrow doorway Mab Meebo assured them led to the rear of the palace. In reckless flight, the humans fended off pursuers long enough to start several fires, as Mab Meebo had suggested. The green men of Nagor were forced to cease their pursuit to put out the flames, to prevent the utter destruction of the palace.

As they ran from the palace, Dat Voga found himself alongside Mab Meebo's friend. "I am glad, Tazzor Gobatt," he said, "that you threw in with us. Were it not for the advent of you and Mab Meebo, we might have been lost."

"It remains to be seen, red man, if that is not still the case! Even so, you are welcome."

Tazzor Gobatt described how he had dragged his friend aside in the ensuing confusion when all attention was diverted to the sailors. He had attacked the ropes that bound his friend, freeing the limbs of the battered man. He had suffered great anguish seeing his comrade in the predicament in which he chose to place himself, but he decided to cast his lot with his friend—precisely as Mab Meebo believed he would.

Their flight was a blur. They backtracked to the rear of the palace, with flames and smoke closing in as their party burst through the door. They descended the cliff to the vent tube without interference. Against the orders of Mab Meebo, little Donza was still there, awaiting them. His excuse was that he feared the humans would become lost in the maze of twisting vent tubes.

Nor was he wrong, as Mab Meebo conceded. It had been years since the green man had explored these subterranean passages, and he doubted if even he could navigate them. The Horzian torches came once more into service, and they fled as swiftly as possible. Most had taken wounds during the fray, except for the women who suffered only chafing from their bonds, and all but the tireless red man neared states of collapse.

Arriving once more at the cliff face below the home of Mab Meebo, they continued upon the perilous path that ran alongside it. In the streets of the ancient stone city above them came shouts and cries as the Palace Guard alerted and rallied green warriors from their homes.

When they came to a certain vent opening, little Donza directed them to enter it. Yet again did they plumb the dark, grainy bowels of the stony island of Nagor. Dat Voga, coming last, expected the prod of a green man's gaff in his back at any moment. When he felt he could not stand being underground a moment more, the vent tube ended just below the edge of the crevasse.

Below the vent aperture was a plummet into inky darkness. They scaled the vertical face to the summit where they saw the ocean to the west. A half haad distant lay the garrison of stony buildings where they had been imprisoned. Nearby lay the entrance to the tunnel to the quays below.

Moving cautiously and looking for sentries, they made it to the garrison without anyone seeing them, for nature had littered their way with rocky outcroppings that afforded them concealment. Soon they were forced into the open as they made for the tunnel to the harbor, and it was here they were discovered. But when the sentries saw the size of the group, they fled up the path toward the stone city.

Chapter Thirty-One

Little Donza Aids Dat Voga

THE HARBOR GUARDS had no sooner fled than they returned at the head of a swarm of green warriors pouring from the city. Lodus Voyvott had regrouped and marched posthaste to head them off.

Dat Voga, bringing up the rear, urged his friends to greater haste. Donza, at the orders of Mab Meebo, sped ahead of the others, for his mother would need his aid in controlling the gantahns. If she had not been successful in summoning the creatures, then they were lost.

Roaring in anger and frustration, the green mob surged forward, weapons bristling. The red man paused to ensure that the others had a good lead, determined to buy them time if needed. As the green men drew nearer, and with his friends well on their way, he, too, darted into the entrance and started down the steep path to the harbor.

The green men were rapidly closing the distance. He could hear their labored breathing, their grunts and curses, the grating of their weapons against the stone of the twisting passage. They were close, and he worried he and his friends might not have enough time to get away before they were overtaken.

An idea occurred to him that might buy them time. He recalled Zikka's account of the radium explosion when the door had been blown off his father's furnace. Dat Voga had two radium torches.

He scanned the walls of the tunnel, for the most part honed smooth by unknown ages of use. At last, he saw that which he sought—a crevice large enough to cram in one of the lamps. He slid the hood up, exposing more of the radium and rummaged in his waist pouch. His questing fingers found what he sought—the fire-starting tool he had brought with him from his own time.

He set it on the highest flame setting, tossed it inside the hood of the torch, and snapped it shut. Sparks and flashes flared in response to the radium compound's exposure to the direct flame, exactly as the radium cake had in the furnace when Zikka's father tossed it in the fire. He crammed the torch into the crevice and ran. Pulling the second torch from his belt, he utilized it to continue his descent.

He had no idea how long it would take for the radium to ignite, or if it even would. Would it detonate, like in Zikka's story? Would it be enough to slow their pursuers, giving them the much-needed time to launch their craft? Had Oola Zofta and Donza been successful in readying the styths? He could not guess, but he wished to be as far away as possible if something happened with that torch.

He was near the bottom when the radium torch detonated. The concussion was greater than he anticipated. Dust and debris flew past him, and the noise was deafening. He had to feel his way forward for the dust was so thick he could not see his hand in front of his face. Fortunately, he was near the exit when the explosion occurred. It would take the green men a while to clear the choked tunnel; he only hoped it was enough to ensure their escape.

His friends were standing beside two styths, looking anxiously for him. He yelled for them to board and waved them toward the waiting styths. He ran to the styth where

Azaria awaited him. She met him and helped him to the hatch. His ears and head were ringing and throbbing from the blast in the confines of the narrow tunnel. Oola Zofta and little Donza already sat at the controls.

Once the red man descended into the interior he collapsed to the deck beside Mab Meebo and Roh-Du-Von. Azaria cradled his head to her breast while Donza saw to the hatch. The styth surged forward under Oola Zofta's prompting of their gantahn, and they were underway, remaining above water while they traveled through the canyon to conserve the meager supply of air in the primitive storage tank.

Atop the cliffs overlooking the harbor, Lodus Voyvott glared down at the fugitives through hate-filled eyes, clutching a throbbing stump where once swung his sword arm. On his hip hung an empty scabbard fashioned by Zikka of Xanator.

Inside the styth, a calm had settled over Dat Voga and his companions after their narrow escape, the only sound that of the water on the hull. It was yet nighttime, and only a soft illumination from the instrumentation filled the interior. Dat Voga had often wondered about these fantastic vehicles of the primitive green men of the past. As they had a few moments to spare, he asked Mab Meebo about them.

"I will tell you the tale," the warrior replied, "because it is illustrative that not all green men are murderous cutthroats. Two and a half centuries ago, an Orovar was captured from a Horzian vessel, an engineer of marvelous ingenuity. To bargain for his life, he told of an astonishing invention he had yet to build due to the time-consuming duties of his station. After relating the idea to Lodus Voyvott, the jed agreed it had merit. He would spare the man's life if he turned it into a reality."

"Thus, did the styth come to be. It was not the creation of a green man, although the idea of harnessing styths to the creatures of the deep had its origins in the twisted cranium of Lodus Voyvott. In fact, a source of motive power is what eluded the Orovar so that he never built the thing. The white men have never learned to control the beasts of the sea like we green men, which is a matter of pride for us."

"But already was Lodus Voyvott the spawn of a liar he is today. No sooner had the Orovar built various designs of these vessels and trained green men in their construction and use than Lodus Voyvott sentenced him to torture and death. Although he made a compact with the man, it was a covenant Lodus Voyvott never intended to keep. The next morning, however, when they went to fetch him, the Orovar was gone. Lodus Voyvott never knew how he escaped. But I know."

Dat Voga eyed the green man suddenly. "It was you," he said quietly.

"Yes, I aided the man's flight. I would have died for that offense had the jed learned of it. I called the gantahn, instructing it where to take the man, and I never saw him again. I have often wondered if he made it back to his people safely. I like to imagine he did."

As Mab Meebo finished his astounding admission, Dat Voga thanked his ancestors for the unique green man. Azaria asked, "Mab Meebo, have your people always lived on that forsaken piece of rock?"

"No. We were seeking new islands when we sailed into the same doldrums that ensnared your vessel. After days rolled into weeks, and no brobdoganth answered our summons, we stripped planking to rig oars and began rowing. Eventually, we called a horde of gantahns, inducing them to tow us to land. They took us to the island.

"We found the cleft in the outer wall, and then the harbor. Taking the passage to the clifftop, we were shocked to find the ancient ruins of the stone city that you saw. We do not know who built them but believe them to predate the known races of Barsoom.

"We settled there, adding homes and incubators as necessary. There we developed our own peculiar oar-driven sailing vessels using material we scavenged from the abandoned vessels in the area in which you yourselves were caught. These hybrid vessels we once utilized for plundering the ships that became mired in the doldrums surrounding the island, which we styled Nagor after an old homeland.

"The adoption of our styths enabled us to foray farther out to sea in search of prey. Many of us might have stomached the lifestyle, were it not for the other changes Lodus Voyvott instituted. It is a natural thing for the green man to plunder the Orovars, who have ever sought to eradicate us. But certain of us came to abhor the degenerated treatment the jed accorded all who fell under his merciless power."

The cabin grew quiet. Initially, the red man did not care in which direction they sailed. But the idea occurred to him to inquire whether they would pass near the vicinity where the *Prachus* had sunk. Mab Meebo was uncertain. Dat Voga had been thinking about the gauntlets. He had asked before if Mab Meebo had seen anyone with such plunder. After he described them in detail, Mab Meebo assured him he had not, and guessed they lay on the bottom of the sea.

The Heliumite sat beside Azaria, where he learned the women had not been mistreated. But they had been told that, as soon as Dat Voga's and Gar-Noh-Dar's usefulness was at an end, the men would all be tortured and destroyed. They had passed through many harrowing ordeals. Now, content to be together, they sat quietly so as not to distract Donza's focus on the gantahn.

Dat Voga's thoughts returned to the gauntlets. Unable to get them off his mind, he asked Mab Meebo if he thought the gantahns would be able to find the shipwreck. Mab Meebo knew then that these gauntlets were important, or the red man would not keep bringing up the topic. By now, little Donza had heard snatches of the conversation and was becoming interested in the lost items.

"The gantahns can find the ship," he volunteered, "for I just asked them. Both were there that day. They know the sea better than a mother knows her son's face and said they can find the wreck easily."

Mab Meebo's face filled with wonder at his son's stunning pronouncement. He asked in a hushed tone, "How far, Donza?"

The boy was quiet, then answered, "We continue as we are for—there is no equivalent for what they told me, but I would guess two or three zodes."

Dat Voga could not believe what he was hearing. "Is your ability so well developed in the reading of the minds of men, Donza?"

"Only for those willing," the boy replied. "Since the time I read your mind, you have blocked any further attempt. But it comes very easily for me with these creatures."

The red man stared at the boy in thought. "Donza, I have a riddle I wonder if you might help me with. There are savants among my own people who could help, but alone, it is beyond me. If I allow you to access my mind, do you think you might help me?"

The little green boy grinned enthusiastically, "Oh yes, Dat Voga! I would be glad to help. What exactly is it you seek?"

He told the boy as much as he dared—about the lock on the gauntlets, and how critical it was that he solve the cryptic. About how he believed the answer resided in his mind, left there accidentally by an evil man named Daxxus Nahl. Dat Voga knew that he asked much of the boy. It could be risky, he knew, for Donza to possess knowledge of the future.

He asked the boy to concentrate on the gauntlets and the conversations he had with Daxxus Nahl that yet ran rampant through the red man's mind. He felt his mind lock onto the boy's. Never had he felt such a strong connection. Donza was, indeed, a telepath of the first order and a savant.

His shipmates in the styth could not possibly guess how

important all this was to Dat Voga, but they knew him well enough to convince them it must be paramount. The man and the boy, eyes closed, slipped into a world of their own. The red man began muttering under his breath, but none could make out what he said.

His voice growing louder with each repetition of the phrase, they at last made out his mumbling words: "I gave this field the appellation of *Soom Spheron*, which is the measurement I gave to its mean amplitude."

He repeated the phrase, his voice getting louder each time. "I gave this field the appellation of *Soom Spheron*, which is the measurement I gave to its mean amplitude. I gave this field the appellation of—"

Dat Voga's eyes snapped open, and he shouted in jubilation. "I know the cryptic of Daxxus Nahl! You did it, Donza!"

Chapter Thirty-Two

OF GANTAHNS AND GAUNTLETS

THE RED MAN GRASPED the green youth in relief, folding Donza's small body in his arms. There were tears of relief in Dat Voga's eyes, for he knew now he could secure salvation for his friends should they recover the lost gauntlets.

A stunned Oola Zofta watched in fascination as the human, with whom her kind had ever warred, exhibited such tender gratitude to her son. No one could guess why Dat Voga was so happy at the idea of retrieving what, to them, were simply baubles no more valuable than any other pair of bracelets.

The remaining distance to where the *Prachus* went down could now not be covered quickly enough for the red man. He became wholly galvanized, having tossed aside his weariness as another might cast off a garment. He went topside to tell Thuria he knew the answer to the riddle they had sought since arriving in this time a year before, waving his arms wildly to hail the vessel.

Thuria grinned widely, her beautiful teeth flashing in the morning sunlight and her eyes filled with tears of happiness and gratitude. "I told you it would come to you, Dat Voga!" she shouted jubilantly.

At last, they heaved-to above the lonely wreck of the greatest ship of the fleet of Hal-Roh-Kim. The gantahns were summoned to the sides of the styths where little Donza and Dat Voga impressed their wishes upon the gentle creatures. As they dove toward the sea floor, the red man also dove, swimming downward as far as he was able.

It was still early morning; they had fought and fled all night. The seabed was still too shadowy for the red man to discern much, but he could see that the depth was not great here, being perhaps a hundred and fifty sofads.

The gantahns, a mammalian creature, surfaced periodically for air. They had scoured the wreck site for zodes. Having been given a clear, mental image of the gauntlets, they knew precisely what their masters sought, and that nothing else would suffice. Dat Voga, surfacing, found anxious faces peering at him from the styth. "What is it?" he asked.

"Styths and sail-oar ships are approaching! They have spotted us and will be here in less than half a zode," Mab Meebo replied grimly.

"Shades!" Dat Voga fumed in frustration. "We're so close!" He closed his eyes in concentration. He felt positive the gauntlets were there and that the gantahns would find them. They just needed time! He thought furiously, then said, "Quickly, Mab Meebo. We need to transfer Thuria and the sailors to this styth, and you and your family must board the other with Tazzor Gobatt. Prepare to dive!"

"We shall not abandon you, Dat Voga!" cried the green man passionately.

"Nor will you. Heed! When these gantahns surface, you shall harness one to your styth and dive. Do not surface until forced to. If we had more time, I would rip the air tank from this vessel and add it to yours, but ironically, despite the capabilities that lie dormant in those gauntlets, time is a commodity we presently lack. When you surface, you will have to be quick—take on air and dive immediately. It has been an honor knowing you and your family, and I hope you find a place where you can live in peace the life you wish to live."

"The honor is mine, Dat Voga. I know not what you plan, but judging what you were willing to risk rescuing Azaria, I know you do not propose suicide. May your ancestors be with you, red man!"

The Heliumite glanced at Azaria and the remaining sailors, each from this time. Thinking of the green man's comment about his ancestors, he smiled. "They already are, Mab Meebo! They already are!"

He looked at Gar-Noh-Dar, reminded of their conversation on the fantail of the *Prachus*, what felt like years ago. He called out across the short distance to the other styth: "Gar-Noh-Dar, do you recall when you approached me on the stern, and I told you to be ready if you wished to be with Thuria? Well, ready yourself, Osar!"

Gar-Noh-Dar frowned as if he sought to recall what the red man referred to. Then his eyes grew as large as Xanatorian bronzes, clearly remembering when he had sought the red man's permission to ask the beautiful maiden to become his mate. Dat Voga had warned him there was but a single path that would allow the osar to become the mate of Thuria. Thus, the man must now know that something momentous loomed.

Dat Voga heard a splash at the side of the vessel and there, within easy grasp, were the gauntlets—each gantahn clutching one in his grinning mouth. With a cry of elation, the young scientist slipped the gauntlets over his arms, buckling them in place as he had that day in the study of Daxxus Nahl.

This time, the gauntlets would provide the power source for returning him and Thuria, and he had decided to take these others with him, back to the future. If, that is, the gauntlets functioned as Daxxus Nahl declared.

The gauntlets had spent weeks on the bottom of the sea.

For all Dat Voga knew, their circuitry was ruined. Perhaps their crucial power charge had dissipated. What if the cryptic was not what he and Donza surmised from their telepathic pairing? What if the cryptic were something they would never guess in a million years?

Thinking of little Donza, son of Mab Meebo, caused him to glance at the other styth. Mab Meebo, having secured the hawser to the gantahn, disappeared into the hatch, but he turned about when he saw his son still upon the deck. "Quickly, Donza! We must dive!" the green man cried in warning to the boy.

But little Donza stood stock-still on the rear of the gently tossing vessel. Then he called across to Dat Voga. "I will buy you more time!" The little green boy closed his eyes in concentration and extended his hands toward the advancing horde, his small body perfectly poised and balanced upon the pitching deck of the vessel.

Dat Voga witnessed the result instantly. A brobdoganth turned upon a passing styth, grasping the vessel in its maw and crushing it. Another horned whale reared into the air and crashed sideways into a nearby sail-oar ship, caving in the side and capsizing the vessel, which fell sideways into another ship and became entangled in its sails and rigging. Gantahns bucked and thrashed, throwing their riders into the tossing sea where many were gored on the horns of the rebelling brobdoganths.

Not all were affected, though, Donza having reached his limit. But his actions gained them precious time. Having observed the chaos amid the green horde, Dat Voga glanced at the styth of Mab Meebo. He was in time to see it dive, the stern sliding beneath the waves. The red man caught a glimpse of Donza's face in a viewport before the styth disappeared. Although they were gone, he threw up an arm in farewell.

Dat Voga looked at the waiting gantahn. Smiling his

thanks, he spoke to the creature telepathically, telling it to follow the other styth. Without a second glance, it sounded and disappeared beneath the waves.

When it disappeared, Bhyda cried out in fear. "The creature abandoned us. We're lost! That was our only means of escape!"

"I ordered it to go because we don't need it," Dat Voga replied. He now focused on the matter at hand. He recalled the conversation with the madman of the gorge. He remembered, as well, the mean measurement of the spheron field. Had he not studied the values of those fields for weeks? He knew those values better than any others he had ever learned.

He triggered the opening of the input glass and was pleased to see the familiar screen. He breathed a heavy sigh of relief when he saw the familiar glow of the instrumentation and realized the circuits had not suffered from their time on the bottom. Daxxus Nahl had built them well.

How many times had he sat before this same screen, entering number after number and word after word to no avail? Why had it never occurred to him to use the ever-so-crucial value of the mean amplitude of the spheron field? He could not say. Taking a measured breath, he began entering the value using standard scientific symbols, because the value was considerable.

In his ear was the slosh of the sea on the sides of his styth, and the voices of the others speaking in hushed tones. Thuria encouraged them to have patience. Roh-Du-Von felt they should have kept the gantahn to escape the oncoming green men who now renewed their advance. Lodus Voyvott's flotilla numbered more vessels than had attacked the *Prachus*, so it was quite formidable.

The red man concluded entering the value and poised his finger over the last button, the one that would ask the gauntlet to accept the entry. If it did not accept it, they would return to the island of Nagor in captivity and be slain after days of torture. The nearest member of the attacking horde closed the gap to but a few hundred sofads. He must be quick. Without further hesitation, Dat Voga pressed the button.

The screen changed, asking for the destination variance and the spatial coordinates. The padwar looked up at Thuria and smiled. "Look one last time, Thuria, upon Throxeus—for we are going home!" And then he began feverishly inputting the required information.

He modified the original spatial coordinates, dropping the elevation by the seventy-five sofads they had been at when they left the Ptarsan gorge. Were they to return to that same point with all of them sitting in the styth they would immediately fall seventy-five sofads to the stone floor.

As Dat Voga completed entering the settings he looked out over the sea one last time, his heart pounding. It was midmorning. Not a cloud was in the sky; the morning light, shimmering on the lapping waves, was so beautiful that his heart ached at the thought that he would never see it again.

Without another tal's hesitation, he snapped the two gauntlets together with their connecting lugs and rotated them until they locked securely, closing the electrical connection. A hum became audible, and an odd lambency in the form of a twenty sofad diameter sphere became visible—a sphere that included the styth, the half-hemisphere of sea with the surrounding air filling the rest of the sphere.

Odar Gan-Toh-Gan shouted, "What is this?"

The others started and sat upright, looking about in confusion. Only Thuria and Gar-Noh-Dar appeared calm—as was Dat Voga. Thuria clutched Gar-Noh-Dar's hands in hers. Azaria, seated beside her chieftain, looked startled, but seeing the outward composure of Dat Voga and Thuria reassured her and allowed her to regain her repose.

The creatures towing the green horde, having approached close to them by now, balked once more, this time panicked by the humming sphere. The brobdoganths reared into the air and many of them panicked and sounded, taking their cruel masters into the deeps to never rise again.

They were less than seventy sofads from the humans when the bluish sphere of the nexus appeared. A lighted indicator glowed on a gauntlet, indicating that the field was fully powered and ready. The red man pressed the control button without further delay.

The scene about them dimmed. Even the sound of the waves lapping the sides of their vessel became muted. Many more of the gantahns and brobdoganths became terrified and dove toward the bottom to escape this terrifying sight, taking scores of green men with them who would never again see the sky. The approaching green warriors faded, but not before Dat Voga saw the looks of incredulity upon their faces.

The morning sky and the sunlit sea disappeared, replaced by walls of stone. Their task completed and their store of power exhausted, the gauntlets shut off. The volume of half of a twenty-sofad-diameter sphere of seawater spilled across a composite stone floor, carrying the styth with it. Once more in Daxxus Nahl's lab, they came to rest against the firmly moored insulators of the power array.

Chapter Thirty-Three

"'TIS THROXEUS, MY PRINCE!"

DAT VOGA HAD DREAMT of this moment a thousand times. Often had he wondered how the scene would unfold when he found himself again in the laboratory of Daxxus Nahl. Now that day had come. Without hesitation, he leaped from the styth, shouting for the others to follow.

He could not acquaint his comrades with the circumstances they must face when they arrived here—a powerful enemy and a radically different world. His lungs were already protesting the lack of oxygen. His friends, too, must be suffering similarly, if not worse.

Although the air in the grotto had not changed since he was last here, he had spent so much time in the past that his lungs had grown accustomed to inhaling that ultra-rich content. While initially he and Thuria had had to monitor their air intake in the past, their lungs had begun to adapt to the richer atmosphere and so were tortured in the rarity of elements in which they now found themselves.

His friends would be confused by this change in the atmosphere, but he urged them on, knowing the powerful Daxxus Nahl would be too much for him to overcome alone. The man's supernatural strength and agility would certainly defeat Dat Voga in his current state, until be became reacclimatized.

He leaped from the vessel, his eyes seeking Daxxus Nahl and Carthoris. He had set the time frame so he would not interfere with his and Thuria's earlier modulation, and to give the array ample time to power down. It was a bizarre paradox, but he did not wish to interfere with their previous escape, which had occurred but a moment before—or a year ago, depending on how one looked at it.

The embattled scientist and the Prince of Helium were still beside the prison cells and near enough to the power array when the seawater that the time travelers had brought with them in the nexus swept the combatants from their feet in its rush across the floor. Daxxus Nahl struggled to stand. Carthoris, still bound, had washed up against a wall and was even then rising to his feet.

The red man's heart pounded when he saw John Carter's son. He shouted, "My Prince, I come!"

Carthoris turned his head toward the familiar voice. "Dat Voga, what happened? I thought you left! Whence came all this water?"

"'Tis Throxeus, my Prince!" Dat Voga replied. Running forward, closely followed by his armed friends, the padwar approached the scientist. "Surrender, Daxxus Nahl! You are outnumbered. We are seven swords to your one. Yield, or you will force us to destroy you!"

The scientist looked perplexed. Drenched in seawater, he stood. The burst of extreme anger he exhibited the last time Dat Voga saw him had in an instant converted into uncertainty. A strange light was in his eyes, obvious to one who knew him as well as Dat Voga. In place of the rage and madness of moments before was confusion.

When Dat Voga had labored under Daxxus Nahl's capricious command, he often sensed the scientist reeled on the rim of lunacy. He had certainly denied himself assistance that might have helped him lead a normal life rather than become the shuttered, self-inflicted exile that he was, living beneath these cliffs, far from the pathways of man. So while

Dat Voga had expected to face an enraged and demented Daxxus Nahl, the fickleness of the man's sick mind had caused him to become confused and introverted. The padwar sheathed his weapon.

"Young Dat Voga? Is that you, then?"

It was little wonder the scientist scarcely recognized the Heliumite, although only moments had passed since he had last seen his former coadjutor. Before him stood a man bronzed from exposure to the sun while at sea. A man whose raven locks, which mere heartbeats before had been trimmed neatly above the ears, now flowed in a thick mane and was bound by a leather band from which hung the feathers of extinct birds.

Upon his body were remnants of blue paint, for at some point the padwar had daubed himself in the fashion of his fellow sailors. His harness was of ancient design, with leather straps swinging from his belt to midflank, while on his feet was a pair of exotic sandals with crisscrossing straps running to his knees. On one hip swung a sword of unparalleled beauty and uniqueness, whose jeweled accents cast glints of light. Protruding from his belt was a bronze torch such as were used by the ancients.

Daxxus Nahl, having forgotten his rage, now became consumed with curiosity. "But you just left! Did the experiment fail? Tell me, Dat Voga, what did you see? What happened? I saw the sky and clouds and moonlight within the spheron field, so I know it was in part successful! I do not understand why you have returned so soon!"

Daxxus Nahl was experiencing the same disbelief at the success of the experiment that Dat Voga had himself felt when he arrived in the past. Neither had he been truly prepared for such success. The Heliumite sensed a shift in the scientist. He motioned to the others to lower their weapons. He felt pity for this man, whose mind slipped in and out of his control.

"Daxxus Nahl, we have spent a year trapped a million

years in the past. Your lock mechanism nearly ensured we would spend the rest of our days there. As you can see, there are others with me who are from that time. It was necessary to bring them, as their time-path had been altered and to have left them there might have revised the future. Your experiment was a success. You have reason to be proud."

Dat Voga knew the Orovars were perplexed, but he hoped they would abide until he could explain. Daxxus Nahl was cooperating, but for safety's sake they bound him. Carthoris retrieved the fallen short sword and Daxxus Nahl's pen-ray device. After they secured the scientist, they released Voss Borgas, the Ptarsan ambassador, before proceeding to the Banaalians.

At the cells of the Banaalians, the padwar turned the dials on their cells that would allow him to speak to them, but which kept the thick glass solid. "You will be taken back to Ptarsas, Zat Simpus, where your perfidy will be revealed to Ptar Ras," he stated. "I should run this sword through your heart, but your sentence is not mine to mete."

The Banaalian, his visage twisted by hatred, sneered in Dat Voga's face. The padwar still wore the harness issued to him from the stores on the *Prachus*. His long incarceration among the inhabitants of Nagor had left him dirty and unkempt, as were all those who stepped from the styth. He presented quite a barbaric sight. To the arrogant prince he appeared an untutored savage.

"And who shall believe the word of a filthy, disheveled nobody like you, over the Prince of Banaal? Do you really think your word will mean anything in Ptarsas? That old fool Ptar Ras will have no choice but to return me to my father. In the end, none of this will matter," the man spat.

Carthoris and Dat Voga, having secured Daxxus Nahl, began releasing the Banaalians from their cells and pinioning their arms. They considered these men prisoners of war after their craven attack in the Trench of Ptarsas. Zat Simpus blustered and threatened. After one such tirade, Thuria, having heard her fill of the man's ranting, stepped up to him, her face as stern as Dat Voga had ever seen it.

"You are a cowardly calot, and not fit to tie the strings on Dat Voga's sandal. I have bit my tongue in the past, but no longer. I shall tell my father, he who has the ear of the Jed of Zoquan, everything, and I shall fill the ears of Ptar Ras with every foul deed ever perpetrated by you. Banaal shall be relieved of you and your father, and it is about time. The despotic rule of the House of Fonn is over, Zat Simpus.

"And, if I mistake not the look on the face of your warrior here, he shall be able to shed some light on what occurred in the gorge, causing the destruction of your ship and crew—a crew of ten, I believe, for whom you are responsible. I do not believe their families will be happy to learn that their fathers, brothers, and mates perished to further your debased desires," she finished coldly.

"Lies! And do you think they shall give any credence to the words of a slave?" laughed Zat Simpus. His eyes became two cold slits. "I will convince Tahn Dih that I was simply having a bad night at that stupid gala of her father's, and we shall begin planning our future. But you, I shall order her to get rid of. That stupid girl, all she cares about is that her coif is in place! She's about as bright as a million-year-old radium bulb and will do whatever I say."

Drawing herself up to her full height, Thuria delivered Zat Simpus a ringing blow, the second he had received since the arrival of the Heliumites to this part of the world. The hand of Prince Carthoris of Helium had delivered the first, while the second came from a wisp of a girl.

The craven prince's face twisted in rage and glowed redly from the slap from Thuria's open palm. Wisely, he knew better than to act on his angry impulse to strike her. The young woman turned her back on him and returned to the side of Gar-Noh-Dar, who, although confused by the altercation, looked prepared to rend Zat Simpus into his major and minor parts at a nod from his princess. For her friends were now his friends, and her enemies were now his enemies.

Dwar Brik Lakko strode onto the command bridge of the *Tycheus*, the flagship of John Carter. "Report, Than."

The dwar slid into the polished seat at his console as he listened to his junior airman's report. He automatically adjusted his radium pistol to a more comfortable position at his side and pulled his sword from its keepers, attaching it to a special stand beside his station, there just for that purpose.

"Sir, we have arrived on the outskirts of Banaal," said wireless operator Than Barr Vondus.

"And it appears we arrived not a tal too soon," the young man continued. "They appear to be mounting a force, sir. Several vessels have taken to air, although none have advanced beyond their city wall, as yet."

"Excellent, Barr Vondus" replied Brik Lakko. "Wire the *Cquikuss*. Have Pakk Bantos remain below the hills out of sight and bring his ship about; make it two haads north of us. Inform Sako Toola of the *Virginian* to notify John Carter. The Warlord may wish to return to the *Tycheus*, if it comes to a fight."

Barr Vondus grinned boyishly upon hearing that John Carter was aboard the *Virginian*. The information came as no surprise. The crew of that vessel had chosen the name in honor of the birthplace of the Warlord, and John Carter never missed an opportunity to visit the ship. He had ridden to Banaal aboard her but wished to be apprised of their arrival so he could return to his flagship.

"Do you think he will return to the *Tycheus*, sir? You know how his face lights up when anyone mentions the *Virginian*!"

Brik Lakko, typically formal when aboard ship and on duty, smiled at the energetic young than. "It does for a fact!

It must be a wonderful place, his Virginia," he mused. Then, turning serious once more, he said, "But we shall let the Warlord make that decision, Barr Vondus. Bring us to a full stop and send your notifications."

With that, Brik Lakko, a man consumed by the burden of his station, grabbed his sword, and slipped it back onto his belt from which he had but a moment ago removed it, and strode from the command bridge to attend some detail of which the lowly than knew naught. Bar Vondus smiled and, shaking his head at his duty-driven dwar, took up his wireless set.

John Carter had decided to take but three of Helium's battleships to visit the Banaalians, preferring the others continue scouting for their missing. As but one of these new ships was adequate to level Banaal if necessary, he felt that three would prove imposing enough to loosen the jed's tongue.

His beloved Dejah Thoris had decided to remain at Ptarsas, believing their missing ambassadors were more likely to be found in that area. She had reasoned that had they been in Banaal, Simpus Fonn would not be similarly seeking his son here as well. Since his princess would be remaining in Ptarsas, John Carter left the bulk of the armada there, for her protection and to aid her with the search.

He had just received word from the *Tycheus* that they had arrived. He had been strolling about the *Virginian*, speaking with her contingent, an occupation of which he never tired. He admired and loved these brave men and never missed an opportunity to immerse himself in their company.

Also, this vessel, whose name alone conjured the Earth-man's admiration, was of interest in that it was the only vessel in the Heliumetic Navy not helmed by a red man, but by a green man called Sako Toola, a Thark who had come highly recommended by Tars Tarkas.

The green dwar was of abbreviated stature for a green man, being only nine sofads in height. Still, he towered over the shorter red men, who, on average, were roughly six sofads tall. But what he lacked in height he made up for in musculature. In banter, John Carter often told the green man he would hate to meet him in a dark alley in Zodanga, for the green man looked as if he could pull a man apart, limb by limb.

As John Carter made his way to his two-man flier, he heard what sounded like the cracks of whips and the booming of distant thunder. Although surprised by the sounds, the seasoned Warlord did not mistake them for anything other than what they were—the staccato crack of gunfire, and the detonations of radium projectiles on the hull of the ship. The foolish Banaalians were attacking the Navy of Helium!

Chapter Thirty-Four

Enter the *Cquikuss*

Klaxons across the *Virginian* blared as enemy fire abruptly struck the vessel, sending pilots scurrying to their fliers and warriors to their deck guns. Needing to reach the *Tycheus* quickly, John Carter broke into a run. Arriving in the hangar, he tossed off the moorings, leaped aboard his flier, and shot from the launch gate. The gate closed behind him, shutting off the sound of the alarm in his ears.

"*Tycheus*, I'm on my way," he announced on his wireless.

"Be careful, John Carter!" warned Brik Lakko. "It seems the Banaalians are intent on giving us a hot welcome."

The Warlord instantly found himself surrounded by gunfire streaming from the hot barrels of twisting and diving Banaalian vessels. Since his advent on Barsoom the man had taken to fliers as though born to them, despite the fact that, when he first came to the Red Planet, aircraft were decades in the future for his native Earth. Thrilled with excitement, he smiled as he threw his staunch ship into vicious twists and wicked turns in his evasion of enemy fire.

Briefly coming alongside a fellow Heliumite hot on the tail of a fleeing Banaalian courser, John Carter waved and grinned at the pilot of the one-man flier. The man's eyes opened wide in surprise when he saw the Warlord navigating the aerial battlefield in his unarmed personal flier.

"John Carter!" the pilot exclaimed in his wireless set.

"Go get him, Padwar!" replied the Warlord, grinning. And then John Carter sped off in a different direction as he sought to return to the decks of his flagship.

Banaalian coursers and their smaller cousins flashed down the sides of the two behemoths like buzzing insects, raining gunfire at any vessel flying the colors of Helium. They had taken the Heliumites by surprise as no one expected them to attack this mightier, modern navy.

"The Ptarsan advisors told us the Banaalians were a craven lot who preferred to attack from ambuscade," commented the voice of Brik Lakko in his wireless, "and to expect to spend our time here questioning them, not fighting them."

"I was thinking about that. A mistaken assumption, obviously," John Carter replied. "Our Ptarsan advisors likely underestimated the conniving mind of the Jed of Banaal. Do we know where these vessels originated?"

"Not at present," Dwar Brik Lakko said.

"And what of the Banaalian ships in the city?"

"Their main aerial force is still sitting where it was when we arrived," the dwar replied.

John Carter twisted and dove to avoid being shot down as a burst from an enemy flier narrowly missed his little ship. "I should have manned one of the deck guns on the *Virginian*," he muttered. "I'm missing out on all the fighting in this unarmed flier. Those fighters on the ground must be a ruse."

Prior to his departing the *Virginian*, Brik Lakko had notified him that the Banaalian Navy vessels were hovering within their walls with every appearance of wishing to parley. The Warlord saw now that this was a feint.

"You're correct, John Carter, those vessels appeared to be exactly that—a trick to make us think they were cooperating. They have some stealthy means we are unaware of to come upon a surrounding host unawares. We just need to find it."

The next instant John Carter entered a steep dive to avoid a Banaalian vessel that was giving chase. He scanned the surface as he dove and happened to spot a Banaalian courser shoot out of a canyon just outside the city. With all its gun turrets rotated upward, the vessel instantly shot skyward toward the belly of the *Tycheus.*

"*Tycheus,* look out!" he cried, but only static met his reply.

Just as he thought he was to witness the doughty battleship gutted by the courser, his flagship's keel batteries fired a salvo and the Banaalian ship disintegrated into fragments, which continued upward briefly from momentum before they slowed and began falling, the ship erupting into flames.

"Poor devils!" the Warlord said as he watched the wretched survivors leap from the burning wreckage, looking like shooting stars as they fell, flaming, toward the surface, their screams going unheard in the enormous din filling the thin air of Barsoom.

Punching a button on his console to reopen his connection to the bridge of the *Tycheus,* John Carter shouted into the microphone. "*Tycheus,* this is John Carter! They're using underground tunnels! Launch the equilibrimotors to fend off the attackers. And have them look for tunnels. I'm coming in."

Brik Lakko stabbed his finger at a communications button on his console and shouted the Warlord's orders into his microphone.

From apertures along the sides of the ship, small, darting figures erupted, dispersing as soon as they were free of the vessel. Veering off both in groups and singly, they flashed through the sky, some diving at the enemy vessels, while others sped groundward. From their wings, automatic fire erupted, spattering the Banaalian ships in a hail of explosive projectiles, sending chunks of metal in all directions, together with dead and dying Banaalian crewmen.

The equilibrimotor pilots were clothed in a tough uniform designed to protect them from flying debris, for these men were intended for up-close attacks. Their heads were encased in back-swept, aerodynamic helms with specially coated viewscreens for both light gathering and glare filtering, enhancing their vision in various conditions.

The controls of the equilibrimotor wings were not located upon the belt as with commercial models. Instead, they were built into control levers descending from the underside of the wings. Using these controls, pilots could regulate their velocity and direction, and utilize various weapons consisting of automatic fire and radium-tipped rockets.

Total bedlam ensued as the Banaalians, in a state of near panic, sought to outmaneuver these new nemeses. In just a few xats, the equilibrimotor warriors destroyed a dozen Banaalian coursers, the first combat use of this new system proving to be a qualified success.

By now, both the *Tycheus* and the *Virginian* were raking the skies with deadly fire of their own, the fleeing coursers relatively easy targets for the battleships' deck guns and keel batteries. John Carter settled his plane on a hangar deck aboard the flagship and, leaping from his tiny flier, raced along a narrow passageway to the bridge. Bursting through the door, he commanded, "Report!"

"Sir!" replied Dwar Brik Lakko. "We routed the Banaalian vessels, but the enemy decoy ships are now headed in our direction, I would guess to cover the retreat of their ships."

"Where is the *Cquikuss*?"

"I sent her exactly where you instructed. She is two haads north, awaiting orders. Shall I contact Pakk Bantos?"

John Carter smiled his grim fighting smile. "I shall wire him myself."

A few moments later the *Cquikuss* swung over the city, her batteries decimating the gun emplacements on the Banaalian perimeter walls. Her long-range deck guns took out multiple enemy vessels, dropping these as flaming wrecks into the city over which they flew.

The effect of the surprise attack was instant, with the

remaining coursers scattering. John Carter contacted the *Cquikuss* and instructed Pakk Bantos to prevent the return of enemy vessels to the city. He then ordered the equilibri-motors and their one-man fliers to trail the escaping cours-ers. They were to force them down and take prisoners, if possible, but if they would not surrender, they were to blast them out of the sky. He did not wish them to return at an inopportune moment.

The sight of these ultra-modern battleships from Helium's navy inspired awe in the hearts of the Banaalian populace as the ships sailed decisively over their city wall—a wall that now did not seem quite so impregnable. They did not realize it, but they had been shown great leniency. Any one of these ships could have leveled their city had they un-leashed, in full, their awful battery of firepower.

Shortly, John Carter, together with the ground force of Tars Tarkas and an escort of fifty of Helium's hardened warriors, marched across an open plaza toward the palace of Simpus Fonn.

The Jed of Banaal, father of Zat Simpus, wearing an angry, arrogant scowl upon his face, awaited the conquering force with a detachment of his royal guard. In the air over their heads, three of the mightiest vessels of war on the face of Barsoom hovered, covering the advance of Helium's beloved Warlord and his warriors.

Once the prisoners were secured, Dat Voga wished to begin the return trip to Ptarsas. But first he and his companions must pass the telepathically locked door that stood between them and the upper reaches of the cavern. He asked Daxxus Nahl for the secret to the lock, but the man had become quiet and refused to cooperate.

Approaching the door, the Heliumite began experiment-ing by passing various thoughts to the door. On impulse, he tried the same key that had proved successful with the gauntlets. After a brief pause, he was relieved to see the door slide into its recess. Daxxus Nahl looked on apathetically, displaying neither disappointment nor interest in his former coadjutor's success.

Dat Voga learned from the older scientist that he had removed all evidence of both the Heliumites' flier and the *Cunning*, Zat Simpus's vessel. He would have liked to have the intact courser in which to make the return trip but, as with the telepathic lock, the scientist resolutely refused to reveal what disposition he had made of the vessels.

Events were progressing rapidly. Although he knew the Orovars must have many questions for him, Dat Voga had not had an opportunity to speak with them. He had asked them to wait until the prisoners were properly secured, at which point he would make everything known to them.

With the prisoners satisfactorily confined and the entry to the surface now open, nothing else prevented them from venturing up the tunnel to the outer world. Dat Voga considered how shocking it would be for his friends to step into the waiting wasteland.

So far, they had contended only with the thin air in the interior of the caverns, which shielded their sight from the current status of the surface of Barsoom. How to tell them these caverns lay far below sea level in the bowels of a former trench? Leaving Carthoris and Voss Borgas with the captives, he led the Orovars to a chamber where he lay everything bare before them.

It took him most of a zode, for he left out nothing. He told them the history of the last million years and of the death of their planet, leading up to the undertaking he and Carthoris had embarked upon. He described how they became prisoners of Daxxus Nahl, of the part Zat Simpus played. He described the brilliance of the maniacal scientist, including his method of remodulating the time field, and explained how he and Thuria came to be on the island where they were discovered by the *Prachus*.

He explained at last to Azaria the understanding of the

moss he had gained while in the laboratory of Arkaff. Gan-Toh-Gan and Gar-Noh-Dar finally understood why this brilliant man, so gifted with skills and knowledge, was, on the other hand, mystified by a simple phlega.

He told them how he came to realize that his involvement during the encounter with the brobdoganth had inadvertently revised the timelines, and the possible consequences. But he could have acted no differently, and later he had the idea to bring them with him to the future, if they would come, to minimize that impact, little realizing how few of them would survive to journey through time.

He explained the differences in the atmosphere now, the distinctions between his body and theirs as far as his and Thuria's lung capacity, and everything else they had ever questioned when he could not answer. He told them everything he and Thuria had ever guessed or deduced about the differences between the past and the present—the things they would discuss at the bow when they were alone.

The padwar held Azaria while she sobbed for her lost world. The expressions of the men were solemn, and Dat Voga saw tears in the eyes of the odar, who seemed to have aged with Dat Voga's revelations. For, never again would the odar command a ship at sea.

They were confused and could not grasp the great passage of time separating them from the world they knew. Gar-Noh-Dar reached out to Thuria, who rushed to embrace the big-hearted sailor. But for Gan-Toh-Gan and the others, there were no loved ones to offer them solace. Dat Voga's heart broke for them. He reached out a hand, placing it upon the shoulder of each man in turn.

"Fear not, my friends," he said, "for I understand the enormity of your loss. When we found ourselves in the past, stranded on the island, all our senses were quickened with the sights we saw. Only then did we truly grasp what had vanished from our world. The madman outside this door intended to determine the cause of the loss of the seas and prevent it, for he wished to remake, for twisted reasons of his own, the surface of Barsoom.

"I can tell you that the longer I resided in your time, I became almost of the same mindset. And then I met Arkaff, and I realized I am no Daxxus Nahl. Rather, I shall dedicate my life to reversing the ruin, beginning here, in my own time, where I now comprehend the causes and effects. I have the germ of a plan to do so that has a place for you all, positions that will give meaning to your lives that you might otherwise find lacking as you enter this strangely changed world."

Taking Azaria's hand in his, he rejoined Carthoris and the ambassador, Voss Borgas. With the prisoners tied to one another, they started up the path that led to the cavern in which they had sought shelter from the attacking Banaalians months before, months that felt like years to Dat Voga and Thuria.

After they climbed for some time, they passed through a doorway, guessing it would let into the cave. Instead, they found themselves in a cavernous hangar in the midst of which sat a flier! The padwar guessed this to be the means the unhinged scientist used to kidnap test subjects, and to take what items he required from the world to maintain the laboratory's needed provisions.

Glancing at the scientist whose face registered not a single emotion, Carthoris boarded the vessel. The design harkened to olden times, featuring the angled stabilizers and bizarre curves of a bygone era. But the ship also exhibited several interesting modifications that were futuristic in appearance and practical use.

Originally an open-top passenger flier, the vessel had been modified with the addition of a unique cabin manufactured from Daxxus Nahl's proprietary materials. Opaque on the outside, from the interior one could see clearly through the hull of the ship. It created an odd sensation, as if one were not really separated from his or her surroundings, but rather flying bodiless through the air.

Carthoris, always a speedy learner of anything that could fly, assimilated the controls in a trice and had the engine quietly humming, with only a few oddly configured controls he found he must examine later to decipher their purpose. He motioned the others to board. The questions uppermost in his mind, however, were not relative to the ship, but how they would exit this chamber.

Surrounding them was solid rock. Upon the far wall was an exit that, upon quick examination, proved to be a door leading up a short ramp into the cavern in which they battled the Banaalians. They could exit this way if they must, but then they would have to walk the seventy or eighty haads to Zoquan, even if they could find their way out of the depths of the gorge.

They boarded the flier, finding the interior of the ship roomy and comfortable. Dat Voga and Gar-Noh-Dar secured the prisoners, and then the padwar squatted on his haunches before the scientist.

"Daxxus Nahl," he said, "your crimes are many and grave. It might go easier with you in the courts of Ptarsas were you to assist us in leaving the confines of this gorge." He said no more and rose to his feet, crouching because the low roof of the cabin did not allow him to stand fully erect. Then he resumed his position at the navigator seat where Carthoris continued to examine the controls.

After a moment's pause, the scientist said, "Now see here, Dat Voga. If you are intent on flying my ship, there is a thing or two you might wish to know."

With a slight smile at the idiosyncrasies of this strange enigma of a man, the former sailor of the *Prachus* turned to face his prisoner. "And what might those be, doctor?"

Chapter Thirty-Five

INTO A DEAD WORLD

TO A CASUAL OBSERVER IN THE GORGE, it might have appeared that a ship emerged from solid stone. The entry to the hangar was so cleverly disguised that one could have stood before the opening and been oblivious to its presence. The path through the rock into the gorge consisted of two turns serving to hide the entrance, the tunnel being cunningly concealed and invisible to the vessel's occupants.

The walls and ceiling of the tunnel were lined with a special material to absorb light and sound, and cast neither reflection nor echo. Finally, set in the end of the tunnel was an immense plate of Daxxus Nahl's vibratory glass, the vibrational rate being activated by a control aboard the vessel. Dat Voga shook his head in amazement at the ever-astonishing inventions of the scientist.

The Orovars were excited and frightened at the prospect of flight, after it was explained to them that this type of vessel sailed the skies, not the seas, of Barsoom. The sailors were fascinated spectators and could not turn their heads quickly enough to view the vistas from the air.

Thuria did much to calm them with her quiet confidence, while Azaria, seated near the Heliumite, appeared as tranquil as if she were in her quarters aboard the *Prachus*. But her

235

wide eyes were riveted on the landscape sliding swiftly by below them.

The men of Banaal were finally grasping the significance of these people, for their white skins, quaint dress, and varied-colored hair and eyes were striking in contrast with the common red skin and black hair of modern-day Barsoomians. They did not understand how they had arrived here, of course, and could but stare in mute fascination.

Zat Simpus had been warned by Carthoris that if he opened his venomous mouth he would be tossed peremptorily from the vessel—and it would not be grounded first. The Prince of Banaal had begun to make a retort, but the glint of steel in the other's eyes warned him that the threat from the Heliumite was no idle one.

Azaria and the sailors watched intently through the viewscreens of Daxxus Nahl's flier. Their eyes were held captive by what they saw a thousand sofads below—haad upon endless haad of rolling desert covered in ochre moss, with nary a drop of water or a sprig of any green growing thing in sight.

Their faces reflected their sadness and dejection upon seeing with their own eyes what Dat Voga had already described. To them, their own time existed but moments before, and they found it confounding to grasp that their beloved seas had been gone for over five hundred thousand years. They found it even more incredible to accept that a man from their own time was responsible.

"Just where in the name of the shades could it have all gone?" an incredulous Roh-Du-Von asked, as he grasped at understanding.

Since Zoquan had been their original destination, they turned their craft toward that city and proceeded with all the speed they could muster, which, in Daxxus Nahl's heavily modified flier, was considerable.

Before long, they arrived at the city of Zoquan, passing over many haads of plantations and groves similar to those abounding in Ptarsas. After being told the distance they had traveled, the Orovars were astounded. What this flier covered in moments would have taken them days astride the back of a zytogonth.

After their arrival, Dat Voga and Thuria learned of the recent appearance of fifteen battleships from Helium, and of the efforts expended by Ptarsas and Zoquan in seeking their missing. Tul Torso, Jeddak of Zoquan, met them personally, extending his arms to Thuria, genuinely affected to see her back safe and sound. They also heard of the overtures of war from the Jed of Banaal, who had all but accused Ptarsas of culpability in the vanishing of his son. The lip of Zat Simpus curled in pompous scorn when he heard the news.

Gaff Vlor, padwar of the *Cunning*, upon seeing the haughty expression smeared across the face of his prince, and having taken all he could stomach from this despot, vowed to disclose everything if it would help stem the tide of war from his city from which nothing good could come.

The prince's wrath at the Heliumites, said Gaff Vlor, had been spurred by the rejection he had received at the hand of Princess Tann Dih. This resulted in his plans to shoot down and destroy their vessel once en route to Zoquan, a trip he learned of from an informant in Ptarsas, in order to be revenged upon the men who had, in the prince's mind, heaped insult after insult upon him. This course Zat Simpus pursued until it nearly destroyed them all.

"The Jed of Banaal and his surly son have dragged my country into a decline ever since Simpus Fonn took the seat of power in a coup," Gaff Vlor said. "The incompetent jed forged enemies of those who would be friends and has nearly destroyed our already meager economy to the point where the people are sullen and ready for a change in leadership.

"We Banaalians have sulked for years under his biting rule, biding our time, hoping against hope that his days might be shortened and that a good man might step forward to replace him. But, unlike most of the modern cities of Barsoom, assassination is no longer rampant in these parts as it was in the past, or Simpus Fonn's shoulders might have felt the keen sting of a dagger ere now."

After Gaff Vlor finished his disclosure, Tul Torso had Zat Simpus removed in chains, the prince rending the air with vituperation against Gaff Vlor, who had decided his loyalty came first to his people and his country, rather than to a jed and a prince who had earned neither loyalty nor allegiance.

For Gaff Vlor, and many others like him, having served under the previous jed, hearkened those days to times of peace and prosperity, while the days under Simpus Fonn were considered dark times of corruption, foul deeds, arrogance, and a steady decline in the welfare of their country.

Daxxus Nahl was escorted to a room from which escape was deemed impossible, where he would abide until he could stand trial for his crimes. Gaff Vlor they invited to remain with them, as he had now taken upon his shoulders the mantle of arbiter of peace for Banaal.

Later, Dat Voga observed the tearful reunion of Thuria and her father, Darfa Quan. After hearing only a few instances of the deeds enacted by Dat Voga and Gar-Noh-Dar in the service of his daughter, the man tearfully extended his arm in alliance to both men. With the death of his mate, Thuria and her brother were all the family remaining to him in the world.

As they spoke and made plans to seek out the flotilla from Helium, the sound of excitement and acclaim were heard. Going to a window, Tul Torso exclaimed, "You will not have to go far to seek the ships of Helium, Prince Carthoris, as they are just outside this window!"

Without the palace, a mighty ship was descending while strung out behind her and farther aloft were eleven others. Where the other three vessels were, none in Zoquan knew.

All within the palace, galvanized by excitement at the sight of the magnificent ships, advanced to meet them. The padwar carried a standard displaying the colors of Prince Carthoris and Helium.

The vessel had not quite completed its landing when a small flier shot from its side and spiraled to the courtyard where it came to rest. Carthoris already recognized the markings on the bow. He called excitedly to Dat Voga, "It's my mother!" And then he bolted to meet the vessel, realizing how fraught with worry she must be.

The others followed, but not too closely, realizing his mother would wish a private reunion with her missing son. Dejah Thoris, Princess of Helium, leaped from the vessel as her boy came to a stop before her and smiled. The first words from his mouth were as typical of him as they would have been of his father: "Mother, how is Thuvia?"

The most beautiful woman in the world smiled at her son through tears of relief as she took him in her arms. She replied, "She is well, my son, but she has been deeply concerned for you. As have I."

"I am sorry I worried you," he replied. He knew his mother well enough to understand that she greatly understated her concerns and fears of the past weeks. Dejah Thoris fairly brimmed with questions. Carthoris was quick to fill her in, and great was her amazement after hearing only a few details of Dat Voga's story. When she met the Orovars, her remarkable statecraft became obvious.

She greeted the Orovars with warm familiarity, asking their names, and where they were from. She treated them as if they were citizens of modern society rather than hailing from a culture that had become extinct thousands of years ago, not wishing to cause them remorse or to feel out of place any more than they already did.

After hearing a few of their adventures, she remembered to tell Carthoris that his father had left that morning for Banaal to seek an exchange with the jed there. Gaff Vlor replied, "And if I know the jed, I would guess that he was attacked!"

Dejah Thoris decided to sail for Banaal to inform her mate of the return of nearly all the missing. After learning that Gan-Toh-Gan had been an odar of a sailing vessel in the past, the title being roughly equivalent to the dwar of the modern-day navy, the princess invited him to come along. An intelligent man, he was thrilled to begin learning the intricacies of commanding a vessel of the air.

To begin the statecraft already completed in Ptarsas, Dat Voga and Voss Borgas remained. With them were Azaria, Thuria, and the other sailors. The Orovars were ignorant of the squabbles of these people, and they all wished to remain with the red man who, besides Thuria, was the only person they knew in this strange and unsettling world.

Chapter Thirty-Six

Hope of the Future

DURING THE WEEKS SINCE DEJAH THORIS set sail for Banaal, Dat Voga had not been idle. At last, he was in Zoquan, the second city with which he was to negotiate trade accords. When not spending time with Azaria, for whom his love and affection grew daily, he worked closely alongside Voss Borgas and the diplomats of Zoquan, ironing out the details of a treaty that would benefit all.

Voss Borgas sent for more copies of the contracts and agreements into which Ptarsas had entered, the originals having been destroyed in their crash in the gorge. After perusing these, Zoquan adopted the same accords, with the only modifications being the names of the individuals and the country.

But there were yet many details and minutiae both large and small to cover and understand. Also, there were discussions to be held with the mining community so that, although the negotiations did not take as long as at Ptarsas, by the time they were complete Dat Voga heaved a heavy sigh of relief.

He had now fulfilled all the duties the Council for the Acquisition of Radium had assigned him. He had discovered, opened channels of communications with, and signed treaties and trade agreements with two of the historically largest suppliers of radium—two nations that many of the outside world had, until now, believed to be extinct.

His task had initially been to continue in the role of ambassador to these two cities after opening diplomatic relations, but now he hoped to transfer that honor to someone else, for he had other, more important work before him. It was all he could do to remain in Zoquan to complete the treaties, as he was impatient to begin what he felt would be the most significant work of his life.

While he was still dealing with the Zoquans, at last came the day when the warships of Helium returned. Almost the instant the dreadnought *Tycheus* landed, John Carter sent for Dat Voga. John Carter had already been briefed by Carthoris but wished the padwar to acquaint him with his findings from the past in person and asked him to meet with him at the palace.

The padwar set out for the stateroom where he had been instructed to meet the Warlord. Arriving a bit early, which some might say was unusual for him, he stared out a window, gazing thoughtfully over the royal grounds while he awaited the others. Tars Tarkas entered, followed closely by two other green men, Dostet Beeda being one of them. Each stooped as he entered the short doorway, for the lintel fell far below the crowns of their heads.

"Dat Voga," addressed the Jeddak of Thark. The tall green man approached the padwar, his lower right arm extended in familiar greeting. They clasped one another's shoulder. Dat Voga was delighted to see him again. Not long past, he and Tars Tarkas had sat in a similar chamber in Helium, where the green warrior imparted his savvy statesmanship to the inexperienced, newly appointed ambassador.

"When we spoke last, I assured you that victory lay within your easy grasp. And here you are! Excellent work, ambassador," he assured the man. "However, I had no idea it would take so long!" The two who accompanied Tars Tarkas grinned broadly at their jeddak's playful taunt, for a green man revels in the torment of others, especially that of good friends.

Dat Voga smiled a self-conscious smile. For sure, the venture had taken longer than anyone might have guessed, but it also turned out better than he had hoped. He had discovered the Ptarsans and their stores of radium, true—but more importantly, he had met the woman who now enslaved his heart.

A few moments yet remained before John Carter would arrive, but the green men were curious as to the rumors they had heard from Carthoris regarding Dat Voga's deeds of the past months. They were interested specifically in the fact that he had purportedly met green men one million years ago. He assured them that he had.

He told them about Mab Meebo, Oola Zofta, and Tazzor Gobatt, and spoke with an especial joy about little Donza. But there was an obvious loathing in his voice when he turned to Lodus Voyvott, Poxx Vorka, Laxx Melda and others of the vile jed's devotees. As he spoke of his discussions with Mab Meebo about the differences between their ancient progenitors and the descendants of the green men, he noted the two traveling with Tars Tarkas casting sideways glances.

"You and Mab Meebo are men of kindred spirit, Tars Tarkas," said the padwar. "Take heart—not all the green men were cruel."

The Jeddak of Thark did not immediately reply, and then John Carter and Dejah Thoris arrived. The green men arose, and Tars Tarkas appeared both thoughtful and distant.

"Tars Tarkas, will you not stay to hear Dat Voga regale us with his deeds in the past?" asked John Carter. "This should prove to be a tale worth the hearing, my friend."

"I asked about the green men mentioned by Carthoris," replied the Thark. "I do not think I ever heard anything more disappointing than the foul deeds of my race in their deportment of members of their own kind, and of young

Dat Voga's innocent friends. Nay, I must be content for the nonce as to our young padwar's experiences. Dat Voga, as to your shipmates, I am truly sorry. For now, I must mull what I have learned."

The three green men filed from the room, Tars Tarkas obviously disenchanted with the path taken by his forebears. John Carter, although realizing instantly that something in Dat Voga's tale had upset his good friend, decided not to delve into that yet. He wished to hear the story page by page, as a story should be told, not piecemeal.

Carthoris had told them a few snatches of his friend's story, but he did not have all the details—and besides, this was a story John Carter and Dejah Thoris wanted to hear straight from the thoat's mouth.

Nor were they to be satisfied with the short version. It took the padwar a week to acquaint them with the entire story, in as much detail as he could recall. To recite the story as accurately as possible, he included Thuria and the sailors in these meetings as well, the recounting of which at times became quite lively.

To say that John Carter and the others were astounded would be an understatement. Yet, the evidence was before their eyes in the form of the crew of the *Prachus*, and Azaria, the daughter of a shipbuilder, who all chimed in to tell the tale, adding depth to the narrative from their different perspectives.

When John Carter heard of their harrowing capture and later escape from the green hordes of Nagor, he understood with sharp clarity what had upset Tars Tarkas. It had been these kinds of ideals and thoughts against which Tars Tarkas himself rebelled when he had taken a mate, and later come to know and love his own daughter, Sola—actions that were beyond the pale for green men.

John Carter was much impressed with the Orovars, and he and Gar-Noh-Dar struck up an instant friendship.

With Thuria by his side, the sailor was as happy as a phlega. With his affable manner, he fit in perfectly with his new, contemporary acquaintances, although he admitted he did not understand everything they said. He had much to learn about the modern world, but his was a keen intellect, and none foresaw him having trouble learning anything he put his mind to.

Dejah Thoris held the Orovars in almost godlike veneration. Were they not her glorious ancestors in the flesh, whom she invoked constantly for blessings, protection, and guidance? But they were not all carefree like Gar-Noh-Dar. The astute princess, wise beyond her years, sensed a sorrow that Azaria had revealed to no one. Encouraged by the Princess of Helium, the Horzian girl confessed a deep longing for her parents, who were now lost to her.

The Jeddak of Xanator, she explained to Dejah Thoris, had told her that when she went missing, her father had begun scouring the seas for his daughter, whom he was doomed never to find. The sad tale caused the heart of the princess to go out to this poor, orphaned waif. The girl begged Dejah Thoris to make no mention of her sadness to Dat Voga, for if it had not been for him, they would have all perished. But she could not help mourning the loss of her family, an ache that had yet to dull.

The sorrow of Azaria came as quite a surprise to the princess. She had always imagined her ancestors during the age of the seas as a happy people, living joyful lives during the gayest time of Barsoom's storied past. The princess became heartbroken for the loss suffered by this girl of another time. She realized now that her progenitors were as flawed and delicate as those of modern-day Barsoom, and with every bit as much proclivity for tragedy.

Odar Gar-Noh-Dar's mate had perished years ago, as he reckoned time, and neither Roh-Du-Von nor Bhyda had family awaiting their return—at least, none with whom they were close. Although they were still acclimatizing to the strange atmosphere, the bitterly cold nights, the loss of the seas, and all the other myriad things that were no more, they were happy to be alive.

They considered themselves fortunate to have escaped the horrid fates that seemed certain one moment, only to be altered by Dat Voga in the next—a man who had piqued their curiosity with his intelligence and friendly character, they had never suspicioned he had at his command a million years of evolutionary advancement.

The news soon reached Zoquan that the Jed of Banaal, Simpus Fonn, and his spawn, Zat Simpus, having been dethroned by the forces of Helium, were to stand trial for their crimes. Gaff Vlor was to testify against them.

In the days following their removal from power, hundreds of Banaalian citizens came forward with tales of corruption corroborating Gaff Vlor's accusations. These were assured that they would not be prosecuted for any crimes committed under order of the jed or his churlish son.

Although the evidence against the pair was soon stacked high enough to sentence them each to death many times over, witnesses continued to come forward. It was as though in confessing the crimes they had committed by order of the jed, they cleared their conscience of deeds they found unconscionable, and that now was the time to seek absolution.

When Dat Voga finished relating the epic saga of his adventures to John Carter and his mate, the intuitive Warlord seemed to sense that the padwar had more to add. "Yes, Dat Voga?" he prompted. "You seem a man on the verge of a revelation."

"I am, sir," the padwar admitted. "Warlord, you have been to Ptarsas. Doubtless you flew over their orchards and cultivated tracks?"

"Yes, I did," John Carter confirmed. "I'm convinced that their like exists nowhere else on the planet, but for here, in Zoquan."

"Sir, it is my belief that, together with the radium we so desperately need from these cities, Ptarsas and Zoquan are key to the remediation of the planet."

Dejah Thoris leaned forward, her keen interest obvious in her expression. "Go on, Dat Voga. Tell us everything you are thinking."

"We know that the moss of Arkaff destroyed the seas. I witnessed a successful test of this in his laboratory myself. Armed with that knowledge, I feel that, rather than flee our dying planet, we should instead fight to save it. I believe if the ochre moss is removed, and vegetation reinstituted into the soils, that with careful monitoring and watering, the surface might be reclaimed."

Everything being circular in nature, he posited, with the introduction of large tracts of green, growing things, the atmosphere would thicken and theoretically there should one day be bodies of water on the surface of dying Barsoom again. He explained that, although the seas were currently dry wastelands, in the future they could rise from the dust of the ochre deserts to flourish again, with proper nurturing.

"And who better to take the lead in fostering this new growth," he continued energetically, "than these—our new friends?"

Yet they could not simply set fire to the moss to facilitate its elimination. It would have to be carefully removed from the soil intact, spores and all, and rocketed to the sun where it would be annihilated, that it might not destroy another world. Were they to burn it, the ash and smoke would poison the remaining air and complete the destruction the loss of the oceans had begun.

To that end, the radium they required from these two ancient pillars of civilization would still be required. But, instead of going to fuel ships in which to flee their world, it would be used instead to reclaim it from the dreadful invention of Arkaff of Xanator.

The padwar was forced to take a brief recess from his duties in Zoquan to return to Ptarsas, where the crazed scientist, Daxxus Nahl, who had sunk into a withdrawn state where he spoke only rarely, was to be tried.

At the sentencing, Dat Voga petitioned for the man's life to be spared. Initially, the jeddak wished to have him executed because the testimony and evidence against him was so severe. To Zoquan and Ptarsas, the trial of Daxxus Nahl, revealing as it did the commissions of his many crimes, explained many disappearances over the course of two thousand years.

They deemed the evil man culpable in the crimes of which he was accused, laying many kidnappings and murders at his silent feet, possibly many he had not committed. But throughout his trial, whether or not he committed one crime or another would never be known with any degree of certainty, for he refused to utter a single word in his own defense.

Chapter Thirty-Seven

Back to Xanator

HAVING COMPLETED HIS LAST OBLIGATION to the radium project, Dat Voga, in the company of Azaria, sped toward Helium with all the considerable velocity Daxxus Nahl's antique ship could muster. When he had spoken with John Carter about his reclamation ideas, he had been assured that every resource necessary would be at his fingertips. John Carter recognized in the padwar the earnest zeal and knowledge to accomplish what the young man claimed to be possible.

The fate of a world hinged upon this last and greatest hope. Still, Dat Voga wished to put his proposal before the Council of Science at Helium and allow its members to confirm the course of action, since they composed an international body formed by the allied nations, which now included Ptarsas and Zoquan—all of which he felt to be key parties in the success of his project.

His duty to complete the contracts in Zoquan had delayed his departure, so that he had yet to return home to see his family since returning to the present. They had, however, received word of his safety and that he would be returning home soon. The padwar experienced all the trepidation a man of any world might when about to introduce the woman he loved to his parents.

He hoped that bringing Azaria to bright Helium would

help console her, for he had begun to sense the effects the loss of her family and her world were having, just as had Dejah Thoris. The beautiful girl from Horz had been careful not to express her sorrow, yet the telepathic bond they shared caused him to sense that all was not as it should be.

Dat Voga's present course retraced that taken by him and Carthoris when they flew in search of the region of Ptarsas. Before he realized it, he was approaching the shores of Xanator. It was the first dead city Azaria had seen, having stayed in Zoquan and Ptarsas since her arrival, both of which were beautiful cities. He started to adjust their course to skirt the city, thinking she might find the sight of it distressing, but she laid a restraining hand on his arm.

"No, Dat Voga. I wish to see this," she said, her gaze still locked upon the scene ahead. Out the viewscreen, the city approached rapidly.

"Azaria," he warned. "It is Xanator."

She nodded. "I know the city lies in ruins now, for you have said so. But I must see it with my own eyes."

Azaria sat lost in thought, presumably reminiscing of the days they had spent walking Xanator's enchanting streets beneath shade trees beside stately structures. The padwar made some necessary corrections to his instruments and the fleet little craft sped forward, leaving haad after haad of desert behind them.

Soon they approached the mighty pile that was once the magnificent city they had visited together only months ago—a happy time that now lay far in the past. The man felt a quick stab when he saw the structures. The ache was sharper than he had anticipated. Gods! The years had been cruel.

They saw the pathetic advance of the city into the ancient seabed, now covered in the ochre moss. The advancing quays were a pitiable reminder of the poor, suffering people who had at one time faced the reality of their dying world in confusion, not understanding what was happening, or why. He tried to determine where, in the remains of the original harbor, the *Prachus* had once berthed, but could not.

Their sleek vessel slid slowly through the thin atmosphere above the city, only two hundred sofads above the ground. Azaria's eyes were moist with unshed tears. She sat, her back ramrod straight, turning her head slowly, seeing clearly the decay of ages and the effects of abandonment.

"It really has been a long time since you and I held hands and walked these streets, hasn't it? I thought perhaps if I saw it, it would bring back the joy of that blessed time we spent here. Rather, it confronts me with the destruction my people unwittingly wrought upon our world! But look, Dat Voga, there!"

The man turned his head to follow the direction in which she pointed. Protruding from the ruins of the palace of Py-Noh-Dok was the sole remaining tower, the one he had asked to visit. He directed the ship in that direction and slowed, at the same time increasing their elevation, for the ancient tower reared its lofty head a hundred sofads above their present course.

When they reached the higher elevation, they could see the horrific destruction the roof and the other towers had suffered, their collapse having gutted the center of the building. Azaria touched the red man's arm.

"Dat Voga, do you think Py-Noh-Dok did as he said? That he immortalized the attack on the *Prachus* in that tower? If memory serves me, this is the same tower you wished to visit, the one that was incomplete when we were last here." In a flash of understanding she exclaimed, "That is why you wished to visit that tower! You knew it still stood in your own time!"

The red man nodded. Before she mentioned the mural, he had already wondered the same. When he and Carthoris flew near this tower, he had been strangely drawn to it, straining to peek inside. He had thought at the time how dangerous it would be to moor to the tower, but now he found himself considering it. On a whim, he nudged the control stick.

The craft drifted toward the tower. To avoid their craft making a racket by striking the tower, the man hit a button causing a glass panel utilizing Daxxus Nahl's technology to vibrate into nothing, and extended a hand to the time-stained wall of what once was polished ersite. On the street below, movement indicated the presence of the white apes—beasts he now considered descendants of Arkaff's bordubors. He thought it fitting they haunted Xanator, from which they were spawned.

As the craft grated up against the tower, Dat Voga brought it to a full stop. Within easy reach lay a window casing, an opening letting into the top of the tower. Could this be the very window from which he gazed upon the distant quays as he strained to see the *Prachus* while she sat in the harbor?

He took a mooring rope in hand and loosened his pistol in its holster. "Come Azaria. This time-haunted tower has called out to me thrice now. It did so as Carthoris and I flew past long ago on our way to Ptarsas, it did so when last you and I were here, and it does so again tonight."

He opened the hatch. In the windows not a single pane remained, so making their way inside was a simple matter. The red man entered first, taking out a pocket torch to scan for unwelcome inhabitants. Making the rope fast to an inner wall to prevent the ship from drifting, he extended his hand to Azaria.

Littering the floor were the relics of a bygone era. They selected a wall to explore, looking for the remains of murals. They were not disappointed. The murals had been completed exactly as Py-Noh-Dok swore they would be and were nearly as vibrant as they must have appeared when new, which Dat Voga attributed to the entry being blocked below, the collapse of the roof having prevented visitors here for millennia.

It did not take them long to find what they sought as they made their way about the great circumference of the tower. Soon, they came upon a scene they recognized, the ominous dark blues and greens of the deep sea drawing their eyes like fofals to a flame. They cleared away many objects standing against the wall so they would have an unobstructed view of the painting.

As they began studying the mural, again it became clearer. There were the fish-men. A prehistoric brobdoganth surged surfaceward, a look of destruction incarnate engraved on its face. The sea swam with pasty fish-men, captured in perfect detail, who pulled men beneath the waves to drown, or to slaughter with fang and talon; the indistinct bottom of a vessel could be seen above.

As they proceeded along the curving wall, the mural continued, and only then did the padwar truly feel the weight of the ages upon his youthful shoulders. For there, in vivid scarlet pigment, he saw depicted a red man, deep beneath the surface. The figure tangled with a fish-man, the pair locked in a grim and silent battle.

Then the tide of the engagement turned as the mural swept around the curving surface of this lone remaining tower of Py-Noh-Dok. Now, the bodies of fish-men floated grimly in the cool waters of Throxeus, which were tinted in brighter and lighter shades of blue, as if the artist wished to depict the scene in a more exultant mood—that of victory.

On the surface of the sea the figure of the red man, his arm extended in a peremptory command, urged on the brobdoganth. The enormous fish turned upon its erstwhile masters, rending and devouring them.

Lastly, upon the fantail of the *Prachus*, leaning over the

rail with her hands extended in fright and supplication toward the red man in the sea, stood the lissome figure of an Orovar maiden who could be none other than Azaria. Her glorious body and hair, and her unmistakably beautiful face, were all captured in wonderful, almost lifelike likeness and detail.

"Shades of my first ancestor," breathed Dat Voga. Azaria, too, was stunned.

It was incomprehensible, yet the paintings were there on the walls before them. And apparently, the historians with whom they had spoken, and for whom they had described the event, had visited the harbor to see the *Prachus* with their own eyes, as the ship in the mural was portrayed with striking accuracy.

When she saw that final panel, Azaria cried out, "Oh, Dat Voga! Father's ship!" And she burst into tears, her slender frame racked with woe and irreparable loss. She had held back her tears for months, but this last reminder unleashed her despair in all its fullness. The man held her tightly. Her face was buried against his chest as he stared at the detailed rendering of the newest ship of the sea trader, Hal-Roh-Kim of Horz.

As he comforted Azaria, his eyes still enslaved by the mural, a sound that had hitherto gone unnoticed impinged on his senses. Shushing her as gently as he could, he strained his ears to their utmost. There! He heard it again!

A raspy sound, a slight exhalation perhaps, from down the deep, inky blackness of the access well, which he had incorrectly guessed to be choked with debris from the collapse of the roof and most inner portions of the palace. White apes were sneaking up the winding hall of the tower!

"Come, Azaria," hissed the padwar. Grabbing her hand, he drew her toward the window through which their waiting ship hovered. They stumbled over various objects littering the floor in their haste, Azaria causing a tall object to fall with a crash. A low, audible growl answered the sound from below, followed by the sound of rushing feet.

Azaria knew not what creatures came from below, but she understood from Dat Voga's haste that they were in grave danger. At the window opening, she stepped out into space toward the waiting vessel. But the ship had drifted, pushed away from the wall, perhaps by Azaria's foot when she had disembarked earlier.

Falling forward with a gasp, she reached outward and narrowly grasped the top edge of the entrance to the ship. Dat Voga's heart leaped into his throat as he clutched futilely at the girl, but fortunately, she had already saved herself.

The man reached out to steady the craft, listening all the while to the sound of thudding feet drawing nearer. After what seemed an eternity, Azaria scrambled aboard. The man started out the window when a deafening roar filled the room atop the tower from behind him.

Those who have heard the hideous shriek of a great white ape at night in close proximity know that it will shatter the nerves of the most steadfast, causing the hair on the neck and arms to stand stiffly erect with a sudden jab of uncontrollable dread. Without a glance behind, Dat Voga dove headforemost across the widening gulf between the tower and the open hatch.

Slamming the hatch shut, he leaped for the controls, then recalled that the ship was still moored to the tower. They could go nowhere! A rough buffet came from the hatch, as of a heavily taloned hand on the hull. Although the beast's vision could not pierce the opaque windows of the flier, Azaria, with the aid of the light-gathering coatings upon the viewscreens, saw clearly the hideous face of the enraged ape.

Its breath fogged the transparent skin of the craft as the woman obtained her first glimpse of this scourge of modern-day Barsoom, the sight of which called instantly to mind the time she had been captured by a bordubor. She knew the beast could neither see her nor reach her, yet still she recoiled backward to the deck of the ship. Involuntarily, she cried out in fear.

Since he could not go outside to release the cord, the padwar punched a button below one of the portals, hoping he could reach the tether with his sword. Risking being grabbed by the great beast, he slid his sword through the vibrating glass as if through tenuous vapor, hoping he could reach it. He slashed at the tether. His ancestors were with him, for with a single slice, he severed it.

The vessel, jostled and buffeted by the antics of the ape, drifted away from the tower. Tossing its head back, the ape faced Cluros, the farther moon, and gave voice to a roar of frustrated rage as its prey darted away into the darkness that had descended over the ruins. Once more had Dat Voga narrowly escaped the doom that haunted this city. Now he determined he would not stop until they were safe in Helium, for he carried precious cargo.

Thinking of that dear passenger, he glanced at the young woman seated beside him. Almost otherworldly was her beauty. The dim radiance of the craft's instruments cast a soft glow on her skin and highlighted the mass of locks descending in waves to shoulder and breast. Although youthful, her body had begun to reveal the curves of maturity, curves that his eyes followed with the apprecia-tion of a man in love with a maid.

He was reminded that he had never declared for her in the customary manner in which a man asks a woman to become his mate. He had thought to wait until they arrived in Helium, but this recent encounter reinforced the uncer-tainty of the future. He could wait no longer, although his heart was in his throat as he choked out the words that he had waited a million years to speak.

"Azaria?"

"Yes, Dat Voga?"

"You know now why I could not declare for you while we were in your time. I feared what might happen were we to become mates in what, for me, is the past. When I brought you to my time, I felt the press of duty to complete the work I had begun. Later, you were understandably grief-stricken over the loss of your family and your world. I did not wish to burden you to make such an important decision while the loss of your world was fresh in your heart."

The young woman's chest rose and fell as her breathing accelerated. Was it the thinness of the air? Was she angry with him? Perhaps she no longer was interested in pursuing a relationship. Maybe the playfulness she exhibited in the early days of their budding friendship was only that—friendliness, and no more.

"And now, Dat Voga?" she barely whispered.

"And now I can no longer wait, Azaria!" he continued passionately, before his courage fled. "This is the present and the future is unwritten, for we are writing it now. My sword lies at your feet, where it has lain since that moment I discovered your bright spirit on your father's ship. Sweet girl, I ask you—will you become my mate? Will you be the princess of my heart and body and soul?"

And then Dat Voga waited with bated breath for the woman of his dreams to answer, just as had countless other youths since the beginning of time, on every planet from the center of the universe to its outermost edge.

Her look was one of surprise, for his pronouncement had come unexpectedly. But her hesitation lasted only long enough for her to comprehend what it was he was asking of her. And then she smiled, and through tear-filled eyes, she said, "My chieftain! I thought you would never ask."

Though a million years had once separated them, Dat Voga kissed the lips of the woman he loved without fear of the repercussions his kiss would have through time. In fact, he looked forward to the cascading effects of that kiss.

The remaining distance to Helium passed quickly for

the two, who had for months restrained their love while the woman grieved and the man answered the call of duty. With seemingly endless days before them, they planned for their future.

He told her of his ideas to remediate the surface of Barsoom utilizing the nigh-miraculous prowess of the Ptarsans and Zoquans, who were apparently created by the gods for the sole purpose of growing things from the soil. As he laid out his plans in animated fashion, he looked into her admiring eyes and felt a surge of confidence and hope for the future, for it was clear from her expression what she was thinking: that if there existed any man on the planet who could conceive these things and make them a reality, it was the man she loved.

Chapter Thirty-Eight

A Daunting Task

MANY MONTHS HAD SLIPPED PAST since Dat Voga and Azaria arrived at Helium, and much of note had happened. A full year had passed since the small group escaped from the laboratory in the gorge of Ptarsas.

The padwar's reunion with his family had been poignantly bittersweet. He was thrilled to be once again in his ancestral home and happy to see his kin, yet never had he guessed how he would feel when he introduced his parents and sister Vala to Azaria, knowing that her own family was as lost to her as if they had never been.

Dat Voga had seen to it that his immediate family was thoroughly versed with Azaria's backstory, for he wanted no awkward questions for her. He knew she still pined for her loved ones, and thus sought to prevent any unkind reminders of the past. Being a scientist, he naturally racked his mind constantly for a way to fill her cup.

Azaria, though, fell instantly in love with his family, and she and Vala, who were of the same age, became fast friends. The day they met, Vala exclaimed, "Oh, Azaria! Your hair! I've never even dreamed of such a color . . . I love it!"

That was all it took. Hand in hand, the two wandered into a garden his father maintained at the back of their property, chattering like a couple of phlegas, just as she and

Thuria once did aboard the *Prachus*. The red man heaved a sigh of relief. He had feared that meeting his family might remind her of her loss. But his charming sister's greeting had been perfect, permitting no time for reflection.

His ideas for the soil-reclamation project had given him the idea for a botanical getaway, a place more like the Barsoom she loved. He had yet to work out the details, but he anxiously awaited the day he could begin. Until then, his current responsibility must be moss remediation. The project must be in capable hands before he could allow himself the luxury of building the retreat, so he decided to delay mentioning it until nothing stood in the way of making it a reality.

Eventually his project of reclamation approached the point that it no longer necessitated the degree of his own presence it had required in the preliminary stages. He had expended a substantial amount of time in a test area with members of the Council of Science, which included experts from Zoquan and Ptarsas. One of the latter was his friend Ran Tasis.

Dat Voga, upon seeing once again his good friend from Ptarsas, decided that none other than Ran Tasis should take his place as overseer of the project, which was now officially under the aegis of the Council of Science as the Project for Moss Remediation and Soil Reclamation.

They had carefully removed the moss from an area consisting of half a square haad. One of the new unmanned, disposable spacecraft, piloted by a mass-produced version of the telepathic brain and fueled with ore freshly mined in Ptarsas, left the atmosphere, watched by the eager eyes of the assembly on magnifying viewscreens. Inside, it carried a payload of moss on a one-way trip to the sun.

They did not wish to risk any of the moss remaining, and this was the only way they could assure themselves that it did not remain upon Barsoom, and also would not accidentally contaminate another world and begin a new cycle of devastation on the soil there.

The telepathically programmed brain, the creation of Fal Sivas, which had figured so prominently when John Carter infiltrated the assassins' guild in Zodanga, had been deemed the most logical solution to ensure that no mishaps occurred in the removal of the moss from the planet, nor in the traversal of the immensity of space that must be crossed to its destination.

The mechanical brains of these ships could be instructed to fly toward the center of the sun, avoiding all obstacles, and the vessels would do so, although obviously they would never reach the belly of old Sol before being destroyed. Scientists all over the planet eagerly watched this first voyager with farseeing telescopes using special filters, as the lone vessel sped its way into the surface of the star, destroying itself along with its cargo of life-sucking moss.

The area where the moss had been removed was reseeded, bringing to bear the almost godlike powers of the people of remote Ptarsas and Zoquan. Already it was yielding the fruits of their labor. Their only regret now was that more seeds of the green, life-giving vegetation lost to time were not available.

Dat Voga knew what it felt like to walk through the waving, now-extinct, primordial grasses of prehistoric Barsoom, and lamented the fact that there were not more varieties of these on hand. But the trees they had from Ptarsas were far better than the moss, and for the first time in hundreds of thousands of years this soil would finally start retaining moisture.

The process of clearing the test area took months of grueling labor to ensure that not a single spore remained. When they considered that more than half of the surface of their world required remediation, some two hundred and four million square haads, they realized it would take thousands of generations to complete the daunting task. Dat Voga would never live to see it, yet he hoped a future Barsoom would eventually be very much like that ancient version in the past with which he had fallen in love.

The effort would require delving into corners of their world that had not been visited in millennia. When they discussed the possibilities of the discovery of other lost peoples and forgotten cities, the eyes of John Carter took on their familiar brightness as he imagined these new vistas begging exploration. The Earthman was always eager to peer over the next horizon toward the unknown.

The evening of that first launch carrying a load of moss to the sun, Dat Voga stood on the balcony outside his sleeping chambers. The suite, located in the Greater Helium's lofty scarlet tower, was a joining gift from the Princess of Helium and the Warlord of Barsoom.

Humbled, the padwar sought to dissuade them, maintaining that it was far too generous. But John Carter insisted that the young man had earned it. He had saved the life of their son from the hands of a madman and given the citizens of Barsoom the hope of saving their world with the information he had brought from the past.

It had been Dat Voga's idea to use the combined technologies of Helium, Ptarsas, and Zoquan for the soil remediation, and his suggestion to use the ships and the mechanical-brain invention of Fal Sivas to facilitate the removal of the ochre moss from the planet. No longer did they plan for a future mass exodus from Barsoom, for that had been supplanted by the hope of saving it. Instead of fleeing a desert world, they now had their sights set on the reclamation of their ancient seas.

Toward this goal, Dat Voga worked nonstop. He discussed his findings at length with the Council of Science, which now included members of Banaal, who had elected a descendant of the previous royal family as their new jed and had themselves now joined the allied ranks of united city-states.

Azaria lay asleep, nestled within silks and furs to ward off the cool night air, to which, she swore, she would never become acclimated, being accustomed as she was to the equatorial warmth of the dim past's climate. They had a beautiful ceremony where they were joined with the golden chains of matrimony, which Dat Voga's family, their mutual friends, and many of the padwar's peers in the navy and Council of Science had attended.

Dejah Thoris, who had become quite close to the beautiful Horzian girl, had insisted on hosting their ceremony at the palace. Azaria had been thrilled to see the sailors from the *Prachus* together with Thuria, who had all traveled from Zoquan for the event. Thuria told her friend that she and Gar-Noh-Dar were planning their own joining ceremony, which they discussed at length.

From where he now stood, Dat Voga gazed in wonder at his beautiful mate as she slept, soft moonlight bathing her features. They were so happy, yet still he hoped to overcome her grief at the loss of her world and her parents. He heard a light rap at their door and, not wishing to have it repeated lest it waken her, he grasped a slender dagger and went to answer the summons.

At the door stood a member of the guard, acting as escort for a man he knew well—Ran Tasis of Ptarsas. Closing the door to their sleeping chamber, Dat Voga escorted the Ptarsan to a small anteroom where they could speak without fear of awakening Azaria.

"Kaor, Dat Voga," Ran Tasis began once they were seated. "I apologize for coming thus unannounced and so late, but I have urgent news I knew you would wish to hear at once. And as it is of utmost importance, I wished to bring it before you myself. Daxxus Nahl is dying. He appears to age years each day, wasting away before our eyes, and our brightest physicians are powerless to stop it.

"As you are aware, after his trial in Zoquan, he was taken to Ptarsas where he also stood trial. After he was found guilty on all charges there as well, our two cities agreed that he would be interned there. On the heels of that internment, a change began to occur that our greatest medical minds have been unable to stem.

"He understands what is happening, and possibly how to stop it, but he will not aid us. All he will say is that he wishes to speak to you. Oddly enough, the more his physical condition deteriorates, the more lucid he becomes. I have come to ask if you will return with me. I realize it might be difficult, but I promised him I would encourage your visit."

The scientist did not need to ponder his answer long before deciding it best that he accompany Ran Tasis to visit his former jailer. He knew not what the enigmatic Daxxus Nahl might have to say to him that could be of such import, but he replied, "Yes, of course I shall come. We shall leave in the morning. I'll bring Azaria along with me so she can visit Thuria and the others."

Chapter Thirty-Nine

Daxxus Nahl Tells His Story

A FEW DAYS LATER found Dat Voga standing at the door of the room of Daxxus Nahl, his late warden and jailer. His hand paused upon the latch. What would he find behind this door? Squaring his shoulders, he rapped lightly and entered. The door closed with an audible *click*, and he heard the Ptarsan guard in the hall lock it behind him.

The room contained skylights set with thick glaze and narrow, vertical slits running up its single outside wall, to allow in light and air. The wall slits were only wide enough to pass a hand through if one turned it edgewise. The Heliumite doubted if it would have bothered the ancient scientist had there not been any sunlight or fresh air at all, as the man had lived most of his life within the stony bowels of the planet, shut away from the outer world.

There were many growing things within the room, vines and such, which climbed toward the skylights. The room was devoid of furniture save for a chair fixed to the floor; this faced the sleeping dais, obviously set in place for visitors. Upon this dais reposed the dying scientist.

Dat Voga could hardly contain a gasp of astonishment when he saw the changes that had been wrought in the man since their last encounter. The figure on the dais could scarcely be recognized as Daxxus Nahl. Gone was the large, youthful, vigorous body with the strength of two powerful men.

He lay withered, his eyes sunken and cloudy. Apparently his hearing had deteriorated as well, for nearly a full xat passed while Dat Voga stood stock-still and took in the scene. Only when the Heliumite found the courage to approach the dais did the withered man note his presence. The man turned his head slowly to greet his visitor.

"The difference in my appearance must be alarming indeed, Dat Voga, to elicit such an expression from you," he croaked. Even his voice sounded aged.

The padwar picked up a vessel of water standing upon one of the immense armrests of the wooden chair and poured a libation for the man. He could not help but recall the time he had been imprisoned in a cell in the gorge, awakening from the induced sleep imposed by this man, who had then fetched him a drink of water from a machine that manufactured it seemingly from thin air.

"I must admit, Daxxus Nahl, it is a shock to see you thus. The last I saw, you some months ago, you—" He stopped, realizing there was no need to vocalize the obvious. He then continued, "What has wrought this great change? Have you no idea?"

"Oh yes, young Dat Voga," the ailing man said weakly, "I know precisely what is back of this. It is the lack of the longevity serum, a supply of which I have been deprived these past two years. And now nature takes her awful course. For seventeen hundred years I took that serum, never realizing it contained a design flaw, an imperfection that destroyed my mind and twisted my mental faculties,"

"I was so satisfied with the longevity and physical enhancements that I allowed those side effects to blind me to the darker ones lurking beneath the surface. And as long as I took the serum, I would have never seen it. There is no telling what might have happened to Barsoom had you not arrived when you did.

"Dat Voga," the man rasped, "there are several reasons why I wished you to come see me. Heed. Soon I shall perish. But before I do so, I wish to attempt to make up to you and others for the awful man I once was. In my current state, I see clearly what I could not see before. I know it may sound presumptuous and arrogant to say what I am about to say, but I have no reason to doubt my abilities.

"I am confident that I would have succeeded in my plan to destroy modern civilization by going into the past and restoring the seas. This, as you well know, would have re-shaped history. I am only grateful to my ancestors that, with the depletion of the serum in my system, my mind has returned, albeit too late.

"I underestimated your mighty intellect. It should have come as no surprise when you told me you had awakened from a dream in which you solved the modulation issue with the nexus. You've the mind of a genius, young Dat Voga. I have no doubt you will go on to do many wonderful things. I wish it had been different, and that we might have truly worked together as peers. After all, can there be any limitations to what two scientists such as you and I, who have conquered time itself, might accomplish?

The padwar decided to enlighten the dying man as to how he had been able to orchestrate the stabilization of the power source. At this point, Daxxus Nahl could do no harm with the knowledge. "You might be interested to know that your spheron filter was the culprit that caused the instability of the field. I had the notion that the field, which in its natural state is as powerful, chaotic, and frenzied as a solar flare, must be used in that same manner. Filtering it diluted its power and unwavering focus.

"Gods, you are right!" choked the dying, old man. His murky eyes stared as if he were back in the gorge before one of his control consoles. "The solution is so simple in hindsight that I never considered it, guessing the solution to be one of infinite complexity. As to why I summoned you, I wish to apologize, as I did to Thuria and Voss Borgas. Carthoris, also, have I spoken with, who has been much in Ptarsas of late. The Banaalians I am not concerned with."

"And I accept your apology, doctor," the young man said earnestly, for he found it difficult to hold a grudge against a man who had been responsible for him meeting the woman he loved. "You were not in your own mind. I am curious, though, as to what drove you to such lengths to revise the past," the Heliumite replied. "I mean, your motive for wishing to revise the past."

The scientist had hinted at, but never divulged, his reasons for the diabolical plot. The old man smiled, closing his eyes in reminiscence. "It was the loss of my true love, Dat Voga. What else might drive a man so?" The smile left his voice, replaced by a wooden tone, as if speaking of something he never thought to vocalize.

"She was destroyed in an instant by an assassin's dagger over fifteen hundred years ago, in Zoquan. I had already invented and distilled the serum of longevity, and we looked forward to multiple lifetimes together. I was successful, I was in love, and in a moment of time, I lost it all. I entered the room just as he slid his blade from her breast—the shiny steel, besmeared with her life's blood. Her beautiful eyes were already losing the light of life as her arms reached out imploringly for me and then fell limp in death.

"I stood between her killer and the door. She was his last victim. None heard the screams of agony the man released over the period of two weeks which, at the time, were as many as I could elicit from him while keeping him alive. Today, I could have kept him alive indefinitely. But he revealed to me everything he knew about who had hired him, and why. They, too, suffered for days on end.

"A rival had sought to eliminate the competition and so sent an assassin to my home, not realizing I was not there. She must have surprised him. Her killer, thinking it was I who had come upon him, thrust his dagger before he made certain of his target's identity. He made a mistake! It was not I, but she! That mistake cost him his life and later, the lives of his entire family were also forfeit, as well as those of the man who hired him. It was these upon whom I practiced the dark arts of torment, for *I* was in torment."

The weakening old man went into a paroxysm of coughing. Dat Voga saw some of the scientist's old fire as he finished his astonishing confession. "Daxxus Nahl, I did not mean to reopen old wounds. I am sorry."

"It is of no import, young Dat Voga," the old man replied. "In a way, it is a relief and a weight off an old man's shoulders to finally confide in someone. No, I am glad you asked the question. It also makes it easier to tell you the rest I have to say."

Daxxus Nahl proceeded to speak of his immense volume of work that, although he had led the padwar to believe he held it all stored in his head, was in actuality carefully documented in a series of journals kept down through the centuries by one who had forgotten more inventions than most could credit to their names.

The old man did not wish this information to be lost to civilization, to rot in the gorge, undiscovered. As part of his atonement, he wished to dedicate his discoveries and inventions toward the amelioration of suffering and the betterment of mankind, the exact things Dat Voga had importuned him so passionately about once upon a time, which at the time caused the scientist to fly into a rage.

"The laboratory, Dat Voga—it is yet intact?"

"Yes, Daxxus Nahl, it is safe," the younger man responded. "The jeddak sealed the laboratory against the future, the current initiative to reclaim Barsoom in an attempt to save our planet and restore the natural wonders of her past taking precedence. Why do you ask?"

"Because," rasped the other. "I wish you to have my journals. Also, I wish to be sealed inside the cave in a state of stasis until such time as society might deem fit to pardon me—if they would ever consider it—at which point I want you to bring me back to consciousness and restore me to health with a redesigned serum!"

Dat Voga was incredulous and said so. "But there is no possibility of getting Ras Thavas here in time to perform the stasis. You might die before he could be located and convinced to come here. He can be quite the most irascible—"

Daxxus Nahl snorted. "That quack? He was an arrogant boor when I met him, and I would not let him touch me! Besides, he might transfer my brain into a white ape, where I merely wish my body placed into stasis. I have a method of my own, perfected fifteen hundred years ago, that utilizes a sealed chamber and a special gaseous compound that I created, believe it or not, to store provisions so they would not spoil."

The eyes of the brilliant scientist stared into space. "I have not used the method for fifteen hundred years."

And then he came to himself and continued. "Now see here, Dat Voga. If you agree, it will remain to you to broach the subject to the Ptarsans and the Zoquans. And toward that end, you might wish to tell them I have volumes on the subjects that are nearest and dearest to their hearts— horticulture. One learns many things in the course of twenty-five hundred years."

The Heliumite found the Ptarsans more agreeable to the idea than he would have guessed. They were already impressed with the man's brilliance, and the thought of the buried knowledge contained in the scientific notebooks he had hidden away they found intriguing. It was agreed that they and the Zoquans would obtain all journals relating to horticulture while the remainder would be turned over to the Council of Science in Greater Helium.

They were adamant, though, that this act did not redeem him nor free him from his debt to society. They agreed, however, that rather than letting him perish in imprisonment within, quite possibly, the next few days, he could finish his term indefinitely in the condition of stasis.

The Ptarsans were now in control of the hidden entry, having had a new, impenetrable barrier installed. The lower cave entrance, which Dat Voga had disclosed to them, was now sealed, and so too were the ventilation shafts. The scientist would not be revived without going through an appellate process with the Ptarsan and Zoquan governments. To all of this, Daxxus Nahl agreed.

Chapter Forty

INTERNMENT IN PTARSAS

DAT VOGA, ASSISTED BY RAN TASIS, loaded a frail Daxxus Nahl aboard the antique flier. Ran Tasis would accompany them to bear witness that Daxxus Nahl entered a condition of stasis satisfactory to the respective governments, and that the promised journals were turned over. The remaining journals Dat Voga was to deliver to the Council of Science in Greater Helium that they might benefit all.

In short order, they found themselves entering the gate in the Ptarsan Gorge, a seal set in place by the Ptarsans, a solid forandus door of prodigious dimensions that could be opened only by sending a series of precise, telepathic frequencies at specific intervals. These frequencies were administered by Ran Tasis.

After the door slid into its recess, the padwar touched a button in the flier that dissolved the original thick glass barrier installed by Daxxus Nahl by setting it to vibrate at a specific frequency. Moments later, they disembarked from the vessel in the cavernous docking bay inside the gorge.

It was with a grim sense of resolve that Dat Voga found himself again treading the paths and ways inside the rent in the planet crust where Daxxus Nahl had built his retreat. Before they ventured too far, Ran Tasis flipped several switches that powered up the electrical systems, including new ventilation machinery, as the old vent system had been sealed off.

The decrepit scientist, unable to walk, was propelled in a contrivance that floated off the floor, using buoyancy tanks filled with the eighth Barsoomian ray of gravitational repulsion. This contrivance Dat Voga now guided through the many twists and turns and down the many ramps, tramping ever deeper into the bowels of the planet.

They passed through the darkened laboratory where Dat Voga spent so many months working with the scientist, past the now-unoccupied cells where he and the others had been incarcerated, when the scientist finally directed them to his former quarters. The Heliumite recognized the room, although he had been in it but once, and that briefly, the time he stole the gauntlets and equilibrimotor belt.

"Would you move that shelf there, Ran Tasis?" directed the hushed voice of the weakened man.

Ran Tasis did as he was bid, moving a tiered shelf to the side after carefully removing the books and objects from the shelves. Behind it was a blank, stone wall carved from the base rock of the cliff.

Daxxus Nahl said, "Cast the key that opens the door to the upper levels, Dat Voga. My mind is too weak. I am failing fast. We must hurry."

As directed, the padwar sent the same frequency he had used with the door that led to the upper areas of the underground complex. With a grating sound, a portion of the wall slid to one side, the miniscule irregularities of the stone face having served to disguise the edges of a door.

When the way was clear, the trio proceeded into the room, in which a soft illumination had been automatically triggered. Dat Voga and Ran Tasis gasped when they saw the contents of the hidden asylum. Along both walls, from floor to ceiling, and for the length of approximately forty sofads, were shelves lined with books.

Dat Voga selected a volume at random, opening it to

find neat hieroglyphs in the writing form of Daxxus Nahl. The journal was titled *The Manipulation of Molecular Datum*. Setting it back on the shelf, he noted that the journals were not placed on the shelves by happenstance, but that devices categorized each section. The volumes contained an immeasurable wealth of knowledge.

While he and Ran Tasis became engrossed, gazing through this library of technological notations, Daxxus Nahl eagerly propelled himself toward the far end of the room, where he paused and glanced upward at a certain shelf. He called out to the Heliumite. "Come here, Dat Voga."

As the padwar stopped beside the fast-failing scientist, Daxxus Nahl pointed a shaky finger toward a shelf. "You must study these." His voice quaked with the effort it took to utter those few words.

Selecting a group of eight or ten volumes from the shelf, the Heliumite was intrigued to see written along one spine the words *My Discovery of the Magno-GraviSpheronic Nexus*. "Naturally, that last volume is unfinished," said Daxxus Nahl weakly. "It is you, Dat Voga, who shall write those final chapters—not I."

Nearby, another volume covered the discovery of the time-modulation variance, in detail. The padwar reeled in astonishment. He held in his hands all the information required to construct a time-modulating power source, including the gauntlet capacitors he yet retained.

Ran Tasis had become fascinated with a large cache of material devoted to horticulture, complete with the descriptions of long-extinct species. The volumes contained seeds in tiny packets bound with the diaries. Ran Tasis gasped as he realized the significance of what he held. To his people, these were priceless.

In amazement, he turned his head toward the aging scientist. "This is astounding. If anyone doubted the veracity of your claim to be twenty-five hundred years old, one need only browse these journals, in your handwriting, and see the seeds of varieties that have been extinct for two thousand years, many of which not a shred of evidence remains but pictures in murals! It is remarkable!"

The old scientist smiled a rare smile. "It is merely a speck compared to the knowledge of the Ptarsans, Ran Tasis. Yet, it gladdens me to see they are appreciated. Now, you two shall have all the time in the world to peruse these diaries, but my time grows shorter by the tal. If one of you will depress this button, we shall begin my internment."

Dat Voga set his load of journals back on their shelf and pressed the indicated button. Silently, a door slid aside to reveal another chamber. Soft lighting, cast from sources on the walls and ceiling, gently encroached on the shadows. But the greatest radiance came from a section of glass embedded in the right-hand wall, a blue glow that cast itself toward the rear of the hidden vault and bathed the chamber in soft luminescence. They entered the vault.

Dat Voga noted that Daxxus Nahl's gaze was glued to the glowing glass panel as he guided him forward. They proceeded toward the rear of the room until they stood before the polished glass set in the virgin bedrock of the gorge.

The two young men started when they saw the perfectly still body of a beautiful, nude young woman. She hovered in midair, her floating hair cascading in all directions about her, not entirely hiding her face, yet not quite revealing it, either. But, although her long, wild locks held the appearance of motion from sheer disarray, not a hair moved from its place, each strand held frozen in a moment of time.

Tiny areas of distortion were visible in the sarcophagus—which Dat Voga now presumed this to be, for the young woman appeared to be deceased. Beneath one perfect, pendulous breast they could see a small incision, yet no blood flowed; nor had it for more than a millennium. Dat Voga knew this woman to be the mate of Daxxus Nahl, slain by an assassin's blade over fifteen hundred years before.

The preservation of the corpse was astounding. The gas

that filled the chamber contained a slightly bluish cast which caused the woman's red skin to reflect a soft, purple color, while her hair had the appearance of a deep purplish-black.

At first, Dat Voga believed some form of lighting within the cavity caused the glow. Then it became apparent that the radiance emanated from whatever pellucid, gaseous substance filled the space. Tiny sparkles of luminescence caused the interior of the sarcophagus to have the appearance of a miniaturized void of star-filled space, giving the woman's body the illusion of immensity in a coffin full of galaxies.

"Daxxus Nahl?" the padwar began to inquire.

"Yes, Dat Voga, you guess right," he croaked. "It is Tala Trerra. Is she not beautiful? Ah, young man, love is such a strange thing. You hate today, and yet tomorrow your anger cools. But when you truly, genuinely love, it is forever. I love that woman as if it were but yesterday that we were joined in a ceremony at her parents' home."

The old man gazed back through the centuries to that distant day. The two others stood there, gazing upon the form of a beautiful woman, struck down in her youth—or at least, the appearance of youth. They stood there in silence with their tongues cleaved to the roofs of their mouths, for it was a pitiful tale, and they knew not what to say to the heartbroken scientist.

Without further preamble, Daxxus Nahl said, "It may require both of you to place me into this receptacle. Pay attention, although the instructions are hardly complex. I prepared for this moment many years ago but did not expect to enter this tomb with the possibility of coming back out. Rather, I envisioned crawling inside and activating the gas, the details of which lie in a volume just outside this room, and joining my beloved in death. Yet now the situation is more complicated."

The scientist then described how it would proceed and exactly what would occur. It was important for Ran Tasis,

She hovered in midair, her floating hair cascading in all directions about her.

as the official representative of justice from his country, to understand the details so he could report back to certain officials in Ptarsas. A gaseous substance, engineered by Daxxus Nahl, would be administered that would render him unconscious—a cousin of the fumes he had released upon the combatants in the lower cavern once upon a time.

Once he lost conscious, the unique preservative gas would be released. This would instantly seal the cells of his body at an atomic level, completely halting any cellular change or decay. Controls on the face of the wall could reverse the process, should that day come.

Alone, the padwar easily lifted the frail and wizened body of the rapidly waning scientist and placed him inside the receptacle upon the slab. With Dat Voga's finger hovering over the button that would resolidify the glass, the same as that used in Daxxus Nahl's prison cells, the scientist spoke his last words.

"I hope to see your face again someday. Mayhap by then you will have figured out what is wrong with the serum. If not, then this is farewell, Dat Voga." The old man closed his eyes and reposed.

Dat Voga pressed the button, sealing the sarcophagus, then proceeded with the instructions as prescribed by Daxxus Nahl, with Ran Tasis witnessing every action. They could tell when the soporific had been administered as they watched the scientist relax. Instruments monitoring his vitals displayed a slowing heart rate. The padwar placed his finger over the final button that would release the gas and preserve the body—only this time it would not preserve a corpse, but a living man.

The Heliumite muttered, "Farewell, Daxxus Nahl." And he pushed the button.

The gas appeared slowly, gathering as if thickening toward the outer corners. It could be detected only because the gas, although at first transparent, caused visible distortions. When it reached the scientist, his body lifted from the floor of the burial chamber as if by invisible forces until it rested in the center, suspended in midair exactly as was the form of Tala Trerra, the gas obviously possessing a gravity-suppressing property.

As the frigid gas pumped into the chamber, it began to assume the same purplish cast as in Tala Trerra's tomb. As if birthed under pressure, tiny corpuscles of light began to glow here and there until Daxxus Nahl's body floated amid miniscule constellations. The body moved about as it settled into a natural position, appearing as light as a balloon. But when a light came on to indicate the sequence had completed, the body moved no more. And then not even a hair on Daxxus Nahl's head drifted in that still place.

Chapter Forty-One

A Letter to Val Statt

DAT VOGA WAS QUIET on the return trip to Ptarsas. He and Ran Tasis had stowed the library of scientific journals on their craft, many of which were destined for the governments of Ptarsas and Zoquan as part of the conditions of Daxxus Nahl's sentence. The remaining volumes were destined for the Council of Science, including the journals Daxxus Nahl pointed out to Dat Voga regarding the Magno-GraviSpheronic Nexus.

These volumes the Heliumite had a mind to retain in his possession to study for a time. He considered the possibility of finishing the incomplete volume, as Daxxus Nahl suggested, since of all living men, he alone held the requisite experience and knowledge to do so. Upon leaving the hangar, Ran Tasis entered once again the secret telepathic code that caused the great door to seal the entrance.

Dat Voga did not linger when he returned to Ptarsas. He and Azaria bid everyone farewell and set out the next morning for Helium. An idea had occurred to him as he had pushed the button that would deep-freeze Daxxus Nahl, an idea that now consumed him and merged perfectly with his plan for the botanical getaway he had conceived for Azaria. He had yet to tell her of it, as he had wished to wait until he worked out the details so that nothing was left to chance.

Now that they were underway, he decided to broach the topic to his beautiful mate. He told her, not for the first time, of the island upon which he and Thuria spent their first six months in Barsoom's primitive past. He told her he had a theory this island lay deep in a remote fastness of ancient Throxeus that he thought had never been settled due to its remoteness. He also repeated Gan-Toh-Gan's words about the island being so far off the course of known shipping lanes that he doubted anyone ever knew of its existence.

"Azaria, I know how deeply you've missed your family. I also know you are not as comfortable in Helium as I am, where I have lived my entire life. I propose that we seek out this island where we shall build a getaway. Ran Tasis gave me examples of trees and plants and vines, and I know how to remediate the land covered by the moss. We could build a paradise there, to which we could abscond for as long as you wish, whenever you feel the need to get out of the city. What say you?"

For an answer, the woman cried and threw her arms about his neck, dragging his face down to hers. "Oh, it sounds wonderful!" she managed between sobs and kisses.

"Then we begin tomorrow," he rejoined happily.

Azaria was deeply touched by the thoughtfulness of his plan, which would obviously entail heroic effort and expense, while at the same time isolating Dat Voga from his own family. As to that, he reassured her, reminding her that with a modern flier there could be nowhere too far to travel, since in a few days he could circumnavigate the globe. For his part, Dat Voga decided to make no mention of the other idea he obtained while in the deep recesses of Daxxus Nahl's laboratory, until he could determine if it was feasible, as he did not wish to give her false hopes.

When they returned to Helium the padwar wasted no time in seeking permission for the trip he and his mate wished to undertake. He spoke to John Carter about it, who instantly reassured him that any resources he required were his for the asking. He reiterated that the entire globe owed him a debt of gratitude that could never be repaid.

Dat Voga told the Warlord about the end of Daxxus Nahl, and his desire to have Ras Thavas examine the body of Tala Trerra, the scientist's dead mate. Although Daxxus Nahl would not approve of involving Ras Thavas, the man was a miracle worker when it came to physiology. If the corpse of the scientist's mate were as well-preserved as Daxxus Nahl had insisted, and the process of her preservation as easily reversed as he swore, it was possible she might be resuscitated using modern science that did not exist in her lifetime.

It was not a subject Dat Voga felt he could broach to Daxxus Nahl, but he thought that, when the day came to revive him—if that day ever came—it would be fitting for the old scientist, who had given into their hands such a wealth of science and invention, for him to awaken and see not Dat Voga's face hovering over him, but that of his lovely mate. John Carter promised to speak to Ras Thavas about the case, although many years might pass before the Ptarsans would release the scientist from his frozen bondage.

Soon, the red man and his beautiful mate were speeding across the wastes of the moss-covered dead sea bottom in the comfortable flier of Daxxus Nahl. Behind them, calibrated to follow and mimic their movements, flew a new ship recently developed that utilized one of the mechanical brains designed by Fal Sivas, the same type used in the new spacecraft now shuttling moss to the sun.

The purpose of the telepathic vessel was to carry the immense amount of supplies, equipment, and building materials, all provided by John Carter and the allies of Helium, who refused to allow the couple to leave with only the harnesses on their backs. The two would require the resources for both comfort and survival while they were gone for what would be months, if not years.

Dat Voga telepathically ordered the supply vessel, a ship

over five hundred sofads in length and carrying tons of supplies, to follow them. It would then perfectly mimic their altitude and seek safe landing when they set down. Azaria was in supernatural awe of the vessel until the red man told her to think of it as if one of their revered ancestors were piloting it. They both laughed.

Old Val Statt, Speaker for the Society of History in Lesser Helium, sat at his desk, mumbling to himself. One hand toyed idly with a fragment of a million-year-old figurine he had recovered near ancient Thark, the great statesman Tars Tarkas having invited the scientist there for archaeological pursuits.

Val Statt had wished to speak with Dat Voga personally before he left on his trip to the desert, the purpose of which had not been announced. But the young odwar, an honorary title bestowed upon Dat Voga by the Navy of Helium, had departed before Val Statt could get word to him, leaving the wizened historian in a foul mood.

"Oh, confound him! What if he perishes out there in the wilds and I never hear his report from his own lips? I need a complete and detailed interview while these things are yet fresh in his mind! Imagine, consorting with ancient Horzians and Xanatorians! It is unthinkable! Gods, I would have wrung his neck if I could but have taken his place!"

The noteworthy scholar had been attempting to meet and speak with Dat Voga for months, to discuss his remarkable journey into Barsoom's past. But first one thing and then another interfered.

"First, the padwar, or odwar rather, was busy finishing negotiations with Zoquan, then came the remediation project, and then, just when I thought things were settling down, there came his new, young mate. Something trivial was always getting in the way, by Issus!"

Siv Datron of Duhor, speaker for the Council of Science, reclined on a chair in front of Val Statt's desk, watching with great amusement the immense frustration of his good friend. At last, exasperated, he said, "Oh, do not be so harsh. It was made no secret, the difficulties his mate was having adjusting to life here. And did not the man work nonstop on the ochre-moss remediation test site? If all goes well, they will return in better spirits. This trip will be good for them."

Val Statt grimaced over his spectacles at his peer before returning to his studied frown.

A brisk knock sounded at the door. Still scowling, Val Statt bid their visitor, "Enter, confound you!"

A lowly than opened the door and peered fearfully into the room. Still but a lad, he seemed appalled to be alone with these two important men who consorted regularly with such powerful dignitaries as John Carter and Tardos Mors. And by the tone of Val Statt's voice, the timing of his arrival was not opportune.

"I apologize, sirs, but I was detailed by Odwar Dat Voga to—" he began.

"Dat Voga? Well, get in here, boy! Quickly now!" Val Statt's tone was one of peremptory impatience.

Carrying a large forandus case and a sealed parchment, the boy first set the case upon the table and, bowing his head courteously, handed the missive to Val Statt. Not bothering to look up, the wrinkled old man said, "If that is all, you may go!"

The young warrior turned swiftly to flee but was brought up short by Siv Datron. "And than? Thank you," said the courteous Siv Datron.

"Yes, sir!" the young warrior replied, smiling now as he quietly closed the door.

Not knowing whether to first open the letter or the casket, they opted for opening the sealed container. Unlatching the clasps, they folded the lid back, gasping at the contents. Within the case lay a collection of items worth ten times their weight in Barsoomian platinum. First was a sword of incalculable beauty and rarity. This could only be Dat Voga's

Xanatorian sword! It reposed in its scabbard and was held in place with tied leather thongs.

Beside it lay a brand-new Horzian radium torch, of the rare bronze design. They knew of the existence of only one other, which was in horrid condition. There were various other items, such as a unique leather harness, showing hard use, but with supple leather, and objects made from the tanned hides of sea-dwelling creatures. In addition, there were daggers, gaffs, short swords, and so forth.

Siv Datron took up the parchment, asking Val Statt, "May I?"

Hardly able to tear his eyes from the invaluable horde before him, that worthy said, "Yes, yes, of course! Read on, Siv Datron, read on!"

Unsealing the parchment, Siv Datron read, "To the wise Val Statt, Speaker for the Society of History." Pausing, Siv Datron quipped, "I am not so sure that I would have led with that myself, but Dat Voga is a generous man."

"Oh, do get on with it," snapped Val Statt. But his face wore the smile of a child with a new toy.

Smiling, Siv Datron continued:

"Sir, I must apologize for the haste with which I departed before we could meet. Rest assured, upon my return, you shall be the first I come to see. I have delayed this quest for months, wishing to ensure the success of the soil-remediation project, which I am happy to report, and as you may have already heard, is progressing fantastically.

In the meantime, I wished to write this missive to detail the items I have had delivered into your care. These items my friends and former shipmates and I wish to place on loan with the Museum of History in Lesser Helium for study and display.

In addition to the items in the case, I am having delivered to the museum the styth in which we returned from the past, a bathysphere of the ancient green men drawn by great beasts of the sea. I suspect you will find it interesting.

Now, the fanciful sword you see before you was fashioned by a man named Zikka, an amazing metallurgist of ancient Xanator whom I had the great pleasure and honor to meet.

Ah, Val Statt, how I wish you could meet Zikka . . ."

And each item, spoken of in turn, detailed a brief history associated with it. The two old men were as schoolboys in their excitement, delicately handling each piece in turn while one or the other would read its description.

"Ah, that Dat Voga is something else, eh, Siv Datron?" said old Val Statt. "I knew we picked the right man when we decided on him for the radium project!"

Siv Datron shook his head.

Chapter Forty-Two

Island in the Middle of Nowhere

It had been months since Dat Voga and his mate left glistening Helium. Periodically, he would send a message to apprise friends and family of their whereabouts. They had spent the last weeks north and south of the equator in search of the island.

The red man began to despair of ever finding it, fearing the volcano had completely obliterated every vestige of the landmass. Then, setting out from their campsite one morning, he spotted a curious feature ahead. For weeks, they had scoured endless flats, with scarcely a low hill to break the monotony. This morning, they spotted a cleft in the sea bottom, with a natural acclivity on one side rising toward a tableland.

It still lay at a distance, but as they drew closer his heart began hammering in his chest. He was staring at the headland from which the brobdoganth had swamped him as it hunted the tusked creature a million years ago. He had fallen into the sea, giving rise to a desire to learn to swim.

The natural acclivity he saw was the same slope he climbed after falling in. Unable to swim, he had sunk to the bottom, where he had been forced to hold his breath as he walked out, spearing a fish along the way. Near the center of the tableland was an unsymmetrical mound—the time-eroded remains of the volcano. One side was lopsided where it had been blown out to sea.

"The headland! By the shades, it is the island, Azaria," he said excitedly. "We've found it!" They landed on the tableland down which he and Thuria had descended during the storm, where they later found a cave that sheltered them. Here, they began surveying for a potential homesite.

The island was certainly remote. There were no changes in topography for thousands of haads surrounding it, the area approaching it being only featureless wasteland. Little wonder people had never settled here. Or if they had, they left no obvious sign of it. There was nothing here to draw inhabitants unless one sought solitude, which it had in plenty.

He looked at his beautiful mate. "Well?"

She flashed him a sudden grin, her teeth sparkling. "I love it, Dat Voga. Where do we build?"

"Let's walk around and decide what view we prefer. I like this little rise just over here. I wonder if I can still find that cave where Thuria and I sheltered while we were here?"

They left their ship and the supply vessel behind and headed toward a low, barren hill he felt would give them a view overlooking the cliffs that plummeted toward the former coastline. The man led the way, telling Azaria how the barren hill was once covered in swaying trees, when he walked into a hard surface and nearly broke his nose.

He cursed and rubbed his smarting anatomy. Moving forward more cautiously, he felt the surface of an invisible wall. He was stunned, and not a little fearful. Perhaps he and Azaria were not alone here, after all? Keeping one hand upon the wall and feeling ahead for fear of stumbling into another imperceptible surface, they explored the periphery.

With no warning, his hand came upon empty space—an opening! The man peered around the edge of the opening and was startled to see a jumble of ruins. From inside, he could see the inner surface of a high wall that completely encircled the small rise, but the wall was only visible *from the inside.*

"What do you make of it?" Azaria asked.

"It's incredible!" he said. "When viewed from the outside, we see only a reflection of the barren ground that lies outside the wall, with the interior being completely invisible. Someone obviously didn't wish to be seen from the coast."

Carefully guiding Azaria through the invisible entry, they stepped into the enclosed area. Inside were the remains of ancient foundations and low stone walls, the sturdy outer wall having remained intact. Whatever had been built of stone remained, but bore evidence of erosion, signifying the ruins were of significant antiquity.

Where the construction material had been less durable, it had long since disappeared, but it had left the pattern of its ancient foundations. The surviving stonework possessed a softened look, as though polished by untold millennia of wind and sand. There was no sign of recent habitation.

"Despite believing this place had never been inhabited, it has, although not recently. These ruins look to date nearly to the time I was stranded here. No matter, there's no one here now. These ruins are of a quaint design, and now that I look at them, the size is what I envisioned we would build. These foundations remain well defined, so I suggest we utilize them, as not having to lay new understructure would hasten the building process. What say you?"

Azaria agreed the plan was sound, so they returned to the ships and landed them inside the invisible enclosure where they began unloading. They would live in the ships for now, until their home was completed. Dat Voga began measuring the ancient foundations, and drafted a striking plan for their home, matching the already-present footings.

Azaria added her own touches to his sketch—architectural features with which she had been familiar in ancient

Horz that had struck her fancy, shapes and angles she had dreamed of having in her own home. With their plans drawn up, they began building.

The padwar was now grateful indeed for the tools and materials with which John Carter had filled their supply vessel. These included beautiful and rare woods from the groves of Ptarsas and Zoquan, donated by those cities, so he might build his mate a home such as she had been accustomed to in her previous life. No expense was spared, and the couple lacked nothing, as Helium and her allies had gifted them with everything they might need, and more.

The two labored for months. Utilizing the existing stonework and the remarkable construction apparatus they had at their disposal, they stayed ahead of schedule. In less time than Dat Voga had believed possible, they finished their home, and then began work on the greenhouses and outbuildings. Ever the scientist, Dat Voga included a laboratory that he might labor at his leisure.

When the time came to outfit his lab, he found he must return to civilization for additional materials. Having the position of the island now fixed in his destination control compass, however, he would be able to make the return trip with ease and rapidity.

He had been studying the journals of Daxxus Nahl, familiarizing himself with all the minutiae the scientist had documented about his Magno-GraviSpheronic nexus, including two volumes dedicated to his spheron-field-harnessing machine that sat far beneath the floor of the abyss. Dat Voga had a sensational plan, but he wanted to fully comprehend what he was getting himself into before he embarked on it.

As he studied what Daxxus Nahl had written about the design and construction of his power source and modulation equipment—these entries being incomplete since he had never notated the specificities—Dat Voga identified many areas for improvement. This finally settled the matter in his mind.

Now having a full understanding of the specifications, he began constructing his equipment, most of which he was able to redesign in a miniature, optimized form, resulting in components small enough to fit upon a workbench.

He modified the array field so he could set the center of the nexus to any coordinate within the boundaries of the power source's limiting radius. Daxxus Nahl had circumscribed the initialization of the field to specifically seventy-five sofads above the center of the insulator array. Dat Voga's system had no such limitation. He could initialize the field in his lab, or outside in the courtyard, and remodulate the contents of the nexus from his control bench.

He also developed a method to adjust the size of the field, within reason. He found that he could encompass most of his complex in the field, but that he could not create a diameter large enough to include the outer wall encircling the rise upon which they had built without risking damage to the equipment. There was a limiting factor in the equipment's ability to handle the necessary increase in power.

Dat Voga found himself wishing he could show his improvements to the system to the one man who could appreciate them—Daxxus Nahl. The Heliumite was unaware of it, but the fact that he had so quickly absorbed and improved upon Daxxus Nahl's invention evidenced his uncanny grasp on physics—an innate understanding that came naturally to him.

He attributed his success in this instance to having worked side by side with Daxxus Nahl and having used the equipment in practical application. But such was not entirely the case. The man was gifted, plain and simple, but he lacked the necessary conceit to attribute his capabilities entirely to his own brilliance, as might others.

He had decided not to redesign the gauntlets—the

capacitors utilized to store nexus energy. After studying their technical specifications, he saw how they could be simplified and downsized. But it would require much tedious, time-consuming work, so he designed his equipment within the parameters of the original gauntlets, which he still had.

The reclamation, both inside and outside their great wall, the origin of which Dat Voga had given up trying to discover, proved more successful than he had hoped. The moss they excavated was sealed in containers they had brought with them. The latter would be loaded aboard spacecraft and disposed of in the now-default manner.

Kneeling in the dust within the parameters of their newly completed ranch, Azaria looked across to where her mate crouched as she did, planting seeds. "Dat Voga?" she asked.

"You have dust on your nose," he said laughing, for gritty soil covered her from head to toe.

Wiping the dust off her nose, and adding more from her soiled hands, she asked, "How are our seeds to grow? We have no canals."

"I had several of Daxxus Nahl's water machines built from the plans I found in one of his journals," he replied. "We shall build them in the millions and use them to reclaim our planet—beginning right here!"

And following instructions supplied by Ran Tasis, they continued and planted many seeds that they hoped to see develop one day into groves.

Chapter Forty-Three

A Visit to Horz

DAT VOGA EXPLAINED THE LAB EQUIPMENT upon which he had labored to Azaria, who was to be his assistant, until she was as well versed in its use as him. They had spent weeks tweaking the setup, preparing for this day.

It was only recently that he had divulged his plan to Azaria, which was nothing short of replicating the nexus in this island lab. His intention was to take her to see her parents, wishing to restore the joy she exhibited when they first met. It was the perfect solution—the only solution. They could remain in the past for as long as she liked, the only stipulation being that they would interact only with her parents. They would take the small flier with them so they might safely and speedily cross the great oceans.

He had not seen his lovely mate so animated in a great while and was grateful to be able to give her this hope. He just prayed nothing went wrong. The machine must work! Should it not, he felt this cloud would always hang over her, she for whom he wished only happiness.

They took their respective positions on the morning of their scheduled departure. Dat Voga squeezed his mate's hand and kissed her. "In moments, my princess, we'll be standing in the equatorial sunshine of ancient Barsoom. The machine is set for a year after when I believe the volcano erupted. The island should be habitable by then, although it may not be quite the same. It will bear the scars of the eruption."

Being equally anxious to see the past again, he excitedly powered up the nexus. They had done so many times, remaining outside of it for safety while he tested the field readings, looking for anything out of sorts. But nothing ever occurred to indicate that it would be anything but a perfect nexus.

The field was much more powerful than the original field he had witnessed in the cave. He had increased its diameter to include their buildings, necessitating the more powerful field. The ground vibrated with the energy. Outside of the sphere, sky, stone, and sand dimmed, to be replaced with the waving grasses and fronds that he recalled growing on this spot.

Before turning off the power, which before had been automatic, Dat Voga walked outside the lab, but remained within the perimeter of the nexus. He examined the surroundings from as close to the field as he dared approach, while Azaria maintained watch at her station.

If anything looked dangerous with this time modulation, he would have her revert to the original settings and power down, preventing them from ever actually modulating here. It was a safety feature Daxxus Nahl had neglected, either in arrogance or because he simply did not care.

Visible everywhere were the marks of the volcano, consisting of ash; broken, twisted, and burned trees; and patches of bare earth. They had discussed the possibility of this. Azaria wished to return as near as possible to the point she had disappeared to shorten the time span of suffering for her parents.

This time modulation was perfect. Already the vegetation battled to regain the foothold it once had. He did not wish to remodulate too soon after the explosion because of the danger of inhaling the poisonous fibers and volcanic residue.

This appeared to be negligible at the selected point in time, however, and he felt they might assist nature somewhat in the vicinity of their homesite.

Dat Voga signaled Azaria to trigger the process to complete their remodulation. As the hum of the Magno-Gravi-Spheronic nexus died, he took her hand and led her outside. They both gasped when they inhaled the richer air—richer and familiar.

Laughing with glee, Azaria ran from his laboratory out into the waving grasses that swayed in a fresh ocean breeze beneath several surviving ferns. A tropical sun illuminated the silvery clouds filling the sky. The red man started to warn the girl of the dangers of inhaling too deeply of the rich atmosphere, but then he smiled and remained silent. After all, this was her world.

Dat Voga saw that from the direction of the sea it would be possible to see their ranch, especially with any nighttime illumination. Since he could not bring the wall here as it exceeded the limits of the field, he would have to replicate it here in the past where it was needed the most. It would not be the first time a ship made land here, he reminded himself, thinking of the *Prachus*.

Fortunately, from the nearby cliffs there was plenty of gergite. Using the futuristic tools at his disposal, he began the task. When he set about to prepare a foundation for the wall, he discovered an irregular ring of exposed stone completely circumscribing their ranch. Seeing that this would save him considerable excavating, he used it, and built a wall he felt would serve his purposes of concealment.

He then applied a coating of the reverse-engineered paint of invisibility, invented by a scientist named Phor Tak, to cover the outer surface so that it, and the buildings it housed, might remain safely unseen from any ship at sea. He left one small opening for them to enter and exit. When he finished, he went to the seaside. Looking toward their compound, he was satisfied that all he could see were the ferns and the cliffs on the back side of their ranch. Of the complex, nary a sign was visible.

As he stood there with Azaria, surveying their work, the woman mused, "You said you don't know who built the wall in the future, yet you've just built a wall identical to it."

"Yes," he said, patiently, "but it's not the same wall, Azaria, only a duplication of it. I cannot explain the other wall, but . . . Wait, are you suggesting that my wall and the future wall are the same? It's not possible. I didn't build it until we arrived in the past. I just finished it today. How could it exist before I built it?"

Azaria had that quality that most intelligent women exhibit who do not allow what sounds logical get in the way of what makes sense. "Well, I'm sure I don't know. But do you recall the star-shaped stone I admired, and you placed it above the gate on the inside? If that stone is in the wall in the future, then that settles it."

Bemused, Dat Voga said nothing further.

The young woman took her mate's hand and began leading him back toward their enclosure. "Come on, Dat Voga. I wish to see my parents—tonight!"

Laughing, they sprinted back to the gate in their wall like children. Indeed, the man felt as lighthearted as a schoolboy. He dreaded leaving this wonderland when the time came but felt a jolt of excitement and joy that they could return whenever they wished.

Through the inky blackness of a prehistoric midnight sky, a sleek flier slid with near silence. Cluros moved slowly and stately through the heavens, but he hid behind too many clouds to cast a reflection on the sleek skin of the futuristic craft while his vivacious mate, Thuria, had already dropped below the nighttime horizon.

But the moons would not have cast their light on this particular vessel, for the outer surface of the craft was not visible. Wearing a fresh coat of the invisibility paint, it sailed through the skies unseen. Over a sea wall and above the highest rooftop, the craft slid. The two in the flier gazed, entranced upon the beauty of the scene below, which was dotted with radium lights and torches.

Azaria was accustomed to flight now, having spent months in a flier as they sought the island. But this was the first time she had flown over the city in which she broke her shell, this being none other than ancient Horz. The woman began to recognize landmarks, and issued instructions to her mate who adjusted their heading.

"There it is, Dat Voga! That is their avenue! Fly lower. Just over that building you'll see a walled garden enclosure belonging to my father." Azaria's excitement was palpable in her tone and quickened breathing.

Beautiful radium-powered botanical lamps were placed about the garden, which fairly burst with wondrous plants and trees and flowers of sundry variety. Upon a wide, pebbled path near a clearing of knee-high grasses, Dat Voga gently settled the ship.

The Heliumite remained by the flier to observe the reaction of Azaria's parents when they saw the daughter they must have given up for lost. The redoubtable Hal-Roh-Kim sobbed as he folded his daughter in his arms. Azaria, weeping with happiness, turned, and smiled through her tears at her mate.

She had told him of fleeing this place, how she refused to be forced into a joining of convenience. Now she was reunited with her family, having taken for a mate, she had said, "the most wonderful man I ever met who could make the impossible possible."

Dat Voga came forward and she introduced him. For the first time, Azaria told her father the story of their days aboard the *Prachus*. The story lasted much of the night, with Hal-Roh-Kim alternately laughing or crying, for the tale was full of joys and woes for him.

He had lost many friends with the sinking of that vessel, but he thrilled upon hearing of the survival of old Gan-Toh-Gan and his son, who were old friends of the family. There were still words left unsaid, but the couple knew they must return to their retreat, so none would see them board the ship in Hal-Roh-Kim's garden and ask her father difficult questions.

They promised to return soon. Azaria wished them to come and stay with them, a visit they immediately began planning. Her parents agreed not to disclose that their daughter yet lived. To the citizens of Horz, she was long dead and gone, and would remain so.

Just before dawn, when the sky seems the darkest, the craft rose and shot out over the restless sea. The destination control compass, recently installed in Helium, worked flawlessly to autopilot the vessel back to the enclosed complex they had built on an island no one ever heard of, that resided in the middle of nowhere in a sea that, in Dat Voga's day, no longer existed.

D AT VOGA STEPPED AWAY from a precipitous ledge that plummeted hundreds of sofads. It gradually turned into a steep slope and continued to descend until it merged with the dead seabed surrounding what had aforetime been an island. After many haads, it flattened into a smooth, featureless plain until it became one with the distant, curving horizon that met the skies over Barsoom.

He crossed a wide plateau dotted with burgeoning saplings and grasses undulating in a light breeze. In the distance ran a series of gergite cliffs, at the foot of which more saplings grew. Here and there were varieties of grasses, ferns, and bushes, brought from the remote past, species that would aid in the reclamation of the planet. Nothing could be seen of his home and living complex, nestled safely out of sight behind a high, invisible wall.

He had put to good use the remarkable science and art of the Ptarsans to give the newly established vegetation a fighting chance. The plants were watered by an aqueduct system fed by the incredible machine invented by Daxxus Nahl for converting whatever molecule to which it was modulated, including the surrounding air, into pure water—which he had noted, ironically, worked exactly the opposite of Arkaff's moss.

He had long since aided the Ptarsans in building these

machines, which they now used to water crops and groves. This single invention had already won the maniacal and eccentric Daxxus Nahl a pardon, for it had done as much to further the reclamation of a world as had the removal of giant tracks of ochre moss, shipments of which were constantly speeding to annihilation in the sun.

Already, he planned a return trip to the sarcophagus of Daxxus Nahl, as soon as he could convince the mighty surgeon, Ras Thavas, to accompany him. Ras Thavas had been reluctant. But, after hearing the whole story from Dat Voga, he grudgingly agreed. Apparently, the dislike between the two great men of science was mutual, but Ras Thavas refused to elaborate on the subject.

Dat Voga entered his gate in the wall, passing beneath a star-shaped keystone that could be seen only from inside the enclosure. The handsome young Heliumite continued around to the back of their home, entered through a sorapus gate, and then paused at sight of his beautiful mate, Azaria of Horz.

The alabaster woman had weaved flowers into her hair, the mass of which she had then bound with a quaint leather band in Horzian fashion, with parts of it braided while other strands flowed free. She had simple designs painted here and there upon her body in the style of the sailors of her father's vast armada, in dabs of yellow and blue.

She walked around what, to a casual observer, might appear to be a shrine, but that a closer examination would reveal to be an incubator, the design of which hearkened to ancient days because it replicated one at her parents' home, the very one, in fact, in which she herself began life.

Dat Voga stood stock-still, captivated by the scene. He closed his eyes and listened as she sang a song as old as stone to a porcelain white egg that lay within that blessed enclosure. "My love," he said at last. "It's about time, is it not? Thuria's joining ceremony?"

The sweet girl, smiling the joyous smile of one whose cup waxes full, replied, "Ah, yes, you're right! We should be going." But then, doubtfully, she started to say, "Dat Voga, do you believe the child—"

He smiled and kissed her worried lips; they had had this conversation before. "The child will be fine, and we shall not be gone long. But wait! I almost forgot Thuria's gift! Issus, if I show up empty-handed, she'll think me an insufferable boor!"

Azaria smiled. "No, she wouldn't, silly! But do go get it. I shall await you here." Humming her ancient lullaby, she turned back to the incubator.

As Dat Voga landed his ship in Zoquan, he noted with admiration the recently completed prototype of a new class of vessel. The craft had been designed by a team headed by Carthoris, long considered the foremost expert in ship engineering on Barsoom.

The sleek lines of the vessel were not lost on the scientist, who recognized Carthoris' brilliance in every nuance. The craft was specifically engineered to utilize the revolutionary engines of Fal Sivas, and to be space-worthy if such were required, and could be configured to carry cargo or passengers.

In its current configuration it would fill the most urgent need of the moment—that of transporting radium ore from the mountains of Ptarsas and Zoquan to processing facilities across the face of Barsoom.

As he and Azaria strode past the vessels berthed at the landing platform, they came abreast of the *Tycheus*, where they intercepted John Carter and Dejah Thoris descending the boarding ramp.

"Dat Voga," exclaimed the Warlord. "I'm sure you noticed the new transport ship. She flew her maiden flight today. But come! Before we go to the joining ceremony, we have time to introduce you to the dwar of the new ship. I believe you might know him."

The young noble saw the pennon of Zoquan fluttering from an airspeed device and wondered, for the vessel had just arrived from a factory in Helium. Together they mounted the boarding elevator, and a crewman touched a button, causing them to immediately shoot upward into the hull. The crewman touched another button that opened the access door onto the command deck.

The room was large and airy, with much fenestration, and Dat Voga immediately loved it, as it reminded him of the glazed promenade upon the *Prachus*. Although the outer hull had been constructed using a mirror-like metal, the floor here was inlaid in oiled skeel and sompus, hearkening to the days of the old sailing vessels, the wood obviously of Ptarsan or Zoquanian origins.

A flurry of activity bustled about the room as crewmen finished last-moment duties, the vessel having set down only xats ago. At first, Dat Voga did not see him, but then there he was, in the full panoply of a dwar—it was Odar Gan-Toh-Gan!

He had not seen the fatherly figure of the odar for almost a year. He had worried periodically about the older man who had spent most of his life on the waves of an ancient sea, as to how he fared here on this dying world after having left one so vibrantly alive. The younger man felt a stab of guilt for not having sought out his old sea odar more often, and for having let so much time pass.

"Kaor, Odar Gan-Toh-Gan! I apologize that it has taken me so long to return to Zoquan—" he began.

Seeing the guilty look on the young man's face, the crusty old odar wisely interpreted the reasons behind it.

"Dat Voga," he interrupted. "From past conversations, and the look on your face, I know you feel responsible for the woe we suffered when we came here and saw the destruction wrought upon the surface of our world. But listen. You did not cause this destruction, my people did. It is not you who should feel guilt, by the shades, it is I! I feel I must apologize to everyone I meet for the loss you have all suffered.

"You saved many of our lives when the fish-men attacked and did so again when Lodus Voyvott sought to destroy us. Rather than perishing in the sea, or upon the torture slab of that despot, you brought us here, where we have an opportunity to atone for what Arkaff unleashed on an unsuspecting world. No, young Dat Voga, it is I who am ashamed. You, my dear friend, were sent by the blessed shades to guide old Gan-Toh-Gan to new ports of call. And for that, you have my gratitude—and my thanks."

Dat Voga faced the man squarely. "But the sea! I know you must miss it. By Issus, I spent one short year there and it haunts me yet."

"Yes, I miss it. Of course I miss it," the dwar assured him. "But, not more so than my beloved mate, whom I shall also never see again in this life. When she perished, the ocean became my mistress. Were it not for my son, I had been dead inside years before I met you. Yet he and a life at sea saved me and gave me purpose anew. So yes, I will always yearn for the sea—but not hopelessly.

"Now, I again have a wooden deck beneath my feet and the same stars and constellations of old still aid me in charting my course, as do Carthoris' gadgets. I have but traded the bosom of the sea for the immensity of the sky. But it does make me proud to welcome aboard my ship one who also has tasted the salt spray of that unpredictable mistress—the sea!"

John Carter sighed. "I too, recall the smells of the sea and can remember as if it were but yesterday the taste of the spray on a tossing deck. For me, it has been many years, though. You two cause me to remember times that have not crossed my mind in decades. I imagine we could swap many stories of our times on the breast of the ocean—she who tames man and beast alike."

"But what of Roh-Du-Von, and Bhyda?" Dat Voga inquired of the dwar. For of these two he had heard nothing of late.

"They are once again my crewmen, all of us being honored to number ourselves among this notable crew," Gan-Toh-Gan replied.

Dejah Thoris interjected, "We should be going. Remember, we have more than one ceremony to attend today." And she smiled at the dwar meaningfully, who stood perceptibly taller.

With a confused expression upon his face, Dat Voga inquired, "What other ceremony?"

The dwar glanced at John Carter, who smiled and said, "It's your vessel. You tell him!"

Gan-Toh-Gan smiled broadly. "The princess refers to the naming ceremony of this vessel, young Dat Voga, an observance of which your attendance would be an honor. If, that is, you and Azaria can spare the time after the joining of my son and Thuria?"

Excited, Dat Voga replied, "Absolutely, Odar! I wouldn't miss it. And, if I may ask, what name have you chosen?" he asked eagerly.

His eyes were misty, and his voice became gruff with emotion when the odar replied. "The *Prachus*."

The joining ceremony of Thuria and Gar-Noh-Dar was exquisite. To fully describe it, and the description do it justice, would take a novel as detailed as one of Daxxus Nahl's journals. Suffice it to say that afterward all swore it to be the most beautiful anyone alive could remember.

Gan-Toh-Gan, now a pilot for Zoquan, stood proudly as he watched the ceremony that forever joined his son to his beloved, feeling a knot form in his throat as he recalled a similar ceremony that mated him for life to his long-dead mate.

Afterward, the closest friends and family of the happy couple joined them in a beautiful wing of the palace of the Jed of Zoquan, where they were all talking and laughing and drinking a delicious berry wine that Odwar Dat Voga assured the jed would put Zoquan on the map of many a merchant.

Azaria reminisced with Thuria of their time together in the past, but mostly they spoke of their hopes for the future. Azaria could not disguise her happy giddiness when she spoke of the tiny porcelain white egg residing in its incubator. She was immeasurably happy now and content in this futuristic Barsoom, for the future looked bright indeed.

Dejah Thoris, standing nearby and watching these two newly mated and happy young women, seemed thrilled to see how much more joyful Azaria was from when she first arrived in this time—a girl who had lost her parents and her world in the blink of an eye.

Dat Voga, a mischievous glint in his eye and a smile on his face, appeared suddenly at Thuria's elbow, the beautiful Zoquanian turning at his light touch.

She discovered then that it was not he who had touched her arm, but rather the soft, moist nose of a bizarre creature he held. The creature instantly recognized the bright-eyed girl from Zoquan and set to mewing and struggling fiercely to escape Dat Voga's clutches, while he comically tried to hold on to the waif in its attempts to get to Thuria. As she recognized the tiny cub, Thuria's eyes grew as large as two antique Xanatorian sovereigns.

"Aava!" she cried, taking the pitiful thing from the man's hands. "Oh, Issus, can it be? But, how? She perished a million years ago! And even were you to have somehow fetched her back with us, that was over three years ago. She would be full grown by now! I don't understand."

Her friend had a hearty laugh, a laugh in which Azaria joined her mate, for she had been privy to the plan. "Do you recall that the cub jumped from the small boat, just as Gar-Noh-Dar and the others were helping us to escape from the island, shortly before the eruption of the volcano?"

"Of course! How could I ever forget? My heart breaks every time I think of that dark moment," she cried through her tears. She buried her face in the soft, downy fur of the dinky cub whose lone midnight black eye roamed nervously about the room, gazing at all the interested spectators to this very odd scene.

"Sweet Thuria, I was there just before we came here. I stood in the jungle and waited for her. I called to her when she came ashore, and she came right to me. I took her up and came straight here. So, you see, she was never slain by the volcano, and she has never grown up, for she is still but weeks old. And now, my dear Thuria, she is safe here in Zoquan with you," he finished, with a wide smile on his handsome face.

Thuria sobbed in relief and joy at the return of the tiny creature that had stolen her heart so long ago and then, she had thought, perished. She smiled her gratitude through teary eyes.

Gar-Noh-Dar, still shaking his head in amazement at his friend, said, "Dat Voga, you are unique in all the world! Only a true and loyal friend would go to the length of traveling through time for a joining gift!"

Dat Voga smiled a roguish grin at his friend. "I have something for you, too, my friend!" Reaching around behind him, he pulled a scabbard from his belt, where he had thrust it so that both hands were free to hold the calban pup. He handed it to his friend, watching his face closely.

Gar-Noh-Dar's eyes widened as they recognized

the scabbard. It was the same that had been fashioned by Zikka of Xanator over a million years before and taken by Lodus Voyvott of Nagor when he fled the scene of battle in the throne room, with the scabbard still flapping from his belt after Mab Meebo lopped off his sword arm. This mate to Gar-Noh-Dar's sword had been deemed irrevocably lost.

"But . . ." he stammered, as confused as Thuria had been a moment before.

Dat Voga said, "I would guess Lodus Voyvott always wondered how this scabbard disappeared from beside his very sleeping dais. The Jed of Nagor should not snore so loudly, as it made pilfering the scabbard from his chambers, within arm's reach of his loudly slumbering form, a simple task!"

Hurriedly, Gar-Noh-Dar unfastened the ornate but modern scabbard upon his hip and withdrew the sword from it. Handing the scabbard to a confused onlooker, he slid his blade back into the sheath Zikka had fashioned to house it.

The action seemed to heal an old wound, giving the man closure to a haunted point in his life. His chest rose rapidly with his emotion, and then he heaved a sigh, still clutching the prehistoric weapon, complete once again. His eyes held the thanks that his tongue was incapable of voicing.

Dat Voga placed his hand upon his good friend's shoulder. "You're welcome, Gar-Noh-Dar. It was the least I could do for the mate of Thuria."

Thuria, daughter of Darfa Quan of Zoquan, having regained her composure, looked at Dat Voga as a thought occurred to her. "Dat Voga, how did it feel seeing her once again? The *Prachus*, I mean," she asked wistfully.

The smile of joy slowly faded from Dat Voga's face and his expression became one of solemn reflection. His eyes looked, not at those around him, but across time, into the past at a distant scene in his memories that only his eyes could fathom. His voice was husky when he replied.

"How can one describe gravity to a shadow, or love to one who has known only hate? I stood there after I caught the cub, watching all of us as we rowed across the harbor. But as interesting as that bizarre scene was, I could not for the life of me tear my eyes from the *Prachus*.

"Shades of our ancestors, but she was beautiful. Even at that moment, with much of her sail hanging in ribbons from the storm, she still looked radiant. I wish you had seen, Thuria, how she glistened in the brilliant sun beneath that cloud-dappled sky."

He fell silent. And then he leaned over and placed his lips next to the girl's ear. "Someday, dear Thuria, you'll see her again, yourself!"

About the Author

Chris L Adams spent years playing guitar in various bands and during that time was more of a voracious reader than a writer. After his last band collapsed, he turned from writing songs to writing stories, including his Barsoom duology, *Dark Tides of Mars* and *Gauntlets of Mars*. In addition to writing, Chris also dabbles in painting; the cover art for his recent novel *A Savage from Atlantis* was created from one of his paintings. Chris resides in Southern West Virginia with his wife and daughter.

About the Illustrator

An award-winning illustrator, Douglas Klauba was born and raised in Chicago, and is a graduate of the American Academy of Art. His paintings have been included in the art annuals of *Spectrum: The Best in Contemporary Fantastic Art*, the Society of Illustrators, and *Imagine FX* magazine. He was Artist Guest of Honor at the 2016 Burroughs Bibliophiles Dum-Dum convention, and he has provided artwork for numerous books published by Edgar Rice Burroughs, Inc., including *Tarzan Trilogy, Untamed Pellucidar, Tarzan and the Valley of Gold, The Girl from Hollywood Centennial Edition, Tarzan and the Forest of Stone, Dark Tides of Mars*, and *A Princess of Mars: Shadow of the Assassins*.

EDGAR RICE BURROUGHS:
MASTER OF ADVENTURE

The creator of the immortal characters Tarzan of the Apes and John Carter of Mars, EDGAR RICE BURROUGHS is one of the world's most popular authors. Mr. Burroughs' timeless tales of heroes and heroines transport readers from the jungles of Africa and the dead sea bottoms of Barsoom to the miles-high forests of Amtor and the savage inner world of Pellucidar, and even to alien civilizations beyond the farthest star. Mr. Burroughs' books are estimated to have sold hundreds of millions of copies, and they have spawned 60 films and 250 television episodes.

Edgar Rice Burroughs, Inc.

A whole universe of ERB collectibles, including books, T-shirts, DVDs, statues, puzzles, playing cards, dust jackets, art prints, and MORE!

Your one-stop destination for all things ERB!

Edgar Rice Burroughs
Dejah Thoris

Edgar Rice Burroughs JIGSAW PUZZLE
Warlord of Mars

TARZAN
LORD OF THE LOUISIANA JUNGLE
A Documentary film about the
1918 Silent Motion Picture 'Tarzan of the Apes'

Joe Jusko's
Art of
Edgar Rice
Burroughs

Tarzan

Edgar Rice Burroughs
The Master of Adventure

ENTER THE
EDGAR RICE BURROUGHS
UNIVERSE

TARZAN
SOAP!

ERB
INC.

VISIT US ONLINE AT ERBurroughs.com

© Edgar Rice Burroughs, Inc. All rights reserved. Trademarks Edgar Rice Burroughs®,
Edgar Rice Burroughs Universe™, Tarzan®, Dejah Thoris®, John Carter®, and Warlord
of Mars® owned by Edgar Rice Burroughs, Inc.

ONLINE ADVENTURE AWAITS AT
EDGARRICEBURROUGHS.COM/COMICS

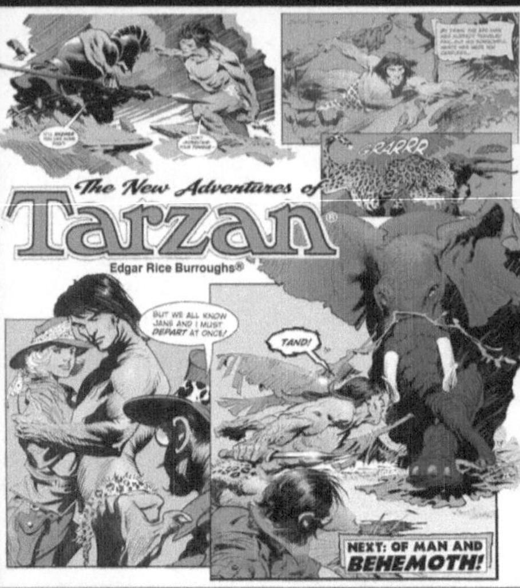

MORE THAN 20 WEEKLY, DIGITAL COMIC STRIP ADVENTURES BASED ON THE CLASSIC CHARACTERS AND STORIES BY THE MASTER OF ADVENTURE, EDGAR RICE BURROUGHS, BROUGHT TO LIFE BY VISIONARY CREATORS!

ERB INC.™

ENJOY THE FIRST 4 ACTION-PACKED CONTINUITY STRIPS FOR FREE!